the Lies
of Bryn van Doren

R.C. MARTIN

Cover Design by Cassy Roop at Pink Ink Designs ©2020

www.pinkinkdesigns.com

To Carrie—Bryn's disc jockey.

Author's Note

I still remember when I dreamed up with the idea of Bryn van Doren. It was early 2017, and I was sitting in the back of a Starbucks. As usual, the concept came to me while I was working on something else. After I wrote it down, I set it aside.

Fast forward a year. The idea of Bryn hadn't yet died (this happens with some of my half-baked plots.) It had, however, become something different. Something more. I'd just finished writing *Severed*, and I thought I was ready to dive into Bryn's story. I wrote an outline. While I was writing it, a friend put together a playlist for me.

I typically only listen to music without any lyrics as I'm writing. Music is often what drowns out background noise, which has the tendency to distract me. For reasons only this book can explain, I needed music *with* lyrics while I wrote it. As I fleshed out my outline, the music became more than inspiration—it became a character in the story.

So, I finished the outline, and I started writing. This lasted maybe a month or two. That's how long it took me to realize, I wasn't ready to write this story. It was like the plot was bigger than me, and I needed to grow a bit before I could do it justice.

Fast forward a year. We're in 2019, now. I thought I was finally ready to write this thing.

Wrong again.

Fast forward into 2020. *Now* I was ready. Which was crazy. I'd started and stopped this project twice already. How could the integrity of it remain the same? Well—I have an answer to that. It was the music. (Okay, the outline gets some credit, too.)

I've dedicated this novel to my friend Carrie because 99% of the music I listened to while I wrote this book was sourced by her. Never before has music played such an important role in my process. It's how the idea I got in 2017, the outline I wrote in 2018, and the manuscript I constructed over the course of three years is now complete and in your hands.

I've since written another novel—and while I wrote it, I *could not* listen to music with lyrics. Crazy, right?

Right—so, you might be thinking, "*Okay… Why is she telling me this?*" Well, I thought a little explanation was warranted before I pointed you in the direction of the playlist I curated for you.

On Spotify, The Official Bryn van Doren Playlist is complete with songs I mention throughout this novel, as well as songs that inspired me the most. I thought I'd share this here rather than at the end, in the event you're the kind of reader who likes to hear what I hear as the story goes along.

Spoiler alert—I've organized the songs in chronological order of the emotional journey of this story. All but the first song, which I kind of dubbed as the theme song for *The Lies of Bryn van Doren*. That said, listen at your own risk.

Okay, enough from me.

Happy reading!

R.C. Martin

CONTEMPORARY ROMANCE AUTHOR

the Lies
of Bryn van Doren

Prologue

ATZEL STANDS ON THE CURB, his right hand casually holding his left wrist as he waits for his employer. The Honduran man is dressed sharply in a black suit, his matching tie snug around his neck. His closed collar rubs against his pale brown skin and is as stifling as it is satisfying, his uniform one in which he finds both pride and gratitude. He mutes the complaints in his mind as he relaxes in the patience which makes him good at his job. Moisture begins to wet the edges of the black, slicked-back locks he keeps trimmed short enough to allow him the professional appearance he deems worthy of his station. He rolls his shoulders, trying to ignore the heat causing his pores to open in an attempt to cool his body.

The bustling city is warm, even under the dark night sky, summer doing its worst in the middle of July. He doesn't need to look up to know he won't see many stars. In the heart of the Financial District, the great beyond is a mystery lost to the grand architecture of the city he's called home for more than half his life. The soundtrack of Thursday night's traffic hums in the background. He listens absentmindedly, knowing he'll be navigating his way through the busy streets in a matter of moments—his vocation of choice for nearly three decades.

Sweat begins to drip down his back as he nonchalantly glances at his wristwatch. It is now five minutes to the top of the hour. Well acquainted with his employer, Atzel knows the importance of being prompt. He's been waiting almost ten minutes, sure when Mr. Morgan said *ten o'clock*, he meant *ten o'clock*. With a few moments left to spare, he reaches for the handkerchief inside of his suit jacket and pats his forehead dry before returning the cloth and resuming his stance at attention.

He smiles inwardly when he spots Khalohn Morgan making his way out of the high-rise building precisely on time. As quiet and calculated as he knows the man to be, Atzel holds a fondness for his employer of five years. While he may not be particularly warm, he has always been kind and fair—even sometimes generous. Atzel, in all his years and wisdom, is certain the power and success which rests on Mr. Morgan's shoulders is a weight he would never wish to bear.

He watches as Mr. Morgan runs his fingers through his thick, dark brown mane of straight hair; the product meant to keep it in place and out of his eyes now worn away after a long day. Without missing a step, he smooths his hand over his tie and looks in Atzel's direction. Atzel, relieved for the opportunity to slip back into the driver's seat of the air-conditioned vehicle, turns to reach for the handle of the back, passenger-side door.

Atzel knows the country in which he resides is greedy and populated with an overwhelming multitude of self-centered people. Somehow, Khalohn Morgan has managed to have all the money anyone could ask for, and yet he still maintains a level of professionalism which repels arrogance and drives his seemingly tireless work ethic. Atzel Zúñiga finds great pleasure and a rewarding sense of accomplishment working for a man he can respect, even if that man never asks him about his day.

Chapter One

KHALOHN WASTES NO TIME closing the distance between himself and his sleek, black Mercedes Maybach S600. After a full, transcontinental day, the sight of the familiar vehicle and his faithful driver reminds him of the pleasures of home he missed while he was away on business. Though, he can't dispute his trip to Tokyo was as productive and lucrative as he'd hoped. The shipyard he's had his eyes on since it came to his attention is now another acquisition bearing his name.

The contract he'd been waiting for, since his plane landed earlier that morning, finally appeared in his inbox a half an hour ago. Ordinarily, he would dive into the numbers associated with his future plans for his new investment straight away; but tonight, he feels he's earned the right to unwind. It's been nearly two weeks since he's had the opportunity to indulge his body's sexual appetite, a truth he wishes to rectify as soon as possible.

"Atzel," he greets politely with a dip of his chin.

"Good evening, Mr. Morgan," his driver replies with a nod.

His slight Honduran accent wraps itself around the curve of every vowel he speaks. He's never admitted it to himself, but it's the finer attributes of the man who travels with him all over the city which Khalohn finds endearing. Being an observant creature who appreciates the details, he's never taken for granted the heritage found in Atzel's manner of speech; or the bags under his eyes, denoting his years of dedicated and tireless service; or the wrinkles that crinkle his skin at the end of his thick, graying eyebrows when a hint of a smile lights up his dark brown eyes.

Khalohn reaches for the button holding his navy-blue Armani suit jacket in place, and Atzel is quick to step behind him and help him out of the garment. Khalohn murmurs a *thank you* as he folds himself into the backseat, and Atzel carefully hangs the jacket on the hook behind the front passenger seat.

Before he can shut the door, Khalohn—not bothering to look away from the phone he extracts from his pocket—announces his desired destination.

"Lower Manhattan, please."

Atzel nods, a gesture not seen yet far from lost as he replies, "Yes, sir."

There is no judgement in his tone any more than there is shame to be found in Khalohn's demand. Neither is there a need for him to offer a more specific end point. There is only one place he ever frequents in Lower Manhattan at such a time of night.

Fifteen minutes after Atzel gets behind the wheel, he places the vehicle in park and hops out onto Broadway. Clandestine's Closet is inconspicuously located between a yoga studio and a high-end home goods boutique. As he steps out of the backseat and up onto the sidewalk, Khalohn pays no attention to either establishment, long since closed for business at this hour. He slips his phone into his pant pocket and then allows Atzel to help him into his jacket. Craning his neck slightly, Khalohn pulls at his cuffs as he admires the light pouring from the windows of the two-story lingerie store he intends to enter.

"Stay close," he instructs, running the back of his fingers along the side of his bearded cheek. "I won't be all night. I'd like a few hours at home before I return to the office."

"As you wish, Mr. Morgan."

With an air of familiarity, and the confidence only money can buy in an establishment such as this, Khalohn climbs the steps leading to the black front door. He crosses the threshold, and the beat of "Jealous" by Nick Jonas reverberates over the sound system—the bass matching the calm rhythm of Khalohn's heart as he maneuvers his way through the racks of woman's underthings. He can feel the staff of both men and woman, dressed all in black attire, eyeing him as he passes without so much as a cursory glance. Not one of them bothers to offer him assistance, well aware he's not interested in purchasing the merchandise available on the main floor.

The thick, black, velvet curtain which hangs across the tall archway at the rear of the store is drawn closed, as it usually is upon his arrival. He parts the heavy material with a small flick of his wrist, slipping through and stepping into the back hallway. As the drapes close behind him, the music that fills the store is dampened. He pauses for a moment, looking over his shoulder to ensure he's alone. Satisfied when the curtains don't part open after him, he shifts his focus.

In front of him are two doors—one on his far left, the other on his far right, each respectively marked *his* and *hers*. With no need to relieve himself, he approaches the large antique mirror situated between the restrooms. The vintage glass is framed in a distressed gold, ornate, wooden frame. To the ignorant, it appears as nothing more than an old mirror in an otherwise modern and upscale themed décor. Khalohn approaches the wall piece and stares right through it.

"Joseph Bonaparte," he speaks, certain the password will grant him the access he seeks.

He listens for the sound of the click, signaling his ability to enter. When he hears it, he gently presses on the left side of the mirror. The heavy, two-way glass eases open, and Khalohn steps over the bottom of the ornate frame and into the parlor of Clandestine's—his intended destination. As soon as he's inside, the mirror eases back in place, locking with another *click.*

"Mr. Morgan," greets the man behind the extravagant, gold reception desk. He doesn't wait for Khalohn to respond before he turns to open a chest mounted on the wall. He extricates the same, long skeleton key Khalohn receives each visit and slides it across the counter.

The man moves with more grace than half the women Khalohn knows. His dark hair is grown long and styled in an up-do which can be ascribed as nothing short of feminine. Yet, with his face void of any makeup, and the tailored black suit he wears showcasing his tall, lean frame, Khalohn has never labeled Stefano as merely queer. On the contrary, it's not difficult for Khalohn to imagine him in an entirely different era. He fits the part of doorman in such a way that makes it almost impossible for one to enter Clandestine's without feeling as though they are traveling through time.

"I trust you will find everything to your satisfaction. Your fee this evening will be the same as usual, and payment will be extracted at the end of your session."

Khalohn nods, knowing how the transaction is conducted. In the last two years, it hasn't changed. Regardless, he doesn't dispute the man. He reaches for the key, slipping it into his pocket as he begins his journey down the narrow stairwell and through the underground maze of the exclusive bordello.

The walls are painted a dark purple, the sconces which hang throughout the corridors so dimly lit, it's as if he's walking through the shadows of secrets only the walls know. Each door he passes is an entryway into a realm of intimate pleasures—pleasures in which only those who have the wealth to indulge may partake; pleasures of those who are not bound by the shame of their indiscretions; pleasures which are so often left to the imaginations of the less fortunate.

Khalohn knows his way through the halls well, the room at the end of the fourth passageway one he has ensured is all but his. When he arrives, he doesn't hesitate to insert the key, twisting it until the lock slides free. He opens the door and steps inside, not bothering to look around as he shuts the barrier behind him. He sets the key on the antique, French side table just beyond the entry, and then begins to shrug his way out of his jacket.

He knows he's not alone, yet he doesn't speak until his jacket is hung and his tie is loosened. As he begins to unfasten his shirt cuffs and roll up his sleeves, he finally looks across the room.

"You may call me Godrik," he instructs, making his way toward the woman seated at the vanity.

She shivers and then peeks at him from over her shoulder as she replies, "I remember."

Khalohn halts abruptly, his arms still lifted as he stops rolling his sleeves. He studies the blonde through the low lighting in the room and knows at once he's had her before. Furrowing his brow, he studies her closer. He can't be quite sure, but the expression in her eye is proof enough. If he hasn't already had her twice, another round would be one he is certain to regret.

"You've been here before," he states.

Slowly, she shifts her body so she's facing him. Crossing one bare leg over the other, she props the heels of her palms on the edge of the stool and leans forward in an attempt to persuade him with her full breasts, barely contained in the red bra which holds them.

"Don't be upset," she murmurs, her voice low in a tone obviously meant to entice him. "One of the girls wasn't feeling well. I told her I'd take her place. I was sure you wouldn't mind." She giggles seductively, running her teeth over her lower lip as she glances down at her lap. Peering at him from beneath her lashes, she goes on to admit, "You seemed to enjoy me both times we were together—and I know I—"

"You need to leave," he interrupts.

"What? Godrik, I—"

Khalohn doesn't allow her to finish as he returns to the door. He swiftly swings the barrier open, staring straight ahead as he mutters, "Out. Now. I won't ask again."

He listens as she finally stands from her seated position and casually makes her way across the room. When she's made it in front of him, she pauses and says, "You'll regret this."

"No," he states, glancing down into her pale green irises. "I won't."

She narrows her eyes at him but doesn't speak another word as she takes her leave. As soon as she crosses the threshold, Khalohn slams the door shut. Frustration courses through him as the consequences of his demand settle in his mind. He scans the room, and his muscles grow tense as the memories weaved within his every sinew remind him of what he won't be feeling for the next hour. The release he was hoping for is now no longer an option—a truth he pays far too much money to endure.

He runs his fingers through his hair and pulls in a deep breath. Closing his eyes, he shakes his head in undeniable disappointment. Khalohn inhales deeply once more, rolling his neck before he shifts his attention down to his arms as he adjusts his shirt cuffs. Once his buttons are clasped, he reaches for his jacket, shrugging it back over his shoulders. Taking up the key far too soon, he opens the door and steps into the corridor.

His anticipation having evaporated, he retraces his steps toward the parlor, the journey not the least bit pleasant. He tries to find satisfaction in the fact that he'll now be traveling home—a place he hasn't been in nearly a week—but his body won't be fooled.

"Mr. Morgan?" Stefano calls in surprise. "What seems to be—?"

"Considering the exorbitant amount of money I pay to frequent that room, I expect my conditions to be met without compromise."

Stefano's mouth falls open in surprise, his flustered state making it difficult for him to find his words. "Mr. Morgan, my apologies. I thought—"

"It is not necessary for you to think. It's simple. I will not accept a woman more than twice. Seeing as you're the one who keeps the records, I expect you to have a far more accurate account than I. Don't let it happen again."

Khalohn turns on his heel, drawing his phone from his pocket as he makes his exit.

"Atzel—change of plans."

Chapter Two

J ESSICA DOESN'T HAVE TIME to panic. She's late.

Jogging the short distance between her and her destination, she reaches for the handle of the old, creaky door and hurries into the back hallway of Moby's Dive. The dimly lit corridor has become quite familiar to Jessica over the course of the last six months. This is why, in spite of her flustered state, she's aware of the walls covered in paint so ancient, she's sure she doesn't want to know what the original color was. They're plastered in an assortment of vintage posters that weren't considered so two decades ago. She's all but memorized every single one. As she passes by the images of bands ranging from classics to one-hit-wonders, she tucks her hair behind her ears and digs into her purse for her phone. With the device in hand, she pauses and adjusts her shoulder strap, typing out a quick text to her best friend.

Huey. Emergency. Our place. Off at twilight.

After she hits send, she peers at the swinging door situated at the end of the hallway. Blowing out a sigh, she combs her fingers through her dark, maple-brown hair, gripping a fistful at the crown of her head as she wills her trepidatious thoughts to take a back seat. Queen's "Fat Bottomed Girls" blares over the sound system, oozing through every crack and crevice between her and the main room—music battling with the roar of the rambunctious crowd awaiting her on the other side. Dropping her phone back into her purse, she shakes away the news threatening to distract her and tries to find her best playful smile.

Tonight, she can use all the tips she can get.

The door swings open as she approaches, and Griffin tosses a towel over his shoulder, his brow dipping in an angry scowl. If she didn't know him to be so mean and self-righteous, Jessica would think the expression sexy.

She has always been confident, in an entirely different world, she'd find her thirty-seven-year-old boss a handsome kind of devil. Standing shy of six feet, his hair a mess of disheveled, brown curls, his eyes the prettiest of dark green, and his chin constantly covered in a thin layer of stubble, it's impossible to deny his Irish good looks. His body speaks of the time he spends lifting crates of liquor every day; and if he never opened his mouth…

"Chapman!" he growls as Jessica breezes by him. "Rafael called out sick, and you're twenty fucking minutes late. What's your excuse this time, huh?"

"You want to chat about it, or you want me behind the bar?" she retorts. As she enters the dive, she doesn't even glance over her shoulder in search of his response. It's not that she's willfully disrespectful or impetuously rude. She simply knows how the conversation will end should she entertain it—with her working her ass off behind the bar.

She tosses her purse underneath the counter and quickly throws her long, wavy locks into a high ponytail. Despite having just arrived, the heat in the room is almost suffocating. She's grateful she opted for her gray, crop-top, off the shoulder, Pink Floyd t-shirt, and her denim, cutoff shorts.

Yet, regardless of the amount of skin she's showing, she knows she'll still manage to work up a sweat.

"Jess—thank *god*," Cassy calls as she looks up from the register. It pops open, and the short, voluptuous blonde is quick to deposit the cash in her grasp before sliding out coins. Her round face is bright, her hairline glistening with a thin layer of sweat. Remembering Griffin's comment about them being one man down for the night, Jessica starts to feel guilty for being late.

"I'm sorry. I—"

"Don't apologize," Cassy insists, leaning over the counter to dole out the necessary change to a waiting patron. She rights herself and blows out a sigh, pushing up her tortoiseshell, cat-eye glasses before she mutters, "You're here now—just *pour*. We've got another two hours with this damn drink special."

Jessica doesn't waste another moment before she rushes to the other end of the bar. Thursday night, drinks are half off until eleven, at which point anyone who is still around is so wasted they don't mind paying full price until the wee hours of the morning. Convinced the busy night will soon drown out her worries, she bellies up to the sticky, mahogany counter and starts taking orders. As "Take on Me" by a-ha comes on over the speakers, Jessica rolls her neck and finds her smile. The beat puts a natural bounce in her step while she pours shots, uncaps beers, and mixes cocktails.

In no time at all, she's lost in a steady rhythm of her own making.

"I'VE GOT TO get out of here if I'm going to squeeze in some sleep before my exams today. You good?"

Jessica forces a smile as she shifts her attention toward Cassy. She looks exhausted. Even the shirt clinging to her curvy body seems worn out after their action-packed shift. The bar doesn't close for another half an hour, but they both know the only patrons left to worry about are the small group of Navy men still throwing darts in the corner. It's always the military crew who stay the latest, like they don't believe in sleep. Jessica reminds herself Griffin will kick them out soon, and then she, too, will be on her way.

"I'm good. Get some sleep," she insists with a wave. "And good luck on your finals."

"Thanks. See you tomorrow."

Jessica watches Cassy as she disappears behind the swinging door. Her thoughts follow after the bosomy blonde, dragging along her envy for good measure. While the two of them are the same age, flirting their way through their twenty-fourth year, Jessica can't help but forlornly acknowledge all that makes them so different.

Cassy is two finals and one semester away from graduating with her fashion degree. It's taken her longer than she hoped to get through school, but Jessica knows her coworker won't be stuck behind a bar for much longer. She's far too talented. As for herself, Jessica has a hard time believing she's got any other option. She has neither the funds to chase after a college degree, nor the luxury of scrimping and scraping as a starving artist. Especially not after the news that fell into her lap earlier the previous evening.

Shaking her head, Jessica stops her tired mind from wandering in a direction she's not ready to traverse. She then takes up the rag on the counter and continues wiping down the vacant surface. Keeping a reign on her thoughts, she finishes up behind the bar and then busies herself sanitizing the rest of the place. A half an hour later, when Griffin comes out to clear the room, Jessica is just finishing her rounds scrubbing tables on the outskirts of the dive.

"Get gone, Chapman. I'll see you tomorrow. You're on the early shift. Don't be late."

Before she can even think of a response, Griffin pushes through the door, headed toward his office. As fast as her tired feet will allow, she returns to the bar to grab her purse. Looping the strap over her shoulder, she digs for her phone and immediately finds a text from her best friend.

Don't like the sound of that. Could use a slice myself. Meet you before dawn, my dove.

Jessica blows out a sigh of relief, certain a few hours with her favorite man is just what she needs. She stops halfway down the hall, pushing open the bathroom door for a quick pit-stop. She stares at her reflection in the mirror, and her chest fills with an anxiety so dense, she can hardly pull in a breath. It's the first time she's taken it upon herself to check her appearance in hours. Except, it's not *Jessica* she sees—it's her life; her responsibilities; her choices, or the lack thereof.

The light over the sink flickers, and the grimy, barely clean restroom seems even more dank than usual. Her exhaustion creeps around the barriers she's been erecting in her mind all night; exhaustion which causes her to wonder if she'll ever be more than the woman she sees reflected in the dirty mirror—if her *life* will ever be more than nights that end with her reeking of liquor and the drunken confessions of strangers.

As she reaches up to free her hair from the droopy ponytail which has long since fallen from the crown of her head, her locks cascade down over her shoulders. She rakes her fingers through the soft, thick strands, trying to bring new life to her appearance. Her efforts are useless, and the weight in her chest grows heavier. If she doesn't get a breath of fresh air soon, her tears won't be stopped.

Jessica yanks the bathroom door open and races out of Moby's Dive. As fast as her feet carry her, she still can't outrun her reality—not her fear, her anxiety, or the ugly sense of hopelessness threatening to make her feel sorry for herself. Nevertheless, she doesn't slow her pace, knowing she's got a bus to catch. She doesn't have time for such useless pity.

After catching the B63 and transferring to B61, it's a quarter to five when Jessica finally arrives on the corner of 39th and 5th—her favorite spot

in all of Brooklyn. As she approaches the entrance of Sunrise Diner &
Donuts, she sees her friend through the window. The sight of him makes
her pause—the image he creates a stark contrast to her own. He's gorgeous,
almost regal, even after a full night of work and sitting in an old diner,
sparsely occupied with the kind of people whose days are finally ending
just before everyone else's begins.

His dark chocolate brown hair is merely inches shorter than Jessica's,
but he's styled it in an up-do so elegant, it rivals her efforts on her best day.
The black suit he wears is expensive, with a label of Burberry or Gucci or
the like, and it fits him perfectly. For a moment, Jessica can't deny her envy.
It's not his *money* she longs for—it's the way in which *Stefano* has managed
to find the ability to fit comfortably in his own skin.

Stefano sips at his coffee, his attention directed down at his phone as
he sits alone in the worn, maroon colored booth. As if he can sense he's
being watched, he looks out the window and spots Jessica right away. The
smile that lights up his face causes her to catch her breath. Instantly, she's
not awash with envy but with love. She stares at him, unable to move her
feet as she's reminded, as frustrating and challenging as life may get, she's
not alone. He would never allow it.

When his smile falls and he slips from out of his seat, Jessica watches
as he deposits his phone into his jacket's inside pocket. He buttons the
garment closed, all the while keeping his gaze trained on her. The muscles
in her chest constrict in warning, and her lips begin to tremble as Stefano
hurries from the diner, obviously aware of what she needs without her
having to say a word. A small voice in the back of her mind calls her to
move, to not allow him to come chasing after her—but it's drowned out by
another voice screaming of her need.

For only a second, she wants someone else to hold her together.

The click of his shoes on the sidewalk beckons her to turn in his
direction, and he folds her in his arms the second her first tear falls.
Neither one of them speaks as she crumbles a little in his hold. She chokes
on her burgeoning sob, clinging unabashedly to his sleek suit. He holds

her tighter, and she loves him harder. Gritting her teeth together, Jessica breathes in the elegant scent of Bleu De Chanel she associates with her best friend, trying to swallow the knot threatening to split her throat wide open.

"Let it out, Jess. It's okay. I've got you," murmurs Stefano as he presses a kiss into her hair.

While his words are meant to grant her permission to fall apart, she doesn't have the luxury of such fragility. She grabs hold of his lapels and pushes her fists against his chest, shoving herself out of his embrace. Her brown eyes catch his hazel ones, and his arms fall to his sides in helpless understanding. Jessica drags in a lungful of air, then another, blowing out each one in a huff. She then sniffles, sweeps her fingers beneath her eyes, and takes hold of one of his hands.

"Jess—"

"Coffee," she states with a shake of her head.

Stefano allows her to lead him back into the diner without question. As he returns to his seat, Jessica catches the attention of their beloved waitress, Wendy. The three of them have known each other for some time now. She's the daughter of the diner's owner and has been working the late shift for the last three years. Despite being a few years younger than Wendy, Jessica can relate more to the waitress's life story than many of her other peers.

When Wendy graduated from high school, she went off to college for a while. It wasn't until she got pregnant by some loser that she came back to Brooklyn. After her baby boy was born, she started working the late shift so she could be at home with him during the day. Her struggle and determination shape her character in such a way Jessica understands and admires. It's why when she asks for her usual order, she does so with a wave and the best smile she can muster.

Stefano waits until Jessica takes her seat across from him before he asks, "What's going on?"

She shakes her head at him a second time, propping her forearms on the table as she leans toward him and insists, "You first. How was your night?"

Stefano tugs his eyebrows together in disapproval, tracing one of his middle fingers around the rim of his coffee cup as he studies Jessica. In spite of his concerned curiosity, he doesn't push her for answers but replies, "There was a bit of a mishap at work—cost me a hefty tip, but it won't happen again."

"What kind of mishap?" asks Jessica with a shrug. She needs another minute to get control of herself. The more Stefano talks, the tighter her grip becomes on her emotional reigns. If she's going to confide in her best friend without breaking down, she needs to be in complete control.

"A couple of the girls traded places without my knowing. It wasn't a switch that went unnoticed."

Jessica nods, not entirely sure how to respond. It took a good deal of time for her to get used to Stefano's chosen career path. It isn't that she judges him for the business he's in, as she supports him in whatever makes him happy. It's just a line of work which is still a bit difficult for her to completely relate to, so they never get into the details of his job's exact responsibilities.

"Come on, Jess. You don't want to hear about Johns, and I've got nothing better to talk about. Out with it."

Wendy approaches the table with an empty mug and a full carafe of coffee. "Hey, Jess," she greets in her thick, Brooklyn accent as she fills the mug. "You two splittin' a slice of blueberry or apple today?"

Jessica looks at Stefano, her inquiry clear in her expression. He quirks an eyebrow at her in minor annoyance and mutters, "Jess…"

"Fine," she tells him before smiling up at Wendy. "Apple, please."

"Two scoops of ice cream?"

Again, Jessica looks to Stefano for an answer, to which he only replies, "Jess…"

"Two scoops. Thanks, Wendy."

"Comin' right up."

As the two are left alone, Jessica reaches for a creamer and carefully peels back the lid before she dumps it into her steaming coffee. She avoids what she's sure is Stefano's steady gaze as she stirs the cool liquid around and around.

"Jess!"

"Would you just—stop saying my name?"

When he reaches across the table and rests one of his hands over hers, she finally stops stirring. Then he murmurs, "Dove," and the words come tumbling out of her as if he's unlocked her mind's Pandora's box.

"Mom got laid off yesterday. And I get it, you know? We knew this would come. Except, *knowing* wasn't enough to prepare us—to prepare *me*." Jessica blows out a sigh, sealing her eyes closed tight as she laces her fingers with Stefano's and grips onto him tightly. He squeezes back, and she scrunches her brow, trying to keep her tears from returning.

"Without a job, we have to figure out what the hell we're going to do about her insurance. And we've talked about Medicaid, but that might not be enough. Not to mention, I've never looked into it in great detail. I didn't think we'd need it so soon. I don't—I don't have a plan, and I feel so stupid for thinking we had more time. We don't and—"

"Hey, look at me. Jess, open your eyes and look at me," Stefano demands softly, giving her hand another squeeze.

She draws in a breath through her nose, holding it in her lungs for a second before letting out a slow exhale. When she opens her eyes, she seeks out his, and her inner anxiety is assaulted by an all too familiar peace. She holds out her other hand, not breaking their gaze, and Stefano extends his own, weaving their fingers together without hesitation. Jessica blows out another slow breath, comforted by his unwavering presence, regardless of the harsh truths she's just spilled all over the table between them.

"Fuck," he finally says.

Jessica doesn't fight the chuckle that bubbles out of her. "Yeah," she nods.

"What do you need? You know, whatever it is—"

"I know. I don't need anything. It's not your problem. I'll figure it out, I just—"

"Not my problem? Jess, you're my best friend, not a burden. You need me, I don't care what it is, you tell me."

She smiles at him, pulling his hands toward her. He leans across the table, following her tug, a small smirk curling the side of his mouth as she kisses his knuckles. There are no words to describe how much he means to her; no explanation grand enough to make sense of the way he can calm her down with promises of which she never intends to take advantage. Simply knowing he's there, no matter what, grounds her.

"There's a reason why, after eleven years, you're still my favorite person," she starts to say. "We don't fuck each other, we don't—"

"—fuck each other's men, and we don't fuck with each other's money. I know. Doesn't change my offer."

"I know."

This time it's Stefano who tugs on Jessica's hands. He turns them, revealing her wrists, and kisses each one before he lets her go. "You're a badass, my dove. You know that, right?"

Raking her fingers through her hair with one hand, she reaches for her coffee with her other. In all honesty, most days she's not sure if she's a badass or merely a stubborn woman who was raised not to take any handouts from anyone.

"All right, it's settled," demands Stefano as he reaches for his own coffee. "Your next night off, I'm taking you to The Critic. I won't take no for an answer. We need to get you to Manhattan in the smallest dress we can find."

"Huey," she laughs, lifting her mug to her lips.

"Not kidding. Deal with your shit, but know I'm coming for you. You need to get out for some fun, even if you won't admit it."

"I'm not off until—"

"Great. It's a date," he interrupts with an impish grin.

As she begins to argue otherwise, Wendy arrives with their pie. Stefano is quick to fill his spoon with a bite. When Jessica opens her mouth to speak, he shoves the utensil in her mouth.

"Ah-ah—it's time for pie, dove."

With nothing left to do, she lets the warm, crumbly, butter crust of the apple pie melt the cool vanilla ice cream on her tongue. Her taste buds rejoice as Stefano extracts the spoon. Any fight she had left in her dissipates.

Chapter Three

KHALOHN STEPS OFF THE elevator and reaches for his billfold, tucked into the inside of his blue, Tom Ford designer jacket. He pulls it free as he crosses the small distance to his suite's entrance. Waving the thin, leather wallet in front of the card reader, the radioactive chip in his access key triggers the lock on the door, allowing him to walk over the threshold. There's a reception desk situated a few feet in front of him, the weekly floral arrangement displayed on the end adorned with hues of summer. The common space beyond the entryway is filled with couches and chairs, the décor rich in shades of navy, brown, and gray. The motion-activated lights power on overhead, following him as he turns and travels toward his corner office on the far-left side of the suite.

He doesn't bother to look between the white columns spaced along the right side of the corridor, sure the rows of desks which fill the bullpen are currently vacant. At six-thirty in the morning, the associates at Khalohn Morgan are not often at their stations. He prefers it that way. There's something about having the office to himself that brings him peace. The silence reminds him how it all started—with him, alone, and nothing more than his willingness to take a risk.

It's been three years since his firm outgrew their previous space, granting him the opportunity to move and lease an entire floor on Wall Street. His is the fastest growing acquisition firm the city has seen in years, and Khalohn has been turning heads and making his name known worldwide. The sound of his shoes, clicking against the concrete floor, bounces off the glass walls of the conference rooms to his left as he passes. Each is filled with its own unique décor, every meeting space designed to house various amounts of occupants. Not one with an eye for design, he hired an interior decorator he could trust. A few million dollars later, he had an office that still fills him with pride each time he walks through it. Building something of *worth* is an aspiration which continues to drive him every day.

He glances at the empty desk located outside his office, the surface of the unmanned station as tidy as it always is. He thinks nothing of it and crosses into his own domain. As he shrugs out of his jacket and hangs it on the steel coat rack beside the door, his eyes roam about the room.

The classic, tuft-backed, chestnut brown, Italian leather sofa, finished with hand-carved legs and clawed feet is situated against his side wall. The navy suede, egg shaped chair beside it is a modern contrast he knows not why he appreciates. On top of the distressed, gray metal trunk, serving as his coffee table, is a stack of contracts he was reviewing the night before. He ignores them for now and glances out the wall of windows in front of him as he makes his way behind his desk, his view that of the sunrise reflecting off the East River. Anxious to dive into the deal that closed the night before, he finds his way to his office chair without allowing himself to get distracted by the vantage point found on the fifty-second story.

He powers on his computer and navigates his way to the files he's been sifting through for weeks. The team of accountants he's had on the Japanese shipyard have reviewed the numbers thoroughly, but Khalohn has always been one to do his own due diligence. Before moving forward with his expansion plan, he needs to be so well acquainted with the shipyard's books he can recognize them in his sleep.

At seven-thirty on the dot, there are two taps on Khalohn's door. He doesn't bother to answer before it opens, and Maribelle enters the room. The slight woman is dressed in a fitted, pale blue, floral print shift dress, her nude heels against the thin carpet beneath them marking the beat of her step as she rounds the front of his desk.

Khalohn glances to his right as his secretary sets down his usual morning tray, complete with an empty mug, a French press full of freshly brewed coffee, and a toasted whole-wheat bagel. He notices her bright red lipstick, darker than the pink she had on the day before, and the string of pearls adorning her pale, slender neck. Her dark, curly hair, streaked with gray, is styled in the same bob she's had since he met her six years ago; and when she smiles at him, the wrinkles around her lips soften.

"Good morning, dear," she says in greeting, clasping her hands together.

Khalohn doesn't mind the familiarity, the longevity of her loyalty and the motherly way she's always doted upon him earning her the right. Dipping his chin in a small nod, he replies, "Maribelle."

"Tell me you went home last night and got some rest."

He looks down at himself, silently pointing out his fresh suit, and Maribelle rolls her eyes.

"Don't patronize me. Don't make me walk to your closet to check your stash, either. I wasn't born yesterday, Morgan."

Fighting a smirk, Khalohn assures her, "I slept. A night in my own bed was necessary."

"Good," she starts to say as she begins to take her leave. "Your lawyers will be here in thirty minutes. Would you like me to buzz you five minutes prior to your meeting?"

"Please."

"Very well, dear."

The scent of the Columbian blend awaiting him is enough to keep him distracted for another moment. He pours himself a cup and takes a sip before indulging in a bite of his bagel. As he chews, he allows his eyes to drift out the window. Instead of the view, his mind is consumed with thoughts of the airlines he's got in his possession. He's not sure which one, but he intends to expand the enterprise in order to include travel by sea—more specifically, luxurious travel by sea. With any luck, his new shipyard will be building yachts in the near future, an idea he intends to propose within the next hour.

Khalohn swallows his first bite and quickly takes a second. He then wipes his hands on a napkin and shifts his attention onto his computer screen. He finishes his breakfast only seconds before Maribelle pages into the room, reminding him of his meeting. Not one for tardiness, he's quick to rise to his feet and don his jacket. After pulling at his shirt cuffs, he runs his hand over his beard and rolls his shoulders upon his exit.

Much of his morning is spent in one conference room or another, sitting in on various meetings. It doesn't go unnoticed the hurried way people leave his presence, anxious to get done the tasks he desires before day's end. There's an unmistakable buzz in the air, the heat of mid-July and the beckoning call of the weekend making his employees borderline restless. He glances down at his watch as he walks toward his office, wondering if it might be better to release them a couple hours early. It's not something he does often, but he's not oblivious to the importance of maintaining a reasonable level of morale around the firm.

"Good. You're back," says Maribelle, disrupting Khalohn's thoughts. He shifts his attention toward her desk, and a hint of a smile tickles the muscles around his mouth at the apparent state of her annoyance. "Your one o'clock is here," she announces.

"Maribelle—*darling*—you wound me," gushes Porter. With one hand planted on Maribelle's desk, propping him up as he leans toward her, Porter presses his other against his chest. "His *one o'clock?* I don't even get a name?"

Unamused, she tells Khalohn, "Morgan, do please get your broker off my desk."

Scoffing in mock offense, Porter straightens and tugs at the bottom of his gray suit jacket. Smoothing his hand down his yellow tie, he retorts, "Broker? Try best friend. As a matter of fact, try *only* friend." He pauses, smirks at Khalohn, and then grins at the older woman before adding, "You know, deep down, you love me, Mari—if for no other reason than because I can manage to drag Khalohn out of the office for a long lunch every week."

"Khalohn, my dear, you work entirely too much," says Maribelle, ignoring Porter as she stands to her feet. "We need to get you out more. Remind me to add it to your calendar." In spite of her straight face, Khalohn knows she's teasing. Walking from behind her desk, she states, "If you don't mind, I think I'll take my lunch now."

"As you wish," Khalohn replies with a dip of his chin. He starts to make his way around Porter, heading for his office, when he remembers his previous train of thought. He stops, slipping a hand into his pocket as he turns and calls out, "Maribelle?"

"Yes?"

"When you get back, send a memo to the office. Early dismissal. Four o'clock."

"Oh, come now. You can do better than *that*," Porter mocks, a playful grin still lingering across his lips.

Khalohn looks at his friend contemplatively, not at all annoyed by his antics. Over the years, he's not only grown quite used to them, but he expects them—knowing Porter Hunt's need for playful banter to be a trait woven into the very fiber of his character.

Drawing in a deep breath, Khalohn shifts his focus back toward Maribelle. He can see traces of the smile she tries to hide from Porter at the corners of her mouth, and he's quick to surmise the woman's thoughts. She's always considered Khalohn a stickler with a rigidity unparalleled in a man his age. While she doesn't question him often, she never hesitates to challenge him to loosen up on occasion. Even though she doesn't hold a fondness for Porter, Khalohn sees she can't argue with him this time.

"Fine. Three o'clock—not a moment sooner."

Her smile breaks free and she nods before she replies, "Very well, dear."

"That a boy," says Porter with a chuckle, clapping a hand on Khalohn's shoulder.

Khalohn shakes his head, paying his friend little mind as he continues toward his office.

Pointing his thumb over his shoulder, Porter insists, "Wrong way, boss man. Lunch is out the other door."

"I've got an email to—"

"As your friend—as your *broker*, I cannot let your ass hit that chair," Porter insists, grabbing hold of Khalohn's shoulders. Despite his smaller frame, Porter manages to pull him back a couple steps. His lean muscle contributing to the undisputed strength in his grip, he shoves Khalohn back out of his office. "You sit down, and we'll miss our reservation. We miss our reservation, and our meeting is completely spoiled."

Khalohn doesn't resist, regardless of his confidence that he could, knowing his efforts would be useless. Porter has always had a knack for interrupting him, if for no other reason than to force him to get a breath of fresh air. Over the years, he's learned to acquiesce—not merely for the simple fact that Porter is far more tolerable when he gets what he wants, but also because Khalohn can't deny the truth. The companionship which exists between them holds value. Different as the two men are, Porter is good for Khalohn. As a businessman and a friend, it's proven to be an irrefutable reality.

"There you go," Porter teases, setting Khalohn free.

They walk side by side, and Khalohn extracts his phone from his pocket, pulling up his email account. Intent on constructing the message still at the forefront of his mind, he opens a new thread and begins to type as he mutters, "Must you flirt with Maribelle every time?"

Speaking through a chuckle, Porter replies, "Yes. It's entirely too much fun."

Khalohn glances up when they reach the elevator bay, watching as Porter hits the call button. "She despises it."

"Maybe, but she *adores* me. In the end, all women do."

Shaking his head slightly, Khalohn resumes typing. "Why do I put up with you?"

"You mean, besides the fact that I've helped to ensure you remain a *very* wealthy man? Or perhaps the fact that I truly am your only friend?"

"You're not—"

"That kid brother of yours doesn't count. You hardly see each other, most likely because he is *way* more debonair than you."

One of the elevator doors chimes open and Khalohn shoots Porter a blank stare as they enter.

"No offense," he snickers, lifting his hands in surrender. He then presses the button for the first floor and says, "I'll admit, he outdoes me, too. Three-time Olympic medalist with swagger? That's hard to beat. Though, I might have had him there for a while, when he was trying to pull off blond hair." He tucks his hands into his pant pockets, his eyes losing focus as he remembers. A shiver of distaste races down his spine and then he shrugs away his memories.

Khalohn's gaze flickers up to Porter's head, his long, dark hair pulled back into a neat bun above the nape of his neck. He's never really understood his friend's desire to grow out his locks. Thinking back to the days of his brother's blond mane, Khalohn can't decide which is worse. Given Blair was barely in his twenties when he dyed his hair and Porter was turning thirty when he started abandoning haircuts, he's not sure the two can be compared. It only takes a moment for Khalohn to come to the conclusion that he doesn't actually care either way, and he shifts his focus back onto his half-constructed email.

"Speaking of your brother, you should reconsider acquiring a few resorts of the *winter* variety."

"I have one," Khalohn replies distractedly. "In Vancouver, remember?"

"Do you hear yourself? One, in *Canada*. How many beachside resorts has Khalohn Morgan bought out throughout the course of your career? You've got to be nearing a dozen by now."

Still busy with his message, he mutters, "Last I checked, my broker's advice was to diversify. I've got enough hotels and resorts to worry about."

"Speaking of, how was Asia, anyway?" Porter asks, the shift in his tone indicating his genuine curiosity. "Where is it you went this week? Shanghai? Tokyo? I can't seem to keep up with you lately."

"Tokyo," Khalohn answers simply. Upon completing his message, he presses send and blacks out the screen of his phone. "It went well. Closed the deal last night. We'll see what the next six months yield."

"Well then. Sounds like congratulations are in order."

Khalohn's shoulders lift in a minute shrug as he shakes his head. The two men step off the elevator, making their way toward the building's main entry as he replies, "Business as usual, Porter, nothing more."

"Nonsense. The weekend is upon us, the weather is forecasted to be incredible, and you're letting your office head home early—that leaves you with plenty of time to prepare for a couple days at sea."

As they emerge into the sweltering heat of midday, Khalohn looks for Atzel and the Maybach he knows awaits them. When he spots the man standing on the curb, he nods in his direction, signaling Porter where to go, all the while reading through his friend's thinly veiled suggestion.

"I've been away for nearly a week. I've got things to see to this weekend."

"Things? Come on, Khalohn. You don't do your own laundry; you don't clean your condo or handle your own grocery shopping—what could you possibly need to see to this weekend that can't wait until Monday?"

"If you want the Monte Carlo for the weekend, why don't you just ask?"

Atzel nods in greeting before swiftly opening the back, passenger door. Khalohn returns the gesture, unbuttoning his jacket as he folds into his seat with ease. When he reaches for his own door, Atzel correctly interprets the act as his permission to hurry around the rear of the Mercedes to open Porter's door.

"I'm not so selfish that I would ever ask to borrow your exquisite MCY96 without first thinking of you," he says, occupying the seat beside

Khalohn. A soft thump fills the car as they're closed inside the vehicle. "It is your yacht, after all. A treasure you so rarely use yourself. It's a travesty, really."

"When I return to the office, I'll notify the crew. I'm sure they can have her ready to set sail within a couple of hours. She's yours for as long as you have the time."

"Thank you. I mean that, and you know it. I hope you also know I'm getting you out on that damn boat at least once before summer's end. It won't kill you to take a long weekend every now and again."

"Excuse me. Where to, Mr. Morgan?" Atzel kindly interrupts.

Khalohn looks to Porter, who rattles off the name of some restaurant before his phone begins to ring.

"Take it," says Khalohn as Atzel pulls into traffic. "I insist."

While Porter speaks, Khalohn tunes out the sound of his voice and stares out the window. For a moment, he doesn't think about business or the work he intends to do over the weekend. He finds himself contemplating Porter's lifestyle—the lifestyle one might presume Khalohn, himself, should be living.

In truth, he is wholly aware of his status. Over the last few years, he's purposefully acquired the possessions which seem necessary for a man of his caliber to accumulate. If nothing else, he has a reputation to maintain in the business sphere in which he thrives. Except, Khalohn's never really found lasting pleasure in the things money can buy. While he appreciates the cut of his tailored, designer suits, and he finds value in the luxurious home he's purchased, while he regularly indulges in the rendezvous he buys at Clandestine's, his list of possessions is not what fulfills him. He has it all, but it's not what drives his efforts.

If anything, the more he acquires only further proves the void he so often feels cannot be satisfied with *things*. Not even the people who surround him are capable of giving his life meaning. It is his productivity, his success, his *name* which fuels his desire to build—not for the sake of money, but for the integrity of worth. He endeavors to immerse himself in the task of finding something of real value and unearthing it. Over and over again, he seeks, and he finds. It is tireless, but it's the path he's chosen, and he doesn't regret it.

Chapter Four

K HALOHN GATHERS THE LAST OF his things into the banker box on top of his desk, then slides the lid on top. He hardly notices the furtive glances being thrown his way, too distracted by his own boldness and the high that makes him feel on edge.

On the edge is exactly where I am—the edge of possibility; the edge of the future; the edge of *everything*.

He doesn't speak a word of farewell to anyone, his mind reeling as he begins to take his leave. He's known, since he enrolled in Columbia's Business School three years ago, he was one day going to forge his own way and start his own firm. Blakney Properties was a steppingstone from the start. It was his first opportunity to get his feet drenched in his area of expertise after he'd earned his MBA. It was his chance to make a home in the city. It was where he belonged—until five minutes ago.

He didn't plan this. He didn't foresee his opportunity landing in his lap like a hot pile of shit he couldn't ignore. His intelligence has long since been undeniable. His ambition is irrefutable. His track record serves as anyone's proof he has always been striving for greater. Yet, this is a risk he didn't know he was ready for—until five minutes ago.

"Whoa. Lohnny, what the fuck is going on?"

Khalohn manages no more than a smirk as he continues toward the elevators. Timothy abandons the small group emerging from their meeting and follows after his friend.

"Lohnny, talk to me, man. What did you do?"

"They wouldn't listen," he states.

He comes to a stop and presses the elevator call button before shifting his attention onto Timothy. They've been friends going on four years now, which is exactly how he knows the box in Khalohn's hands isn't evidence he's been sacked—it's a sign he's quit. Nevertheless, the expression on his face speaks of his disbelief. Khalohn doesn't blame him. He can hardly believe it himself.

"What did you do?" Timothy repeats.

"They're going forward with the deal. It's such a short-sided decision, it's stupid. They think that chain of resorts will make them billions—but it will cost them more. This place is a sinking ship, Tim. Maybe not today, maybe not tomorrow, but the executives who are calling the shots can only get by on dumb luck for so long. I can feel it."

"So, what?" Timothy shrugs his shoulders, dumbfounded, and looks at his friend helplessly. "You're going to throw a tantrum and quit your job? Are you nuts? You're a smart man. I know you, and I get it. You want more than this— but what you're doing is reckless."

The elevator chimes and Khalohn looks over as the doors slide open. Shaking his head, he boards the lift car, Timothy on his heels. "It's risky, I'll give you that—but it's not reckless. I've got it worked out. I'm doing this, Tim."

"Doing what?" he asks incredulously. He presses the button for the first floor with more force than is necessary, then grabs hold of his hips as he stares at Khalohn.

"It's time I go my own way."

Timothy coughs out a humorless laugh and replies, "You're insane. You *know that, right? And what are you going to tell Hollie? Happy one-year anniversary. I quit my fucking job. Bet she'll love that."*

Khalohn grows silent as he clenches his teeth together. He knows better than to lash out at his friend—even if he believes the man has crossed a line. As they descend to the lobby, the cacophony of truths and lies neither of them have dared to broach since the night of the Morgan union permeates the veil of his silence. As far as Khalohn is concerned, Timothy had his chance to speak his piece, and he didn't—which remains his problem, not Khalohn's.

"I know how to take care of my wife."

Timothy reaches up and presses his fingers to his temples as he pulls in a deep breath. "I just—I don't think you've thought this through. You're not impulsive. You're—"

"I'm going to do this," Khalohn interrupts as the elevator doors open with a chime. "Watch me. Hell, you ever get the balls to leave, you can join me."

"Khalohn? Khalohn!" Timothy calls as Khalohn makes his exit.

His efforts are weak and futile. Khalohn's mind is made up—and no one can stop him.

"Lohnny? Lohnny, are you home?" Hollie speaks as she unlocks the door to their small flat and steps inside.

Their unit is hardly bigger than a shoebox, so she doesn't have to look hard before she spots her husband as he paces back and forth in their bedroom. When he hears her, he stops in the doorway and holds up a finger, his other hand pressing his cellphone to his ear.

"Tomorrow, then? Ten o'clock?" he asks, his blue eyes locked with his wife's gray ones. "Thank you. See you then."

Khalohn steps out of their room as Hollie shakes her head at him in confusion. "Tim texted me—he said I should check on you as soon as I could. I—are you okay? What are you doing home so early? Our reservations aren't until nine. I thought you'd—"

"I quit," he announces, spreading his arms open wide. "They pulled me into the office this afternoon and fed me some bullshit about this deal I've been working on. They're going against all of my advice. I tried to fight them, but in that moment, I had never felt such clarity about anything."

"Clarity?" Hollie murmurs as she reaches up to bury her fingers in her hair. She shakes her head and scrunches her brow as she inquires, "Clarity? You just—you just quit your job without discussing it with me because you felt clarity?"

"Hey." Khalohn's voice is soft, and he's quick to close the distance between them. Curving his hands around her cheeks, he stares deep into her eyes and whispers, "I know it sounds crazy, but look at me—look at me. Am I not the same man I was this morning?"

"Lohnny, it's almost Christmas."

"Baby, look at me."

He pauses as he continues to gaze into her eyes, waiting for her to see him like only she ever has. When she sighs and lets go of her hair, he knows her fear of the unknown has begun to subside. Khalohn presses a kiss to her lips, but neither of them closes their eyes. Hollie rests her hands at his sides and beseeches him for more with her silence.

"The deal I told them not to make, they're making it. But my proposal— my deal—they're tossing it. I'm going to take it. I'm going to do this. Start from scratch. Make a name for myself."

"The resorts in the Bahamas? You're going to—you're going to buy a chain of resorts that's going bankrupt? At Christmas? Lohnny, with what money? We're doing fine, but you just quit your job, and we don't have—"

"I've got a meeting with the bank tomorrow. And my financial advisor, he thinks I can do it. If I liquidate all my investments—"

"Oh, my god. Lohnny, you're scaring me," Hollie breathes as she rests her forehead against Khalohn's chest.

"Hollie—baby," he mumbles, tilting his head until his lips are pressed into her silky, blonde hair. He smooths his hands along the strands and then holds the back of her neck. "I'm doing this for us. You hear me? I'm not in this alone, and I know it. If I thought the risks far outweighed the reward, we wouldn't be having this conversation. You have to trust me. Do you trust me, baby?"

A soft sound erupts from the back of her throat as she presses her head against him harder. She then lifts her head, in search of his eyes. The expression on her face speaks of her apprehension; but as she circles her arms around his middle, he knows she's with him.

"I'm scared," she admits on a whisper.

"I will not fail. Regardless of the outcome, I will not fail you."

Hollie leans into him even as she reaches up with one of her hands to cup his smooth cheek. "I know. It's why I married you." Holding him tight, she declares, "I love you."

"I love you back."

A beat of silence passes between them, and then she traces one of her fingers across his lips as he watches hers turn into a small smile. "This better not be my anniversary present."

Laughing, Khalohn presses his lips to hers and mumbles, "You know I can do better than this. It's why you married me."

Chapter Five

J ESSICA SHAKES HER HEAD, the end of her ponytail brushing across the back of her shoulders as she tries not to mumble to herself in irritation like a crazy person. In spite of her perfectly timed ride on the R train—traveling to and from the pharmacy—her errand has left her running late. She's convinced, had she not been forced to explain herself three times to Dr. Freeman, beseeching him to alert the pharmacy Beth needed her prescriptions refilled two and a half weeks early, she'd be on time. As it stands, she'll be at least twenty minutes late. She's already fighting the urge to roll her eyes at Griffin's reprimands.

With Beth out of work and the month dwindling to a close, the Chapman women have been doing their best to make ends meet whilst trying to plan ahead. Knowing Beth can't go without her bronchodilators and her steroids, their best plan of action has been to acquire the necessary medications in preparation for the upcoming month. August will bring with it a new set of challenges. While they are hopeful the application process to get Beth on Medicaid won't cause too much trouble, they're unsure how much help the program will be in their situation. Even more,

Beth's meds aren't their only worry. As much as Jessica doesn't like to think about it, a month's worth of back-up meds is merely a drop in the bucket, but it's the best they can do for now.

She travels at a clip somewhere between a walk and a jog as she hurries down Bay Ridge Avenue, heading for home. Her skin grows slick as her pores open in an attempt to cool her down. It's no use, with the sun still high in the sky and evening doing little to chase away the summer heat. Even though changing into a fresh top will likely do little to help, she's already mentally sorting through her stack of clean shirts, in hopes of finding one to change into quickly before leaving for work.

When she reaches 7th Avenue, she holds her purse to her side and jogs around the corner. Light on her feet, she races up the steps to their apartment building. After successfully punching in the code to grant her entrance through the front door, she bypasses the elevator and quickly climbs her way to the third floor.

"Mom?" she calls out the second she crosses the threshold into their humble abode.

It's a one-bedroom, one-bathroom unit located on the edge of Bay Ridge, nestled in the southwest corner of the borough of Brooklyn. Beth moved into the quaint living space six months after Jessica settled into a place of her own with Stefano. When Jessica packed her bags two and a half years later, intent on making her home with her mother, the thought of a bigger unit hardly crossed their minds. With medical bills to worry about, they've simply managed to make it work—like always.

The sofa, situated in the middle of the living room, doubles as Jessica's bed. Sleeping on a pull-out mattress isn't ideal, but she never complains. Neither does she neglect to stow away the bed each morning, giving them the semblance of more space—which is nothing shy of a difficult feat. The gray walls are covered in framed photographs, documenting Jessica's life in the most endearingly cluttered way possible; and every corner is filled with the stacks of books Beth has been collecting for years. To Jessica, they are a constant reminder of the life she wishes she could give her mother—a life filled with rest and days upon days of nothing more than murder mysteries, suspense thrillers, and wine.

Before Beth can respond with her words, Jessica hears her cough as it sounds from the kitchen. Making her way in that direction, she drops her purse beside the sofa, digging out the paper bag full of meds along her short journey.

"In here, baby," Beth manages as Jessica approaches the arched entryway.

For reasons neither of them has ever been able to justify, the walls in this particular room are painted a soft pink, which causes the white-washed cabinetry to catch one's eye. The old, white-oak table that's been around for more than fifteen years is pushed up against the wall across from the sink and the stove—making it nearly impossible to open the refrigerator door all the way, so long as someone is seated on the left side. As awkward as the piece of furniture might be in such a cramped space, Beth has always insisted upon it. Her argument has consistently been that *dinner* can hardly be considered *dinner* without a *dinner table*. Currently, she occupies the chair on the right, her attention glued to the outdated laptop they've had since Jessica was in high school.

Without even having to ask, Jessica is sure her mother is busy looking for a job. She's been at it for two whole days now, and she's wearing her discouragement like an ugly sweater draped around her slightly rounded frame, the garment one she's trying to convince the whole world is comfortable. Staring at the forty-three-year-old woman, who looks closer to fifty than either of them would like to admit, Jessica's heart feels heavy. She wants to tell Beth to take the night off and relax, but she knows the plea would be useless. Jessica is also conscious of the fact that there's no way her job a Moby's Dive will sustain them for very long. They need whatever income Beth can supply.

Shaking her head at herself, Jessica pulls in a breath and gives herself a mental kick in the rear. The last thing she needs is Griffin threatening her job, too, which means she can't slow down—not for another second.

"Got your meds," she announces, holding up the paper sack. "I'll put them in your nightstand, okay? I've got to run. Do you need anything?"

Beth looks away from the computer and combs her fingers through her thin, chestnut, brown hair, streaked with gray. Offering her daughter a small smile, she mutters, "Thanks, baby—I'm good. Get out of here. I'll see you in the morning."

Jessica forces a small smile of her own before she turns and hurries for the bedroom. She doesn't take in the details of her mother's room, having long since memorized them. She does take note of the book resting on top of the nightstand. *The Crooked Staircase* by Dean Koontz is open, face down, the binding showing signs of Beth's multiple trips through the pages. While she's appreciative the man wrote a book capable of capturing her mother's attention over and over again, and though she's grateful there's something familiar and consistent Beth has found to occupy her mind enough to find rest at night—Jessica wishes Beth didn't need to seek out the tried and true in an attempt to escape the unexpected and daunting reality that arrived before either of them were ready.

After closing the small drawer of the nightstand, she returns to the living room, where she digs through the laundry basket full of clean clothes. When she finds her loose-fitting, black tank top, with a faded and distressed rendition of the American flag printed down the length of the front, she doesn't waste any time switching it out with the t-shirt on her back. The cut of the neckline dips low, exposing the small, top swell of her breasts, and she decides it's a sexy as she's capable of for the evening. Tucking the front into her short, holey jean skirt, she then reaches for her purse and starts for the door.

Jessica craves a night at home, but she doesn't let her mind so much as entertain the longing.

"Bye, mom. Love you," she calls out as she takes her leave.

"Love you, too. Have a good night at work," Beth replies before Jessica closes the door.

She races back to the subway and manages to arrive just as her ride comes to a stop. Relieved, she boards the R train and then pulls out her phone and her earbuds. For the next fifteen minutes, she wills the music that flows through her ears to relax her muscles and quiet her mind. It feels like it's been a long day, and yet she's barely getting started. She needs a release—someplace to expel the worry and stress which seems to be wrapping itself around the muscles in her shoulders and neck before solidifying in such a way that makes it difficult for her to move with all the dexterity she requires to feel *human*.

Jessica rolls her neck and then her thoughts take her back a couple nights. A small smile plays at her lips as she remembers Stefano's promise to get her into the city the next night she has free. Even though that's days away, the hope of an escape looming in the distance—short lived as it might be—provides her with a jolt of determination she needs. When she arrives at the 9th Street Station, even though she doesn't stop her music, her mind shifts in a different direction as she hurries for the bus stop. By the time the B61 arrives, she's already searching the internet for a job.

She doesn't know when she'll have time to sleep if she finds herself a second gig; but slumber seems like a small sacrifice to pay in return for a little peace of mind and a smaller measure of pressure on Beth. As unfair as it is, Jessica knows her mother's worsening condition was a contributing factor to the loss of her job. The practical part of Jessica's mind is frustrated that after more than twenty years of service, the plant could let Beth go, as if it were nothing—as if her loyalty and her dedication didn't make her better than half their staff.

On the flip side, reason also has room to argue in Jessica's mind. She can't help but to feel relieved the workplace that brought about all this trouble in the first place is finally a matter with which they need not concern themselves. Except, the trouble still remains that Beth didn't leave after her diagnosis for a reason. She doesn't have experience doing anything else. With her lungs as damaged as they are, her options are limited. If it weren't for her medication, showering alone would put her into a coughing fit with the power to render her useless. Even if Jessica does find a second job, it's no secret between mother and daughter, it won't replace the income which has been lost. Whatever job Beth might mange to find will likely still leave them scraping by.

During her twenty-minute bus ride, Jessica screenshots a couple leads to follow-up on as soon as she gets the chance. Upon arriving at Van Dyke Street, just a block away from her destination, she puts aside her job hunt and jogs the whole way to Moby's Dive. There are small beads of sweat gathering along her hairline as she bursts through the back door not even two minutes later, but she ignores them. Shutting off her music, she tosses her phone and her earbuds in her purse. She tries to slow her breathing as she journeys down the dingy corridor leading to the bar.

She's so focused on reaching the door, she doesn't hear Griffin when he yells her name from his office as she passes. It isn't until he all but growls at her from behind that she turns and acknowledges him.

"You think you can walk in here twenty fucking minutes late and then ignore me? You think you own this place, Chapman? You fuckin' don't."

"I'm sorry, okay? I'm here now," she murmurs, too exhausted to put up more of a fight before she turns toward the door once more.

"I'm not done with you," Griffin retorts.

Jessica jolts to an abrupt halt when she feels his hand grab hold of her elbow. His grip alone speaks of his warning. She looks down at his fingers, digging into her flesh, and then into his dark green eyes, where she finds another warning.

"Get your shit together or you're out. I mean it. I'm sick of your excuses."

An unexpected ire rises up inside of Jessica, setting her chest on fire. As it burns, the thick, billows of smoke it produces clogs her throat and steals her words. All the while, her heart beats angrily inside of her chest, knowing he doesn't know the half of it.

Without a word, she jerks her arm, intent on escaping his hold. To her surprise and relief, his grip loosens before his hand falls away. With still nothing to say to the man, she turns on her heel and pushes her way through the swinging door at the end of the hall. When she emerges into the bar, "It's My Life" by Bon Jovi blares over the sound system, and she closes her eyes, wishing she could turn around and flip Griffin the finger. He knows nothing about her; nothing about her situation; nothing about her *excuses* and the plaguing effect they play in every aspect of her life. He's certainly the least of her worries and far from the center of her universe.

"Jess—you made it," greets Cassy, beckoning Jessica to open her eyes.

She spots the spunky blonde as she leans against the bar. The crowd in the room is light at this early hour, making Jessica even more annoyed about the run-in she just had with Griffin.

"Hey, you okay?" Cassy asks. Her eyebrows pinch together in concern.

Convinced she doesn't have the spare energy to feed the fire that burns inside of her, Jessica pulls in a deep breath. She then shakes her head and rolls her stiff shoulders before forcing on her best smile. Then she does the only thing she can think to do.

She lies.

"Yeah. I'm good. Totally ready to kick Saturday night ass."

Chapter Six

"IDID IT. FUCKING FINALLY!*" Stefano declares as he bursts through the* front door. *"I told that bastard of a boss I was done, and I walked my happy ass out of that god-awful, pretentious, bigoted dump of bar. Jessica, my dove, I was a fucking man today. God—it was heavenly. Now, I have no idea whether or not I'll be eating crow's shit tomorrow, but right now, I have not one shit to give,"* he continues, his words spilling out of his mouth a mile a minute.

His voice resounds through their apartment as he announces, "You see, I met this woman—no. She was more than a woman. I swear, the sophistication that ran off her shoulders was irrefutable. It was fucking amazing *is what it was. And she—"*

Stefano jolts to a halt when he fills Jessica's bedroom doorway. As she sits in the middle of the floor, half her wardrobe shoved haphazardly inside of her suitcase, she can barely hear her own thoughts over the panic that seems to be screaming relentlessly in her mind. The pitch of her fear is so ear-splittingly high, it slices straight through her—from her head all the way down to her belly.

Jessica's unaware of the way her body is swaying from side to side as she presses one hand to her stomach while the other is clasped tightly around her mouth. Tears race down her cheeks, but she doesn't notice them. She's too busy trying to keep her jaw locked shut. She's afraid if her mouth opens, her panic will manifest in a cry and spill through her lips in a perturbation so profound, she won't be able to silence it.

"Jess?" Stefano breathes her name, and the sense of his presence as he eases into the room tickles the nape of her neck. She knows she should speak. Her subconscious is aware Stefano won't know what to do with her in her crumbled state any more than she does. In the seven years they've known each other, she's never felt so afraid. So unsure. So directionless.

"Jess?" he whispers, sinking to his knees.

His soft voice penetrates through the cacophony of her panic, and Jessica seals her eyes closed tighter as she lets go of her stomach and reaches for him. She catches hold of his shirt, but she doesn't have to tug before he's right there— folding her in his arms. The instant her head makes contact with his shoulder, she can feel it as Stefano holds her together. Her agitation begins to cower in his presence, and she blows out a huff as she frees her mouth from the prison of her own fingers. Reaching for his side, she shifts enough to grab onto her best friend. He squeezes her tighter, and she manages a deep breath.

"Jess? What happened? Fuck. Talk to me."

Jessica pulls in a shuddered breath, lifting her head until her forehead is pressed to the smooth skin of Stefano's neck. The warmth he emanates seeps into her pores and reminds her she cannot succumb to the cold threat of death—not so long as the people she loves more than anyone in the world still have breath flowing through their lungs.

"Damnit," she curses, her fingers tightening into a fist around his shirt.

"Dove—come on. You're freaking me out."

"Hold me tighter. Please." Her voice is hardly more than a whimper as she begins to feel the tears that continue to pour from her eyes.

"Jess, I'm two seconds away from crushing you."

In spite of her consternation, Jessica manages a half-hearted chuckle as she shakes her head in disagreement. "We both know I've got you beat in the strength department."

"Says the one bawling her eyes out in the middle of the floor," he argues, his arms constricting around her tighter. "What the fuck, Jess?"

Burrowing into him even closer, she finally confesses, "It's my mom. She's sick, Huey. She's really—she's really sick." She chokes on her sob and shakes her head in a failed attempt to ward off her devastation.

"Sick? Sick how? I thought—I thought she just had bronchitis or some shit."

Another cry ripples through Jessica's insides as the truth settles heavily on her chest and guilt starts to seep into her bloodstream. She feels the toxin begin to course through her body as she thinks back over the last six months and the cough she let her mother tell her was nothing. Jessica can hardly bear the feel of her own pulse, each heartbeat reminding her of the life Beth Chapman sacrificed everything to raise.

"God—I should have done something. I shouldn't have listened to her. I should have—"

"Stop," Stefano demands, giving her a shake. It isn't until he constricts his arms that Jessica realizes her own attempt to wiggle out of the comfort of his embrace. "Don't go making this about you," he insists, not unkindly. "Now, what's wrong with her?"

She nods, pulling in a deep breath as she manages to grip onto her runaway emotions. She then tells him, "She's got—chronic obstructive pulmonary disease. It's—it's in her lungs. Her cough—Huey, it's not going to go away. COPD isn't curable. The best they can do is give her meds to help make it easier for her to breathe—but it's going to get worse. They can't even figure out how long she's had it. Fuck, she works at a damn chemical plant. God—she's been there my entire life. Why didn't I ever—"

"What? Tell your mother to change professions? Like it's that easy?" Stefano murmurs, his lips brushing against her temple.

She blows out a sigh, grateful her best friend has always been good for a reality check. He's the only one in her life who knows when she's too weak to fight her own self-pity. He's the only one with the unique capability of making her see reason when it's the furthest thing from her mind. She respects him for being

*bold; for reminding her she's got to be better than her circumstances. It's a battle
she's been fighting her whole life, and to lose is unacceptable.*

*Be that as it may, Jessica feels the potential of loss in ways she isn't prepared
for. In her mind, on repeat, she hears her mother's doctor as he delivers her
diagnosis. She feels Beth squeeze her hand, only the pain she feels at the pressure
is around her heart.*

"Huey, I can't lose her. I can't."

*Stefano hesitates, and she feels it as he lifts his head away from hers to look
beside them.* "You're moving out."

*This time, when she tries to pull away from him, he lets her go. She rests
one of her hands flat against his chest, raking her fingers through her hair with
her other as she whispers,* "I need to be with her. I need to make sure—"

"You don't have to explain. I get it," *he assures her, resting his own hand
over the top of hers.*

"Wait…"

*Jessica crinkles her brow and lifts her gaze to meet his hazel stare. Feeling
slightly calmer and more aware of the moment in which she finds herself, she
tries to piece together what she thinks she might have heard not even five
minutes ago. Her eyes travel away from his handsome face and down toward
his chest. The crisp, white fabric beneath her hand is her confirmation Stefano
has recently come from work. Only, his tie is loose and sloppy.*

Sniffling, Jessica shakes her head and mutters, "You quit your job?"

A sly smirk curls the corner of his top lip as he nods. "Yeah."

"Your timing is kind of shit, Stefano."

"Please," *he says with an eye roll.* "We both know I don't need your rent."

"Yeah, well, we both know how Stefano despises needing Hugh's money."

*He nods, curling his fingers under hers as he holds her hand to his chest and
retorts,* "This isn't about me, dove. Besides—I've got a job interview tomorrow.
If it turns out to be legit, I won't need to bother with Hugh at all. Shit—if I'm
lucky, maybe I'll finally be able to pay to be rid of Hugh all together. It's high
time Stefano became legal."

Blowing out a huff, Jessica tries to pull herself together. She wipes her face dry and reigns in her emotions. Deep down she knows, whatever happens moving forward, it's her turn to be the strong one; it's her turn to be the caretaker; it's her turn to step up and put herself second, like her mother did twenty-one years ago. It's the least she can do. She owes her mother more than she could ever repay.

With this in mind, Jessica shakes off her moment of helplessness and shifts her focus onto her friend. Cognizant of her mounting responsibilities, she decides to tackle her problems the only way she knows how—one at a time. Lifting up onto her knees, she squeezes his hand and insists, "Okay. Tell me about this job interview."

Stefano studies her for a few seconds before he shakes his head at her. "No."

"What?" *she asks, knitting her eyebrows together.* "What do you mean, no?"

"You're tough as nails, Jess, I'll give you that—but even you can't handle this conversation without the help of a little wine." *Before Jessica can conjure a response, Stefano is on his feet. He smooths out his pants and then looks around at the mess she's made in her frantic attempt to pack.* "I'm going to run around the corner and pick up a couple bottles. When I get back, I'll fill you in while I help you pack. Then we'll get drunk and dance it out. You down?"

Jessica doesn't fight her smile as she admires the pretty man who stands before her. If she didn't know him half as well as she does, she'd swear he was hiding a halo underneath all that hair.

"Any chance you could add an apple pie to that grocery list?"

"Mmm. Pie and port. I like where your head's at, dove. I'll be back in a few."

By the time Stefano returns to the apartment, Jessica has managed to clear her small closet of all her belongings, and the mess she had been drowning in earlier is merely a memory. The pie Stefano brings home is cold, but it's a gift she won't take for granted from the one and only man who has never left her side. While they pop it in the oven to warm it up, Stefano helps her clear her things from the bathroom. She doesn't have much. Their space would never allow it, and her tips from her waitressing gig don't carry the reputation of ever going very far.

When her bags are packed, stacked neatly beside the door, Jessica looks around at their little piece of Brooklyn Heights, crestfallen she'll have to leave.

"I know that look. That look calls for pie. Come on, it's ready," Stefano insists. He takes her hand and leads her into their small kitchen before he uncorks a bottle of tawny port. After he pours them each a glass, he hands her a fork, and they both dig into the pie without bothering to even slice it properly.

"Okay. You've stalled long enough," Jessica mutters with a mouthful. "Who's this woman you were blathering about? And what's the job?"

Stefano takes a slow sip of his wine, staring at her all the while over the rim of his glass. Jessica quirks an eyebrow at him, and he swallows loudly before he sets aside his wine and looks her straight in the eye.

"Her name is Beatrice Deveaux. She came in for a drink and—"

"Wait, you met her at work? You hate the patrons at—"

"Yeah, I know. Trust me. Half of them remind me of my father. The other half are practically clones of my overly entitled grandmother—but she was different. I swear, she walked into the room, and I felt it."

Jessica stares at him dubiously, her fork stuck in the pie as she murmurs, "If I didn't know better, I'd think you had a thing for her."

"Oh, shut it," he grumbles as he digs for a bite of his own. "You do know better, and this woman is old enough to be my mother."

"All right. So, what's her deal?"

Stefano pauses again, shoveling a fork-full of warm, apple filling into his mouth, his hazel gaze locked with Jessica's brown one as he chews. She squints at him suspiciously, and he shifts uncomfortably under her perusal.

"Stefano!"

"She runs an underground business," he blurts. "I didn't get a lot of details. She didn't want to talk about it out in the open. But she told me she'd pay three times as much as I was making and, if all goes well tomorrow, I could start immediately."

"An underground business? What kind of underground business? What would you be doing? Stefano—"

"Listen, it's as I said, I don't have all the details. But what she told me is she's been looking for a gatekeeper. She said she'd been watching me for a couple weeks and thought I'd be perfect."

"A g—a gatekeeper?" Jessica stutters, her tone dripping in disbelief. Without missing a beat, she reaches for his glass of port. "I think you don't need this. I do. From the sounds of it, I'm going to be taking care of my sick mom and my insane best friend."

"Give me that." Stefano snatches his glass away from Jessica, who manages a small giggle, in spite of her mounting worry. "I know it sounds crazy."

"Huey…" Jessica starts and then stops. She sets her fork down and reaches her hand out, signaling for him to do the same. He does, giving her fingers a slight squeeze as he places his palm on top of hers. "I know it's been frustrating for you to find your place. You are—extraordinary and exceptional and unique in so many ways. And as much as I know you hate it, you can't escape the fact that you were bred for a certain kind of lifestyle. I know this sounds like something strange enough to be right up your alley, but—"

"It's a risk. I know. But you weren't there. You didn't meet her, Jess. I'm telling you, there's something about her. I can't put my finger on it, but just the possibility alone…" His voice trails off as he looks down at their conjoined hands. "This might sound crazy, but this is a leap I'm willing to make. Even if, at the end of it all, I have to be Hugh for a little while longer."

"Okay then," says Jessica with a resolute sigh. She lets go of his hand and reaches for her fork once more, her attention focused on the pie as she tells him, "I'm going with you tomorrow. And don't even try to stop me. No way am I letting my best friend go on some weird-ass interview for some underground gatekeeper job all by himself."

"I'm a big boy, Jess. I think I can manage an interview in the middle of the day—underground or otherwise."

"Yeah, well, I don't need to be worried about you and mom. I'm coming to ensure I can check one of you off my list. Like I said, you can't stop me. Now, drink your wine. I could use a buzz right about now."

Stefano smirks at Jessica as she shovels a big bite of pie into her mouth, and then he downs the rest of his wine in a large gulp. Setting his glass on the counter, he starts to make his way out of the tiny kitchen, smacking her backside as he passes.

"Pour me another. I'm going to turn on some tunes."

JESSICA CLINGS TO Stefano's arm as they stand out in the cold, mid-morning air, staring at their destination's storefront.

"A lingerie store? She wants to meet you here?"

"This is the address," Stefano confirms.

"This just got kinky."

"Come on," he chuckles. "It's freezing, and I don't want to be late."

With a nod, Jessica allows Stefano to escort her into Clandestine's Closet. As soon as they pass through the front entrance, her eyes are everywhere, taking in the elaborate space. In spite of the warmth that fills the establishment, as Jessica lets go of Stefano's arm, she hugs her coat around herself, feeling slightly embarrassed by some of the apparel out on display. While she's certainly no prude, she's never found herself in the market for underthings quite as decadent as the items laid out before her. It's not so much her sexual experience so much as it is her socioeconomic status that makes her feel out of place.

"You okay?" asks Stefano, pulling Jessica from her thoughts.

She looks up at him and offers him another nod.

He dips his chin in response before assuring her, "I'll be back. I'm going to find Beatrice."

"Good luck."

As soon as he walks away, "River" by Bishop Briggs starts to play over the sound system. Jessica looks up at the ceiling, smiling to herself as the beat begins to wash over her. She's never been one to believe in signs, but she can't deny a good song. As it continues to play, she allows her eyes to dance around the store once more. Willing herself to relax, she decides to embark on a little exploration of her own.

One song transitions into another as she wanders around the shop. She allows her fingers to glide over the material of the garments she likes, all the while knowing she could never afford to buy any of the items. Even if she could, she'd never attracted the kind of man who would appreciate her delicate tastes. She's known more fumbled, back room, half-clothed sexual encounters than she'd like to admit. Even so, as she whiles away an hour, she lets herself imagine a time and place where such underthings would befit an evening or two.

She's making her way down from the second level of the boutique when she spots Stefano as he steps out onto the main floor. She can tell right away he's looking for her, so she calls out his name in a mock whisper, catching his attention before offering him a wave. The grin that splices his face tells her all she needs to know, and she hurries down the stairs to meet up with him. The instant she's in reaching distance, Stefano takes her by the hand and begins to drag her out of the store.

"Wait—Huey, slow down," she laughs, clinging to his arm with her free hand in an attempt to keep her balance. "What happened?"

"Jess," he mutters, speaking through the biggest smile she's ever seen on his face. Without slowing his pace, he exclaims, "Fuck Beyoncé. I work for the real Queen Bea."

Chapter Seven

KHALOHN WIPES HIS FINGERS ON the napkin in his grasp as he continues to chew the last bite of his meal. After discarding it with the plastic container in which his lunch was delivered, he continues to read over the documents his lawyers sent over earlier that morning. When his cell phone rings a moment later, it takes him a second to shift his attention onto the device before he proceeds to answer.

"Hello?" he mutters in greeting, his mind still torn between the task in front of him and the caller in his ear.

"Boss man, I've got news."

Khalohn can hear Manhattan's late afternoon traffic playing in the background on the other end of the line, and he's certain Porter is on the move. He also surmises, given his straight-forward announcement, he's in between appointments. The only time Khalohn can expect Porter to be direct is when he's fully immersed in business mode. He'll never deny how much he appreciates when his broker, not his friend, desires his time. After all, it is their business relationship that made way for their friendship in the first place.

"I'm listening," Khalohn replies.

"Pier House Resorts—heard of them?"

His attention now completely captivated, Khalohn leans back in his chair, a slight scowl tugging at his brow. His eyes focus out the window across from his desk, but he doesn't see the view as he mulls over the name Porter just spoke. Khalohn spent many years with his sights set on a number of resorts all over the world. When he began to branch out in an attempt to grow his enterprise and expand his footprint, he found he had little time to keep abreast of vacation homes as much as he used to.

"Sounds vaguely familiar, but I can't say I know anything specific."

"Chain of hotels along the Gulf. Coincidentally, *golf* is one of their selling points—that and their spa packages. Don't have a bunch of details in regard to what's going on behind the scenes, but saw they took a hefty dip in the stock market this morning. Thought you might like to look into it."

Khalohn sighs, flicking his wrist as he checks the time. His afternoon is stacked, and he plans on being in meetings until early evening—the first of which is to begin in less than an hour.

Hearing the reluctance in just one breath, Porter chuckles in Khalohn's ear. "There's nothing wrong with making a quick buck, especially not with a family-owned business that's likely in the midst of a scramble, trying to save their asses. You know I wouldn't bring it to your attention if I didn't think it worth your while. You've got a lot of big deals in the works—deals that take *ages*—look into this one."

"Yeah. Thanks for the tip."

"I am good for something," he retorts, his smile evident in his tone. "Catch you later."

Khalohn doesn't even have to think of a response, Porter quickly disconnecting the call. Before his cell phone hits his desk, he's got his office phone in his hand.

"Morgan?" Maribelle answers a second later.

"Please get Lorelai in my office. Preferably within the next five minutes."

"I'll see what I can do, dear."

She disconnects before his headset is even nestled into its cradle, but he thinks nothing of it. He shifts his scrutiny back onto the documents which occupied his attention not even five minutes ago, scouring them until a knock sounds at his door. He calls for the person on the other side to enter, and he looks up when he sees Lorelai rounding the front of his desk, her heels marking the beat of her step until she comes to a graceful halt.

She tucks a bit of her cropped dirty-blonde hair behind her ear and then casually slips her fingertips into the pockets of her fitted, navy ankle slacks. The white blouse she wears is sleeveless with a lace overlay, extending all the way up her chest and around the base of her neck. Similar to their first encounter, Lorelai exudes a confidence which mirrors her bold choice of attire.

Khalohn doesn't take in her details, noting only that she appears as poised and prepared as she has been since he hired her, a year and a half ago. Past experience fills him with the assurance that while she might appear to be unprepared to take any sort of instructions from him, he can count on her to deliver precisely what he wants in the time frame in which he needs it.

"Pier House Resorts—have they ever been on your radar?"

She tips the corners of her lips down as she shakes her head at him. "No, sir. Should they have been?"

"It's what I'd like you to find out. Dig up anything and everything you can about them. Apparently, they took a hit this morning."

A smirk turns one side of her mouth in the opposite direction. Lorelai nonchalantly pops out one of her hips as she inquires, "Do we smell blood in the water?"

"You tell me. Two hours."

Her smirk stretches into a grin. She then nods her head and begins to take her leave. "Yes, sir."

Khalohn watches her go, a small part of him humbled by the

happenings of the last several minutes. There was a time when he was Lorelai—the associate sent on a hunting endeavor. Now his phone rings with a tip and he's able to send someone else to do the grunt work while he sees to other matters.

That small piece of him, who can acknowledge his acquired position and the power found in his station, is soon silenced by his own tireless work ethic, which reminds him his afternoon is full.

Too full to warrant the time for a recon mission.

He shifts his focus once more, intent on preparing himself for the meetings which will consume the next few hours of his day. Maribelle calls five minutes before he's due to report for a sit-down with his CFO. He slips into his jacket, smooths a hand over his beard, and pockets his phone prior to making his exit. Two hours and three meetings later, he's almost forgotten the task he doled out to his shark of an associate—that is, until he sees her push off the wall she was leaning upon while she waited for his meeting to be adjourned.

Khalohn doesn't even have to ask, and he's got an iPad in his hand. Neither does he have to glance down at it as Lorelai follows him back toward his office. With her hands casually tucked into the pockets of her slacks, she informs him, "Pier House opened their first hotel and spa upwards of twenty-five years ago. Father and son headed the project on a piece of real estate which had been inherited. Three years later, they were in the black and looking to expand. *Ten* years down the road, and they had five resorts and enough money to set up trust funds for all the little Jimmys and Janes they'd been popping out; not to mention a nest egg large enough for the old man to retire.

"Fast forward to six months ago," Lorelai insists as the two of them come to stop a few feet away from Maribelle's desk. Khalohn's brow furrows in interest, offering the woman another second of his undivided attention before he begins to open up the documents saved to the *Pier House* folder in order to glance at her evidence.

Continuing with her diatribe, Lorelai informs, "The son who started it all dies in a tragic boating accident. Sad as it was, someone had to step up. As family businesses are prone, there was a squabble for the vacancy—Jimmy and Jane duked it out, and it got nasty. *Headlines* nasty. In the end, Jimmy won. Makes me wonder, had Jane fought a little harder, if the whole thing wouldn't be going to shit right about now. They're hemorrhaging money, sir. Without seeing their books, I can't say with all certainty, but their dive in the stock market this morning exposed them. It's a fucking blood bath."

Khalohn hums, his eyes taking in the numbers in front of him. What he sees is textbook research. The facts are there, as plain as day. If they don't act soon, someone else will—if they haven't already. He hands the device back to Lorelai and demands, "Make contact. Set up a meeting."

"Am I running point on this?" she asks, quirking one of her perfectly manicured eyebrows.

"Pull me in if you need me."

With a confident, lopsided smile, Lorelai begins to back her way in the direction from which they came. Holding up the iPad in mock salute, she replies, "Yes, sir."

As she turns around to hurry back to her desk, Khalohn calls out, "Lorelai?"

"Mr. Morgan?" she murmurs, turning only enough to look back at him from over her shoulder.

Knowing what it means to surrender this deal into her hands, his tone is stern and coated in a not-so-subtle warning as he demands, "*Don't* need me."

Lowering her eyes, Lorelai dips her chin in a slight nod of acknowledgment before she takes her leave.

"You're getting better at that, you know?" says Maribelle softly, earning Khalohn's attention.

"At what?"

"Letting them fly," she answers with a small, enigmatic smile. "It's good to see you let go of the little ones. Granted, I don't think you'll manage to leave the office any earlier having assigned that one into her care, but I appreciate the small victories right alongside the big ones."

He grunts, not willing to admit how right she is, and closes the distance between them. With ten minutes before his next meeting, his only intention for returning to his office is to check on any messages.

"Anything important cross my desk while I was out?"

"Important? No. But the reports you requested should be in your inbox. Also, your housekeeper called. Something about a mix-up at the dry cleaners. Your suits won't be ready until tomorrow."

"Fine. Thank you," he replies as he continues toward his office.

Khalohn is just sitting down to log-on to his computer and take a look at the reports Maribelle mentioned when his phone begins to ring. Upon seeing Porter's name lighting up his screen, a smirk pulls at the corner of his mouth.

"Morgan," he answers.

"You're going after it, aren't you?"

"Chances are the current CEO is nothing more than a rich kid who didn't know what he was getting into when he stepped into daddy's shoes. Now all he sees is his family's fortune draining from the hole they've got in their hull. At the right price, he won't be able to help himself. It's like taking candy from a baby."

Porter chuckles as he mutters, "*Savage.*"

"*Smart*," Khalohn retorts with a shake of his head.

"Tomato, *tomato*—either way, you owe me."

"I *pay* you," he replies with confused scowl.

"Tonight. I need a wingman, and you're it. Besides, after Tokyo—after the Monte Carlo—I owe you a drink."

Fighting the urge to roll his eyes, Khalohn mutters, "After the Monte Carlo, I don't see why you need a wingman." There's no doubt in his mind his yacht was occupied by no less than half a dozen women over the long weekend. He knows to tip his crew generously after Porter has been out to sea. There's no telling what the clean-up is like.

"The weekend is over, my friend. Today's a new day. Now stop fighting me. We both know you're overdue for a night out."

"Fine," Khalohn concedes. He rakes his fingers through his hair, more concerned with getting Porter off the phone than a night spent away from home. Before Porter can get a word in, he goes on to clarify, "I pick the place."

"Done. Text me where. I'll meet you at nine."

IT'S TEN MINUTES after the top of the hour when Atzel pulls up to the curb in front of The Critic—located on the banks of Hell's Kitchen. The high-end club is one Khalohn has been able to tolerate in the past, all the while certain what he seeks for his own personal endeavors won't be found within the establishment. It is a setting by which a compromise is often found on nights like this one. It's no secret to either of them how much Porter enjoys playing *the game*.

While Khalohn finds it almost as painful to watch the hunt as it is to participate himself, The Critic is worth his time for more than one reason. Not only is it a place Porter likes to frequent, but it's also a space in which a number of notable, wealthy New Yorkers find themselves on occasion— their VIP status an actuality which must be *seen* to be accepted. Much as he wishes he could deny it, rubbing shoulders with the right crowd never hurt his reputation as a businessman not to be forgotten. And when schmoozing with the elite gets to be too much, The Critic serves a scotch smooth enough to make the trip worth his while.

Atzel opens Khalohn's door, and he's quick to step out and onto the curb. Glancing at the line of people who wish to get into the nightclub causes him to remember how much he despises being surrounded by women the likes of which he's encountered far too many times. He sees it, even now, as a couple women eye him from head to toe. Flattering as one might think their attentions are, all they see are his details. The cut of his tailored Gucci suit, the shine of his Tom Ford oxford shoes, and the face of his Montblanc timepiece. In their eyes, he isn't a man so much as he's a bank account—and this is not a notion which has ever brought him pride. As he looks away from them, he pulls his phone from his pocket. After a couple of hours in the club, an indulgence of his own will be warranted. Ironic as it might seem, the extravagant amount of money he invests in his frequent rendezvous doesn't cause him to see those women in the same light in which he views the ones in the crowd. When he walks into that room, he is not a bank account, but a man intent on doling out pleasure as he seeks his own. His reputation precedes him in more than one arena—underground, the generosity they speak of holds no monetary value.

Dismissing Atzel kindly, he begins to place a call to an all too familiar number. The line rings only once before Stefano's voice greets him from the other end of the line.

"I'd like to make a reservation. Eleven thirty. Khalohn Morgan."

"Of course, Mr. Morgan. And I assure you, the mishap which occurred on your previous visit will not happen again."

"I would hope not."

Without another word, he disconnects the call, slipping his phone back into his pocket as he makes his way toward The Critic's entrance. Bypassing the line, he approaches the bouncer who stands at his post, beside the second set of front doors. Khalohn need not do more than slip the man his name, and he is granted entrance. He heads up the stairs to the VIP lounge and spots Porter right away. He's standing at the crowded bar, grinning as he leans down to hear the words of whatever woman is speaking into his ear. Khalohn fights the urge to turn around, uncertain why Porter ever thinks he needs a wingman.

When his friend sees him, he raises his free hand and waves him over. It takes only a moment for Khalohn to close the distance between them. As he comes to a stop, Porter straightens, revealing the face of Naomi Gray. She is who most would categorize as gorgeous—Khalohn included. For him, it's not her narrow, lithe, and delicate frame which he appreciates so much as the unique features of her face, not a bit of it crafted by human hands.

Her wide smile and large, round eyes are enticing; the dark freckles dusted across the light brown skin of her nose endearing; and her long, thick, wildly curly black hair simply exotic. Nevertheless, what she has to offer has never been enough to tempt Khalohn. Even if he were interested in the complications of a romantic entanglement—a sentiment which has not been true in years—her lifestyle is not one he's ever been drawn to. She's a Grammy award winning, two-time platinum record artist and a long-time friend turned client of Porter's.

"Naomi, you remember Khalohn, don't you?"

She rolls her eyes and nudges Porter's shoulder with her bare one before she replies, "Don't be cute. I remember all of your friends—especially the hot ones." Naomi smirks at Khalohn teasingly, and he can't help but return the expression. Their history is not extensive, but her attraction is always an offer she's unafraid to lay on the table, regardless of the fact that he never takes it. "How are you, Khalohn? It's been a while."

"More than a year, I'd guess," he responds, tucking his hands into his pant pockets.

"Yeah. It feels like I've been everywhere but home in a while. I had my nationwide tour, my international tour—then my managers had me in L.A. to be a judge for the pilot season of a show I'm not allowed to talk about yet. Anyway, when I saw I had a free week, I booked my flight back before anyone could add something to my schedule," she admits on a sigh.

"But you're here now," Porter says, playfully bumping his shoulder against hers. He then turns his focus onto Khalohn before he says, "Of course, this means she's totally fucked up my plans last minute. She's always been the worst cock-block I've ever been up against. Wingman or no wingman, this mission has turned into a damn social hour. Either way, I hope you'll stay—let me buy you that drink."

"Obviously he's staying. He just got here. Right?" goads Naomi.

With a subtle nod, Khalohn agrees, "I can stay for a drink or two."

Being a man of his word, Khalohn nurses two orders of scotch for the next hour and fifteen minutes. The majority of his time is spent in conversation with Naomi. As they sit at the bar, they discuss her travels, the two of them reminiscing about their shared habit of allowing their jobs to prohibit them from honestly experiencing the foreign places they frequent. All the while, in spite of his earlier comment, Porter loses interest in their chosen topic of conversation when he finds a woman he deems worthy of his attention.

"Don't tell me you're leaving so soon," Naomi demands as Khalohn closes his tab.

"I've got someplace to be," he states simply, standing to his feet. "It was good to see you—but I have monopolized your attention for long enough."

Rolling her eyes, Naomi replies, "Porter came to play, and it looks like he's found a willing opponent. You're not monopolizing anything I haven't offered freely." She reaches for his wrist, her touch as delicate as her plea when she murmurs, "Stay."

Khalohn pauses for a moment—not because he has any intention of staying; not even because he feels regretful he's not the slightest bit enticed by her beauty. While he's confident one night with Naomi would bring them both pleasure, he is equally as certain there would be no value in their exchange. To sully their cordial relationship would be unnecessary. In an effort to maintain their easy rapport for future encounters, he takes a second to calculate the appropriate response to her request.

"You and I both know you've had eyes on you all night. The seat I vacate will be occupied before I reach the door. Goodnight, Naomi."

He turns, slipping out of her hold with ease as he makes his way toward the exit. When he emerges into the warm, humid air of night, he stands on the curb and waits for Atzel. Upon his driver's arrival, he doesn't bother waiting for the man to get out in order to open his door and fold himself into the backseat.

"Lower Manhattan," he instructs, adjusting the watch on his wrist.

In truth, while Naomi could never persuade him into her bed, the feel of her hand still lingers on his skin. It stirs within him the desire to touch and to be touched. Khalohn stares out the window, his thoughts racing back to the last time he'd heard a woman moan for him. A frown pulls at his brow when he realizes he can hardly remember anything other than contracts, lawyers, and meetings consuming his time over the last few weeks. This awareness, coupled with the memory of his last visit to Clandestine's, fills him with an impatience and a hunger he's not willing to deny.

The fifteen minutes it takes to reach their destination does not pass quickly. Upon their arrival, Khalohn pauses long enough to allow Atzel to exit the vehicle in order to perform his due diligence and open the back door. Taking advantage of the quiet, empty space of his Maybach, Khalohn draws in a deep breath in an effort to will his mind into a state of calm submission.

"I won't be all night," he tells Atzel as he steps out onto the curb.

"Understood, sir."

Smoothing a hand down the front of his jacket, Khalohn relaxes before he journeys into the building. He doesn't pay any mind to his surroundings as he walks through the store into the back. When he enters the grand foyer of the underground establishment, he offers Stefano no more than a nod of acknowledgement before collecting his key.

As he finally enters his room and sets the key down on the side table by the door, he immediately searches for the woman. Unlike his last encounter, he finds her seated in the wing-backed chair in the sitting area to the right of him. She sits up straighter when their gazes meet, and he knows right away he's never had her before. He can sense the uncertainty of her breath as his eyes travel down to her chest. Her breasts, held in the sheer black lace of her bralette, heave with her short, shallow breaths.

Without a word, he eases his way out of his jacket and hangs it on the rack beside him. She doesn't look away from him as his eyes drink her in while he loosens his shirt cuffs and rolls them up his forearms. The promise of what awaits him ignites his arousal, and his pants become uncomfortable as he tugs at his tie. Enlivened by the sensation, he slowly begins to make his way toward her.

"You may call me Godrik."

Chapter Eight

*E*ffortlessly, Nathan spins the cocktail shaker around his palm. Catching it when it's right-side up, he discards the cap and pours the sweet, apple martini into the glass in dramatic fashion. He slips a thin slice of apple on the rim and pushes it toward the woman on the other side of the bar, all the while entirely engrossed in his own thoughts.

The woman thanks him, but her words are lost in the same airwaves as the music which resounds throughout the room, Nathan's attention focused on the man three stools down. The bar hand doesn't know his name, but he doesn't need it—he knows the man's drink. Old fashioned, made with the finest bourbon they've got. It's the only thing he's ordered in the two months Nathan has been keeping tabs on him. Yet, in an establishment such as this, his taste in bourbon isn't what catches the bartender's attention. The exclusivity of this particular underground sex club, on the banks of Hell's Kitchen, all but guarantees the crowd is made up of only the elite, which means he pours top shelf liquor all night.

It's not attraction which causes him to study Old Fashioned discreetly. While Nathan can appreciate the cut of the man's suit and the cool way his eyes *seek out his prey each visit, the bar hand surmises he and Old Fashioned have more in common than the stranger knows. Above all else, it's his awareness the stranger doesn't quite belong which causes him to study his subject.*

Fortunately for Old Fashioned, Nathan knows a place more likely to suit the man's tastes. If he was the jealous type, he would keep his mouth shut, knowing the information he has will never be beneficial for himself, in light of his significantly inadequate pocketbook. But he isn't—and he reminds himself of the commission which will come his way with the referral. Even more, as a man not without compassion, Nathan decides it would be better for his karma to put Old Fashioned out of his misery. If their roles were reversed, he'd be indebted to his subject for offering him another way to find what he so desperately craves.

Noting Old Fashioned's drink is nearly gone, Nathan goes about fixing him another. When he's finished, he grabs a cocktail napkin and a pen. After scribbling down the address and the necessary code word, he grabs the old fashioned and walks the short distance to the stranger's place at the bar.

Aware of Nathan's presence, his cool, blue gaze turns away from the dance floor. His eyes fall toward the drink Nathan pushes his way, the glass gliding across the bar atop the cocktail napkin. Shaking his head slightly, he lifts a hand and insists, "No, thank you."

Not deterred, Nathan props his elbow against the bar and leans toward the man, inching the drink closer. He then brazenly admits, "I know your game. I've seen the calculated way you pick your women. I know you like them as sober as they come, and you're not one for small talk." *Lifting the glass from the napkin, he drops his eyes, implying the stranger should do the same. When he does, Nathan goes on to say,* "I know a place. Lower Manhattan. It's private. It's immaculate. It's easily ten times more than you'll pay here, but there is no hunt; no foreplay—only business transactions that get you to your end game, if you're willing to pay the price."

Old Fashioned's pure blue eyes stare at Nathan, his mind obviously at work as he processes what he's just heard. He looks down at the napkin once more and then asks, "Beatrice?"

"Clandestine's Madam."

Old Fashioned quirks an eyebrow at Nathan, causing a smirk to tug at the corner of the bartender's mouth.

"Like I said, no hunt. No foreplay. No games."

The stranger shakes his head, the expression on his face one of suspicion. "I don't—"

"You have no reason to trust me—but by sending you there, I'm losing the generous tip you're good for every time. The girls are clean and well taken care of. Ask for Beatrice when you arrive. Five minutes in her presence, and you'll understand what you're in for. Something tells me you won't regret it."

The man hesitates, furrowing his brow as he reaches for the napkin. Holding it between his fingers, he inquires, "Napoleon the Great?"

Nathan chuckles, righting himself behind the bar before he replies, "She's got a thing for French flair. When you arrive, walk straight to the back. There'll be a mirror. Say those words, and it'll grant you entrance. Ask for Beatrice," *he repeats. He takes a step back, his attention already captured by a waiting patron four stools down.* "Tell her Nate sent you. And you're welcome."

KHALOHN DOWNS THE rest of his drink, clenching his jaw closed tight as the bourbon burns the back of his throat, racing toward his stomach and warming his insides. His eyes flick toward the bartender who passed along the curious, albeit intriguing information regarding what sounds like little more than a brothel. Khalohn hesitates a moment longer, wondering if he's that desperate. Then he remembers the stranger said he'd pay easily ten times more than he currently pays for his lackluster membership at the establishment which never yields a guarantee.

One last look around the room and Khalohn knows, while he might not be desperate, he's far too fascinated to discard the tip.

He reaches into his wallet, pulling out a fifty-dollar bill. Placing it under the drink he never intended on drinking, he stands, pockets the cocktail napkin, and maneuvers his way through the club toward the exit. He sends Atzel a text as he emerges into the cool, October air, and the Maybach pulls up to the curb less than five minutes later.

"Headed home, sir?" asks the Honduran as he opens Khalohn's door.

"Lower Manhattan," he announces before taking his seat.

When Atzel buckles himself behind the wheel, Khalohn rattles off the address from the cocktail napkin. With no more than a word of affirmation, Atzel shifts the Maybach into drive and merges into traffic. Twenty minutes later, Khalohn finds himself looking out his window, his eyebrows tugging together in confusion. The storefront for Clandestine's Closet leaves no doubt he's happened upon a lingerie store. He can't say for sure what he was expecting, but a woman's underwear boutique never crossed his mind.

He double checks the address as Atzel opens his door and then steps up onto the curb. Tilting his head back, he peers through the windows of the second story, the bright lights from inside illuminating the sidewalk on which he stands.

"Stay close," he instructs, feeling dubious. "I don't know how long I'll be."

"Of course, Mr. Morgan."

As Khalohn approaches the front door, he glances to his right and to his left, noting the businesses on either side of him are closed for the night. He takes one step into the establishment and pauses. Everything is white—the floors, the walls, the modern chandeliers, the display tables—the lack of color obviously meant to draw all attention to the assortment of undergarments displayed throughout the store. In contrast, the sales associates are dressed in all black. However, it's not their attire Khalohn finds striking, but their behavior.

It's nearly midnight. While "Rumor Has it" by Adele plays over the sound system, the bass reverberating around the room, there are no customers to recognize the song. As Khalohn begins to make his way toward the back— remembering the bartender's instructions—not one of the associates offers him any assistance. While he has no intention of buying anything, he wonders how they seem to know this to be true.

Upon reaching the middle of the store, Khalohn notices the heavy, velvet, black curtain blocking off the rear of the establishment. As he makes his way toward it, he's tempted to look over his shoulder, curious if his actions are being watched. He resists. Intent on appearing confident in his endeavor, he simply slips through the curtain without a backwards glance. On the other side is the mirror he was told he'd find. The large, antique mount is not at all like the contemporary fixtures found in the whitewashed store at his back.

He furrows his brow and peers through the glass, seeing nothing but his own reflection. For a moment, he wonders how he got here. It all seems preposterous—Khalohn Morgan, wearing a ten-thousand-dollar suit, standing in front of a mirror, hoping to find something of value. It's ironic. It's disappointing. Suddenly, he feels ridiculous.

Staring through his reflection, he begs himself to acknowledge why he made the trip. To think there's anything on the other side seems otherworldly. He glances to his right and his left, wondering what he truly sought to gain by coming. The idea that he can find what he seeks on the opposite side of a mirror is a fantasy, and he doesn't believe in fairytales.

But to come so far without uttering a word?

He thinks back to the club he just came from and sighs. If he was duped, his only other option is to claim defeat for the night and head home. When he ponders the associates and their behavior as he passed by them on his way through the boutique, he can't shake the feeling there's something mysterious about the atmosphere in which he finds himself. Reaching up to run his hand over the side of his beard, he shakes his head and does the only thing he can think to do. He utters the password.

"Napoleon the Great."

He freezes at the sound of the click, signaling a loosened latch. Leaning forward, he realizes the mirror has shifted the slightest bit, and he can't stop himself from extending his hand out to touch the distressed glass. It gives when he pushes, and he knows not what to think as he eases open the door and steps into the room on the other side.

What can only be described as a foyer is decked out in dark purple walls, the interior trim and crown molding a distressed golden hue. The matching, antique sconce lighting scattered around the space provides enough illumination to be considered useful; the large chandelier hanging in the center of the ceiling casting what one might consider a romantic amount of light.

"Good evening. Welcome to Clandestine's."

Khalohn's attention quickly shifts toward the sound of the smooth, tenor voice coming from the opposite side of the elaborate reception desk. The man who greets him is impeccably dressed, yet with a certain style which makes Khalohn question if he's unrealistically traveled into an entirely different time.

"I presume, having found your way through the door, you have come with a specific request?"

Shrugging away his distracting amount of intrigue, Khalohn clears his throat and steps toward the man as he replies, "I'd like to speak with Beatrice."

A mischievous smile curls the corners of the man's mouth, and he nods before he murmurs, "Of course. Please, follow me."

With more grace than Khalohn has ever possessed, the receptionist steps out from behind his station and heads for the narrow set of stairs leading toward a long, dimly lit passageway. It's Khalohn's rapt curiosity which causes him to trail behind the man. There's a soft melody playing overhead, but it isn't loud enough to drown out the sound of their heels against the floor or the moan Khalohn is sure he hears slipping from underneath one of the closed doors they pass. His heartrate picks up speed as he wonders if he'll get what he came for after all.

Along their journey, Khalohn peers over his shoulder and down the long hallway. The underground establishment is far more extensive than he imagined it could be, leading him to question his own doubts. He refocuses his attention in front of him just as his escort comes to an abrupt halt. Khalohn watches as the man raps his knuckles against the closed door, and they both wait silently for a response.

Much like the click he heard after muttering the password a moment ago, he hears the latch of the barrier give before the receptionist pushes it open. Instead of crossing the threshold, he merely extends his arm in invitation. Khalohn glances his way, smoothing his hand over his tie before he walks by him and steps into the room.

The walls are painted the same rich shade of purple as in the hallway. On the right side of the room is an elaborate fireplace, with an elegant mantel which appears to be hand carved. Hanging on the wall above it is an oval mirror with an ornate, golden frame. There's a curved, lavender, velvet, tuft sofa and a glass coffee table with gold trim in front of the fireplace. There's also a butler's tray which holds what appears to be an abandoned tea service. On the left side of the room is a dining room table, complete with four round-back, velvet cushioned chairs. The wall behind it is embellished with an array of paintings—all in various sizes and shapes, each in its own golden frame.

"Bonjour. Do please come in. I assure you I don't bite."

Instantly, Khalohn's attention is drawn to the woman standing behind the black, French writing desk situated in front of the large armoire, which takes up much of the rear wall. In her heels, she appears to stand just shy of Khalohn's six-foot frame, her body narrow and, in Khalohn's opinion, too small. The suggestive look in her green eyes, and the little smile which highlights her pronounced cheek bones, reminds him he's not here for her. Furthermore, as he takes in the cut of her dress, the diamonds around her wrist, and the heavy pendant dangling from her neck, he knows one thing for sure—the bartender was wrong.

"Stefano," calls Beatrice, her eyes still admiring Khalohn. "A round of scotch, if you don't mind."

"Right away, madam."

Making his way toward one of the chairs on the opposite side of the madam's desk, Khalohn is certain he doesn't need five minutes in the woman's presence to make up his mind. Five seconds, and he's already come to the conclusion that whatever she has to offer, he won't regret his visit.

Chapter Nine

JESSICA CHECKS THE TIME ON her phone, stifling a sigh of resignation when she realizes she's not going to make it. Ignoring the knot of anxiety twisting her stomach, she shoves the device into her purse and then rakes her fingers through her hair.

"Jess—" Beth starts to speak, her voice hardly louder than a wheezing breath. "You don't—"

"Mom, I'm not going anywhere," Jessica insists. She reaches for her mother's hands, resting in her lap, and clasps her fingers over them. They'd waited to see a doctor for two hours. Now that her mother is finally closed into a room, she isn't about to leave. It had taken her almost as long as they'd waited to convince Beth to even come to the Urgent Care—but Jessica knows better than to take any reckless chances.

Beth stares at her daughter, and Jessica can hear all the things her eyes are saying. She knows how helpless her mother feels; worse, she can see how weighed down she is, shouldering the belief she's somehow a burden. Jessica squeezes her fingers reflexively, silently trying to convey there's nowhere else in the world more important to be than exactly where she is. She doesn't have the words to properly express that not only is Beth not a burden, she's worth a lifetime of inconveniences. Not to mention, the interview she's going to miss would be for nothing if Beth ends up hospitalized—*or worse*—from an untreated cold.

"Jessica," Beth begins again.

This time, she's interrupted by a soft tap on the door before it swings open. A handsome Indian doctor in green scrubs enters the room, Beth's chart in his grasp. This time, Jessica doesn't stifle the sigh of relief that rushes from her healthy lungs, grateful for the man as he gets straight to the point. It's Jessica who explains her mother's worsening symptoms, as Beth's head cold has descended to her chest over the last several days. The man listens patiently, looking from Jessica to Beth to the chart and back at Beth before he gives her chest a listen.

Jessica isn't aware how tense her shoulders are until the doctor returns his stethoscope to rest around his neck and tells her she was smart to bring Beth in for treatment. Her muscles relax, causing her arms to drop down her sides as he writes Beth a prescription for antibiotics and an oral steroid. Jessica doesn't complain about having to make another trip to the pharmacy before her shift at Moby's Dive, too content to have gotten a competent physician.

As she and Beth take their leave, she wonders how difficult it might be to convince the restaurant she was to have interviewed with that afternoon to reschedule. Beth's extra meds aren't something for which either of them planned. To say they could use another source of income would be a gross understatement.

It takes forty minutes and two transfers to reach the subway stop closest to their apartment, where they part ways. At Jessica's insistence, Beth returns home while Jessica journeys another twenty minutes in the opposite direction to the pharmacy. By the time she gets her order filled and returns home, she knows she'll be late for work. She doesn't even bother changing her clothes before she rushes out the door. The short black skirt that clings to her thighs and the cream-colored silk blouse she tucked into it aren't exactly *dive bar* material. In fact, chances are high she'll ruin one of the only nice shirts she has during her shift, but there is no time to give a damn.

With her feet still tucked into a comfortable pair of walking shoes, Jessica doesn't hesitate to make a run for the bar as soon as she steps foot off her bus. She's not at all surprised to find Griffin waiting for her halfway down the grungy hall—his shoulder propped against the doorjamb of his office, his eyes glued to his wristwatch. He doesn't even bother to look her way before he mutters, "You're fired, Chapman."

What little breath Jessica has in her lungs disappears as her feet stumble to an abrupt halt. Her jaw falls open, but no air passes through her lips as she gapes at Griffin. After a moment of silence, he tilts his head just enough to glance at her. He then pushes away from the door and heads for the bar.

The sight of his retreating figure pulls Jessica out of her daze. She gulps down a breath and then hurries after him. "Wait," she calls, adjusting the strap of her purse on her shoulder. "Please, don't—"

"Heard enough of your shit," he hollers from over his shoulder. "You were warned. I'm done."

"No. Griffin, you can't—" Her strides grow longer and faster, and she manages to catch his elbow before he pushes through the swinging door to the main room. "I had an emerg—"

He spins on her, the simple movement causing her to let go of his arm. They are standing so close, he seems to tower over her, as if he's grown a foot since the last time they stood toe-to-toe in that very hallway. Never has she felt tempted to cower under his glare, until right then. In that moment, she realizes her fragile world is resting in the palm of his hands.

She can barely breathe as she pleads, "Griffin—"

"Did I stutter?" he all but growls. "Get the fuck out of my bar. You don't work here anymore."

He turns once more, and her heart sinks all the way down to her feet. Stunned still, she stares at the door he passes through, leaving her shattered world in his wake. She doesn't know how much time passes before she manages to take one step and then another, shuffling in the direction from which she came. It isn't until she exits the building that a heavy sense of reality begins to slither through her insides. The balmy evening air, thick with the humidity wafting from the bay and the stench of the heated contents of a nearby dumpster, is enough to make the certitude of what just happened so tangible, she can feel it like a sickness churning in her belly.

Pressing her hand to her stomach, she thinks of the hours spent in the Urgent Care across town. The image of Beth sitting patiently yet miserably in wait flashes before Jessica's eyes, and she's convinced she can't return home. Not now. The last thing she wants to do is bring bad news to their doorstep. No—she can't heap more hopelessness on top of all the other setbacks she and Beth are dealing with. She can't go home until she figures out one hell of a plan B.

She buries her fingers in her hair and inhales deeply. Blowing out a heavy sigh, she closes her eyes and then sucks in another breath. Her need for oxygen and fresh perspective is so desperate, she hardly notices the rancid smell in the air. Once she feels stable enough to walk, she heads back to the bus stop. She doesn't know where she's going until after she pays her fare and takes a seat at the back of the next bus. There are tears pooling behind her eyes, but Jessica ignores them as she pulls out her phone. If there's one thing she's sure of, it's that she doesn't have time to cry.

Our spot. Soon as you can. I know you're probably working tonight. I'll be waiting.

Jessica sends the text, resting her hands in her lap as she awaits a reply. All the while, she stares out the window, concentrating on her breaths and ignoring her rising sense of panic as the distance between her and Moby's Dive stretches farther and farther. Even though it's less than five minutes, Stefano's reply seems to take forever to arrive.

That's not ominous at all…

Jessica stares at their text thread. She wants to reply with something witty or confident, but she doesn't have it in her to make light of her current situation. What she needs is a job—or two—and the assurance that everything's going to be okay.

See you at twilight?
I'll be there, dove.

"MORE COFFEE?" ASKS the waitress, her tone barely concealing her irritation.

Jessica can't remember her name, but she doesn't have the wherewithal to be distressed about it. She glances up at the woman, offering her a small nod, not the least bit concerned she's been occupying the same booth for hours, downing nothing but cup after cup of coffee.

"Hey, Miranda," calls a familiar voice, heavy with her characteristic accent.

Both Jessica and *Miranda* watch as Wendy approaches with a fresh carafe of hot coffee.

"I've got her."

Jessica hears it as Mirada mutters *thank god* under her breath before she turns to leave, but it barely registers.

"Here before me? That's new," Wendy says, filling Jessica's cup. "Where's your other half?"

"He'll be here," replies Jessica through a forced smile.

"Everything okay?"

With a sigh, Jessica places her phone face down on the table. She's been looking for work all night, submitting countless applications. With her battery life down to less than twenty percent, she wonders if she can stomach the idea of taking a break. In the back of her mind, she can't escape the truth that every minute she's not working is another setback followed by another and another.

Closing her eyes, she grips her fingers around her mug and holds the hot porcelain, willing herself not to succumb to the hopelessness which has been taunting her. Even denying her weariness has grown exhausting. Just the thought of surrendering to despair seems like an all too enticing reprieve.

"Do you ever feel like—you can't win? Like, being one person is not enough?" she practically whispers, her eyes still shut tight.

Wendy coughs out a quiet laugh and then rests her hand on Jessica's shoulder. "All the time, Jess. All the damn time."

Finally opening her eyes, she looks up at the waitress and asks, "What do you do about it?"

"The only thing I can do. I keep goin'. I keep *tryin'*. I keep fightin'. Whatever it takes." Wendy gives her shoulder a squeeze. "Then I eat pie. Speakin' of which, can I get you some? On the house."

Jessica manages a half a smile and nods. "Sure. Thanks."

"Apple pie a la mode, coming up."

In spite of her favorite treat, Jessica's state of mind doesn't improve over the next couple of hours. After her phone dies, she stares unseeingly out the window, allowing her thoughts to wander. The optimism she felt upon waking the previous morning has died a little, then a little more as one thing after another has led her to the very booth in which she fights the urge to wallow. It's hard to imagine how anything short of a miracle can provide all she and Beth need.

No sooner has the thought crossed her mind than she feels a pair of hands cover hers. She inhales deeply, smelling his Bleu de Chanel before she looks up into his hazel eyes. All at once, and for the very first time, the man who sits across from her is more than the boy she met in high school. He is more than her best friend. He is the answer to a question she has never thought to ask. He is her opportunity to throw herself into the unknown—her chance to do *whatever it takes*.

He is the gatekeeper.

She isn't aware of his voice until she sees his hand in front of her face, his fingers snapping her out of her thoughts. As if the sharp, staccato sound is like a bullet breaking through an impenetrable barrier, Jessica gasps, the air which fills her lungs forcing her to sit up straighter. For the first time all night, she's awash in hope.

"Hey, you okay?" asks Stefano.

"Yeah. I mean—I am now."

"What happened? I got here as soon as I could. Luckily, it was a slow night. I—"

Cutting him off, Jessica moves her hands so she's the one gripping hold of him as she states, "I just got an idea. Oh, my god—I don't know why I didn't think of this before."

Stefano's perfectly manicured eyebrows tug together in bewilderment. "Think of what?"

"You can get me a job. I could work for Beatrice. My schedule would hardly change, and my income would—"

"Wait, what? No, stop." Stefano jerks his hands out from underneath Jessica's as he physically shrinks away from her. "If you're saying what I think you're saying, the answer is *no*. Absolutely not."

Not deterred in the slightest, Jessica leans across the table toward him, her eyes frantically searching his as she demands to know, "Why not? I know I'm not, like, a model or anything, but I've got the right—"

"Damnit, Jess—you're beautiful and we both know it. That's not what this is about." Mimicking her stance, Stefano closes the distance between them and whisper shouts, "But if you think, for one goddamned second, I'm going to let you sell your body for—"

"For my mother?"

She coughs out a humorless laugh, wondering if she's come unhinged. Clearheaded enough to understand Stefano's reaction, she can admit to herself what she's proposing is crazy and unlike anything she would have ever considered before. But now that the idea has taken residence in her mind, she can't fathom a better chance to rise above all the setbacks which have been piling up as of late.

"You need money? I'll give it to you. Just *ask*."

"I don't want your money, Huey. I want your help."

"What's the difference?"

Taking hold of his hands once more, she holds on tight and murmurs, "You *know* the answer to that."

"You don't know what you're asking of me," he replies with a shake of his head. "Hell, we barely even talk about my job, and now this?"

"I'll make enough to cover my expenses and mom's, right?"

Stefano hesitates before begrudgingly admitting, "More. Way more."

Her fingers grip his even tighter, her heartbeat picking up speed as she pulls herself even closer. "And you trust her. She's your Queen Bea, so you can trust her with me, right?"

His face contorted into a deep frown, Stefano blows a sigh through his nose, touching his forehead to hers. "You'll never forgive me if I let you do this, dove. I can't."

"It's my body." As she says the words, the tears which she has been holding at bay all night begin to fill her eyes—only now, they fall for completely different reasons. "It's my *healthy* body. If I don't do everything in my power to help my mom, I'll never forgive *myself*. And if you won't help me, I'll just have to do it without you."

"Damnit, Jessica," he grunts, pressing his head against hers harder.

"Tell me I'm wrong. Tell me there's another job out there that'll hire me tomorrow and offer me better pay. Tell me, and I won't ask you to do this."

They sit in silence for what feels like forever. All Jessica can hear is the sound of her blood rushing through her body as her heart pounds in anticipation of Stefano's reply. Finally, he pulls away from her enough to lock his gaze with hers.

"Fuck," he whispers.

She smiles and then lifts her seat out of the booth in order to reach his cheek. She presses a kiss against his smooth skin, lingering long enough to breathe, "Thank you."

Chapter Ten

STEFANO STANDS IN FRONT OF her door and hesitates a minute longer. He pulls in a breath through his nose, exhaling it slowly as he smooths a hand down the length of his black, floral Versace silk tie. It's been years since he's mindlessly succumbed to his propensity to fidget, his confidence all but eradicating the habit. Within the underground palace in which he stands is where he once shed the last of his false identity and finally stepped into the fullness of his true self. Only now, he can barely help straightening the lapels of his black Versace suit—the irony of fiddling with such fine material not at all lost on him.

Staring at the closed door, he remembers the call he received from Jessica yesterday afternoon. Her test results came back negative. Stefano did not doubt they would, but he couldn't deny he had hoped the time it would take for his beloved friend to see a doctor would be the appropriate amount of time to change her mind.

It was not.

The thought has occurred to him, more than once, to lie. He's even gone so far as to play out the conversation in his head—the conversation where he would tell Jessica that Beatrice would not allow her to be a part of her *collection*. The reason behind her decision would be simple; for the intimate friendship which exists between himself and Jessica might, after all, prove to be a great conflict of interest. He's concocted a number of examples in which Beatrice believes it would disrupt business if he, as the gatekeeper, could not separate his professional self from his personal self. Being so familiar with the Johns, who whisper the password to gain access night after night, he's in a unique position to be impartial with whom Jessica is paired with; or perhaps the aftermath of an encounter would yield erratic behavior for either of them. He is convinced he would be able to sell the lie effortlessly, but the ease of such a deception does nothing to make it easier to execute.

In truth, there is no denying Jessica's predicament, her character, and the lengths she will go to dig herself out of the hole in which she finds herself. Stefano knows he has only two choices: to play by her rules—or his.

Having accepted his love for her needs to be expressed with the integrity found only in the truth, he poises himself to execute the best alternate option he can think of. Certain he is in no position to lie to his dearest friend, he instead intends to not let his entire idea go to waste. As the gatekeeper, he is not short of the power of *knowledge*. Without further ado, he raises his closed fist and knocks gently on the barrier between him and the *queen* of Manhattan's finest bordello. He's beckoned to enter before he even has a chance to drop his hand down his side.

Steeling himself for a decision he will not be able to take back, he rolls his shoulders and enters Beatrice's office.

"Bonjour, darling," she greets, barely looking up from the records she's addressing at the moment. "What is it you need at this early hour?"

Stefano swallows hard, taking a few hesitant steps toward her desk before he replies, "There's someone I think you should meet—a woman I believe would be an extraordinary addition to your collection."

"Oh?" She stops what she's doing, folding her hands as she looks at

Stefano with an undeniable sense of intrigue. Her dark auburn, shoulder-length hair falls dramatically on either side of her face—the strands as straight and sleek as ever. But it's her painted red lips, shaped in a pouty-*oh* fashion that hints at her interest.

Never before has Stefano spoken of a recruit, but his position has earned him a level of trust few on Beatrice's payroll can claim. After all, he is her eyes and ears. He knows, before he says another word, his Queen Bea will not simply hear him out, but welcome Jessica with open arms.

She's a fucking diamond—and Beatrice will agree.

"Hello?" Jessica answers, almost breathlessly. She clutches the phone to her ear with both hands, even though she can hear just fine. She hasn't spoken to Stefano since the day before. The twenty-four hours she's waited has done nothing to abate her nerves.

"I got you a meeting," Stefano starts to say. "You're to meet me out back in two hours."

Jessica nods, despite his inability to see her do so, and mentally maps out how she'll make it to Lower Manhattan in that specified time frame. She's getting ready to verbally agree when her friend continues speaking.

"Listen—"

She can *see* his face simply *hearing* the tone of his voice. He's on edge, and Jessica knows it. Furthermore, she loves him for it. It would be a lie to say she hasn't been on edge about this whole idea since the moment they left the diner a couple of nights ago. Even still, whatever hesitation he feels, she's determined not to let it fill her with doubt.

Peering over her shoulder, she glances in the direction of the apartment's only bedroom, where Beth is resting. It doesn't matter how on edge Jessica might feel, she won't back down. She can't.

"If you're really going to go through with this, I have one condition," Stefano states, forcing his way back into her thoughts.

"What—what is it?" she stammers as she tries to refocus.

"Twice and you're out," he demands. "The first night will get you enough to settle what's hanging over your head now. The second night will give you some cushion—enough for you to take the time to find a job that doesn't involve you…"

Jessica closes her eyes in a long blink, shaking her head slightly as she reopens them. She can hear Stefano still talking in her ear, but she can't comprehend what he's saying. When she finds her own words, she interrupts as she mutters, "I'll get that much?"

As far from naïve as she knows herself to be, she never imagined her cut would be as significant as Stefano seems to be implying. Well aware of the designer of his suit and the brand of his aftershave, Jessica has always been able to see how well Beatrice treats her staff—but *two nights?*

Speaking softly, she goes on to say, "I think you may underestimate my situation, Huey. *Dire* about—"

"Not all Johns are created equal, Jess; but I know the clientele. I know who has the deepest pockets."

"We're talking *thousands* of dollars," she hisses, cupping her hand around the mouthpiece of her phone.

"Jessica." The way Stefano utters her name, she understands he's running short on patience. More than her awe in regard to the glimpse he's given her into his world, he's concerned about the condition he's laid on the table. He confirms her suspicions when he repeats, "Twice and you're out. Agreed?"

Jessica says nothing at first. Her silence isn't a sign of her attempt to mull over his condition; rather, the thought of making *that* much money in only two nights makes it difficult for her to pull in a breath. The *how* makes it difficult for her to exhale. Until the second her phone rang, everything she's been contemplating the last couple of days has been little more than a *plan*.

For a second, she wonders if she can agree to his terms. Looking around the small box of an apartment she calls home, she can't help but to imagine how much better off they might be if she could endure more than a couple nights…

Oh, god, she thinks, her stomach tightening when she realizes exactly what she's entertaining. *Do you hear yourself, right now? This is sex, we're talking about—sex with only god knows who.*

She swallows hard, grasping at the out Stefano is offering her. There's something about hearing him put words to her future actions that causes her heart to thud loudly in trepidation. As confident as she is in her decision to follow through with her plan, she can't overlook the truth. She has no idea what she's really getting herself into. Even more, she prefers it that way. To think on it too much might lead her to change her mind, and she can't afford to make that kind of mistake. There is comfort in knowing her best friend *does* know what awaits, and he's granting her just enough access to get what she needs and nothing more.

"Jess, I'm not fucking around here. You get in and you get out. This is temporary. You promise me that, and I won't walk right back into Bea's office and tell her you've had a change of heart."

"Fine," she whispers. Closing her eyes, she shakes her head and forces in a deep inhale. As she blows out a sigh, she nods and says, "Twice and then I'm out." After she says the words, she becomes cognizant of the relief she feels at the prospect of such a short commitment.

"Great." Stefano's tone is drenched in sarcasm, causing a small smile to play at the side of Jessica's mouth. She knows, even though he has offered his help under strict conditions, he doesn't want her doing it at all. His awareness of her stubborn nature is the only reason they're having this conversation—and for that, she can't help but to love him a little more.

"Huey?" she calls out softly. He doesn't respond, but she doesn't need him to. "Thank you."

"Don't. Don't thank me for this. *Not this.*"

Her small smile fades, and she offers him another nod he can't see. Staring down into her lap, her heartbeat now pounds with a measure of fear. He loves her too much to let her walk into this without him, but the thought of him looking at her differently after is a possibility she hasn't considered until now.

"Huey…"

"I know," he responds gently. "I'll see you in two hours. Don't be late."

He hangs up before she can even say goodbye, but she doesn't hold it against him. She forces in another round of deep breaths before she starts to get ready. An hour later, she's quietly slipping out the front door in a black bodycon halter dress, her hair falling in big curls down her back. Her makeup is darker than she'd usually wear for an ordinary job interview, and the hem of her dress a whole lot shorter. She's not thrilled about catching the R-train during rush hour dressed the way she is, let alone explain herself to her mother. She skips the latter and forces herself to get over the former.

After checking her bag for the heels she plans on changing into upon reaching Clandestine's, she takes one final glance at her front door and then starts for the subway. Along the way, she slips her earbuds in and tries to lose herself in music. At first, she's hardly conscious of what she's listening to, too consumed with thoughts of where she's going and why. When she goes through the motions of transferring lines, boarding the N train as routinely as any native New Yorker, it's not long before the speed at which she travels out-races her thoughts. She lets them go, closing her eyes as she seeps so far into the melody of the song in her ears, all she can feel is the rhythm beneath the lyrics.

When she arrives at the alley behind Clandestine's Closet, Jessica stops to change her shoes. She tosses her earbuds into her purse, then slides into her best black platform heels. Raking her fingers through her hair, she throws her curls down her back and sweeps her fingers across her forehead, in an attempt to wipe away the thin layer of sweat gathered there. Knowing she's running short on time, she ignores the knots in her belly and strides toward the spot Stefano instructed with as much confidence as she can muster. The closer she gets to her destination, the harder it is for her to keep her cool.

Just two nights, she reminds herself with a shake of her head. *For mom—the woman who gave up everything for me. I can do this. I can do this for her.*

The back door of Clandestine's is hardly different than any of the other doors that line the stretch of establishments along Broadway; however, the black door marked with the white cursive font of the store's name seems to loom over her forebodingly. For a moment, Jessica stares at it, well aware that as soon as she crosses the threshold, she'll be stepping into a forbidden realm she never thought she'd know.

Well—when life throws a punch, you don't cower in the corner. Reaching for the handle, Jessica reminds herself, *You fight the bitch with everything you've got.*

She practically hears Stefano's sigh before she sees him. He stops his pacing as soon as they lock eyes, and Jessica wonders how long he's been walking in circles in wait.

At first, he says nothing. He stares at her intently, his hazel eyes dark with a meaning she knows better than to interpret. Finally, he takes hold of her hand, squeezing her fingers tighter than is comfortable. She doesn't mind.

"I've never been so annoyed at how goddamn gorgeous you are," he mutters as he stomps down the hallway. "Come."

She trails after him without argument, too out of sorts to be flattered by his words. Rather than escorting her toward the door at the end of the corridor, they walk a short distance before he takes a sharp right. With a long skeleton key, he opens what looks like a closet door, revealing a stairwell. But it's no ordinary stairwell. The walls are painted a dark purple, and the antique lamps mounted on them—illuminating their path—seem beautifully out of place. When they reach the bottom of the stairs, Jessica becomes fully aware she's descended into an entirely different world.

Her feet slow without her permission as her eyes dance around the narrow, rectangular room. It's immediately obvious she's in what must be a staging area. Rather than a rich purple, the walls are painted lavender.

The added texture makes the paint look old yet beautiful, and the three, gigantic, gold chandeliers in the middle of the room cast a soft light on every workstation. It's got a *backstage at a fashion show* vibe, but far classier, more elegant, and—*Victorian*. Lining both sides of the room are a variety of mismatched, antique vanity table sets. They're each elaborately hand carved with embellishments that seem both out of place and yet perfectly suited to the rest of the décor. No one occupies any of the stations at the moment, and the lamps at each spot are darkened, but Jessica's belly flutters as she imagines the room full of women.

Taking in the cream-colored chase lounges in the center of the room, accented with gold and complete with pale purple throw pillows, Jessica grapples with a measure of confusion she wasn't expecting. There's something about the gorgeous, French-Victorian room juxtaposed with the purpose behind why the room exists that doesn't quite add up in her mind. The ambiance she stumbles through feels more akin to a courtesan of a story book—fantasy stripping the scene of any grime and disorder— not a prostitute in the twenty-first century.

Prostitute? Really? Shit, Jess.

"This is where the girls get ready. When you come in, any open vanity is fair game. We've got clientele in here every night, but none of the girls work more than two or three nights a week, so there's no need for anyone to get too settled," Stefano informs her.

Jessica nods, latching onto his words in an attempt to forget her own.

Stefano leads her through a heavy velvet curtain, and they step into a long hallway. Jessica's jaw falls open a little as she stares down the length of the corridor. It's quite apparent the world in which she has entered is larger and more extravagant than she ever imagined. She wonders exactly how big the place is. Before she can ask, Stefano is standing in front of her, his face void of its usual warmth or carefree demeanor. He takes hold of her chin, and she shuts her mouth as she stares up into his eyes.

"I won't ever forgive myself for this," he starts to say.

"Stef—"

"Just remember what we agreed."

She nods as much as his hold will allow and whispers, "Two nights."

"And Beatrice doesn't need to know," he warns.

"Of course not."

Stefano sucks in a deep breath through his nose, his grip still firm on her chin. He then plants a solid kiss against her forehead and lets her go. He runs a hand down the length of his tie and turns toward the door directly across the hall. Jessica watches as he rolls his shoulders before knocking. Her stomach twists as she hears a voice calling for him to enter followed by a *click* signaling the door is open. She can barely breathe when Stefano steps inside, leaving her alone in the hallway.

He gone too long and yet not long enough. When he reappears in the doorway, Jessica recognizes she's no longer in the presence of *Huey*, her closest friend in the world. No, she's being beckoned by *the gatekeeper* of Clandestine's. He turns, leaving enough space for both of them in the doorway, sweeping his hand into the room as a sign for her to enter. Her stomach drops, feeling heavier than it has all day. She doesn't know how she manages to pick up one foot and then another, only that she finds herself in Beatrice's large, gorgeously decadent office a moment later. Her eyes are everywhere, taking in the details of the room, until she hears the click of the door behind her.

A small gasp passes through her lips, her whole body jerking as she turns her head to find she's been closed in—Stefano no longer in sight.

"I should have known."

As fast as her head snapped to peer behind her, Jessica's attention is drawn to the woman across the room. For as long as she's known about Beatrice, she's wondered what the madam might look like. Extravagantly beautiful as she always imagined the woman to be, the gorgeous creature before her almost takes Jessica's breath away. While Beatrice is no longer young, she is strikingly radiant. One look at her, and Jessica understands the elegance that exudes from every corner of the establishment is a manifestation of the woman who runs the place.

When she begins to make her way from behind her desk, Jessica remembers she has spoken. Before she can find the words to reply, Beatrice speaks again.

"He said you were an exceptional beauty. But you, my dear, are positively exquisite."

Jessica looks down at herself, self-consciously smoothing a hand over her flat belly and the best dress she has. It's useless to compare herself to *the Queen Bea*, but she finds it hard to believe Beatrice—in the sleek and stylish dress she's wearing—could consider her *exquisite*.

Nevertheless, she wills herself to find her manners and her voice as she replies, "Thank you."

"Come," Beatrice instructs, motioning toward the sitting area in front of the fireplace. It's filled with cream candles of all shapes and sizes, each of them lit now, the light of the flames dancing within the confines of the fire pit. "Sit with me. Let us chat for a moment."

Jessica manages a small smile in response before she makes her way toward the Victorian couch in front of the coffee table, adorned with a delicate tea service. She shakes her head as she sits, still boggled by all she wasn't expecting. Beatrice sits on the opposite end of the sofa, crossing her ankles as she rests her folded hands on her knees. Jessica tries not to fidget, sitting up straight and reminding herself to breathe.

What seems like a long moment of silence stretches between them. Each second that ticks by makes it more difficult for Jessica to sit still, but she reminds herself to remain calm. Nevertheless, she finds it impossible to keep her gaze locked with Beatrice's intense stare.

Finally, the silence is broken when the madam simply inquires, "Why are you here?"

Sitting a little taller, Jessica admits, "I need a job."

A small laugh causes a rueful smile to play at Beatrice's lips. In the strangest way, Jessica doesn't feel patronized when Beatrice replies, "This, my dear, is not a job. What you give is not something you can ever get back.

The exchange is not even within the same realm of equivalent currency. So, I ask you once more, why are you here?"

All at once, Jessica feels herself relax a little as the actuality of Stefano's *Queen Bea* manifests completely in front of her. This time, she finds the confidence to admit, "I need the money."

Beatrice tilts her head, studying Jessica more intently, and then says, "Try just once more."

Intrinsically aware she does not know what Beatrice expects her to say, and afraid she's on the verge of losing her opportunity to do what she has been preparing her mind to do for the last several days, her posture falls. Certain she has nothing more to lose, she decides to tell the truth.

"My mother is ill. She can't work, and my attempts to care for her are not enough. I need this." Dropping her gaze into her lap, Jessica stares at her fingers as she fidgets and goes on to say, "I need the money, and I don't care what it costs me. It's for my mother. I would do anything for her."

Beatrice doesn't respond immediately but takes a moment to consider Jessica's answer. When she draws in a sharp breath, Jessica peeks up at the elegant woman from beneath her lashes.

"Very well," she says, matter-of-factly. "I have three rules. *Une*: When you are called upon, you show up as expected. If, for whatever reason, you cannot, you will be subject to probation for a month. *Deux*: my clients pay a great sum in order to keep their visits completely confidential. You are not to do anything that would sabotage that trust. *Trios*: So long as you are within the confines of these walls, you belong to me—and I take great care of what is mine. If any man so much as threatens to harm you in any way, I want to know about it. I do not condone harassment of any kind, and I am against violence, unless it is consensual and ends in two orgasms. *At least*. Are we clear?"

The small bit of relaxation Jessica latched onto only a minute before vanishes as her stomach turns at the mention of *violence*. Her spine straightens as she lets the substantiality of the situation sink in. While Beatrice obviously cares about the safety of her *women*, Jessica would be lying if she said the thought of even the possibility of physical harm had crossed her mind. There are so many other scenarios she's still trying desperately to wrap her head around.

She forces a swallow, sealing her eyes shut tight for a second. Shaking her head once, she reminds herself there is no other way.

Two nights. It's only two nights.

Prying her eyes open, she forces herself to meet Beatrice's inquisitive stare as she finally responds, "We're clear."

"Good."

Promptly, and with more grace than seems possible, the madam stands to her feet and glides her way toward the door. Jessica looks from the recently vacated spot on the couch to the door twice, wondering if she, too, should follow in her footsteps. By the time she makes up her mind and lifts herself from her seat, she sees Beatrice is engaged in a hushed conversation with Stefano. She decides not to move but to wait for a summoning, all the while watching the exchange, straining to hear what is said between them.

"Draw up the NDA, the appropriate waver, and her pay contract," she hears Beatrice instruct. Stefano replies with what Jessica assumes is an affirmative, then murmurs something she can't quite catch. She watches closely as Beatrice clasps her hands together behind her back, inclining her head slightly as she tells Stefano, "Proceed."

He chances a look in at Jessica, her only clue that he seems nervous for some reason, and then refocuses all of his attention on Beatrice. This time, Jessica manages to hear him as he suggests, "I recommend we offer her to Mr. Morgan. After the mix-up a couple weeks ago, I believe he would appreciate the gesture. I also think we can increase his usual fee by informing him he'll be the first client to touch her."

Jessica's stomach turns, knowing *she's* the piece of property Stefano is referring to—as if she's nothing more than a shiny new toy. Swallowing hard, she presses both of her hands against her belly, willing herself to suck it up. As she pulls in a cleansing breath, she remembers Stefano is her best friend; moreover, he knows the men who frequent this place better than anyone. He wouldn't suggest something if he didn't think it worth the effort. She also reminds herself she's not in some cheap hotel in a shady part of town, and Beatrice isn't a classless pimp.

Jessica is coaxed from her own thoughts as the woman hums her approval. She then goes on to say, "Arrange it. Prichard has had his fair share of first nights. Besides, the last time he got a new piece from my collection, he demanded a twenty-five percent return as she was a blubbering mess by the end of the night. But this one..." Beatrice taps an inquisitive finger against her painted red lips as she pauses. "When you propose the pairing, increase his rate by fifty percent." She turns, as if to address Jessica, and then changes her mind. Lifting a finger thoughtfully, she looks to Stefano once more and adds, "For both nights. I have no doubt he'll wish to indulge to the full extent of his limits."

Jessica looks between Beatrice and Stefano, certain more has been exchanged between them than she can understand. She wonders what it was the madam was going to say before her voice trailed off.

What is it about me she's so sure of?

Who is Mr. Morgan? Or Prichard?

God—am I really going to do this?

"Yes, madam," Stefano agrees, breaking through her thoughts.

She dips her chin affirmatively and then turns again toward Jessica. "Come, my dear. It is time we make this official."

Jessica wastes no time walking toward them, curious as to what happens next. She need not ask as Beatrice places a hand on her back and gently guides her into the hallway. Stefano smiles at her, taking hold of her waist as he begins to lead her down the long corridor.

They don't get far before Beatrice insists, "Make sure Evelyn is the one to style her."

"Of course," says Stefano from over his shoulder.

"And Jessica?"

Both she and Stefano come to a stop, each of them looking back at the woman.

"Yes?" she murmurs a bit apprehensively.

"That name will never do. Charming as it may be, there are no *girls next door* here. Think of another, yes?"

Nodding her understanding, Jessica replies, "Okay."

"Off you go."

Beatrice disappears into her office, and Stefano continues to escort her down the hall. He gives her hip a squeeze and she looks up at him, entirely unsure of what to say.

"If all goes to plan, you'll get two nights with the most coveted John in this place, and you'll make a fucking killing."

Overwhelmed by all that's been said and done in the last fifteen minutes, Jessica doesn't know how to process what he's saying, let alone respond. Instead, she asks, "But—what now?"

"Now you spend an hour with Evelyn. You are not officially a part of the Queen's collection until you are outfitted with enough lingerie from Clandestine's Closet to appeal to any man."

"Oh," she mutters breathlessly.

"Don't worry. This is the fun part."

When they reach the end of the passageway, he leads her up a short flight of stairs, abandoning her long enough to press a button. At his touch, the mirror on the wall opens up, and Jessica stares in awe as he takes her hand and guides her through it. Her jaw goes slack when she realizes they are in the back hallway of the lingerie boutique.

Coughing out a laugh, she tells Stefano, "I really should have asked you more questions about your job over the last couple of years."

He offers her a small smile, parting the heavy black curtain between them and the store. "Come on, Jess."

HE CATCHES EVELYN'S eye from where she stands, straightening merchandise near the front of the store. He dips his chin in a subtle sign of acknowledgment, and a soft smile graces her face as she proceeds to walk toward them.

"Don't worry about the prices on anything, you can have what you love and what Evelyn agrees to," he says, speaking to Jessica, yet keeping his gaze trained on the woman heading their way. She jerks her neck, tossing her long, black bangs out of her eyes, her short bob swaying around her chin with the action. "And you must answer any questions she will ask honestly. It's important."

"Questions? What kind of questions?"

Jessica's voice forces him to find her eyes, and he stares at her for a second. Without even thinking about it, he sweeps her long hair over her shoulder and down her back as he gazes at her. One of her pretty brown eyes is slightly smaller than the other—the only flaw on her entire face, and almost entirely imperceptible at that. He's always considered it the universe's way of maintaining balance in the world. It wouldn't be fair for her to be completely perfect.

"Stef?"

"What you share with her will be your only chance to give voice to your sexual boundaries."

Her mouth falls open again, and he taps it closed just as they are joined by one of Clandestine's finest stylists.

"Don't worry. This is the fun part," she says in greeting.

After passing Jessica along to Evelyn, Stefano stands back and watches as the women venture into the land of lace and leather, all the while wondering if he's made the right decision.

Smoothing back a nonexistent stray hair, he draws in a sharp breath and turns on his heel to return to his desk. With each step he takes, he hopes with every ounce of his being his plan will come to fruition. If there's one thing he knows for sure, it's that there's no one better for his beloved dove than Khalohn Morgan.

Chapter Eleven

"**W**HAT WAS THAT ABOUT?" *Timothy asks. He stands from his desk abruptly, hurrying into the walkway with Khalohn as he makes his way back to his own seat.*

Khalohn doesn't bother trying to hide his grin, glancing at his friend as he replies, "Oh, just a chat."

"Bullshit," Timothy scoffs, keeping pace with Khalohn's rapid stride. "Turner Jefferies calls you into his office for a private meeting after the all-hands, and you expect me to believe he wanted to talk golf?"

Khalohn scowls playfully, stopping just short of his destination as he says, "Golf? I don't play golf."

"Stop being an asshole. Are you really not going to tell me?" He shoves his hands into the pockets of his slacks, which are at least a size too big for him, making him look young in that disheveled kind of way. Khalohn doesn't blame the guy, acknowledging they're all still a little wet behind the ears. Even with their master's degrees and the name plates on their desks, they're new financial analysts at Blakney Properties, paying their dues.

I might just be a little ahead of the curve—exactly as I always intended,

Khalohn thinks to himself as he makes his friend wait another moment in suspense.

"You're a dick," Timothy says before he starts to turn away.

"Oh, come on. I'm just kidding. It's good news." He crosses the remaining distance to his chair and takes a seat, swiveling toward the man as he leans back comfortably. Timothy doesn't miss a beat, rounding the side of Khalohn's desk before propping himself close enough for them to hear each other in hushed tones.

"So, spit it out already."

"He's taking me under his wing," Khalohn confesses with another grin.

His excitement is uncontainable. While it has always been his plan to latch onto someone with influence—someone who could get him on the fast track, where he could learn not just by watching but by getting his hands dirty—he never imagined it could happen so fast. It also shocks the hell out of him the someone with influence who will take him in and show him the ropes is not just some big shot with tenure, but the CFO himself. At only twenty-four years old, Khalohn is beginning to see the fruits of his labor. The long days, late nights, and endless stream of numbers are paying off.

"You've got to be shitting me," mutters Timothy, not masking his dumbfounded expression.

"I shit you not. He said he saw what I did on the Blue Lagoon proposal, and I've been on his radar since."

"Wait." Timothy folds his arms across his chest, squinting at Khalohn skeptically. "Is he putting you on the Rickman Properties deal?"

"Grunt work, mostly," Khalohn replies with a nod. "But if that's not a foot in the right door, I don't know what the hell is."

"You son-of-a-bitch," he replies on a laugh, shaking his head in disbelief.

Smirking, Khalohn shrugs. "Yeah, well, you're not wrong."

Timothy stands at his full height, looking down at his friend as he mutters, "Guess this means happy hour tonight is off?"

"I'm out. Grunt work waits for no man. Besides, if I'm late home another night this week, Hollie'll kill me."

"We can't have that, can we?" he teases snidely. "I'll leave you to it, golden boy."

Khalohn shakes his head dismissively as Timothy starts back for his desk. Somewhat relieved to be left alone to his tasks, he shifts his attention to his computer and the reports that arrived in his inbox since he left Turner's office. He allows himself a moment to replay their conversation. A sense of pride fills his chest until it's almost full. He's confident no one has worked harder than he has, because no one's ambitions can match his.

Khalohn is sure of this not because he's pumped full of arrogance, but because he knows he'll never have the life he's chasing unless he goes after it. For the first time in his history, he has an opportunity to create a future that can't be destroyed or manipulated by anyone. It's what he's wanted for as far back as he can remember. It is what drives his efforts and buoys his integrity. He has every intention of succeeding, one full day's worth of work at a time.

He's so focused on the projects he's been assigned, he hardly notices as his teammates leave for their weekly Thursday night happy hour. As the office grows quiet, his attention becomes sharper, until he's completely lost track of the time. He barely even notices he's hungry, only distracted from his tasks when he hears the cleaning crew enter the office. Looking at the time and seeing it's after eight o'clock, he curses under his breath before he starts to pack up for the day.

He lifts an arm to hail a cab just as soon as he steps out of his office building. He expels a sigh of relief when he catches a ride in no time. He calls out his destination in Chelsea to the driver before he's even got both feet inside the vehicle. As they're on their way, he pulls out his phone and sees the three messages Hollie sent him over the last hour.

Are you working late again?
Should I eat without you?
Okay, well, I want Italian so, hope you don't mind. And I hope I don't have to eat it alone.

The last message was sent only twenty minutes ago, and he's quick to send her a reply, hoping he's not too late.

Sorry. Lost track of time. Italian sounds amazing. On my way.

Even in spite of the traffic, Khalohn gets dropped off on his block only fifteen minutes later. He starts to make his way to their apartment building but stops when he sees a flower vender on the corner. Jogging over to the man whose plastic buckets of arrangements are almost empty, Khalohn pays for two bouquets of daisies and then races toward home. His phone alerts him to a message as he climbs the stairs to the fifth floor, but he doesn't bother to check it.

He fumbles with his keys for a second at his door before he's able to grant himself entrance. He drops his bag and his jacket in the corner, just beyond the threshold, kicking the door closed as he searches the small flat for his wife. He spots her, sitting at their two-seater dining room table, squeezed into the far corner on the opposite side of the kitchen.

Without bothering to look up from her plate of half-eaten food, she murmurs, "If I didn't know any better, I'd assume you'd found some other woman you liked more than me."

"But you do know better," he says, making his way toward her. "There's no one else I love more than you."

She sighs, the sound implying he's right and she can't deny it. When she finally lifts her gaze to meet his, a small smile crosses her lips. She then rolls her eyes and stands to her feet. Closing the distance that remains between them, she reaches for the flowers, immediately bringing them to her nose.

"You are so annoying," she whispers into the daisies, peeking at him from beneath her lashes. "But there's no one else I love more than you, either."

"I'm sorry," he insists, sliding his arms around her waist. She yields to his touch, crunching the flowers between them as she leans into him. Khalohn presses a kiss against her forehead before he mutters, "It was a big day."

"Define big," Hollie insists.

"Big, as in the CFO calling me into his office today after our all-hands

meeting and telling me he intends on making me his protégé." He watches as his wife's mouth falls open in shock, causing a small laugh to rumble from his chest. Smirking down at her, he says, "He may not have used those words exactly, but he might as well have. He's bringing me in on a project no analyst in his first year could even dream of touching."

Hollie sighs again, exasperated, and then tugs her bottom lip between her teeth. She shakes her head at him and then semi-repeats, "You are so annoying. And now I want the details." Pushing her way out of his hold, she heads toward the kitchen as she tells him, "Your plate's in the oven. I'm going to put these in water."

He follows after her, grabbing his plate of spaghetti and meatballs as he begins to verbally replay the conversation he and Jefferies had behind closed doors earlier that day. He's so wrapped up in defining what this opportunity means for his career progression, he barely gets more than a bite in by the time Hollie carries her vase full of flowers to the table. They sit together and she props her elbows on the table, resting her chin in her hands as she smiles at him. It isn't until he recognizes the knowing glint in her eyes that he realizes he hasn't stopped talking in nearly ten minutes.

"Sorry." He shrugs and repeats, "It was a big day."

"I don't think there's anyone in the finance industry as excited as you are about their job. You fascinate me, Lohnny Morgan."

Khalohn takes a bite of his dinner and then shoves aside his plate. Stretching his arm out across the table, he holds open his hand in invitation. Hollie looks down at his palm before sliding one of her own over his. Wrapping his fingers around hers, he aligns his gaze with her gray one as he assures her, "You know everything I'm doing I'm doing it for us."

"I know," she replies with a subtle nod.

"I mean it," he insists, gripping her hand tighter. "The late nights, the long hours, it's not because I don't want to be here with you. I promised myself a long time ago I would make something of myself. Then I met you."

"The best thing to ever happen to you," she teases softly.

He pauses, the silence meant to remind her what she's said isn't a joke *but the truth—a truth he never intends on forgetting. He then lifts her hand, turning it so as to press a kiss against the back of her palm.* "We're in this together. Everything I'm working to build, it's for us. For our future."

Her playful expression fades, and she reaches out her other hand to sandwich his. "I know, baby." *Extracting her fingers, she points at his plate and instructs,* "Finish your dinner and then take your wife to bed."

"As you wish, Mrs. Morgan."

Chapter Twelve

KHALOHN STARES OUT THE floor-to-ceiling window in front of which he stands, his gaze focused over the tops of city buildings and out at the calm East River. His mind is quiet, as is the office he has chosen to inhabit for the last several hours. He doesn't think about the financial reports he scrutinized while at home over his morning coffee. He doesn't bother to worry about the contracts he read and signed following an invigorating hour of exercise. Neither is he concerned with the truth that he left home and came to his office soon after lunch on a Saturday afternoon in order to clear his mind.

There's something sacred about his piece of Wall Street. Fifty stories into the sky is where he knows he can always be himself. Within the confines of his offices, he is expected to be only one person. His success depends on it, and that truth provides a comfort he hasn't been able to find anywhere else. For Khalohn, *home* has always come with obligations, false hopes, broken promises, and shattered vows. Even a decade after a dissolved marriage and countless nights in the penthouse he's never once shared with another, it isn't so much comfortable as it is familiar. It upholds his status more than it showcases who he is.

When his phone rings from inside of his pocket, he doesn't immediately move to answer it. As if slowly trudging his way through the abyss of nowhere he's been occupying in his mind, he blinks until he recognizes his reflection staring back at him by way of the spotless glass. Finally unfolding his arms, he reaches into his slacks and draws out his still ringing device. Curious to see *Clandestine's* is trying to reach him, he swipes his thumb across the screen and brings the phone to his ear.

"Khalohn Morgan," he answers routinely.

"Yes, hello, Mr. Morgan. This is Stefano. I'm calling as Clandestine's would like to offer you an exclusive special, of sorts."

"I'm listening," he assures his caller, looking beyond his reflection now.

His gaze drifts toward the Brooklyn Bridge as Stefano goes on to inform him, "As a way of showing our appreciation for your continued business, and in hopes of expressing our sincerest apologies for our most recent mix-up, we would like to offer you the pleasure of an evening with the newest woman in Clandestine's collection."

Khalohn's brow dips in a slight frown as the words take shape and form meaning in his mind. He then turns away from the window entirely as he asks, "She's not been touched?"

"It will be her first night," Stefano answers smoothly.

His frown deepens even as a spark of excitement ignites within his chest. The thought of spending the evening with a woman he's never had before awakens his carnal desire, which has been dormant—buried under a week's worth of days so busy the hours seemed to have gotten lost in a blur of activity.

But held in his silence is a caution he simply cannot ignore, regardless of the need which has been aroused.

"Is she a virgin?"

"No, sir. Beatrice does not accept—"

He nods, shifting his body back toward the window as he interrupts, "How much?"

"Right, well, she'll be an additional five thousand on top of your usual fee. This will apply to both nights, should you wish a repeat encounter."

Khalohn barely considers it, the thought of being with a woman who has yet to be purchased exciting him in a way he hasn't felt since he first discovered the underground establishment.

"That'll be fine. I presume this can be arranged for tonight?"

"Yes. Yes, of course," he replies exuberantly.

"Ten o'clock, then."

"Until then, Mr. Morgan."

Both men hang up at the same time, Khalohn staring at his phone for a moment before returning it to his pocket. With his evening plans now made, he no longer finds himself wanting to wade back into the recesses of his mind, lost in the view draped in front of him. He returns to his desk and picks up his copy of *The Journal*, resuming the article he abandoned. When he starts to grow hungry, he decides he's finished with the print. He then makes two calls—one to his favorite Thai restaurant, and the other to Atzel. Ten minutes later, his office as undisturbed as it was when he arrived, he takes his leave.

As he approaches the Maybach, his paper underneath his arm, he nods at his faithful driver, who holds open the backseat door with an extended hand. Khalohn gives him the paper before folding himself into the vehicle, and they are soon zipping through the streets, heading for the Upper East Side. On their journey, he directs his gaze out the window, watching as the evening sun casts shadows throughout the city. It's quiet—the absence of the weekday buzz seeping into the silence of his smooth ride—the heat from the first days of August sending the city dwellers to the Hamptons or out onto the water surrounding their corner of the world. In the silence, his mind drifts in remembrance of the phone call he had a couple hours earlier.

Khalohn wonders what treasure he may be unearthing later that night. He's never been offered the rights of first touch before. Even more, he's never even considered asking. If he's being honest with himself, he's willing to admit such a detail has not mattered to him until now. More than a woman's tenure at Clandestine's, he simply wishes not to have her in his bed over the two-night limit he has set. He's not taken the time to consider how much he's invested in his sex life or how Beatrice manages to maintain her *collection*. He doesn't care. He's paying for the best money can buy; he expects not to be disappointed, and Beatrice has been delivering for two years. Now this.

He's not arrogant or ignorant. He knows his reputation in the extravagant underground world he inhabits as frequently as he likes. The thought of ruining this woman for any other who may darken the various doorways of the clandestine space almost brings a smile to his face. He promises himself he'll take his time with her, worshiping her body as the untarnished offering he believes her to be.

When Atzel opens his door upon reaching their destination, Khalohn gets out and informs him, "I'm going out tonight. I'd like you to return in two hours."

"Yes, Mr. Morgan."

Without further instructions, Khalohn climbs the steps toward the double doors that grant him entrance inside. As he passes through, a slim Asian man hurries by him. He's barely into the lobby when the concierge behind the large front desk greets Khalohn with a warm smile, his teeth strikingly white in contrast with his smooth, dark skin.

"Good evening, Mr. Morgan," he says, his British accent somehow adding to the deep, rich tone of his voice. "Your dinner has arrived. I was just getting ready to have it brought up."

"No need."

"Very good, sir," he says, holding out the closed paper bag with his white gloved hand.

Khalohn thanks him, taking his dinner on his way to the elevator. The doors slide open without a sound, shutting only after he's keyed in the code granting him access to his unit. The smell of noodles, spicy chicken, and shrimp fills the lift car, and his hunger increases. There's a small chime when the elevator reaches the fifteenth floor, where he steps out, heading through his foyer and straight for the kitchen.

He spots the half-completed crossword puzzle from last week's *Sunday New York Times* right where he left it, abandoned on the corner of his expansive marble island. He unpacks his dinner, snapping the wooden chopsticks apart with ease, not even bothering to sit down before he takes his first bite. As he chews, he focuses his attention on the black and gray boxes on the folded newsprint. He's surprised when his dinner is gone. Flipping his wrist, he notes the time, then allows himself another ten minutes to complete the puzzle.

He's done and in the shower in eight.

In spite of the extra time he spends on his beard, he's dressed and ready to leave with twenty minutes to spare. He could be on his way with no delay after two simple calls, but he walks to his office instead. Logging into his computer, he decides to spend a few minutes glancing at the emails he neglected earlier in the day. He sees an unread message from Lorelai and clicks on it right away. Over the last week, she's done a fine job of handling the Pier House Resorts proposal. As he peruses her notes, he's sure it won't be long before contracts are drawn up and prices are negotiated. He was right to let her take the lead.

Khalohn replies to her email with one of his own, following up with a few instructions. Once it's sent, he finds he has another five minutes to spare. With no patience remaining, he closes his computer and starts for the elevator. It's no surprise, when he steps out of the lobby, Atzel is already waiting.

JESSICA STARES AT HER reflection in the gorgeous vanity mirror, trying to pretend it's not *her* looking back. She hears laughter between two of the women sitting somewhere behind her, and it makes her anxious. Even though she has no reason to believe they are laughing at her, she wouldn't blame them if they were.

Huffing out a sigh, she closes her eyes and rakes her fingers through her maple hair—curled to perfection. The locks fall down her back, the soft strands brushing against her exposed skin. A chill runs down her spine at the remembrance of her mostly naked state in a room with nearly a dozen other thinly clad women. She swallows hard and darts her tongue out, wetting her maroon painted lips.

"First night's always the hardest."

Jessica's head jerks in the direction of the woman who just spoke. Beside her, seated on the cushioned stool with her attention focused on her own face, is a blonde bombshell applying a generous amount of mascara. She doesn't even bother to look in Jessica's direction as she goes on to say, "Just relax. Don't overthink it. You do, and you'll be like sandpaper. We aren't paid to be like sandpaper."

At a complete loss for words, Jessica's lips part but nothing comes out. She simply stares at the woman. She's wearing a bright red, silk cover-up, her thick, wavy locks dusting her shoulders. She's the image of a pin-up girl—curvy, voluptuous, confident. When she's finished with her lashes, she gives Jessica a sidelong glance. Her blue eyes are dark—made even darker by the heavy makeup that surrounds them; and in spite of the serious expression on her face, there seems to be a glimmer of softness in her gaze.

Tossing her tube of mascara aside, she leans across the space separating them and extends her hand. "Dahlia."

"Jessica," she replies timidly, accepting Dahlia's gesture.

A smirk curls the corner of her mouth as she lets Jessica go. "No way Beatrice is letting you keep that name. Am I right?"

"Yeah," says Jessica, managing a half-hearted smile.

"Most of us don't use our real names anyway."

Before she has a chance to ask whether Dahlia is her real name or her *stage* name, she feels a warm, familiar hand on her shoulder. Jessica looks up and sees Stefano. Instantly, she crosses her legs and folds her arms over her chest. She doesn't need a mirror to know her cheeks are burning in embarrassment, and she's surprised by her sudden urge to cry. Frantically glancing into her lap and at her feet, she wonders where she put her robe.

Stefano squeezes her shoulder gently, and she sucks in a startled breath when her gaze locks with his once more. He frowns at her, and she can sense his confusion without him having to say a thing. He's seen her in a towel before, and they both know it—but this is different. She's never felt more vulnerable in front of him than she does now. She looks away again, certain she needs to get herself together.

I chose this, she reminds herself.

A rush of tears floods her eyes when she feels him slip her black satin robe up her back, draping it over her shoulders. He then wraps himself around her, pressing his cheek to hers. When she shifts her gaze toward the mirror across from them, she finds his eyes staring into hers. For a moment, neither of them says anything.

In a voice wrapped in more compassion and love than she deserves from him, Stefano asks, "Who are you, dove? You need a name."

Her lips tremble, but she presses them together firmly, willing herself to be as brave as the man at her back. He doesn't want to do this. She knows how much he wishes he could have changed her mind. Still, his hazel stare is giving her strength as he effortlessly expresses more support than she has the right to hope for.

Swallowing the knot in her throat, she offers him a slow nod. She'd been thinking about it all day—who she wants to be within the walls of Clandestine's—and her mind is already made up.

"Bryn. Bryn van Doren."

He quirks an eyebrow at her. In spite of her lingering fear, his expression forces a little laugh to bubble out of her. With a shrug, she says, "Seemed appropriate."

"Can't argue that. Come on," he insists, pressing a soft kiss against her cheek. "It's time."

THE MIRROR BEFORE him releases, and Khalohn presses his fingertips against it lightly. He slips through the narrow opening, allowing the door to close automatically as he heads toward the front desk. Tonight, Stefano doesn't even turn to extract his room key from the cupboard on the wall but slides it across the smooth, golden surface from behind which he stands.

With his fingers still holding the key captive, he doesn't utter his usual greeting. Khalohn studies him passively, not curious enough to question his change in demeanor, yet noting it just the same. When Stefano finally speaks, he reminds Khalohn, "She's an extra five thousand."

"I haven't forgotten," he says in reply, reaching for the skeleton key. He frowns slightly when Stefano doesn't let go. He looks from the key to the gatekeeper, saying nothing as he waits for an explanation.

The man's hesitation is quite uncharacteristic, and what could potentially be interpreted as a warning in his steady gaze does not go unnoticed. This excites him. As unnecessary as it is for Khalohn to be reminded of what awaits, their silent exchange does exactly that. Knowing he's only a short distance from the woman he intends to ruin, he decides he will wait no longer. Not allowing Stefano a chance to express whatever words may be on the tip of his tongue, Khalohn yanks the key from his grasp and starts for the stairs.

He's standing in front of his private suite less than a minute later, and he doesn't dare linger in the hallway. He opens the door and steps inside, not bothering to look around as he shuts and locks the barrier behind him. He sets the key on the antique side table just beyond the entrance and then begins to shrug his way out of his jacket.

He knows he's not alone, yet he doesn't speak until his jacket is hung and his tie is loosened. As he begins to unfasten his cuffs and roll up his sleeves, he finally looks across the room. He sees her sitting at the vanity, and his heart beats harder inside of his chest. For a minute, he neither moves nor speaks. He has no intention of rushing his way through their night. Not one tempted by impatience, he allows himself to admire her from afar.

Her feet are tucked into a pair of shiny, black, platform stilettos—her long, slender legs crossed at her ankles. She's wearing a pale pink bra covered in black lace, and he doesn't have to look to know her panties match. Her long hair has been swept behind her shoulders, but even in the dim lighting of the room, he can tell it's as thick as it is smooth. All that withstanding, it's her hands clasped tightly in her lap which draw Khalohn's attention.

She's staring at her fingers, not glancing up at him once as the seconds tick by in silence.

She's nervous, he observes to himself, allowing his arms to fall to his sides.

Instinct beckons him to tread softly, so he does. Slowly, he closes the distance between them, studying her every step of the way. Over the *click* of his Tom Ford double monk-strap shoes, he can hear the sound of her breaths—growing shallow as he draws near. His chest swells, the air in his lungs mingling with something else—something more potent than oxygen.

Power.

It seeps into his bloodstream, coursing through his veins, consuming him like fire. It's impossible to combat, and he can't tell if he's salivating in anticipation or in response to her scent. She smells not sweet or decadent; it's not as obvious as all of that. He inhales deeply as he comes to a halt only a foot away from her, and he feels his dick as it begins to harden.

Suddenly aware he's in danger of losing himself to his carnal nature, he reigns himself back in and continues with his signature routine. "You may call me Godrik," he instructs.

A hint of a smirk twitches at the side of his mouth when he notes his voice is softer than normal—as if the moment demands it. It's a heady feeling, the sense of power inside of him battling with his control, all the while succumbing to whatever it is *she* exudes in the air.

He watches as she squeezes her fingers anxiously before offering him a quick nod, her gaze still trained at her lap. He waits another second, wondering if she'll look at him. When she doesn't, he slips his index finger beneath her chin. Gently, he lifts her head, eliciting a soft gasp. His gaze locks in on her mouth, and his penis twitches at the sight of her painted lips—the top half thin and delicate, but the lower half perfectly plump. He doesn't stop himself from grazing the pad of his thumb beneath the bottom edge. The feel of her quickened, hot breath against his skin beckons him to take a good look at her.

When their gazes align, the distinct, warm brown of her irises exposes an innocence within her as potent as her curiosity. What he sees in her dilated pupils isn't fear, but something far more complex and almost mysterious. It is irrefutable he must have her. It isn't that she's the most beautiful woman he's ever seen. While she is exceptionally fine, he cannot put her on such a pedestal. It's too finite—too *cliché*. In truth, he doesn't quite understand what it is he sees when he looks at her. All he's sure of is he has no desire to look away. Even more, as he stares into her eyes— watching as she stares back in return—he recognizes his own desire for more than the satisfaction of one night.

It's as obvious as a business transaction he'd be stupid not to take. The woman within his reach is not to be taken swiftly or selfishly. There's something in her gaze, something which cools the fire of power heating him from the inside out; something that beckons him to explore her—to unearth the value found in her quiet, unflinching gaze.

With his finger still poised beneath her chin, and his thumb still pressed against the soft skin below her lips, he cannot brush away his doubt any more than he can ignore it—the doubt which begs the question: *is this merely due to the fact that she's yet to be touched?*

He doesn't know. He cannot know. All he can do is obey his calm, quiet intuition. As aroused as he is at the sight of her gorgeous body and her pretty face, it is not within his temperament to ignore the mysterious nature of his conscience. It has taken him to heights he never could have reached without such consideration, and he's learned to trust the still small voice inside of him.

He's inclined to believe *this* woman is to be savored.

"And what shall I call you?"

Jessica has to force a swallow in order to wet her throat, her shallow breaths making it dry. Just as she's about to tell him her name, she stops herself before the truth passes through her mouth. She licks her lips, unable to tear her gaze away from his, even in spite of her nerves.

He's handsome—surprisingly so. She doesn't quite know what she was expecting. Perhaps someone less polished and poised, someone slicker and skeevier. Whatever it is she imagined, it doesn't come close to resembling his unmistakably attractive face or his perfectly blue eyes. There's something about him, something quiet and almost *hidden* that makes her almost not afraid.

Almost.

Her heart is beating so hard, the sound of blood rushing through her ears makes it difficult for her to concentrate—for her to remember she's not in a cheap motel, but a luxurious suite filled with antique furniture and elegant details. The man standing before her moves, speaks, and *touches* with a confidence she doesn't understand. The warmth of his hand at her chin is a reminder that the source of his *power* in the room they inhabit is found in his bank account. As she stares at him, trying to find her voice, her anxiety takes on a different shape. No longer is she simply worried about a stranger touching her—she's terrified she might not be enough.

He moves his thumb again, this time taking it higher and gently sweeping it across her bottom lip. "Your name," he demands softly.

"Bryn," Jessica breathes, forcing the word out.

He says nothing in reply. In fact, he stares at her so long, she wonders if he can somehow see through the lie she's just told him. When he drops his hand away from her face, her stomach plummets, apprehensive about what might happen next. Then he takes a step away from her, and then another. Jessica's breathing picks up speed, until she's almost panting as she watches him.

He's leaving, she thinks frantically. *He doesn't want me? Shit, what do I...*

Her thoughts trail off into a jumbled mess of incoherent emotions as Godrik slowly strides to the wing-backed chair in the sitting area to her left. He picks it up, turning it toward her, and then eases down onto the seat. She forces herself to swallow, gripping her hands so tightly it hurts, wondering if instead of leaving, he'll ask her to get on her knees. He runs the back of his fingers down the side of his bearded cheek, admiring her contemplatively. Jessica wills herself not to squirm as she waits for him to say something.

"Dance for me."

Jessica sits up straighter, her grip around her own fingers loosening as she replays his request in her mind. She rehears him twice, but that doesn't stop her from murmuring, "What?"

Godrik rests both of his arms on the arm rests of his chair as he repeats, "Dance for me."

Relief washes over her like a cool tidal wave, and she gapes at him as she tries to wrap her mind around this unexpected turn of events. She doesn't have time to make sense of any of it before her brain kicks her into action. She stands on shaky legs, certain she must do as he asks before he changes his mind.

"I—"

She stops almost as soon as she starts, silenced by the way his eyes take her in from head to toe, in what can only be described as tamed hunger. She doesn't know what to make of his gaze. Her timid ego dares to feel beautiful while her conscience reminds her it's not about that; all the while, there's a soft whisper of a voice in her mind that alerts her to a small measure of respect she feels toward him.

She can't explain it, but there's something in his eyes…

Suddenly, she gets an idea and remembers what she had started to say. Focusing on the task at hand, she continues, "I'll need music."

Without a word of protest, she watches as Godrik reaches inside of his pocket and extracts his phone. He unlocks the screen and taps his thumb against the device a couple times before holding it out for her. She hesitates for only a breath before she crosses the short distance between them and takes his offering.

Turning her back toward him, she searches within his chosen app for the song that popped into her mind a moment ago. When she finds it, she draws in a deep breath, allowing herself to embrace that familiar sense of calm she gets just before the song starts. She's never put on a show like this before, but it doesn't matter—every time she dances, no matter where she is, the music always takes her someplace else. Someplace safe. Someplace like *home*.

She presses play, turning up the volume full blast. "Dangerous Woman" by Ariana Grande starts to play as she sets the device on the vanity table. A small smile spreads across her lips as she lets the rhythm of the song sync with her body's internal metronome. The lyrics start, and she steps out of her heels, kicking them out of her way before she begins to sway her hips. It only takes a couple lines, then her fear is gone, and all that remains is the music.

Khalohn's eyes widen when Bryn turns to face him again. She whips around with so much intention he's taken by surprise. As the music plays, her body moves in such a way, it's as if she belongs to the song and the song belongs to her. What he thought might be a slow, fumbled, and *merciful* attempt to get her to relax completely backfires in the most merciless fashion.

The woman who dances for him is not the woman she was in the silence. She's breathtaking. She's sexy. She's confident. She's *fearless*. Bryn doesn't take her eyes off of him as she seduces him with every inch of her body. She dances with all she's got—even her hair seems to be part of the choreography. And that's exactly what it looks like, expertly punctuated choreography meant to drive him out of his mind. By the time the song comes to an end, he's uncomfortably hard and on the verge of losing control.

She's on her knees when the next song begins to play. The change in sound causes her to snap her attention toward his phone. She rakes her fingers through her hair, pulling it out of her face. Khalohn can tell whatever it is that took over her before is now gone. The panting woman on the floor is the vulnerable beauty he knows as *Bryn*.

Khalohn stands abruptly, certain if he doesn't leave, he'll do exactly as he promised himself he wouldn't. He crosses toward the vanity, takes up his phone, and silences the device instantly. He slips it into his pocket and then looks down at Bryn. If she were any other woman, and if this were any other night, the bulge trying the seam of his tailored slacks would be satisfied without delay—but she isn't any other woman, and he can't trust himself. Not with her. Not tonight.

Without a word, he dips his chin in a curt nod and then heads for the door. He grabs his jacket and the key, leaving her behind without a backwards glance. He ignores the erection in his pants, not bothering to don his jacket as he pulls out his phone and calls Atzel. He left less than twenty minutes ago, and Khalohn can hear the surprise in his tone as he promises to make a swift return—but Khalohn doesn't pay it any mind. He disconnects from the call as Stefano comes into view.

A worried frown tugs at the man's perfectly manicured brow. Khalohn speaks before he can give voice to his concern. "Tuesday. My usual time. No one touches Bryn between now and then."

A subtle, pleased expression releases the tension in Stefano's brow as he replies, "Of course, Mr. Morgan."

It isn't until Khalohn steps out of the lingerie boutique and into the humid night air that his hardened appendage starts to go soft. As his mind takes him back not even five minutes, the image of Bryn's fingertips dragging up the length of her toned legs before swiveling her hips and dropping to her knees, her hair whipping back and forth as she worked the floor—there's no going back. He's hard as stone, and he knows he'll have to deal with his heightened sense of arousal before he can sleep. He doesn't relish the thought of getting himself off, but he also can't deny the truth.

That was the best damn fifteen grand I've spent in weeks.

Chapter Thirteen

JESSICA'S LAUGHTER DIES AS SHE looks across the crowded bar and sees Penn. It's obvious he's just arrived by the way he impatiently flags down the bartender. Jessica can't help but to stare for longer than he deserves, his good looks irrefutable, even if the sight of him causes a sneer to pull at her top lip.

"Oh, fuck," mutters Stefano—enunciating the curse word in such a way that somehow gives it more emphasis.

Remembering the drink in front of her, Jessica pulls her attention away from her ex and takes another sip. She polishes off the cosmopolitan, wishing it was more vodka and less juice all of a sudden. What she wants is to feel the burn of liquor as it passes over her tongue and down the back of her throat, not the burn of remembrance, which feels more like indigestion than anything else.

"Are you okay? What do you want to do?" Stefano asks, compassionately rubbing his hand over her bare shoulder and down her arm. "I can order another drink right now and go throw it in his face."

A small laugh forces its way out of Jessica's mouth, and she compels a smile as she looks to her best friend. He's gorgeous in his royal blue suit with matching blue accents. His dark hair is slicked back into a French braid, the end knotted *at the nape of his neck. He looks far too poised to ever do such a thing as waste a perfectly good drink to humiliate Penn, but Jessica knows he will if she even so much as gives him an approving* look. *She shakes her head, allowing her eyes to flicker across the bar for another second.*

This time, Jessica notices Penn is with another woman. He smirks at something she says before sliding his fingers through his own, cropped, wavy blond locks. Jessica seeks out Stefano's hazel eyes in search of solace. It's been six months since she and Penn split up. She should be over it—and in many ways she is—but sometimes she can't help but to think of the awful things he said to her the last time they spoke.

He is the sole heir of his father's fortune. His family comes from what Stefano often refers to as old money. *Born with a silver spoon in his mouth, Jessica had been surprised she and Penn hit it off so well. After almost a year of dating, she realized their entire relationship had been more of an act of rebellion than of love. When it came time for Penn to start thinking about where he intended to go for law school, he began to change. All at once, Jessica wasn't good enough anymore.*

Her stomach twists in regret as she remembers how much of herself she invested into him. Then she feels the acidic residue of both disgust and sorrow when she re-hears him telling her she would never amount to be enough for him and the man his father expects him to be.

"Hey." Stefano cuts through her thoughts as he tenderly puts both of his hands around her face. She blinks and refocuses on his kind gaze as he goes on to say, "You are so much better than that bastard deserves. You know it, I know it, and whatever cold, entitled heiress bitch he invites into his bed will remind him he knows it too. You have nothing, absolutely nothing *to be ashamed of, Jessica Shae."*

The smile that pulls at her mouth is genuine this time, and she rests one of her hands over his as she leans into his touch. "Thanks." She inhales deeply and huffs a sigh as she gently breaks his hold of her face and says, "Maybe we should just get out of here."

"It's not fair," he pouts, cutting his eyes across the bar. "I haven't been able to get you out in weeks. We've barely been here an hour."

"I'm sorry," she murmurs over the sound of music and conversation in the packed club. While she can't deny how much she usually enjoys their nights out at The Critic, the thought of Penn spotting her and then parading another woman in front of her is revolting. "We could go for pie," she suggests hopefully.

Stefano studies her for a long moment and then smiles at her slyly. "How about one more round. Shots."

"Huey, I—"

"Come on," he pleads, squeezing her hands earnestly as he stands to his feet. "I'll be right back. Order whatever kind you want. When we're done, we'll go. I promise."

"Fine," she all but groans. She hardly gets the word out before he's making his way across the dance floor of the swanky club. When she loses sight of him, she beckons the bartender and tries not to look over at Penn for a third time. Fortunately, she doesn't have to wait long. After ordering two chocolate cake shots, she turns her back to her unsuspecting ex.

By the time Stefano returns, she's got both of their shots in hand. The grin on his face as he approaches causes her brow to dip in suspicion, but she doesn't give voice to her confusion as she hands him the shooter glass.

Holding his up, he declares, "To being bad."

He then clinks his glass against hers and downs it instantly. Jessica hesitates for a moment, then follows suit. Before she can ask him what he's up to, she hears it as "Sorry, Not Sorry" by Demi Lovato starts to play over the sound system. Her eyes find his immediately, and his grin returns, along with a mischievous glint in his gaze that cannot be denied.

"Show him, girl. You know you want to."

It's all he has to say. When a laugh bubbles out of her, Jessica can't contain her smile. He's not wrong. The beat starts to grow through the course of the first verse, the rhythm practically seeping through her skin as the melody becomes one with her blood stream. She stands to her feet, unable to resist the urge.

Stefano yells out in excitement as Jessica saunters to the edge of the dance *floor. As soon as the chorus starts, her body takes over. Her tight, short dress and her stiletto heels don't hinder her movement in the slightest, her mind telling her what to do and when as she freestyles. The way she uses her hips invites the attention of a couple of ignorant men who try to reach for her as she dances. Rather than ignore them, she plays off of them, using them as props as she moves from one man to the next. It's not long before her tactics have earned her a crowd of interested onlookers. Their eyes only spur her on more. Fully in character, she performs her heart out, expressing everything she's feeling through dance.*

Two and a half minutes later, a round of applause erupts as she gasps for breath—her heart racing and her adrenaline heightening the excitement of the moment. With both of her hands, she rakes her hair out of her face and down her back, graciously smiling and nodding at the onlookers as she returns to the bar, where she left Stefano. The pride that shows on his face causes Jessica's heart to swell. As she takes his hand, signaling she's now ready to leave, she doesn't stop herself from glancing over at Penn. He looks back at her unabashedly, his mouth agape almost unknowingly. Awash in her own sense of pride, she winks at him before escorting Stefano toward the exit.

"Oh, my god—his face!" *Stefano practically shouts as they step out into the chilly night air. He bursts into laughter, and Jessica joins him as he throws his arm around her shoulders. "That was priceless, dove. Absolutely* priceless."

"Felt pretty good, too," Jessica admits, circling her own arm around his narrow waist.

"You were made for that dance floor, darling. Fucking made for it," he says with a satisfied sigh.

Jessica gives him a squeeze, leaning into his side as she lets his words fall to their feet. She looks down at the sidewalk as they stroll aimlessly, trampling over his declaration. Her smile fades a little, but she tries not to get lost in the old temptation to wallow. Fact of the matter is, he's not merely saying what she wants to hear. He's giving voice to what her heart has known to be true since she was barely six years old. They don't talk about it much anymore, but she doesn't fault him for the slip. The moment, coated in alcohol and revenge, makes the sentiment all but inevitable.

Tomorrow, she'll wake up back in the real world—where her bank account and her life circumstances make the dream of dancing full-time only that. A dream. But for just a little while, as the night races toward dawn, she allows herself to cling to the high of speaking her truth in the one way in which she's always been able.

Chapter Fourteen

J ESSICA'S HEART SKIPS A BEAT when she hears the doorknob twist to
grant someone entrance. Her head snaps in the direction of the room's
only passageway. She holds her breath until she sees Stefano slip between
the small opening he allows before he locks them both inside. For a split
second, she's relieved. Her muscles relax, causing her body to slump a little
where she's still sitting, in the middle of the floor. When Stefano draws
closer, she catches a glimpse of the expression tugging at the features of his
smooth face, and her muscles tense up again.

Halting only a step away, he studies her with a frown. He then looks
around the room before meeting her gaze. Her head still in a fog, Jessica
can't make sense of what she's feeling, let alone what *he* might be thinking.
He looks even more perplexed now than he did when he first walked in.
Jessica doesn't realize she's holding her breath in anticipation of *something*
to give until he demands to know, "What the hell just happened?"

She expels a sigh, tearing her eyes away from his as she stares into
her lap. She shakes her head, unable to make sense of it herself. Replaying

the last few minutes once, and then twice, and then three times, one truth emerges from the haze of confusion she's wadding through.

I thought that would go…differently.

"Jess!" Stefano takes a knee in front of her, snapping his fingers to catch her attention.

She lifts her face and swats at his hand as questions start to clog the back of her throat. "He barely touched me. Am I going to get paid? Do I have to—be with someone else?" A frown tugs at her brow, matching his expression. "Did you tell him I could dance?"

"What? No," he replies incredulously.

"Well, *that's* what happened. He came in, he told me his name, he—he sat in that chair and he told me to dance for him."

Stefano says nothing in reply, his mouth falling open in what could be shock or awe. Jessica isn't sure; but now that she's found her words, she can't stop until she's told him the whole story.

"I thought he might ask me to—I don't know. But it was like some sort of sign. It felt like a moment of kindness. Except—when I was finished, he just…*left.*"

She looks to Stefano for some sort of explanation. He doesn't say anything, which brings Jessica back to her previous line of thinking. The idea that she wasn't what Godrik wanted makes her palms sweat. She's not sure what she's more worried about—that the man Stefano all but handpicked for her hadn't touched her—or that the man with the secrets hidden in his perfectly blue eyes, eyes she almost trusted for reasons that don't make sense, hadn't touched her.

She'd mentally prepared all day to give herself to a man she didn't know, then in walked Godrik. What feels like the very real possibility he'll refuse to pay for a night with no *happy ending* makes Jessica's heart race anxiously.

After more silence than she can stand, she reaches up her hand and snaps her fingers in Stefano's face. "*Say* something. Please!"

Gently taking hold of her hand, he moves it out of his face in order to stare into hers as he murmurs, "You just made eight thousand dollars, and all you did was dance?"

An involuntary laugh bubbles out of Jessica before she catches herself. She covers her mouth with her free hand for a second. That's about as long as she can hold her tongue. Sliding her hand down until her fingers are splayed across the exposed skin of her chest, she exclaims, "What? I made—I made *what?*"

"Eight thousand. It'll be wired into your account Monday morning."

"Holy shit," she says on another laugh.

Pulling her hand out of Stefano's grasp, she submerges all of her fingers in her maple locks as she lets the actuality of eight thousand dollars sink in. She shakes her head in disbelief and then closes her eyes as she remembers the man who is responsible for such a large amount of funds. Her eyebrows knit together, and her hands fall into her lap as her moment of hysteric surprise slowly morphs into sober realization.

I need more. Eight grand is amazing, but I'll need more—and something tells me I won't get off so easy next time.

Even in the midst of such a reality, made even more evident in the room in which she still sits, Jessica can't ignore the thrill of what she's done and what it means. Not just for her, but for her mother—for their future. In one night, she's made more money than she would have been able to take home from Moby's Dive in *months.*

"I can't believe it," she says softly, looking at Stefano.

"Me neither. He's never—" He cuts himself off and looks away from Jessica. She interprets his sudden silence immediately.

In this room, she is not his dove more than she is an asset. In this moment, Godrik is not a man to be gossiped about. He's a client whose secrets are protected. As much as she wishes she could be privy to the rest of Stefano's unfinished sentence, she acknowledges she has no right. She surrenders to the gatekeeper out of respect for her friend.

"So, what now? What happens next?" she inquires.

His hazel eyes cut back to look at her, but he says nothing as he admires her in thought. Before she can grasp even a hint of what he might be thinking, he rises to his feet and smooths his hands down the front of his jacket.

"You get dressed and you go home," he answers matter-of-factly. "If he wants you another time, you'll be notified. I should be getting back to the front."

"If?" She stares up at him before joining him as she stands. "Beatrice made it seem like maybe—do you think he won't? And if he doesn't, I'll get someone else?"

His face softens as a hint of desperation glints in his eyes. "Jess—"

"No," she states, stepping toward him. It takes her no effort at all to see what he's thinking—what he's *hoping*. "Two nights. I know you hate that I'm doing this, but we both promised. Two nights. I just, I need to know if you think it'll be Godrik or someone else."

Stefano's eyebrows knit together at her use of the name *Godrik*, and she wonders if the two men are not on a first name basis. Her suspicions are confirmed when he replies, "If *Mr. Morgan* would like another night…" He pauses and sighs resolutely before he changes his mind. "*When* Mr. Morgan would like another night, you will be the first to know. For now, go home. The night is yours." He presses a kiss in her hair, just beside her temple, and then starts to take his leave.

"Huey?" she calls out before he can get too far.

He stops, turning only enough to see her from over his shoulder.

"Thank you." She knows he doesn't think he deserves any appreciation for what he's done for her, but neither of them can negate the truth. Her first night went better than either of them could have imagined. Regardless of what the future might hold, she's more certain now than ever it'll have all been worth it.

"I'll call you tomorrow."

When he leaves, he doesn't bother shutting the door behind him. Jessica watches him go, but it isn't until he's out of sight that his words really sink in.

The night is mine.

After she tucks her feet back into her heels and slips on her robe, she becomes aware of a boldness that washes over her as she exits the room. She shuts the door behind her, her hand lingering on the knob as she remembers the handsome man who first opened it not even a half an hour ago, changing her life in ways he will never know.

A small smile plays at her lips, and she lowers her chin, hiding the expression from no one as she starts down the hall. She feels wired. The thought of going home doesn't seem realistic. There's too much excitement still lingering in her veins, and she needs to get it out.

Upon reaching the ready room, she finds her way back to the vanity station she occupied before. Sitting on the cushioned stool, she flips on the lamp and then stares at her reflection contemplatively. Earlier, she had been looking at herself, trying to pretend she was someone else; trying to pretend she was *Bryn van Doren*. Now, as she spots the fire still simmering in her brown eyes, she realizes she hasn't felt more like herself in ages. The woman she was in that room—the woman who danced for Godrik—that wasn't Bryn. It was Jessica. It was a version of herself she hasn't slipped into for so long, she almost forgot what it felt like.

Cognizant of exactly how she wants to spend the rest of her night, she reaches for her purse. She sets the bag in her lap and digs through it for her phone. When she finds the device, she searches her contact list and finds Kierra's name. She constructs a text and sends it without thinking twice about it. Immediately after, she wonders if her old friend will even give her the time of day. As she stares down at her screen, waiting for a response, she goes so far as to question if she's still allowed to call Kierra a friend at all.

She shrugs her shoulders, as if to shrug away her negative thoughts, worrying her lip as she continues to wait. If nothing else, the life coursing through her after the show she just put on is a reminder that what once made the two of them close still has the power to reunite them. One minute goes by, then another, until Jessica convinces herself a watched pot never boils. Setting aside her phone, she slips out of her robe and shimmies into the dusty-rose romper she wore to Clandestine's. As soon as she's finished tying the drawstring at her waist, her phone alerts her to an incoming text. She's quick to grab the device and unlock the screen.

New phone. Who dis?
Just kidding! OMG, Jess! Where you be, girl?
We're on our way to Sound Effects. You in?

Relieved to have gotten such a favorable response, and with an invitation to a club she hasn't been to for months, Jessica sends a rapid reply. Promising to give her a call upon arrival, she gathers the rest of her things and starts for the rear stairwell.

She's halfway across the room when she hears someone say, "Leaving so soon?"

Jessica stops in search of the woman's voice. When she looks to her right, she watches as a blonde woman stands slowly from her seat and turns to face her. The sheer robe she wears drapes all the way to the floor, but she parts it open as she takes hold of her hips, exposing her bright red lingerie and her well-maintained physique. At first glance, Jessica can tell she's at least a couple years younger than the stranger; but it's not the woman herself who beckons the hair on the back of Jessica's neck to stand on end. It's the tone in which she speaks, as if she knows something Jessica does not.

Her pale green eyes rake up and down the length of Jessica, her piercing gaze making her feel as uncomfortable as if she were still only half dressed. With the most arrogant sneer she's seen in a long time, the blonde mutters, "He must not have liked you."

At a loss for what to say, Jessica merely stares at the woman, slightly dumbfounded. As if her lack of response seems to prove some sort of point, the stranger lifts her chin and looks down her nose at Jessica. Feeling uncomfortable under such a judgmental perusal, she decides to continue on her way. The woman says nothing to stop her, but her words follow Jessica as she climbs the stairs leading to the back exit.

She ascends slowly, wondering why the pale-eyed woman would say anything to her at all. Had she simply wished her a goodnight, she's sure she would have found the blonde beautiful. Now she knows only that whoever she was cannot be trusted. Sneaking through the doorway at the top of the stairs, then stepping into the vacant hallway, Jessica stops to consider the meaning behind what the woman said. She stares at the door from whence she came and wonders if there's any validity to what the woman implied. While Godrik seemed to appreciate the looks of her, he didn't seem interested in exploring her body in any way.

The sound of a door slamming in the distance rattles Jessica, causing her to abandon that train of thought. Certain she should leave before she's spotted by the wrong person and forced to explain her presence, she hurries for the exit. The moment she walks outside, the heat of the day still clinging to the air in darkness, she reminds herself it doesn't matter that Godrik didn't touch her. He paid his fee.

He didn't demand a refund, like that other John I heard Beatrice mention during my interview. Godrik paid, and I made eight grand in one dance. One. Freaking. Dance.

Her smile of realization returns, but this time she doesn't hide it. This time, as she heads for the Canal Street subway station, she allows herself to feel it.

Chapter Fifteen

KHALOHN GLIDES THROUGH THE water towards the opposite side of his pool, slapping his hand against the wall before he turns to swim another twenty-five meters. After two hundred meters of the breaststroke, he pulls himself up onto the edge and sits with his feet in the water as he works to catch his breath. Staring into the pool—the muscles in his arms and legs complaining of fatigue, and his lungs demanding an explanation for his need for speed—Khalohn asks himself if he requires another couple of laps. He drags a hand over his mouth, wiping away droplets of water from his beard, then smooths a hand through his hair, remembering the day before.

Monday morning, he woke thinking of Bryn. As if she had infiltrated his dreams, he woke with a desire that was soon followed by an erection caused by the memory of her body as she danced for him. He tried to set aside his desire and ignore his body's demand for a sexual release by increasing the intensity of his usual Monday weight session in his private gym. While it had gotten his blood moving in a different direction, it did little to quench the thirst she had created in him.

All morning, he contemplated calling Clandestine's to reschedule his next visit for that very evening. Never had he woken up two days after a session longing for a woman the way he longed for Bryn. He chalked it up to the fact that he hadn't yet touched her. It was that reminder which forced him into a cold shower. He intended to take his time with her, which meant he needed to be in control. Even with his mind made up to practice patience, it wasn't until he was able to immerse himself in work that he was able to operate with a clear mind.

Now, as his breathing grows steady, he can't ignore the excitement of knowing tonight he will touch the woman who has managed to consume his idle thoughts. There's an almost palpable satisfaction in his intention to bring her pleasure the likes of which she will experience in no other room at Clandestine's. With every other woman he's had, his reputation has proceeded him; however, his reputation means nothing to a woman who has not had to endure the selfish demands of the other clientele. He is certain he's not wrong to believe the average buyer to roam those underground halls is more concerned with what can be taken rather than given. But he remembers her eyes—Bryn's curious and timid brown eyes—not tarnished by the hardness he's seen more times than he can count.

It's not the timidity you remember. It's not the curiosity or the innocence, either, he tells himself.

Dropping his chin to his chest, he shakes his head and then submerges himself in the cool water. As he flips onto his back, he presses his feet against the wall and then propels himself backwards, his arms stretched out over his head. When he's gone as far as his momentum will take him, he begins to wind his arms, racing toward the opposite side of the pool. Somehow, he knows it'll be a hundred and fifty meters before he can chase away the impatience which has resurfaced with the memory of the *fire* he saw in her brown-eyed gaze. From across the room, he had seen it—her passion. Unbridled. Unafraid.

That's what he wants. That's what he craves.

That's what I'll take before I'm finished with her.

reaches up to sweep her hair behind her ears. Khalohn hides his smirk, certain he already knows what she'll say, but not wishing to clue her in to that fact. "I know you told me not to need you on this, but—"

"Dinner. Tomorrow night. Eight o'clock. But I expect you to bring it home."

"Yes, sir," she replies with a curt nod.

She starts to make her exit, and he shifts his attention back onto his computer as he calls out, "Have Maribelle make the reservation."

"Certainly."

Before his attention is fully captured by the task he was in the middle of only moments ago, his thoughts drift toward another reservation. He checks the time, noting he's only eight hours away from his scheduled appointment in Lower Manhattan. He then glances at his calendar, satisfied to see his upcoming evening is filled with plenty of distractions, in the form of international conference calls to Japan. Aware he has far more valuable ways to spend his time, other than to daydream about the ways in which he will indulge his sexual appetite later, he shoves all thoughts of Bryn out of his mind and gets back to work.

JESSICA SITS ACROSS the table from Beth in their tiny kitchen, peeking over at the tired, middle-aged woman every few minutes. While her mother is searching for work on the outdated laptop she's been using for that one reason going on weeks now, Jessica is doing the same on her phone. At least, she should be. Her mind is too distracted to focus. She would be lying if she denied her sense of urgency has been usurped by something akin to doubt.

The large sum of money she was promised has been sitting in her account for the last two days. She's logged-in to her bank app more times than is necessary over the course of the past twenty-four hours, but she can't help it. Neither is she quite ready to touch it. Well aware she will eventually spend every dime, she is also conscious of the fact that she needs

In spite of the extra time spent in the pool that morning, 1
arrives to work before the rest of his staff begins to trickle in.
the sun is high, casting shadows throughout the streets of the Fi
District, the office is buzzing with activity. Khalohn spends the firs
of his day in meetings with analysts, listening to presentations, going
projected growth charts and dissecting public information reports
early afternoon when he finally returns to his office to check emails
messages. Maribelle brings him his lunch, reminding him he's hungry. S
offers him a knowing smile, speaking not a word as he thanks her on h
way out. He's almost finished with his meal when she pages him on hi
desk phone.

"Lorelai is requesting a moment in regard to Pier House Resorts."

"Send her in," he insists, wiping his hands before pushing aside the
remains of his salad.

He hears the muted sound of Lorelai's heels against his carpeted floors
before she rounds the front of his desk. He says nothing as he sits back in
his chair, and she doesn't wait for him to prompt her to speak. Knowing
what it means to have been granted an audience with him, she slips her
hands into the pockets of her fitted, bright yellow, cropped slacks, and lays
all her cards on the table.

"They know who we are, they've seen our proposal, I've done a hell
of a lot more than my due diligence in record time, but they're not ready.
There's blood in the water," she says with a shake of her head. It's obvious
she's irritated, but he knows she's not finished. She's relentless, which is
why he put her on this deal in the first place. She goes on to say, "But it's
family blood, and the CEO has voices in his ear who have greater influence
than anyone on his payroll."

Khalohn nods, having been exactly where she is in the past. "This is
about trust."

"Yes, which is why they're insisting on an informal sit down. We're not
the only ones hunting them. They'll be in the city until Thursday. Look,"
she starts before she pauses. Extracting her hands from her pockets, she

to be careful about how it is distributed. While she certainly has to plan ahead, figuring out how to get the funds to last as long as possible, she also has to utilize it in such a way that it won't cause Beth to be suspicious about where the money has come from. *Technically,* neither of them has a job.

It has occurred to Jessica, more than once, she could lie and tell her mother Stefano dipped into his pocket in order to help them out. In the end, she always arrives at the same moment—the memory as vivid as if she were still sitting at the center of it. She sat across from her best friend at the diner and insisted she would see her own way out of their financial troubles. It's who she is. Jessica has decided, if she is going to lie, she needs to lie as the woman her mother raised her to be.

Right. That makes so much sense. Because she definitely raised you to be a prostitute.

Unable to stifle her sigh of frustration, Jessica lets it out and then drops her phone along with her forehead down onto the table.

That—that right there is why I can hardly think straight.

More than the logistics involved in spending the money, and more than the lies she keeps tucking into the cracks of her story, she's troubled by the doubt that arises every time Godrik struts into her thoughts.

Are two nights going to be enough? Could I offer myself up for another? Four nights. Five—mom and I would have so much money, I could convince her to stop spending every day sitting at this table, looking for work that isn't there. But what would it say about me if I was willing to take that chance? And how many men would that be?

She closes her eyes when she feels Beth begin to stroke her fingers through her hair comfortingly. Her delicate touch makes Jessica feel better and worse at the same time. As much as she hates lying to her mother, she is convinced it'll be worth it in the end. She allows herself to truly *feel* Beth's fingertips as they graze her scalp all the way to her ponytail before she pulls away and starts at Jessica's hairline again. The repetitive motion puts her at ease, all the while reminding her she's not a prostitute.

At least not yet.

A grimace tugs at her face at the sound of the antagonizing voice disguised in her own tone. She squeezes her eyes closed tighter, breathing in deeply as she forces herself not to lose the feeling of her mother's touch.

As she continues to wait on Stefano's call, she acknowledges it's only a matter of time before a *prostitute* is exactly what she will become. One more night, or a dozen, it will make no difference. Yet, that realization no longer carries the fear which accompanied it a week ago. As naïve as it is to admit it—one pair of blue eyes and one demand for a dance has caused her to reassess everything. Every day since Saturday has brought with it a dose of curiosity that has caused an anxious anticipation she never expected.

Godrik has proven to be nearly impossible to put out of her mind. It's his pretty blue eyes she stares at in her mind's eye whenever he's actively consuming her thoughts. But it's not merely his good looks which have her thinking about him repeatedly throughout the day. More than the cut of his tailored button-down shirt or the shine of his fancy shoes, more than the confidence he possesses in a single finger or the intensity of his stare, she's found herself replaying and analyzing the way he treated her on Saturday night.

I was his for the taking, but he didn't take. He gave. *Even if he doesn't know it, he gave me a piece of myself I never thought I'd find in that room.*

Over and over again, she reminds herself that next time will likely not be the same. No man in his right mind would throw thousands of dollars her way just to watch her dance. Even so, the idea of seeing him again doesn't scare her. As terrifying as it is for her to admit, even to herself, she is looking forward to the next time they'll be in the same room together. If nothing else, she has somehow arrived at a place where she assumes he can be trusted. If he is to be her first, she'll have more to be thankful for than regretful of. Her certainty is weakened only by the truth that Godrik Morgan is nothing more than a stranger.

But there's something about him—something he keeps close—something he hides—something I want to see.

As romantic and unrealistic as it sounds, Jessica doesn't care. She allows herself to entertain such thoughts and to flesh out the fantasy she has created for *Bryn van Doren*. To look at it any other way would be to admit the people who roam the decadent halls of Clandestine's aren't people at all, but puppets and puppet masters. That, or something far worse and debase.

Had Godrik been anyone else, she might be dreading Stefano's call; she might feel used and disgusting and faceless. She is convinced she wouldn't be entertaining thoughts of breaking the deal she made with Stefano to quit after only two nights—but he had seen her. Godrik allowed her to be seen. And as he watched her dance, she saw a piece of him, too. Overpowering her cowardice is her desire for *more*. More money, certainly, but it doesn't stop there.

He isn't a monster, whoever he is.

"Why don't we take a break, hmm?" suggests Beth, pulling Jessica from her wandering thoughts.

Furrowing her brow, Jessica is relieved her face is hidden. She can feel it as a blush invades her cheeks, causing her skin to burn in both embarrassment and self-reprimand.

Good god. Am I really thinking about screwing some stranger with my mom sitting two feet away from me?

"We've been at it for a while," Beth continues, obviously oblivious of her daughter's thoughts. "Watch a movie with me, baby. I'm having dinner over at Jackie's tonight, but we've got some time before then," she says, speaking of her best friend.

After a slight pause to gather herself, Jessica lifts her head only enough to be able to prop her chin on the table. Beth's fingers, no longer in reaching distance of her hair, trace along the side of Jessica's face before she closes the laptop and nods her head toward the next room. For a few seconds, Jessica just stares at Beth.

She studies the details of her mother's face—the thin lines that fan around the edges of her eyes and the corners of her mouth; her pale pink lips, which haven't seen a lick of lipstick since Jessica walked across the stage at her high school graduation. She stares and sees the woman who hasn't had a chance to live enough life, but who has spent years working tirelessly to make ends meet.

Both of them are at a time in their lives where they should be out on their own, figuring out who they are—other than a mother who loves her daughter or a daughter who adores her mother. But they're trapped in a small apartment they can barely afford. Worse, Beth is trapped in a body that will likely never be well again. Yet, even in the midst of what feels like a frustratingly dead-end situation, Beth wants to watch a movie before she spends the evening gabbing away with Jackie.

"I love you, mom," Jessica whispers.

"I love you, too, baby." Pushing herself away from the table, she stands to her feet and asks, "Should I make us some popcorn? And what should we watch?"

For a minute, Jessica doesn't respond. She watches as Beth maneuvers her way around the small kitchen, doing exactly as she's been doing for the last twenty-four years—making the best of things. As she stares silently, realization washes over her like a gentle breeze.

Two nights. It's all I get. It's all I want. Just enough to give me a chance to start again. I'm not a prostitute. My mother raised me so much better than that. I owe her the world, built on sweat, blood, and tears—not sex, lies, and broken integrity.

Two nights.

"Jessica?"

"Yes. Sorry. Yes, to the popcorn," she insists, finally sitting up straight. "And I'll let you pick the movie."

She's barely finished her sentence when her phone starts to ring, vibrating against the table. Even though she's been waiting all day for this particular call, the sight of Stefano's work number lighting up her screen causes her breath to catch in her throat.

"I—I need to take this," she tells Beth distractedly as she picks up the phone. "I'll be back." Hurrying from the kitchen, she slides her thumb across the screen and presses the device to her ear. "Hi," she finally answers. In a hushed voice, she goes on to inquire, "You're calling from work, so I'm guessing..." She doesn't quite know how to finish her sentence. Thankfully, Stefano doesn't force her to.

"Mr. Morgan will arrive tonight at ten. Your call time is nine o'clock."

"Okay. I'll be there."

"I know. I'll see you in a few hours."

"Stefano," she says before he can bid her farewell.

"I'm here," he assures her.

"Our spot? Tonight?"

He's silent for a beat. In the silence, they have an entire conversation. Without saying the words, she's admitting and he's accepting tonight won't be the same as her first night. Whatever happens within the confines of the elegant blue room belonging to one Mr. Morgan, she'll need her best friend afterwards. In the silence, she admits he's been right all along, and he accepts she has been right, too.

"I'll meet you at twilight, dove."

When Jessica returns to the kitchen, her phone still clutched in her hands, Beth is at the stove popping a pot full of popcorn. She looks to her daughter, smiling softly as she asks, "Is everything okay?"

"Yeah. That was, um—it was Stefano. I think I'm going to go out with him later. I'll probably leave around eight or so."

"I think that's a good idea. You could use a night out to get your mind off things."

Grazing her teeth guilty over her bottom lip, Jessica nods, averting her gaze. When Beth asks her to fetch a bowl, she stifles a sigh of relief, glad for the opportunity to escape the lie—at least for the length of a movie.

Beth chooses a tried and true favorite, and the two of them curl up on the couch as they watch *Dirty Dancing*. When it's over, Jessica cleans their popcorn bowls and straightens the room while Beth changes to head out to her friend's place. Jackie's been around for as long as Jessica can remember.

She's got a place with her live-in boyfriend up in Queens. While Beth isn't the biggest fan of Jackie's partner, she puts up with the guy for her closest friend. They've been as thick as thieves since the day they met at the chemical plant.

Beth leaves around six. In order to escape her own thoughts, Jessica hops in the shower to get ready for her trip into the city. When it's time for her to depart, she draws in a deep breath, reminding herself this'll be the last night she'll have to lie to her mother about where she's going. Her mind is made up. She has no intention of breaking her promise to Stefano any more than she intends to break the promise she's made to herself.

She leaves her guilt behind and starts her journey toward Clandestine's.

KHALOHN STAYS AT the office until it's as quiet as it was when he arrived. While he's got a few analysts who are known for burning the midnight oil, he spots not one as he takes his leave. But who is or is not still on the clock is not at the forefront of his mind. As he makes his way toward the elevator, he acknowledges his thoughts are already far from work.

Resigned to the truth that Bryn has a way of infiltrating his thoughts in a way no other woman has in years, he doesn't fight it. He knows it's temporary—his routine making any woman who inhabits his bed hardly more than a fleeting moment. It appears life has given him an opportunity to embrace a level of excitement that doesn't happen every day. He's stumbled upon a treasure of sorts, the value of which he has yet to assess. Tonight, he intends to unearth his finding and extract from it what he desires.

Atzel stands patiently beside the Maybach as Khalohn makes his way out of the building. When he's a few feet away, the Honduran man turns slightly to open the passenger door, his movements as practiced as the breaststroke Khalohn executed in the pool what feels farther away than that morning.

"Atzel," Khalohn greets politely.

He unbuttons his jacket as he steps into the vehicle. Absentmindedly, he takes note of Atzel's polished shoes as the man replies, "Good evening, Mr. Morgan."

The sound of Wall Street's traffic is hushed with the soft thump that accompanies a closed door. Khalohn's attention is drawn out the window, and he doesn't bother to look elsewhere as he instructs Atzel to take him to Lower Manhattan. For the duration of his ride, he thinks briefly of his schedule for the remainder of the week, his mind unable to tack down a single thought for longer than a few seconds.

When he's only a block away from his destination, the streets almost as familiar as the map on the palm of his hand, he closes his eyes and pulls in a slow, deep breath. He exhales unhurriedly, reminding himself of the control which personifies him. He opens his eyes just as Atzel opens his door, and he steps out onto the curb without hesitating.

"Stay close. I don't intend to stay all night."

"Yes, sir," Atzel agrees.

Khalohn dips his chin in a slight nod, buttoning his jacket in the same swift manner. Without another word, he strides toward the front entrance of Clandestine's Closet. The boutique still boasts of a few browsing costumers, but they pay him no attention as he makes his way through the store. He chances a glance over his shoulder only after he's allowed the heavy, black curtain blocking off the back hallway to fall closed behind him. When he is sure he is alone, he approaches the antique mirror, uttering the password just loud enough to be heard. It clicks open a second later, and Khalohn checks his surroundings once more before slipping inside.

Stefano stands behind the golden desk, poised with the same graceful air as always. As Khalohn approaches, it dawns on him that everything about his evening is as ordinary as it usually is. His routine is punctuated with the same reliable and predictable details which define it. The woman he is about to encounter is the one piece of his evening he cannot predict. He's underestimated her before, but he has no intention of letting that happen again. His experience has taught him, to assume he knows the likes of Bryn is reckless—and he's never been a reckless man.

"I trust you will find everything to your satisfaction," says Stefano, sliding his private room key across the counter. "Your fee this evening will be the same as your previous visit, and payment will be extracted at the end of your session."

Khalohn nods his understanding and reaches for the key. He notes the gatekeeper's slight hesitation, similar to their last encounter. Stefano removes his hand from the key before Khalohn can think too hard about it. Slipping the possession into his pocket, he continues toward his ultimate destination. His strides even, yet purposeful, he allows himself to embrace the anticipation he feels as it builds with each step. When he arrives at his door, he wastes not a moment before he grants himself entrance. After he locks the two of them inside, he doesn't take off his jacket or loosen his shirt cuffs. He doesn't fall into the rhythm of his usual routine, his curiosity blindsiding him with the urgent desire to see her.

Much like their previous encounter, he finds Bryn perched on the stool directly across the room. Her face is hidden from him as she stares into her lap, not bothering to look over at him even as he tries to tempt her with his silence. Rather than her fingers grasping desperately to one another, Bryn's hands are resting calmly atop her bare knees. There's something unpresumptuous about her stance, and a quiet sense of appreciation invades Khalohn's mind.

Without taking his eyes away from her, he sets the skeleton key on the table beside him. Slipping out of his jacket, he studies her, his fascination increasing as he tries to call to mind a single woman who has occupied the room the way she seems to be able to. In an inexplicable sort of way, she manages to consume the entire space with nothing more than her essence. It's as if his memory of her and the way she moves surrounds them both, permeating the air they breathe. Khalohn has no idea what she tastes like, but his mouth begins to water as he hangs his jacket. He has no idea what she looks like completely naked, but as he unfastens his cuff links and begins to roll up his shirt sleeves, his skin begins to perspire; like the anticipation he feels is beyond what his body can contain for even a moment longer. As he starts to cross the room, he allows himself to feel impressed.

They always look at me. A coy smile. A flirtatious laugh. An enticing touch drawing my attention to what she considers to be her best asset. Every woman who has ever entered this room has always looked at me. Begging me in a single glance. Pleading for me to live up to the whispers that fill these underground halls. Trying to convince me she is worth more than two nights in my bed. If not on our first encounter, without a doubt on our second, they always look.

But not her.

This time, when he stops a mere foot away from her, it's not her chin for which he reaches. Wanting her to meet his gaze in her own timing, he grazes his fingertips through her hair. Just as slowly as he sweeps the silky, thick strands behind her ear, she lifts her face enough to peek at him from beneath her eyelashes. For a moment, he feels triumphant. A slight scowl causes his eyebrows to twitch, and he questions what he possibly has to feel triumphant about—*I've done nothing,* he admits. Regardless, the feeling cannot be denied, and he wishes only to amplify its effects.

He traces his fingertips, still lingering at her ear, along the curve of her jaw toward her chin. With every inch of skin he covers, her face lifts a little more, until her warm brown eyes are open wide and staring at him in quiet wonder. In the silence that continues to fill the space between them, he pauses, enraptured by the reflection of himself in her eyes. He doesn't know who it is she sees when she looks at him, and the uncertainty that exists in her knowledge of him makes him feel as though he's been given an opportunity. She is his conquest—his untarnished treasure—her value hidden in pleasure he fully intends on unearthing and exploring. Yet, captured in her eyes is an unspoken gift, one he is sure she has no idea exists.

It's not just her body that's not been touched. Her mind is pure. She's not been taught to play a part. She's not been forced to learn the game. I am not a client with a reputation. I am her first. I am the unread definition.

For the first time since he was offered the woman who sits in front of him, he fully appreciates what he's been given. He thought he knew, but he didn't. Even more, if he had not left so abruptly three nights ago, had he given in to his impatience, he would never have known. The triumph that fuels his excitement now is not unearned.

A chill races down Jessica's spine as Godrik's touch travels up her chin and onto her lips. She doesn't know what to make of him. She can practically smell the power and control he possesses; but it's not an unpleasant scent so much as it is an intoxicating aroma that causes her stomach to tingle in anticipation. As he stares at her, his touch as gentle as if he knew her, she allows herself to get lost in the fantasy that Bryn belongs to him. She convinces herself that if tonight is to be her last within the extravagant world of Clandestine's, she will allow herself to seek whatever pleasure she can find.

So long as I'm in this room, so long as he's looking at me like that, I'm not Jessica. I'm Bryn.

Godrik's fingers linger on her lips, and Jessica's stomach clenches anxiously as she opens her mouth for him. For a moment, fear takes hold of her, but she closes her eyes and forces herself to pretend. Before she can change her mind, she darts out her tongue, in search of his warm skin. In an instant, she can hardly breathe. Faster than she could possibly anticipate, he leans over and hooks his arm around her waist, yanking her to her feet and pressing her flush against his chest.

Jessica's eyes fly open, her hands instinctively clutching at the man's shirt as she tries to catch her breath. The strength found in the arm wrapped around her and the solid muscle she can feel pressed against the entire length of her torso makes it nearly impossible for her lungs to function.

"I won't hurt you," he says, speaking for the first time.

Trusting his words to be true, Jessica nods. Still, she doesn't relax against him until his lips find hers in a decisive kiss. He doesn't open his mouth as he allows the kiss to linger, and he doesn't force her to open hers. As if to make his intentions perfectly clear, he slips his free hand around the back of her neck, gently tickling the hair at her nape with his fingers. When he has her wholly in his grasp, he pulls his mouth away from hers.

Jessica's eyes flutter open. When her gaze collides with Godrik's stunningly blue stare, she wonders when her eyelids lost the fight to his touch. Then he kisses her again; and it dawns on her, she is powerless against his lips and the way the whiskers of his beard tickle her face. With him so desperately close, her senses are so utterly confused. He smells incredible—masculine and fine, yet somehow deliciously delicate. His hold is firm and unyielding, but she is not frightened because his kiss is honest.

Godrik is a stranger. Except, in spite of her inexperience with situations such as these, Jessica is even more sure now than she was before that she is safe in his space. If their first night together wasn't enough to prove it, the self-control she can feel in his touch does. She doesn't have to know him to be aware of his respect for her.

This isn't my first kiss. I know an animal when I taste one, and he isn't.

When Godrik pulls away for a second time, Jessica's heart pounds in her chest as the extent of her confusion begins to sink in. Her mind is caught between her instincts to fight or to fly. She can admit what she's about to do is unnatural and wrong. She also can't deny the verity of her situation. She could have been given to anyone who might have done ungodly things to her—who might not have promised with an intentional kiss that she would survive the night unscathed. Knowing such a truth fills her with a sense of obligation.

Fight, she whispers in her mind. *Fight the doubt and don't run. Let him have what he wants. Let him have Bryn.*

Forcing her body to comply, Jessica leans into Godrik, silently granting him permission to take as much as he's paid for. Instead of touching her further, he lets her go and takes a step back. Before she can question him, he walks around her, toward the bed. A perplexed frown tugs at her brow and each corner of her mouth as she watches him toss the decorative pillows onto the floor before pulling back the covers, revealing a set of royal blue, silk sheets.

Meticulous.

When he's finished, he turns toward her and instructs, "Get in."

Khalohn takes pleasure simply watching her as she makes her way toward him before slipping out of her heels and climbing onto the bed. He can still taste a hint of her on his lips, but he tries not to think of it, lest he lose hold of the short leash he has on his patience. He hadn't meant to kiss her. He rarely feels the need to do such a thing. He's always considered it an intimate gesture meant only for the moments so ravaged with greed, it could be disguised as desperation. Nevertheless, he can't take back what has already happened. If he's being honest with himself, he doesn't want to, either. His touch had the desired effect, even if it did come with the consequence of wanting more.

Bryn crawls just out of reach onto the mattress, settling herself on her knees. She looks to him for further instruction, and he requires no extra time to ponder before he tells her, "Lie down."

She does as she's told, resting her head on one of the two pillows he left on the bed. He watches her, all the while unconsciously making the decision to not unfasten the buttons of his shirt or to loosen the buckle of his belt. He merely unties his shoes and discards them before crawling onto the bed with her.

Bryn's breath quickens as he straddles her legs with his own, his body hovering over hers. Intrinsically aware there's only one acceptable way to begin, he brings his mouth to her ear and whispers, "Relax." He then begins to pepper kisses down the length of her neck, across her collarbone, and between her small, pert breasts. Despite his gentle command, as he drags his mouth across the smooth plane of her flat stomach, Bryn's chest heaves with labored breaths.

Intent on ensuring he only takes what is desired, he pauses to look up at her from where he's settled in between her legs. Without taking his eyes off her face, he reaches down with his right hand and glides his fingers up the inside of her left leg. The sound that escapes her lips when he presses two fingers against her panties at her center is indecipherable. Fully immersed in his quest for noises the opposite of ambiguous, he slowly pulls her panties to the side and finds the bundle of nerves he intends to use to coax her arousal. To his surprise, she needs little encouragement. The next sigh that graces his ears is accompanied by the act of her legs falling open for him.

Her sigh—almost too quiet for his own ears—travels straight to his groin. As his length begins to harden, filling up what little space remains in his slacks, he loses his grip on his patience. Remorselessly, he chases his pleasure by way of hers, pressing her legs open further as he makes room for his mouth.

A few minutes later, when she comes on his tongue, the sound she makes is so soft, so beautiful, so uncontrived, it halts him. Barely lifting his head, he glances up at Bryn's face, and the breathless expression she wears almost knocks the wind out of him. Her cheeks are pink, and her eyes are filled with an awe which seems to mirror his own. Except, instead of the triumphant feeling he was after, Khalohn is now certain that while he could take from her until she has nothing left, he has glimpsed the depth of her value. While he thought he understood he'd been given a woman with whom he should take his time, he finds he has been presented with a choice. He can stay or he can go.

It takes him only a moment to accept that if he stays, he will stay all night—and that is a choice he cannot afford, *time* a commodity he cannot earn back. Another night, however, is an option far more affordable. With this in mind, he drops his gaze down to her exposed center. He doesn't think twice about leaning down to kiss her there. His lips barely graze her slick, swollen skin—a promise masquerading as a tease. Easing her panties to right, he then presses a soft kiss on the inside of her thigh and climbs out of the bed. With his back turned to her, he adjusts himself in his pants and then reaches for his shoes.

Jessica sits up, her heart racing as she watches him. She can barely think straight, the memory of his mouth so poignant, even as she closes her knees, she imagines she can still feel his wet tongue, his hot breath, his soft beard.

Oh, my god, she thinks with a shake of her head. A blush rushes to her cheeks, and she seals her eyes closed tight. A small voice in the back of her mind shouts to be heard, warning her that for the second time, the man she's supposed to have sex with is leaving. Except, rather than take his own pleasure, he has done the exact opposite. The warning in her mind is difficult to hear through the lingering fog of euphoria clouding her thoughts.

Never has she experienced oral stimulation as gentle and intentional the likes of which Godrik Morgan is capable. It was as if his sole purpose was to make her melt into the mattress, until her only option was to surrender to the feeling of his touch.

Hearing the click of his shoes against the floor, heading toward the door, Jessica is brought back to the present. She gasps, feeling both confused and panicked in equal measure.

"Wait," she calls out as Godrik reaches for his key.

He says nothing in reply but merely turns to glance back at her.

For a second, she doesn't know what to say. His silence unnerves her, and his quick departure fills her with doubt. The memory of his affection fades a little, cowering as she draws her knees up, curling her body into the smallest version of herself. It takes her another second to find her voice in order to match words with the feelings that seem to be robbing her of the lingering effects of her pleasure.

"Is—is there something wrong? Something wrong with...me?"

"Not in the slightest," he assures her.

He leaves without another word, but she manages to breathe a sigh of relief.

If she hadn't been looking into his eyes, she would have missed it—his beard hiding the slight movement at the corner of his lips. But she hadn't missed it. She saw what could only be described as the merciful—almost *tender*—expression soften those perfectly blue eyes.

Not in the slightest.

Dropping her chin to her knees, she frees a quiet laugh, recognizing the moment can be punctuated with no other sound.

I just made another eight grand—and all I had to do was come.

After her laughter dissipates, the silence she's left with sends a chill down her spine. Her gaze takes in the details of the extravagant room, and the relief she felt moments ago wanes. For a second, she feels lost between the realm of *real life* and an incredibly bizarre *dream*. The silken sheets beneath her, the dark blue walls with gold trim around her, the beautiful preserved, antique furniture, the chandelier hanging from the ornate ceiling in the middle of the room—it doesn't feel real. She closes her eyes and turns her head, until it's her cheek resting atop her knees. In the darkness behind her eyelids, she can feel Godrik's mouth between her legs. Another chill runs down her spine, this time for entirely different reasons. She furrows her brow as she holds hers legs tighter.

Was that real?

It's over. Two nights. That's what she promised Stefano. That's what she promised *herself*. Now that it's over, the whole experience seems too good to be true. Too fanciful to be *real*. She seals her eyes closed harder as she considers the sacrifice she's made. She's earned sixteen thousand dollars. She offered up her body, and the man who bought it took nothing. Instead, he *gave* so much. Rather than guilt, she finds herself grappling with *curiosity* and *desire*.

There's no space between her knees, but she presses them together anyway—her sex pulsing in memory of the pleasure she was given by the mouth of a stranger. Jessica's hard nipples tingle, and she tugs her lower lip between her teeth, biting down in remembrance of his beard scraping against her sensitive flesh as he dipped his tongue inside of her.

What's wrong with me?

A soft moan fills her mouth before she shakes her head, in an attempt to discard the memory. Pressing her forehead to her knees, she feels a knot as it begins to form in her throat. She tries to swallow it as she asks herself, *Why do I want more?*

STEFANO'S SPINE STRAIGHTENS when he hears the fast approaching footfalls of a John. He looks up from his task, turning his gaze toward the short staircase, bracing himself. As the gatekeeper, he is certain there are seven men locked behind seven doors with nine women—one of which is his beloved dove. He knows the clock has not yet reached half past ten, and the last John to have arrived did so not twenty minutes before. His awareness of the clientele leads him to believe there should be no footfalls echoing along the corridor for at least another hour. When he sees Khalohn Morgan hit the first stair, Stefano pulls in a deep breath in an attempt to control his rising sense of panic.

"Mr. Morgan, is everything all right?" he asks, careful to keep his tone professional.

Khalohn stops in front of the reception desk and places his skeleton key atop the guest book opened in front of Stefano. He then reaches into his jacket pocket and extracts his wallet as he says, "Friday night. Eleven o'clock. Same woman."

Stefano loses hold of his professional air as his mouth falls open. He's stunned into silence at Mr. Morgan's request for Jessica for a third night. He can't think about what such a request might mean before the man in front of him pulls a wad of cash from his wallet and places it next to his discarded room key.

"No one else touches her between now and then."

Stefano doesn't look down at the tip he's been given. Neither does he speak a word before Khalohn turns and heads for the exit. It isn't until he's almost made it to the door that Stefano's mind recognizes the full extent of what Mr. Morgan's request will entail.

A third night.

Rather than his shock that Mr. Morgan would prefer Jessica for yet another night, he realizes the deal he made with Jessica will be broken. For a split second, he feels torn between his roles. He doesn't know whether to be a best friend or a gatekeeper.

"Wait," he calls out, hardly remembering Khalohn won't be able to take his leave until he's released the latch on the door.

Mr. Morgan says nothing as he stops and glances back over his shoulder. One look into his familiar blue eyes, and Stefano realizes he doesn't have a choice. He is to be both the gatekeeper *and* a best friend. Khalohn is not a John who can be denied. He is, by far, among Clandestine's top VIP members. And yet, he and Jessica made a compromise. Stefano is intuitive enough to surmise, given Mr. Morgan's reputation, she's yet to be taken. As much as he would like to leave it at that and refuse another night, he must settle for the next best thing. He doesn't think about the consequences which might be doled out by Beatrice at his actions. He simply makes up his mind he'll deal with whatever comes his way as he barters with his best friend's body.

"She'll be double your normal fee next time." Stefano doesn't deny the price he demands is not so much for the sake of Jessica's financial benefit but for the small hope Mr. Morgan won't part with twenty thousand dollars for a single night with a woman he could have had already.

Khalohn doesn't speak his reply. He jerks his chin in a nod of affirmation and then continues toward the exit. Stefano presses the button that opens the hidden door, and he stares after the man, slightly dumbfounded. At the sound of the clicking latch, signaling he's now alone, he drops his gaze down at the items Khalohn left in front of him. He picks up the cash first, counting out fifteen hundred dollars.

Ten percent. He counts the bills again to be sure. Mr. Morgan has always been a generous tipper—but he's never tipped more than five percent, least of all on a fee higher than his usual. Pocketing the cash, Stefano takes up the skeleton key and abandons his station. He doesn't hear the music playing softly through the halls, or the faint sound of pleasure slipping beneath the doors he passes. All he can think about is the equation in his head he can't figure out.

He doesn't think twice before he inserts the key in Mr. Morgan's door and frees the lock. For the second time in a row, he breaks the gatekeeper code of conduct, which is to allow the women fifteen minutes alone in the room before they are released. He doesn't care if Jessica isn't decent. Furthermore, he suspects she must be. Mr. Morgan wasn't in the room long enough to do a damn thing.

Jessica gasps, her head snapping up from atop her knees upon his entrance. He closes the door behind him, taking her in before he settles his gaze on her brown eyes, obviously glazed over in confusion. He doesn't know what to say. The longer they stare at one another, the more uncertain her expression becomes.

"Huey," she starts on a whisper.

Stefano shakes his head, signaling her silence, and takes another step into the room. He wants to ask her what happened; but just as torn as he was with Mr. Morgan, he remains with Jessica. He ignores her use of his nickname, remaining firmly in his skin as Stefano—the gatekeeper.

"He's requested another night. He never requests a third. Never."

Jessica's spine straightens, her eyes growing round with an expression Stefano can no longer interpret. "He hasn't—"

"You and I made a deal," he interrupts, not wishing to hear what Mr. Morgan has or hasn't done in the sum total of thirty minutes he's spent with her. "But he's not a client I can refuse."

"I'll do it," she murmurs, her voice so soft he's only sure of what she's said by the shape her mouth makes around her words.

He pauses, squinting through the dimly lit room at what might be a kiss of color brightening Jessica's cheeks. He forces himself to look away from her altogether before he replies, "I didn't foresee this. I don't know what you do to him, but he wants you—regardless of the cost."

As soon as he's spoken the words, a pang of guilt slices through him.

She's priceless, and he won't allow himself to forget it—regardless of the circumstances.

Softening, he brings his eyes back to meet hers. "Swear to god, he's the only one I'll let touch you, Jess. But the second you want out—"

"I'll be okay. I promise. He makes me feel..."

Her voice trails off, and he knows he shouldn't wait for her to finish the sentence, let alone beg her to. Nevertheless, he doesn't look away from her as he accepts his need to know. He needs to be reminded she won't break under the weight of her choice—a choice *he* has allowed her to make.

"He makes you feel what?" murmurs Stefano.

"Not afraid."

He offers her a small nod and then turns his back to her as he reaches for the door handle. "I'll meet you in the hall when you're ready."

"Huey?"

He turns his head so she can see his profile, but he directs his gaze down at the floor as he waits for her to continue.

"Twilight?"

Stefano glances at his chest, thinking of the fifteen hundred dollars tucked away in his breast pocket. In that moment, he knows he'll not only pay for their coffee and pie—he'll slip her all of what's left over.

"Of course, my dove."

Chapter Sixteen

*I*T'S LATE WHEN KHALOHN INSERTS *his key into the lock and twists the deadbolt open. He can't remember the last time he was home before nine o'clock—but he also can't remember a time in his life when he's felt more alive. It's been a year since he's gone into business for himself. The work has been difficult and sometimes arduous, but the foundation he's strived tirelessly to build has been worth it. He's starting to turn a profit at a rate which seems unheard of at this stage in the game.*

He's surprised when he closes the door behind him and finds Hollie sitting on the couch, with a half empty glass of wine in her hand. "Hi," he greets simply, locking up behind himself.

"Nice of you to come home."

Khalohn halts, glances at the bottle of wine he surmises must be at least half gone, and then decides not to respond to her statement. He doesn't want to fight with his wife. Any argument she may wish to hurl at him wouldn't be completely unfounded. He's aware the last year has taken a toll on the both of them—but his motives have not changed. Neither has his heart.

"I'm sorry I missed your call this afternoon. Is everything all right? How was your day?"

"Don't. Don't do that. Don't be nice to me," she demands. She sets her glass on the coffee table and stands to her feet as Khalohn shrugs his way out of his coat.

"Hollie, let's not do this now. It's late. You're tipsy. Let's just go to bed."

"You want to fuck? Is that it? If you take the bait—if you say what you're thinking instead of sweeping it under the rug for later, you know I won't let you near me—is that it?"

Frustration niggles the back of Khalohn's neck as his exhaustion settles into his bones. He lifts a hand and scrubs it down his cheek, covered in a day's worth of stubble. He's been here before. They've fought it out before. Tonight, he doesn't have the energy.

"Hollie, this is not about sex. You don't want me to touch you, I won't— but I won't fight with you, either. If you want to finish your wine, by all means, don't let me stop you. I'm not hiding anything, not sweeping anything under the rug, I merely inquired about your day, which you seem not inclined to discuss. I'm going to take a shower and then head to bed."

He's halfway to their bedroom when she screams, "I fucked Tim. You want to know about my day? I met him for lunch, and he took me back to Blakney's office and fucked me in the supply closet."

Khalohn stops abruptly, his back to his wife. Her outburst hits him in the chest like an invisible force, meant to knock the air from his lungs. His organs burn until he finds the wherewithal to inhale. He draws in a deep breath through his nostrils. Before he can blow it out, Hollie continues.

"It wasn't the first time. The first time was Fourth of July. You said you'd be home that weekend, and then you got stuck in the Bahamas. I felt guilty—but Timothy, he couldn't stay away. You know what he says? He says you were the obvious choice. He said, all those years ago, when I first met you both, he never stood a chance. It's why he never said anything. Why he never admitted he's loved me since the moment he laid eyes on me. He said it was finally his chance, and he wasn't going to let me go twice."

Khalohn's eyes fall closed as her words wash over him. The truth of her betrayal ignites a chain reaction beneath his skin. He can feel it as fury chills his blood, turning his veins to ice. In an instant, his body is numb. He can hear his pulse—slow and steady—as his mind falls silent. The world around him seems to come to an unhurried stop. A scowl pulls at his brow, and he realizes he can no longer hear his wife as she speaks.

He's alone. It's a feeling he's experienced before. It welcomes him, like an old friend he hadn't planned on meeting again. The clutches of his familiar companion soothe him into a state of calm which makes no sense. On his next inhale, Khalohn breathes in an awareness he recognizes—the truth that in this world, the person he can rely on the most is himself. No one, not even his wife, can be expected to fully appreciate who he is and love him anyway. It's a lesson he learned as a child; one he's been trying to forget for years. In this moment, he understands it is inescapable.

It isn't until he feels the palm of Hollie's hand strike his cheek that he opens his eyes.

All at once, the world begins to spin again.

"Are you even listening to me?!" she cries.

His eyes lock with hers, and he watches as her tears streak down her cheeks before they drip from the edge of her chin. He doesn't resist the urge he feels to reach up and gently brush the back of his finger along her face. He perceives her pain, and he doesn't dispute it. He loves her, and he finds no vindication in her broken state. He sees beyond the truth she's laid before him.

For the first time, he understands the depths of her needs—needs he cannot meet. His ambition, his drive, his vision, his plan, it has him on a path from which he cannot stray. To do so would be to betray himself—and as his wife and his closest friend have seen to that already, he will not do the same. He's on a mission, a mission he thought they were on together. He understands now it isn't a mission she believes in. Or, perhaps, she simply lacks the strength or the courage to see it through. Either way, her love for him has proven to be a cracked foundation on which nothing can stand.

"I'll take the couch."

"Excuse me?" she hisses, jerking away from his touch.

"I'll call my lawyer tomorrow. I'm sure he can refer someone on your behalf, as well."

"What? That's all you have to say? I tell you I'm having an affair, and you add me to some to-do list like I'm some meaningless task—"

Her accusations spark his ire, and the ice in his veins shatters as he bellows, "No—you're my fucking wife! A wife whose loyalty has been sullied and nailed to the bedpost of another man. You made your choice. Repeatedly, as I understand. Now I've made mine."

"Khalohn," she calls as he starts to make his way around her. "Khalohn!"

"You could have told me." He spins in the opposite direction and points a finger at her as he mutters, "I'm a fair man, not some pig-headed brute. You didn't have to lie and cheat while I was building something—building something for us."

"Oh, don't give me that bullshit! You're hardly ever home. If you were, you'd have heard me tell you I changed my mind. I don't need all of this. If I'd have known—"

"If you wanted out, all you had to do was ask!" Taking a step toward her, he stares into the depths of her soul and demands, "Look at me. Fucking look at me. I would have let you go. That's how much I love you. Now it's too late. This is not the partnership I agreed to. Every time I look at you, I'll see him. You're not the wife I want. Not anymore."

Chapter Seventeen

K HALOHN REACHES FOR HIS phone without bothering to glance away
from his computer screen, the ringtone recognizable as belonging
to only one. As he presses the handheld speaker to his ear, Maribelle's
exasperated tone clues him in to her annoyance as she simply says, "I'm
sorry, dear."

She doesn't have a chance to say much else before Porter strolls into
view, and a hint of a smirk teases the corner of his mouth. He tries his best
to conceal it from the man who is practically grinning as he unbuttons his
suit jacket and takes a seat on the leather sofa adjacent to Khalohn's desk.

"No apologies are necessary, Maribelle."

"Oh, someone must apologize for that man—today, it might as well
be me."

She disconnects and Khalohn quirks an eyebrow at Porter as he
returns the phone to its cradle. This elicits a mischievous chuckle before
the broker shrugs and admits, "She makes it far too easy. She only has
herself to blame."

"So you continuously insist." Shifting his attention back to the task at hand, he informs his friend, "I need a minute and then we can go."

"That won't be necessary. While I hate to cut our weekly meeting short, I figured you wouldn't mind the excuse to stay and work on—whatever is you've got prioritized for the afternoon. I'm going to the Hamptons this weekend. My car's waiting for me downstairs as we speak."

"All right," says Khalohn, looking at the man with a scowl. "If that's the case, you could have called and canceled."

"Yes, but then I wouldn't be able to attempt to persuade you to come with me. You know I'll show you a good time."

"And you know I'm not going to the Hamptons this weekend."

Porter leans forward, propping his elbows on his knees as he insists, "I cannot, in good conscience, leave you here for another boring, predictable weekend alone. Convince me I'm wrong, and you'll be free of me until next time."

"My life is not *boring*," mutters Khalohn dryly. "I've got a company to run—"

"Which you do splendidly," Porter interjects. "In fact, you're so fucking good at it, you've got a room full of people out there doing your bidding, which means *you* can take a weekend to kick back, relax, and enjoy more than a little female attention. You come with me, and even the ones with rings on their fingers will be throwing themselves at you."

Khalohn's even temperament is nicked at his friend's comment, earning the man nothing but a scowl in response.

"Okay. Bad form. You're right," he acquiesces, standing to his feet. Porter buttons his jacket as he crosses the room, stopping in front of Khalohn's desk. "All I'm saying is, it's too damn hot to spend your weekend holed up in the city. There won't be any pretty little things in bikinis around here."

"Maybe not, but I won't be left wanting for female attention. I never am."

A slow, sly smile pulls at the corner of Porter's mouth as he slips his hands into the pockets of his linen suit. "No, I suppose you aren't." With a shake of his head, he starts to take his leave as he says, "The women I have in mind are a lot cheaper. You ever feel like slummin', you know how to reach me," he teases. "See you next week."

Khalohn listens as Porter leaves, but he doesn't mutter a farewell. Neither does he watch him go, his friend's comments taking another turn around his thoughts. While Porter has a vague idea of how Khalohn feeds his sexual appetite, that's all it's ever been—an *idea*. If he knew how much money Khalohn's invested into a steady stream of women for the last couple of years, he's sure he'd never hear the end of it.

Lifting his gaze, he stares out the windows across the room. His thoughts shift not to the steady flow of cash he's invested in Clandestine's— but the fifty thousand dollars he'll have spent on one woman in the span of only seven days. For a moment, he loses control of his thoughts, his memory fogging up his mind. He can hear Bryn's shallow breaths; feel her soft skin against his lips; taste her arousal on his tongue. He remembers the warmth between her legs, and how quickly he discovered how she liked to be taken care of. His mouth starts to water as he replays the generous manner in which he used his tongue, and the soft moans she sang for him all the while.

Khalohn closes his eyes as his erection fills the crotch of his pants. He inhales deeply through his nose, forcing his mind and body into submission. A frown of frustration tugs at his brow, and he shakes his head at himself. When he opens his eyes, he looks to his computer, recognizing he should get back to work. Bryn is a fantasy. In his annoyance with himself, he acknowledges if he's not careful, his quest to unearth the full value of their transactional relationship will make a fool out of him. He admits to himself she arouses him with a memory simply because he hasn't yet found his own release. He's allowed her to excite him—leaving him suspended in anticipation.

Tonight, he reminds himself. *Tonight, the fantasy will play out.*

Khalohn discards his thoughts of Bryn as he re-submerges himself into his previous task. It's Maribelle who takes it upon herself to make sure he gets lunch, and he eats it at his desk before his scheduled afternoon conference call. When hunger rumbles his stomach again, he decides to stop for the day. As he leaves the office, he hardly notices how quiet or how late in the evening it is.

Upon arriving at his penthouse, he heads straight for the fridge. He sorts through his options of prepackaged meals, settling on a chicken dish he slides into the oven. As his dinner cooks, he discards his suit jacket and takes up the previous Sunday's crossword puzzle, finishing it just as the timer sounds on the oven. He eats his dinner standing up, looking out the tall windows in the dining area beyond the kitchen. It's nearly eight by the time he's finished, and he makes his way to his study to work for a couple more hours.

With the sun all but set, he switches on the light, the sleek, modern light fixture hanging from the center of the room casting a warm glow in the otherwise dark space. Three of the four walls are lined with built-in shelving units painted charcoal gray, the fourth wall containing two tall windows. His desk is to the right of the door, the mahogany piece simple and classic, outfitted with little more than a lamp, his home computer, and a few files tucked with contracts he's still mulling over.

Behind his large, leather, ergonomic chair hangs a canvas awash in shades of blue and gold—some of the only color brought into the room. A matching canvas is hung on display on the opposite side of the room, between the shelves filled with books and the knickknacks his interior designer found fitting in the space. Just off the center of the room is a tweed-gray couch, situated in front of the flat screen television that's mounted to the left of the door. Khalohn turns the big screen on, adjusting the volume down low before he sits behind his desk.

A while later, after he shuts his computer down and turns off the television for the night, he makes his way to his bedroom. He takes a quick shower before donning a pair of blue slacks and a white, mock-collar button-up shirt. He allows his mind to revisit thoughts of Bryn as he loops a belt around his hips and dons a watch with a matching leather band. He slides his bare feet into a pair of brown leather, Brunello Cucinelli loafers, grabs his wallet, and is out the door.

As he rides in the backseat of the Maybach, Bryn becomes all he thinks about. Rather than the pleasure he doled out upon their last encounter, he recalls the smaller, seemingly insignificant moments. The way she parted her lips as he grazed his fingers across the smooth skin of her face. The feel of her tongue as she sought to taste him. The look in her eyes when he yanked her off her seat and into his arms—and the expression on her face when she called to him before he left.

Is—is there something wrong? Something wrong with…me?

He replays her questions on a loop as it occurs to him the message he's sent. The longer he ponders it, the more aware he becomes that she's twice been granted access to his private quarters with a certain expectation, and he's never so much as loosened a button on his shirt. Given the lack of conversation exchanged between them, he can understand why she would think he's somehow dissatisfied with what she has to offer, even in spite of his answer to her question. In point of fact, she can't be further from the truth.

He thinks ahead to the night that awaits him and the complexities of the situation he's created. He's been privy to her nerves; and while he's confident he can dissolve any uncertainty he's planted within her, he makes up his mind that he'd like to dispel her doubts in a way he never has before. The longer he considers it, the surer he is of his decision. Out of the ordinary as it may be—so is she. So is their arrangement. Furthermore, he has glimpsed her value, and he knows better than to tarnish it.

JESSICA STARES THROUGH her reflection in the vanity mirror as she thinks over the last several days. With the cash Stefano insisted she take, after they shared a slice of apple pie at Sunrise Diner & Donuts a couple of nights ago, she's got more money in her bank account than has ever been there at one time. In less than thirty minutes, she will be earning another ten grand. As much as she needs the money, and she's under no illusion she can talk herself out of needing it, she hasn't quite been able to talk herself into *spending* any of it.

Burying her fingers in her hair, which she'd taken the time to curl before her commute into Manhattan, Jessica seals her eyes closed and asks herself the same question she's been trying to figure out since the moment Godrik walked out of the room on Tuesday night.

Why me?

She's been prepared to sell her body. At least, she thought she was. What she wasn't and still isn't prepared for is Godrik. It isn't merely the curiosity he's sparked inside of her. It isn't the way he turns her on, or how confusing it is for her mind, her body, and her heart to be in three completely different worlds when it comes to the man.

All right. Maybe it's a little bit about that, she thinks as she pulls in a deep breath. *He's handsome. And while I've never seen him naked, he's good with his hands. He's really good with his mouth, and I'd have to be dead not to be turned on by him—even if my heart is confused, because I've never had sex with someone I didn't care about; even if my mind is confused because the sum of what we are amounts to an exchange that's more monetary than anything else; even if he is a stranger.*

Even if he's spoken a sum total of five sentences to me.

Jessica pulls in a sharp breath through her nose and rights herself. This time, when she stares at her reflection, she sees herself. She *studies* herself. For reasons she can't begin to comprehend, Godrik Morgan thinks she's worth an obscene amount of money. Given she hasn't so much as touched him—which she understands is the whole *point* of Clandestine's—she's certain she's not worth the price tag Stefano placed on her. The price tag to which Beatrice agreed. This certainty makes her feel guilty—guilty enough to let more than seventeen thousand dollars sit in her bank account untouched.

It also makes her feel more than a little bit afraid. A couple nights ago, she'd told Stefano Godrik makes her feel *not* afraid. But that was post orgasm. And not just any orgasm, but one gifted with a slow, sensual, intentional build that came complete with a payment of eight thousand dollars. She was in shock. After a few days of being able to think of little else, she's convinced herself tonight will be different. In her mind, there's no way Godrik will pay double his normal fee without demanding something in return. Though, it's not the possibility of more which frightens Jessica— it's the possibility that he'll finally have his way with her and realize she isn't worth the thousands upon *thousands* he's invested in her.

She shakes her head at herself and shifts her gaze down to her body. There's nothing to smooth out, but she adjusts the straps to her navy blue, lacey, bralette bustier and traces her fingers across the front of her matching, lacey, bikini panties to busy her hands. In the back of her mind, she believes if she turns out to be Godrik's most expensive disappointment, she'll be free. With the money she'll have earned in just a week's time, she'll have some *breathing* room. She reminds herself this'll allow her to look for a job. A *real* job. A job that won't make her mother ashamed of her. A job that won't make her best friend stare at her in an expression that reads both worrisome and awestruck.

Except, if she listens closely to the soft whisper of a voice in the back of her mind, she hears the truth. She doesn't want to be a disappointment. She can't explain why. It's not that she has feelings for Godrik. That's impossible, as she knows nothing about him—other than he's the type of man who pays for sex. That alone *should* be reason enough not to harbor any twisted thoughts about satisfying him. Jessica can only imagine how many women were in his bed before her. Then again, she is wholly aware she has no right to judge. Not when she's putting herself in his bed—no matter her reasons.

She stares down at her hands, now clasped in her lap. In a moment of surrender, she acknowledges to herself that it's complicated. It's all so very complicated. She owes him her body, and nothing more; and yet, she wants to give him more. She wants to give him what he has given her.

"Fuck," she whispers as her eyes fall closed.

"There's a rumor going around."

Jessica's head snaps up as she looks to the vanity station to her left. Dahlia, the curvy blonde who was kind to her on her first night, must have arrived only moments ago. Jessica was so lost in her own thoughts she didn't hear her as she settled in and began her own preparations.

"Um, I'm sorry?" murmurs Jessica.

"Beatrice is classy. She runs an upscale operation. Well, as upscale as one can get in this line of work. But don't for a second let yourself think the women of Bea's collection aren't catty. We are. We so *totally* are."

Jessica folds her arms across her chest, unconsciously hiding herself, not entirely sure what's happening. Dahlia smooths her fingers underneath her eyes, sighs, and then turns to look at Jessica before she continues.

"I don't mean to scare you," she says.

Jessica doesn't offer any type of response. She wants to believe Dahlia, but she also doesn't understand the meaning behind her warning.

"Okay, I'll admit, it's not all nails and fangs. For some of us, we've got each other's backs. Beatrice is all of our greatest ally. She's our boss, yes, but she takes care of us. I wouldn't say many of us are *friends* beyond these halls, but we know the score like no one else does, you know? And we talk. About the men. The ones we like. The ones we have to watch out for. It gets catty when the ones we like prefer someone else. It's stupid and petty but—it's hard to escape. Comparison. Competition."

"I don't…" Jessica starts to say, shaking her head in a physical expression of her confusion. "I don't understand what you're getting at."

"Godrik. He's not just a John. He's a legend. Even if you aren't his preferred flavor, he'll take care of you at least once. Twice if he likes you. Twice if he *adores* you—but only twice. Only ever *twice.*"

Dahlia tilts her head to the side, her gaze taking in Jessica as if she's never seen her before. An impish grin pulls at her lips, revealing a confoundingly beautiful albeit dubious smile. Jessica's only response is to blush.

"I don't know you, but you've got my respect in spades. No one, and I mean *no one* has had Godrik Morgan *three* times."

Jessica opens her mouth to explain she isn't *that* special, and she hasn't *had* Godrik once, let alone twice and gearing up for a third; but before the truth comes out, her curiosity stops her, and another question tumbles out of her mouth.

"How—how does anyone know who my John is?" she murmurs softly, feeling a little embarrassed.

If ever she's felt like a novice, it's now. Regardless of the previous two nights she's frequented Clandestine's, she knows very little about the other women or the innerworkings of the club. As far as she's aware, Stefano and Beatrice are the only ones who know which woman is in which room on any given night.

Dahlia's smile stretches wider as she informs Jessica, "The rooms require preparation and cleaning. They're cleaned the morning after use. They're prepped an hour before use. Girls around here pay attention. The Legend is one of only two Johns who has a room belonging to him and only him. That room has been prepped three times in the last seven days— and none of us have been requested, which leaves...*you.*"

Before Jessica has a chance to respond, Stefano enters the room. Instinctively, she reaches into her bag and pulls out her plain, short, black satin robe, slipping her arms through it and hurriedly shrugging it over her shoulders. It's the third time Stefano has come to collect her in order to escort her to Godrik's room; it's the third night he's seen her in lingerie the likes of which she never thought she'd be able to afford. As she ties the belt tightly around her middle, she recognizes it doesn't matter that they used to live together. It makes no difference that he's seen her in as little as a towel. It doesn't matter—*none of it matters*—because the scraps of fabric that cover her now are like chains. They are a heavy burden that is the truth of her circumstances, of their agreement, and the indiscretions which have led them to this moment.

"Bryn," he mutters, offering her his hand.

Jessica's heart constricts within her, and she allows herself to enjoy the feeling at the sign of Stefano's mercy. In one word—with one name—he's reminded her that in the ready room, with the rest of Bea's collection, and throughout the halls of Clandestine's, she's someone else. She's not his dove, she's the fantasy belonging to Mr. Morgan.

At least for another night, she thinks as she slips her palm against the one he's offered.

"Bryn?" Dahlia comments, her right eyebrow lifted in intrigue.

"Bryn van Doren," says Jessica as she stands to her feet.

Dahlia shakes her head before she shifts her attention back onto her vanity mirror. All the while she whispers, "Respect."

"What was that about?" asks Stefano as they step into the quiet hallway.

Thinking about her exchange with the voluptuous blonde, Jessica glances down at her strappy, black, stiletto sandals as she places one foot in front of the other. She remembers how she introduced herself as Jessica the first time they met, and she realizes she still doesn't know if *Dahlia* is the blonde's real name.

Is anything real in this place?

Stefano squeezes Jessica's fingers, and she brings her gaze up to find his. She can read the assessing way he's studying her, and she forces a smile as she shakes her head at him.

"Nothing," she replies. "It was nothing. Shop talk, I guess."

Neither of them says another word as they approach Godrik's suite. Stefano unlocks the door and grants her access, but he doesn't cross the threshold. For this, Jessica is both grateful and disheartened. She closes her eyes as he shuts her inside, and she wills herself to get over it. She doesn't want his encouragement. Doesn't need it. Neither does she wish to see his worry or apprehension. As she slips out of the robe, laying it over the back of one of the couches, she shoves aside who she *is* and slips into the skin of who she needs to be.

Tonight, she sits on the cushioned bench at the foot of the bed. She's not sure what time it is, but she's confident she'll have no more than fifteen or so minutes before she's no longer alone. She crosses her legs and stares at her surroundings, trying to let the setting swallow her up; trying to forget who she is; trying to immerse herself fully in the fantasy. Soon, her eyes fall closed and she drifts into a memory.

She remembers the taste of Godrik's kiss.

She remembers the heat of Godrik's mouth.

She remembers the generous way he uses his tongue.

When Jessica hears the insertion of a key in the door a few minutes later, her eyes fly open. She's no longer nervous—she's *wet* and wanting, and she doesn't allow herself to fight it.

As Godrik enters the room, rather than stare down at her hands, she looks over at him. Right away, she notices he's as casual as she's ever seen him. He's in a button-up shirt, tucked into a pair of tailored slacks. Still, he looks like money. But there's something more. Something different about this version of casual. The fabric of his shirt hugs his broad shoulders and accentuates his narrow waist. She can tell, by the way his pants fit from his hips down to his ankles, his thighs are solid and strong. When she wonders what he might look like beneath his clothes, she embraces the thought, clinging to the fanciful notion, willing herself to be brave.

For a moment, he doesn't move. Godrik stands at the door as his eyes complete a body scan. As soon as his blue eyes find her brown ones, he reaches behind him and locks the door—all the while keeping his gaze trained on her. Jessica doesn't notice he's holding something in his hand.

As he crosses the room, silently and intentionally, her heart starts to beat faster. By the time he's standing in front of her, she can hear her blood *whooshing* through her body as if someone is pounding a drum inside her head. When he holds out his free hand, palm up, Jessica looks at his offering before hesitantly sliding her fingers across the plane of his slightly calloused skin. As soon as her palm kisses his, he wraps his long fingers around hers and tugs. Instantly, she's on her feet. She hardly has a chance to acclimate herself to their proximity or the delicious smell of him—a smell, she's decided, that can't be found in a bottle, but only wafting off of him with every decisive move he makes—before he drops her hand and reaches behind her.

Jessica can barely feel it as his hand brushes against the tips of her hair while his fingers work to unhook her bustier. It takes him a *second*. When the hooks are free, he slowly traces his fingertips up her naked spine and then around to her left shoulder. His eyes still trained on hers, he drags his fingers across her shoulder, catching the strap of her bralette. Jessica is hardly aware of her breaths, now more accurately described as *heaves* as she gapes up at him. However aroused she was seconds ago, it's completely overshadowed by a rising sense of panic. She knew this night would be different—but the substantiality of it staring straight at her alerts her to the truth that she's not ready.

Ready or not...

Her bralette falls to their feet, and Khalohn finally tears his eyes away from hers in order to look down at her breasts. The faint sound of her rapid breaths becomes more apparent at the sight of the quick rise and fall of her chest. He notices her pink nipples are hard, and he slides an arm around her back, splaying his hand across her warm, soft skin as he dips his head and captures one of her peaks into his mouth. Bryn gasps as her back grows rigid. Khalohn swirls his tongue, and she emits the faintest mew. Then he sucks, and he feels it as her body starts to melt at his touch.

He takes his time, savoring the taste of one breast before showering an equal measure of attention on the other. By the time he's done, her hands are clutching the fabric of his shirt at his sides. When he lifts his head, Khalohn searches Bryn's face. Her lips are still parted, her breath still rapid, but her eyes seem darker. Warmer. Softer, yet with a tinge of what might be doubt or apprehension. In her gaze, he sees exactly what he wants—exactly what he plans to unearth—and his penis starts to harden at the thought.

Remembering his gift, still clutched in the hand dangling at his side, he takes a step back. As if the loss of his touch is a reprimand uttered in the silence, Bryn's eyes grow wide, and a bit of the warmth he saw only a moment ago starts to disintegrate. In a split second, he recognizes her reaction as the sole reason behind his gift. Tonight, any doubts she harbors about how much he wants her, he plans to eradicate.

For reasons she doesn't think she needs to explain, the moment Godrik steps away from her, Jessica wonders if he'll leave. Before she can decide what another swift disappearance might do to her ego, Godrik lifts his hands and spreads open a gorgeous, sheer, floor-length, black lace robe. She can't fully grasp the beauty of what's right in front of her before Godrik reaches behind her, holding the garment down low. This is all the hint Jessica needs to guide her hands into the sleeves of the robe, and she gazes down at the material as he lifts it up and over her shoulders. The sleeves are wide at her wrists, and the material is light and airy as it grazes the length of her legs.

"This stays on," says Godrik, sliding his hand inside the robe and across the small of her back. Jessica jerks her gaze up to meet his as he goes on to instruct, "and the shoes." He pulls her against him, and her breath catches in her throat as his hand slides down over her panty-covered behind. Reflexively, Jessica's hands shoot up, her palms colliding with Godrik's hard abs, and she wonders if she'll ever be able to catch her breath.

"Take my shirt off, Bryn," he tells her. His voice is so low, she can feel the vibrations of it at her fingertips almost as well as she can hear it. Her hands curl around the fabric of his shirt anxiously, and she licks her colored lips as her eyes drop down to his chest. Jessica's heart takes off, beating faster than she can ever remember as the thought of Godrik *shirtless* fills her mind. Her hands begin to tremble as she takes the fabric in her grasp and tugs. The hem of his shirt is freed from the clutches of his belt, and she slowly starts to loose his buttons, beginning from the bottom.

A small voice tells her to go faster. Somewhere in her subconscious, she understands if she doesn't pick up the pace, she might send the wrong idea—the idea that she's terrified and has absolutely *no* idea what she's doing. While part of that is accurate, there's also another part of her that's not terrified in a fearful way, but in a completely aroused way. She can't go faster because her hands are shaking so hard, she can't catch her breath, and the last thing she wants is for Godrik to turn around and bolt from the room. *Again.*

She's halfway up his shirt when he dips his chin, tilts his head, and presses his mouth to hers. A kiss, in and of itself, is unusual for Khalohn—especially during foreplay—but he can't help himself. Again. Or, more accurately, he doesn't want to. Her trembling hands and her slow ascent up his shirt serve as further reminder that she is *precious*, and she is his to ruin. This is why he flicks his tongue out, tracing her bottom lip. Bryn opens for him on a gasp, and he barely stifles a groan as he reaches up to bury his fingers in her hair, kissing her deeper. Fisting his hand at the back of her head, he holds her where he wants her, plunging his tongue into her mouth. She surrenders almost immediately, twisting her tongue with his, emitting another faint mew.

Jessica's hands stop moving, her fingers stop trembling, and her lungs stop working when Godrik pulls at her hair, tilting her head just so, and kisses her silly. She kisses him back not because she doesn't have a choice, not because he's paying her to do so, but because she's never been on the receiving end of a kiss so spectacular in all her life. It's hard, and wet, and *deep*—and the things he does with his tongue are her undoing. She can hardly breathe, so lost in his kiss. As she starts to grow lightheaded, she finds herself leaning into him, sliding her hands beneath the flaps of his shirt, against his smooth, hot skin, and around his waist. She hardly notices when the hand at her behind disappears.

Khalohn finishes the work of unbuttoning his shirt, all the while indulging in Bryn's mouth. He's now fully erect. In the back of his mind, he acknowledges he can't remember the last time he was so turned on by a *kiss*. Her thick, long hair is like silk between his fingers. The feel of her arms around him—her soft breasts and hard nipples pressed against him—he knows he'll have to reign himself in before he loses all control, all of it over faster than he'd like.

His hand comes back, sliding across the small of her back, down over her rear before he grabs a handful and squeezes. Jessica's body curves against his, and the feel of his erection against her hip makes her moan. So consumed by Godrik's kiss, she forgets who she is—who *he* is—and chases after the longing he's awakened, making her skin tingle as her belly flips and her heart pounds. She drags one of her hands around his side, up his solid abs, over a smattering of chest hair she barely registers, around his neck, and up the back of his head. Burying her fingers in his thick, soft hair, she presses into him further, coming up on tiptoe, hoping against all hope he'll never pull his mouth away from hers.

At the feel of her fingers scraping against his scalp, Khalohn disengages his own from her hair and reaches his hand down to join his other. At first, he only pulls her against him tighter; but as she arches her body into his, their lips still locked, a whisper of a grunt tickles the back of his throat as he leans into her, his hands gliding down the back of her thighs. Bryn gasps, sucking in his exhale when he lifts her from her feet. Immediately, she curls her legs around his hips, and the arm around his side disappears before she uses it to cling to his shoulders—all the while, their kiss is not broken.

Blindly, he carries her around the foot of the bed. With one arm still wrapped about her, Khalohn plants a knee on the side of the mattress, positions her against the decorative pillows at the head of the bed, and lays her down. When he finally severs their lips, Bryn's eyes fly open. Her brown irises are dark, *molten*, and hungry. Welcome as her stare might be, she freezes as he begins to pull away from her. He shakes his head once, but he's not thinking about whether or not he's shaking his head at himself or shaking it at her—signaling what's on his mind. There's only one thing on his mind, and that is to find his way inside of her before whatever doubts or inhibitions he just fought off make a comeback.

Jessica's gaze follows Godrik as he lifts himself away from her and stands beside the bed. She hardly remembers how it was *she* who was supposed to remove his shirt when he yanks the fabric from his body.

Then, as if her heart has gone dormant and her libido has infiltrated the command center of her brain, a surge of wetness hits her between her legs at the sight of his bared chest. The smattering of dark chest hair between his pecs does *not* go unnoticed, and the hardness of his abs is explained by the defined muscles she sees. She barely has the wherewithal to grow anxious as Godrik loosens his belt, unbuttons his slacks, and discards his pants with his shoes—too transfixed by the way the muscles that make up his biceps, his chest, and his core move as he moves.

Godrik steps toward the nightstand next, and Jessica's throat grows dry at the sight of his length making a tent of his black boxer briefs. She pays no mind to what he's after as he yanks open the drawer before he closes it. The longer she's in bed alone, the more crowded her mind becomes. Her sexual desires start to make room for her apprehension, and a fog of confusion begins to billow in her mind's eye just as Godrik climbs onto the bed, his body straddling hers. Then he captures a nipple in his mouth again, and the fog of confusion starts to dissipate as her eyes fall closed and she *feels* him begin to worship her body.

And that's exactly what this is.

He drags his lips from one breast to another.

God, that's exactly what this is…

Bryn arches her back, and Khalohn does another swirl of his tongue around her nipple before he begins to kiss his way down her belly. When he reaches her navel, he traces the tip of his tongue around the circular indent, and he doesn't miss the way her hands fist the comforter beneath them. The sound she makes as he tastes the skin above her panty line about saps what little patience he has left, and he's up on his knees a second later. A second after that, her panties clear the heels of her strappy, black sandals.

It takes no longer than the blink of an eye for panic to interrupt the fog of Jessica's heightened arousal. While she's still wearing her shoes and the robe Godrik slipped over her shoulders a few minutes ago, she feels no less naked than she is. For the first time, he's taking everything he's paying for, and it registers that she's *naked* in front of a complete *stranger*.

But then he descends, gently spreading her legs before his mouth is there. As he tastes her, a twisted sense of familiarity chases away her panic, and she gives in. Again. Only this time is slightly different than the last. It's good. It's *really* good—but he's not so gentle, and she thinks she likes that better. Her hands, holding two fistfuls of comforter, yank at the fabric as her back arches and her eyes fall closed. When she moans, it's because she can't help it. His tongue is demanding, coaxing the height of her pleasure to the surface. Then he's not using his tongue at all, but his fingers. This, she can't deny, she likes, too. So much so, as he curls his digits inside of her, Jessica is certain she's on the brink of an orgasm.

Then his fingers are no longer there.

She opens her eyes just in time to see Godrik lift himself over her. She blinks, noticing his hardened length has been freed from his underwear and sheathed in a condom. So distracted by her own arousal, she can't make sense of when that happened. She blinks again, and before she has time to *think*, he's inside of her.

She gasps loudly, her eyes open wide, her knees fall open, her back arches so severely her nipples graze across Godrik's chest, and she swears she can feel him so far deep inside of her, she wonders—fleetingly, irrationally, yet blissfully—if he's grazed the nerves of her spine.

Khalohn stills for a moment, enraptured by the look on Bryn's face and the arch of her body as he fills her completely. She whimpers when he eases his way out; then as he surges his way back in—her hands are on him, one at his shoulder, the other at his side, her fingers digging into his skin as she starts to come.

"*Christ,*" he hisses, grabbing hold of her hip and holding her trembling body steady. He yanks himself out and slams into her once more.

"*Godrik,*" she breathes.

Godrik...

He replays the sound in his head as he stares into her liquid brown eyes, glued to his as she pants for breath. He lifts his hips, pulling out yet again, and when she's still coming on his return thrust, he knows one thing for certain. He's just unearthed his treasure. It's mesmerizing. It's precious. And they've only just begun.

Chapter Eighteen

JESSICA STARES AT THE DOOR through which Godrik has just taken his leave, the wrinkled, silky sheet pulled up over her chest in one hand, the lacey, floor-length robe clenched in her other. She's at a loss for words, her mind adrift in the alternate reality that is Clandestine's. *More* even—the elaborate fantasy in which she is Bryn and she belongs to a man she knows nothing about.

Her fist tightens around the sheet as she tries to shake her thoughts into order, bringing her back to real life. Unfortunately—or *fortunately,* she can't decipher between the two—her mind is still foggy with the thick, billowing cloud that is the result of four orgasms delivered over the course of an unknown number of hours. Godrik had worked her up with his mouth, then his fingers, before he made her come with his extraordinary cock. And that's exactly what it is, she's convinced. Nothing short of magnificent.

Her second orgasm came by way of his mouth. While she had been so turned on and wanting enough to wish to use her mouth on him as well, he wouldn't let her. Instead, he licked and nibbled, teased and coaxed, worshipped and explored her body until he was inside of her again, and orgasm number three—orgasm number two for *the legend* she now understood him to be—caused them both to collapse in exhaustion.

After a short doze, Godrik got his money's worth and worked them both to the height of passion one last time.

Now, her body sated, relaxed, and tired, her mind muddled and confused, Jessica can't take her eyes away from the door. When Godrik climbed out of bed and started to get dressed, she didn't know what to do. She remained stretched out in bed, watching as he donned his clothing in such a way she believed he was doing his clothes a favor, instead of the other way around. When he was finished tucking in the hem of his shirt, he returned to her only to plant a wet kiss in the soft sensitive spot just behind her jaw and beneath her ear. He'd made it all the way to the door, had his key in hand, when she realized he was going to leave without saying anything at all.

"Wait," she recalled herself saying, her voice hoarse as she sat up in bed, covering her chest with the sheet. When he turned to look at her, his perfectly blue eyes softer and warmer than she'd ever seen them, she realized she didn't know *what* she wanted to say. Frantic for an excuse to get him to say something, she spotted the robe he'd given her at the foot of the bed—the robe he'd stripped off after orgasm number two—and snatched it up with her free hand. "You forgot," she murmured feebly, her eyes catching his once more.

"It's yours."

That's all he said before he was gone.

It's mine.

The thought circles itself around her mind over and over again. Part of her wants to bring it to her face and bury her nose in it so she can breathe in the scent of *them*. In the back of her mind, she finds this to be an odd desire—but that realization is dwarfed as she remembers the power of Godrik between her legs, the weight of him on top of her body, and the taste of him still lingering on her lips. Drawing her knees up to her chest, she brings the robe to her face and drops her nose into the lacey material. She doesn't think about putting on her underwear. She doesn't question what time it is, or how many minutes tick by as she replays the sensual kiss Godrik delivered before he left.

When Stefano knocks on the door before entering, her head shoots up and her eyes fly open in search of his. As soon as her brown eyes find his hazel ones, the fog of her post-orgasmic daze is shattered.

For a second, neither of them speaks. Neither of them moves. Unlike the previous two times he's come to collect her after Godrik's departure, the expression on his face broadcasts his careful assessment of her, filled with caution mingled with guilt. It isn't lost on her, even in the silence, he's trying to figure out if she's still whole, or if his dove is broken.

Finally, Stefano asks, "Are you okay?"

If his presence broke the daze, his *voice* shatters her guard. Suddenly, there's a knot in her throat she can't fully explain. It hurts her to swallow it down, but she does, offering him no more than a nod in reply.

"Get dressed, my dove. I'll be outside when you're ready."

She offers him another nod in response and then he, too, makes his way out the door. As Jessica slides from between the sheets, her limbs start to tremble. She can't exactly make sense of what her body is doing, but she doesn't try to figure it out. Not now. Not within the walls of Clandestine's. She finds her panties and slides them on before doing the same with her bralette. She doesn't think twice about putting on the robe Godrik gifted her, wrapping it around her tightly and securing it with the solid, silk belt. She doesn't bother with her heels, anxious to be out of the room, but hooks the straps between her fingers before grabbing the satin robe she'd worn into the room.

As she steps out into the hallway, she tries to ignore the question which brings a wrinkle to Stefano's brow. To do this, she shifts her attention to her feet before she starts to make her way down the hall. He doesn't protest but locks the door behind them and catches up with her.

They're silent all the way to the ready room. Jessica doesn't know what time it is, and she doesn't much care. All she's aware of is the room's vacancy. As they approach the vanity station where she's left all her belongings, she reaches for her oversized purse, focused on grabbing the t-shirt and jeans she wore upon arrival. When Stefano rests a warm hand on her shoulder and gives her a squeeze, she swallows. She's trying so hard to keep her thoughts at bay. It isn't until she feels the saliva barely find its way around the knot in her throat that she realizes it's still there.

As Stefano starts to pull away, she stops digging through her belongings and grabs his hand, keeping it on her shoulder. After a moment, he turns his wrist, positioning his hand to be able to wrap his fingers around hers. She grips him tightly and then finds her voice.

"Can I—can I stay with you tonight?"

She's still shaking; why, she can't explain, but she needs the time and space to figure it out. What she doesn't need or want is to wake up in the apartment with her mother if she is still losing her shit.

Stefano doesn't speak a word. His clothing rustles before he's dangling a key to his place in front of her. "I won't be long. An hour or so. Leave the light on for me, yeah?"

Again, she nods as she takes hold of his key. He then presses a kiss against her hair at the crown of her head before he lets her go. When she's alone, she goes through the process of getting dressed without looking at herself in the mirror. Certain, at the very least, her hair must be a disaster, she finger-combs her limp curls into a high ponytail before she takes her leave. By the time she's made it out into the warm city air, she's so ready to be away from the place, she wastes no time hailing a cab. Twenty minutes later, after she's paid her fare, Jessica finds herself entering Stefano's apartment building at 365 Bond Street.

Since he started working for Beatrice, he's moved up in the world. Or, more accurately, he's scaled up. When he moved out of the apartment they once shared, it didn't come as a surprise to Jessica. She knew Stefano was high class. While she's sure he could afford a place in the neighboring borough, she also knows he'll never move there.

You can take the Brooklyn out of the boy, but you can't take the boy out of Brooklyn.

Backwards, but true.

As Jessica rides the elevator to Stefano's fourth-floor luxury apartment, she embraces the measure of comfort she feels being someplace familiar. Someplace safe. Someplace where she'll always find love.

Stefano lives in a corner unit, the tall windows that flank his small kitchen and adjoining living room looking out into the street. His curtains are open, but this doesn't stop Jessica from dropping her bag on his sleek, glass, four-seater dining room table before she starts stripping out of her clothes. She leaves a trail of her belongings in her wake, and she's naked before she reaches the huge master bathroom—or, at least, huge for an apartment in Brooklyn. She opens the door to his glass enclosed walk-in shower, turning on the water before she steps aside in order for it to heat up. She frees her hair from a ponytail only to twist it into a tight knot on top of her head. As soon as it's secure, and the water is hot enough to steam up the glass, she steps under the spray.

It's in the shower where all the thoughts she's been shoving to the side start to overpower her. She clinches her fists and closes her eyes, trying to remain calm as she let's the water sooth her. It's no use. Her thoughts are too frenzied to allow such a thing. She remembers Godrik's kiss. The feel of her fingers in his hair. The feel of his beard as it scrapped against her soft flesh. The cut of his body, and the strength he possessed. Her belly tightens and her eyebrows knit together as she recalls the way he fisted her hair and kissed her deep. The way he refused to accept her attention, too busy showering her with his. The sound *he* made when *she* came around him, and the look on his face when he toppled into ecstasy right along with her.

And there it is, she admits with a gasp.

A chill races down her spine, and she releases her fists only to wrap her arms around herself. In spite of the heat steaming up the bathroom, she shivers at the realization that she liked it.

No...I didn't.

Her eyes fill with tears.

Damnit, that was the best sex I've ever had in my entire life.

When a sob erupts from deep within her, she sinks to the floor, leaning up against the back wall of the stall as she covers her face with her hands. She allows herself a minute, and then another, admitting to herself that no amount of water can wash away her guilt and shame. She'd sold her body to a stranger—and she *liked* it. On that floor, pressed against the cream-colored tiles, she can hardly stand being in her own skin. She doesn't recognize herself. As she cries, her mind berates her, flooding her head with memories of every decision that led her to believe she could do what she's done. In the end, she acknowledges she had no idea what she had agreed to. Not really.

When the water starts to turn lukewarm, she finally stands and washes her body. The stall fills with the aroma of Stefano's bodywash, but she hardly notices the masculine scent, wishing only to get out of the shower in order to crawl into bed. After she's rinsed clean, she frees a groan when she notices she forgot to grab an extra towel. Naked and dripping wet, she leaves footprint puddles across the bathroom to the small closet housing Stefano's extra linens. She dries herself off and wraps herself in the plush, fluffy material of his big, gray towel before she makes her way into his bedroom.

She heads directly to his dresser and digs through his drawer until she finds what she's after. Soon, she's donned a worn, charcoal-gray tank top that fits her just right—which means it hugs Stefano like a second skin—the front reading *Fifty Shades of Gay* in bold, rainbow print font. Sans underwear, she then slips into a pair of silk pajama bottoms. These are too big for her, but she pulls the drawstring tight before she climbs into bed. Hugging one of his fluffy throw pillows close, she doesn't care that she's left every light on in every room, or that her damp towel is carelessly left on the hardwood floor, or even that she's left the front door unlocked. All she can think about is how big of a slut she is.

She doesn't know how long she lays alone before her exhaustion catches up with her. But as soon as she starts to close her eyes, all she can see is Godrik. Imagining his blue eyes, made darker by the extent of his arousal, forces her own back open in a flash. She hugs the pillow against her chest tighter as she pulls her bottom lip between her teeth. She bites down hard, willing herself not to cry.

An undiscernible amount of time later, when she hears Stefano enter his apartment, she closes her eyes and sees a different face. *His* face and the way he was looking at her when he walked through a different door. She listens to the click of his dress shoes against the hard floor. He starts and then he stops. Over and over again. It doesn't take her long to realize he's picking up her clothing. Upon his entrance to the room, she furrows her brow deeper, refusing to open her eyes. She's not ready to face him again. Not now. Not now that she understands what he'll see when he looks at her.

She blows out a slow breath when she hears him in the bathroom, getting ready for bed. It takes him a while, as per usual, but she's still not prepared when he's finished. After she hears the light switch and they're shrouded in darkness, she finally dares to open her eyes. He climbs into bed with her, and she can tell he's let his mane free, his long hair draping over his shoulders. For a few minutes, he lays opposite her, his hands folded beneath his cheek, his eyes trained on her. She can't make out the hazel color of his irises, but Jessica doesn't need the light to feel his stare. She rolls her lips between her teeth, keeping her mouth shut tight in an effort to squelch her emotions. More than anything, she's grateful for his silence.

Finally, he carefully reaches for the pillow she still hugs to her chest. Jessica doesn't fight him, but releases it, listening as it makes a soft thud when Stefano tosses it over the side of the bed, and it lands on the floor. Still not speaking a word, he wraps her in his arms. Jessica draws in a shuddered breath as she tucks her face in his neck, and he exhales a calm one. With one arm around her shoulders, he places a hand at the back of her head, holding her to him.

She starts to cry only when her body reminds her the slim arms, flat, lean chest, and delicate frame wrapped around her is nothing compared to the broad, sculpted, solid man who held her only hours before. The man she's sure she'll never be able to scrub out of her brain.

The man I'm not sure I want to scrub out of my brain.

Shit. I'm such a slut.

JESSICA DOESN'T REMEMBER falling asleep or the feel of Stefano getting out of bed in the morning. When she wakes up, the plush mattress beneath her body, the fluffy pillow caressing her cheek, and the soft jersey sheets tangled around her legs are all the reminder she needs that she's not at home, on the pull-out couch that's seen better days. The floor-length curtains, which cover the tall windows across Stefano's bedroom, are mostly closed; but a sliver is enough for the bright, summer sun to slice through the room, alerting her Saturday is well on its way.

Blinking her eyes open, Jessica is temporarily engulfed in the blissful comfort found before awareness. For a moment, she's merely in her best friend's bed, her body relaxed, even if her head feels foggy and tired. As sleep starts to drift further and further away, the state of her mind begins to chase away the loose muscles of her body. She tenses, clutching her pillow for something to hang onto as she's slammed with a fresh wave of guilt and shame. It tugs her under, and she seals her eyes closed tight as she mentally flails to find solid ground.

Shoving aside memories from the previous night, she tries to remember her *why*. The dawning of a new day beckons her to shift her thinking, to remember the deposit she's sure to find in her account if she were to look in that very moment. But such awareness doesn't make her feel any better. It doesn't change what she's done or how good it felt. The light of the sun peering down through the oceanic amount of confusion she drowns in seems farther and farther out of reach.

Shit. I'm a slut, she thinks, wishing to give up her fight and just drown.

"Your mom called."

Jessica is pulled from her thoughts at the sound of Stefano's voice. She shifts her gaze and finds him leaning against the doorframe of his bedroom, his long, dark hair unruly from a night of sleep and spilled around his shoulders; his chest bare, and his silk pajama bottoms hanging low around his narrow hips; his hazel eyes, leaning toward dark green at the moment, calculating as he stares at her—and a steaming mug of coffee clasped in his elegant hands.

She doesn't respond, too distracted by the look in his eyes. Last night, under the blanket of twilight, she could hide from his judgement. The sun, meager as it is with the drapes drawn closed, leaves no room for hiding.

Her silence doesn't seem to be something he minds as he goes on to say, "I answered. Told her you were here; that I wanted your company last night."

He lifts his mug to his lips and takes a slow swig. His gesture is one she understands is full of mercy. She should have at least sent a text to her mother last night, but she hadn't thought of that. Yet, regardless of Stefano's kindness, it's impossible for him *not* to see her sluttiness. Not now. Not after what happened.

When Jessica doesn't speak, he swallows and then turns to make his way out of the room. She doesn't move, both relieved and apprehensive for the gift of more time alone. She's familiar with how this will go. Last night, Stefano didn't make her talk—but she'd cried herself to sleep in his arms. She isn't going to get to leave without a thorough conversation; a conversation she dreads, no matter how much she loves and trusts him. *Because* she loves and trusts him.

When Stefano reappears in his doorway, not even thirty seconds later, any reprieve Jessica feels vanishes. He nonchalantly brings his mug to his lips a second time with one hand, using his other to hold up the lacey garment from last night. Jessica's stomach drops. She pushes herself up, supporting herself on her hands as she continues to stare at him.

"He gave this to you," Stefano says, breaking the silence.

This stays on.

Jessica remembers Godrik's words as he pulled her against him.

And the shoes.

Swallowing hard, Jessica offers Stefano no more than a nod. She doesn't know what to say. Even if she did, the heat crawling up her spine and wrapping itself around her neck feels like a noose.

"Gifts are prohibited. Bea's rules. Her collection of women makes a lucrative living. Johns aren't meant to *woo* what does not belong to them."

Her mouth falls open, as if she's going to say something, but then nothing comes out. The searing heat around her neck begins to creep into her cheeks. Her first reaction is to be embarrassed, his comment like a reprimand that simply *proves* she's done something wrong. Before she can wrestle her embarrassment into submission, she's smacked down by another emotion—*disappointment.* She clamps her lips closed, shakes her head, and closes her eyes, trying to pretend Godrik's kind gesture meant nothing. Only, the more she thinks about it, the kinder the gesture becomes.

It's yours.

He hadn't said much. Not the whole night, and especially not about the robe he'd given her—but in her mind, it doesn't negate the fact that, every time she's been with him, he's given her something. That first night, it was dance. The second, it was an orgasm. When he came to her for a third time, she knew he would take more—and he did—but before he did, he *gave.* Then he gave, and gave, and gave some more.

Her blush grows warmer and she forces her eyes open in an attempt to escape her memories. When she locks eyes with Stefano, who is still *clearly* waiting for a response, she forces herself to speak. "He's—he's not…" Her voice is hardly more than a hoarse whisper, lower than usual from lack of use. "That's not…" She can't finish her sentence, not entirely sure *what* the gift meant or how she feels about it being taken from her.

"I'm not going to report it. It's yours, Jess."

She tries to ignore her relief and says nothing as Stefano saunters into the room and tosses the garment to the foot of the bed.

"Come on. I made coffee." He doesn't wait for her to respond before he turns and heads for the door. Just as he crosses the threshold, he calls out over his shoulder, "There may or may not be a couple slices of apple pie out here, too."

The small smile that dances across Jessica's mouth can't be helped. Her heart swells, and she acknowledges if she *has* to talk about it, at least there will be pie.

Without second guessing herself, she slips from between the sheets, leaving the robe, and makes her way to the bathroom. She takes a couple minutes to splash her face with water, rinse out her mouth, and tug down her knotted bun, which fell loose in the middle of the night. The release of its hold feels good to her scalp, and she combs her fingers through her hair, leaving it in disarray. Bedhead is acceptable before coffee. She hardly looks at her reflection throughout all of this and is happy to escape it as she turns and walks out of the bathroom, through the bedroom, and into the open main room, where Stefano is already sitting at his dining room table set for two.

He watches her as she carefully pulls out the chair opposite him and sinks into it. Not knowing how to begin, Jessica chooses not to. She uses both hands to reach for her steaming mug of coffee and takes her time indulging in her first sip. A full two minutes of silence transpires between them before Stefano sets down his mug, props his forearms against the table, and leans toward her.

The compassion and love she sees reflected in the warm pool of his hazel eyes makes her want to shrink back away from him as he inquires, "Are you okay?"

Lowering her mug away from her lips, she hugs it to her chest and considers the question. It's the same thing he asked her in the wee hours of the morning, at Clandestine's, when she was naked, covered only by a top sheet. Now, wrapped in his clothes, she feels no less exposed. She's convinced she's not worthy of his careful treatment of her. Regardless of how much he loves her, it hurts her more the way he's *pretending* not to see right through her.

With a slight shake of her head, she replies, "You don't have to do this."

"Do what?" he murmurs, knitting his eyebrows together in confusion.

"Take care of me. Try to make me…feel better."

"Yes. Yes, I *do*. Fuck, Jess—I'm the reason you're here. I'm the reason you cried yourself to sleep in my arms last night. I *let* you—"

"This isn't your fault," she interrupts, setting her mug on the table. She reaches for her fork with one hand, using the other to pull her fingers through her hair. Her gaze trained on her utensil, she turns it round and round, avoiding Stefano's stare.

"I *agreed*. I let this happen."

"I would have…" Jessica's face scrunches as she tries to stave off the overwhelming emotions she felt before sleep. Forcing herself to speak, to let the truth eradicate whatever guilt or misguided sense of responsibility her friend is shouldering, she continues, "I would have done it with or without your help. You know that. I forced your hand."

"Bullshit," he scoffs. He reaches across the table, covering her hand with his, effectively putting an end to her fidgeting. "You're gorgeous, and Bea wouldn't have been able to deny that, but I could have convinced her not to—"

Yanking her hand out from underneath his, she raises her gaze as she hisses, "It doesn't matter. It's done. You don't get to feel sorry for me, Huey."

"Dove—"

Jessica slams her fork down against the glass table, the sting at the back of her eyes an announcement that she's got more tears left to shed as she erupts, "I *liked it!*" Even as her tears start to well up, her face growing red in shame, she stares at her best friend and admits, "He fucked me better than I've ever been fucked *in. my. life.* The man hardly speaks, but he worshipped my body like I was some goddess and *he* owed *me* something rather than the other way around. I didn't fake an orgasm *once*. Not *once*." She blinks, and her first couple of tears race down her cheeks, allowing her to see the stunned expression on Stefano's face. With a gasp, she almost chokes on a sob as she realizes all she's said. Closing her watery eyes, she bows her head and mutters, "I'm a slut. I let someone *pay* me for sex, and I liked it. No. I *loved* it. So, you see? You don't have to take care of me. I don't deserve it. Not from you."

She doesn't open her eyes or bother to look up as she tries to get a grip. Even when she hears Stefano scoot his chair back. Even when she feels his presence at her side. Even when he squats down next to her, resting his hands against her thigh.

"Jess," he whispers, giving her leg a squeeze. "Jessica, *look* at me."

"I can't," she breathes.

"Fine. Then listen. You're not a slut, do you hear me? I know you. Better than anyone. I know how many men you've slept with. Hell, we both know your number is smaller than mine. If anyone's the slut here, it's me."

As much as she wants to find validity in his statement, she can't. Still, what he says beckons her to open her eyes, even if only to scowl down at him as she declares, "It's not the same."

"No. You're right. Remember that guy Carl? All looks and no skill. Didn't get me off. Selfish bastard. Had to take care of myself after he passed out."

"Huey, stop," Jessica pleads. "It's *not* the same."

For a second, he obeys. When he reaches up to graze the backs of his fingers down her cheeks, drying her tears, he proceeds to ignore her and says, "He's hot. Don't need to see him naked to know what's underneath those clothes would be enough to get me off with nary a wink." He offers Jessica a sly smirk, and her cheeks turn rosy as she shakes her head at him. "I'm just saying, there's nothing wrong with being attracted to him. Not to mention, I *chose* him for you *because* of his reputation. I knew he'd be good to you."

"But—"

"No. No buts, Jess. He made you feel good. That doesn't make you a slut, it makes him good in the sack. And—look, you know I don't believe in karma, but the whole reason you're doing this is so you can take care of your mom. Maybe this was the universe's way of giving you a fucking break."

Jessica doesn't respond right away. She stares into the eyes of her friend, daring to glimpse her reflection from his perspective. The longer they stay silent, the longer he remains next to her, the more his words penetrate, creating a crack in the wall of shame she built around her in her sleep. As her thoughts fill with memories of Godrik—his generosity, his silent power, his indisputable prowess—she peeks through that crack and sees what's on the other side. *Beth.* The woman for whom she would do *anything.* As her guilt begins to wane, the foundation of her shame begins to crumble, and she reaches for Stefano's hands.

He weaves his fingers between hers, and she stares down at their connection as she murmurs, "What if he asks for me again?"

She can hear the smile in his voice as he gives her fingers a squeeze and replies, "Dove, if he asks for you again, he'll no longer be a legend—*you* will be."

Feeling strangely buoyed by the thought, she peeks at Stefano from beneath her wet lashes. Miraculously, a small smile plays at her lips when he pulls one of her hands toward him, turning her wrist so he can press a kiss there.

"We'll also have to come up with a reason to explain to your mom why you've got money falling from the sky."

Jessica's smile falls as she dips her head and lifts her shoulder, pressing her cheek against it with a sigh.

"You're also free to tell him no. Your contract permits you to walk away at any time."

When her stomach twists uncomfortably, she pulls her hands away from Stefano and sits up straight. Shoving aside the acidic feeling of disappointment which accompanies the thought of never touching Godrik again, she tucks a bit of hair behind her ears and clears her throat.

"Our coffee's getting cold," she says, reaching for hers.

At first, Stefano doesn't move. Jessica can feel his eyes on her, but she refuses to acknowledge him; refuses to acknowledge what she's sure he interprets in her swift change of subject. He knows her far too well, but she doesn't care. She doesn't want to talk about it. She *can't* talk about it. Not anymore. Finally, when he stands, pressing a kiss on top of Jessica's head, she stifles a sigh of relief, grateful for his silent reprieve.

Chapter Nineteen

KHALOHN WAKES LATER THAN usual on Saturday morning, the sun pouring into his bedroom through the windows he neglected to cover before sleep. He's so distracted by the physical proof of being *alone*, he doesn't concern himself with checking the time our looking out at the morning. He tucks one hand behind his head as he lays on his back, staring up at the ceiling, *remembering*.

He's been a client at Clandestine's for a long time. Long enough to lose count of the number of women he's taken to bed. Long enough for most of the women to blur together into faceless, lithe bodies in various shades of luxurious underwear. Long enough that he shouldn't wake up the morning after a night of sex thinking of nothing but her face.

He remembers the look in Bryn's eyes, darkened and smoldering, her painted lips round and open on a gasp, her back arched and her hardened nipples grazing his chest when he entered her for the first time. In that moment, she was wholly his—his in a way no one ever had been before. He could feel it in her grip, her hands clinging to him in raw and transparent *need*. It wasn't surprise. Not entirely. He's sure of this because it wasn't the only time he felt it as the night turned to morning and he owned her body again and again.

The longer Khalohn spends immersed in his memory, the more aroused he becomes, until his erection is mocking him. He ignores his longing, all the while wondering if he can arrange to have Bryn again that very night. Then he remembers how much he spent on the four orgasms he delivered less than twelve hours ago. Using his free hand, he reaches up and rubs at his eyes with his thumb and forefinger. Another night would be another twenty thousand. Twenty thousand would bring Bryn's ongoing tab to seventy thousand dollars. It would be a careless investment—regardless of how delectable she tastes; how perfectly their bodies fit together; how turned on she makes him with the little sounds she makes; or how utterly *gorgeous* she is stripped completely bare.

Gorgeous enough to get my dick up three times in a single session with hardly any reprieve.

Hell—gorgeous enough to get my dick up when she's not even here.

He sighs, a part of him wanting to be careless. He never is. Not to mention, it's not as if he doesn't have another twenty thousand to spend frivolously. Yet, knowing the transaction would be just that—*frivolous*—he comes to his senses. Furthermore, he knows one more night won't be enough. The need he saw and felt in Bryn when he slid inside of her wasn't one sided. He knew it then. He acknowledges it now. It isn't Bryn he's hesitant to invest in—it's *how*.

As confidential and convenient as Clandestine's is, seventy thousand dollars could get him a private apartment in Manhattan for almost an entire *year*. Khalohn stops at the thought, allowing it to circle around his mind for a minute. The hand at his face moves up, until his fingers are submerged in his hair. The longer he thinks about it, the more figures start to compile in his head, until he knows *precisely* how he can invest in Bryn in a way that would benefit them both.

He lingers in bed just long enough to plot his plan of attack, and then he's up, phone in hand, heading toward his office in nothing but his underwear. Once in his oft used domain, he sits down behind his desk and opens the bottom drawer, where he finds a copy of the NDA and contract he signed with Beatrice years ago. He goes over it carefully, the details murky after all this time. When he's assured his latest business proposition won't violate any agreement he's made with Clandestine's, he unlocks the screen of his mobile and searches his contacts. Upon finding the number for his real estate agent, he pushes a call through straight away.

"Diaz," the man answers on the second ring.

"Khalohn Morgan," mutters Khalohn in greeting.

"Mr. Morgan, good to hear from you, sir. What can I do for you?"

The men don't speak often. Khalohn's personal property needs are few and far between. Neither are the two men friends. Nevertheless, Khalohn is well aware of the weight his name bears and the value Walter Diaz understands comes with a simple phone call.

"I'm in the market for an investment property. A condo or loft space. Single floor plate. Near or around Lower Manhattan."

"I'd be happy to help you with that, Morgan."

"I'm only interested in a quick turnaround," Khalohn insists, his gaze shifting out the window and what he can see of the Upper East Side from his vantage point. "Ready to occupy. Can I expect a list of properties by this afternoon?"

"I can guarantee that list within the next four hours."

"Then we'll be in touch."

They disconnect, and Khalohn doesn't second guess his motives, his intentions, or his plan. If everything works out in his favor, it'll be money and time well spent.

When Jessica wakes up Sunday morning, Godrik is still at the forefront of her mind. She sighs, as if in resignation, resolved to the fact that she can't *un-feel* him anymore than she can *undo* what's already been done—the choices she's made, the body she gave, the pleasure she took...

Her gaze jerks to the closed door of Beth's bedroom at the sound of her wheezing cough, and Jessica's resignation turns into something else. Something unapologetic. The moment she walked into their apartment the previous afternoon, it was as if she fell face first into acceptance, her shame and guilt bruised and battered with her landing. The cramped space she shares with her mother, the meager assortment of food in the fridge, Beth's medicine in the bathroom, it was enough to bring Jessica wholly into reality. Not just the reality in which Godrik isn't her lover but a man using her—but a reality in which *she* is using *him* just the same.

Wading through her lingering thoughts of Godrik, Jessica gets out of bed and makes her way to the kitchen. She rummages through some of the groceries she splurged on the day before and finds the box of green tea she thought her mother might like. She puts on a pot of water to boil and gets down a clean mug, placing a fresh bag of tea inside as she waits on the water. Leaning up against the counter beside the stove, she folds her arms across her chest and tries to think of something *other* than Godrik. She thinks of the more than twenty-six thousand dollars she now possesses and the best and smartest way for her to spend it.

By the time the water is boiling, Jessica has decided she'll pay for the next four months of rent. She'll then set aside an allotment of funds to cover their utilities and groceries for the same amount of time. Once she's factored in the cost of Beth's monthly prescription drugs, she breathes easy, realizing she'll still have plenty in the event of an emergency. That also gives her a few solid weeks to find another job. A *good* job, one that'll help her take care of her mother so she can focus on staying home and resting.

As Jessica steeps the tea bag, watching as the water turns yellow-ish green, the unique comfort that comes with a sense of *security* makes her thoughts go lax. Soon Godrik is weaving his way through her mind again. She sorts through the more subtle moments they've shared and the things he's made possible for her. In a twisted way, he's responsible for her finding any semblance of peace of mind. Moreover, he's flipped a switch inside of her she'd turned off a while ago. It's like he's woken her up, and with a mind not so muddled with worry—even if only for a while—it's given way for her to acknowledge a desire that's been dormant for a while now.

She recalls the night she spent out at the club with Kierra nearly a week ago, and the longing that tugs at her heart is enough for her to make up her mind. She decides she'll head to the studio later that afternoon. It'll be a splurge, paying for a few classes; but with such a surplus in her bank account, she can't reason her way out of it.

Jessica squeezes a bit of honey in Beth's tea and then walks across their small apartment until she's standing in front of the closed bedroom door. She knocks softly before granting herself entrance, smiling sweetly when Beth looks over from where she's laying in the middle of the bed.

"Morning, mama," she greets softly. "I made you some tea."

"Thanks, baby. That—" She's interrupted by another round of coughing as she sits up. Jessica tries not to whence at the sound, which seems to come from deep within her mother's chest. Beth draws in a desperate breath after the coughing has subsided, propping herself against her pillows as she reaches for the mug. "That's sweet of you," she finally finishes.

"Why does it sound like your cold isn't getting any better?" asks Jessica.

She hands her mother the steaming mug and sits facing the woman on the side of the bed. Beth shakes her head and then takes a sip before she answers, "You know how it goes. The cough is always the worst, but it signals the tail end. Just takes me a little while to get over it is all." She studies her daughter over the rim of the mug as she takes another sip, then adds, "Don't look at me like that. I'll be fine, Jess."

Holding tight to the secret she's doing everything she can to make sure her mother is right, Jessica forces a small smile in response. Wanting more than the comfort of financial security, she stretches out across the bed, resting her head in her mother's lap as she drapes an arm across her thighs. When Beth starts to run her fingers through Jessica's long locks, Jessica relishes the feeling and closes her eyes. Again, she remembers her *why*, and any lingering sense of shame or guilt is shoved farther and farther away.

WALKING INTO MIAH Michael's Dance Studio on the south side of Tribeca is like coming home. Jessica can feel the energy in the building as if she's entering into an entirely different atmosphere. There's an electric current bouncing off the walls, the loud chatter in the lobby almost drowning out the overhead music. The familiarity of that space and time between classes, people coming and going, makes Jessica's heart beat faster in anticipation. She looks around, searching for a familiar face, but finds none. Even so, she feels no less welcome. There are no strangers in dance. These are her people. This is where she belongs.

"Jessica?!"

She twists her neck at the sound of her name, her long ponytail whipping around until the tail drapes against her chest. She barely has time to register the sound of that excited voice before Kierra has her wrapped in a tight embrace.

"Oh, my god, what are you doing here?"

Jessica is grinning when her friend pulls away, only to grab hold of her bare arms—as if she'll bolt at any moment. Kierra's mop of dark brown curls, with a ton of honey highlights, is pulled into a thick puff on top of her head. Her jade-green eyes, so striking against her pale brown skin, are alight in excitement; and the smile that's spread across her face—bright in and of itself, with her straight, pearly-white, movie-star teeth—seems to make her whole face sparkle.

"I felt like dancing," she answers with a shrug, a motion exactly the opposite of how she's feeling. "I wasn't sure what classes were offered this afternoon, but I don't really care."

"Girl, you know Miah," she insists, letting go of Jessica only to fling her arm across her shoulders. "It's Sunday afternoon. There's only one thing she feels like teaching Sunday afternoon..."

Kierra quirks an eyebrow at Jessica and they both say in unison, "Hip-hop."

"She is going to *flip her lid* when she sees you. It's been forev-a!"

"She's going to laugh her ass off when she sees me," Jessica counters with a shake of her head. "I'm so out of shape. I'm sure she'll kill me today."

Miah is one of the best choreographers in all of New York. For Jessica, getting to dance under her instruction is an honor. It was always hard to afford studio time, but both Beth and Jessica scarified as much as they could to make it happen—until there weren't enough pennies to scrape up to make it work. It broke her heart when she had to give it all up. Being back in the studio lifts her spirits so high, she feels like she's floating.

It was in one of Miah's classes where Jessica met Kierra. Kierra is among the most talented ballerinas in the city. After high school, she was able to train at the Joffrey School of Ballet, and now she performs as a principal dancer with the Parson's Ballet Company. If she wasn't such a pleasure to watch, Jessica would envy her success. There was a time when all Jessica wanted was to be able to dance for a living.

She shakes away the thought that if finances weren't an issue, maybe she'd be the contemporary dancer she feels like she was born to be. There's no sense in dwelling on what *might have been*. For now, she's merely grateful for the opportunity to join a class *at all*. Even if it is an advanced class.

Even if it will totally kick her ass.

Miah offers a variety of classes, from hip-hop to contemporary to ballroom. She's got some amazing instructors on her payroll, and she herself is called upon to choreograph for music videos and movies quite frequently. The fact that her classes are even remotely affordable is proof she's got a big heart and she wishes only to foster a community of dance to keep the art alive.

It hasn't been so long that Jessica has forgotten Miah's weekend classes are mostly for the advanced group. Aside from a couple offerings on Saturday morning, Miah caters her weekend to dancers who spend Monday through Friday in whatever art schools or company practices they're in. The weekends are for the rebels—her *favorite*—the ones who want to step outside their norm and dance to a different beat. This explains why Kierra is here.

She's classy as hell, in her pointe shoes and tutus, but the girl likes to get down, Jessica muses as they make their way to the check-in desk.

"Hey, Miah! Look what the wind blew in," Kierra calls out, stealing Miah's attention from a conversation she's having.

Miah's flirting with fifty, her spikey hair tinged with gray, her light-blue eyes framed by crow's feet, and the skin under her neck slowly losing its elasticity—but the smirk that tugs at the corner of her mouth at the sight of Jessica is all the proof she needs to know the choreographer is still just as spunky as she remembers. She's thin, but not overly so, and stands no taller than five-two. She's always said she's too short, which is why she got into choreography.

"Well, I'll be damned." Miah shakes her head and stares, as if in awe, her previous conversation all but forgotten. "Jessica Chapman," she breathes.

The way she says her name makes Jessica's nose tingle, the only warning she needs to know she's on the verge of tearing up. She swallows hard and bites the side of her lip, willing herself not to cry. It's been a long time. *Too* long. In a single stare, with not a word spoken, the two women say as much.

"Get this girl signed in, Dave," she insists, not even bothering to look at Dave. Jessica assumes she's referring to the man standing hunched in front of the computer, but she doesn't look away from Miah to confirm. "On the house today."

Snapping out of her trance, Jessica pulls away from Kierra and replies, "Oh, no, Miah. I'm—"

"On the house, gorgeous," she semi-repeats, arching a demanding eyebrow. "Pay your way next time. And *next time* I want you in my contemporary class. And *next time* better not be two years from now, you hear?" she asks, pointing a finger at her.

This time, at the threat of tears, Jessica's only chance at combatting the excess moisture is to blink as fast as she can.

"Yes, ma'am," she murmurs.

"Good," says Miah with a wink.

When Kierra loops her arm around Jessica's elbow, pulling her toward the main studio space, she leans over and whispers in her ear, "Welcome back, Jess."

An hour and a half later, Jessica is covered in sweat, her whole body burning with the awareness of how out of shape she is; but she can't remember the last time she felt so exhilarated. After signing up for Miah's contemporary class late Wednesday afternoon, she leaves the studio with Kierra feeling *jittery*.

"Kierra—that felt *so good*."

"Hell yeah, it did," she replies on a chuckle. "Hey, how about a smoothie? That spot a couple blocks from here?"

"I'd love that."

No sooner are the words out of her mouth than Jessica's phone begins to ring from inside her purse. As they start toward the smoothie place, she pulls out the device to see who's calling.

"It's Stefano. Sorry, I'll just be a sec."

"No worries," Kierra assures her with a single shoulder shrug.

"Huey, guess where I just came from?" she asks, almost breathless.

He pauses for a beat and then says, almost reverently, "Miah's."

Giggling, Jessica smiles at Kierra and replies, "Yeah. How'd you know?"

"Only one thing makes you that happy, dove. And—fuck—I don't want to rain on your parade, but..."

"But what?" she asks, her smile slipping a little at his tone.

"Mr. Morgan. He's requested you. Tonight. Eight o'clock."

Unintentionally, her feet move at a slower pace as her entire body reacts to Stefano's statement. Her post-class jitters are burned up as a different kind of heat courses through her body. She directs her gaze down at the sidewalk on which she treads, grateful for the exertion of the last hour, for it all but masks her blush at the thought of being with Godrik again.

He still wants me, she thinks as her stomach tingles.

She doesn't want to read into her excitement. She doesn't want to think that *excitement* at the possibility of another night in his arms is what she feels, as if the guilt of her actions is nothing more than a memory already forgotten. She doesn't want to read into what it all means, so she doesn't. Not yet.

Clearing her throat, she murmurs, "Okay. I'll—I'll be there."

"You're sure? You can say no, Jess."

She bites her lip, unable to ignore the fact that *no* never crossed her mind.

"I'll be there," she repeats.

"Clandestine's new legend," he whispers before he disconnects.

"This'll only take a moment," Khalohn informs Atzel as he steps out of the Maybach and smooths his hand over the crisp fabric of his pale-blue button-up. "Ten minutes."

"Very well, Mr. Morgan," replies his driver with a sharp nod.

Khalohn looks up at the store front of Clandestine's Closet, wondering if he'll have this view again soon, or if he'll find himself on an indefinite hiatus from the underground bordello. Knowing better than to guess, he heads up the stairs toward the entrance, making the familiar trip through the store. After murmuring the password, he's granted entrance, and he doesn't hesitate when Stefano offers him his room key. He barely looks at the man, which is why he misses the careful stare casted his way as he passes by with hardly more than a glance. His mind is preoccupied. It's been a busy twenty-four hours; and in spite of the hour, on the tail end of his weekend, he's got more than a little business he needs to see to before the day is done.

When he approaches the door to his room, he forces in a deep breath, steeling himself for his next encounter. *Control* is something he needs to keep in his possession. He's not oblivious. He is quite aware the loft he's in the process of purchasing, the proposal he's about to deliver, the speed at which his *need* has spurred him to act—it is proof that *Bryn* and the value she holds is enough for him to loosen the reigns he's usually so careful to keep close. Before he opens the door, he reminds himself that while the choice will be *hers*, the power is still *his*.

He inserts the all too familiar skeleton key, twisting the lock free before he opens the door and steps inside. Out of habit, he doesn't look for her until he's locked them inside and discarded the key on the antique table. That done, he casually slides his hands into his pockets before he searches the room. As soon as he lays eyes on her, his fingers curl into fists in a desperate attempt to keep hold of his restraint.

Utterly gorgeous, he thinks, keeping his mouth closed as he pulls in a deep breath through his nose.

Jessica's hand grips the wing of the armchair fiercely in a desperate attempt to keep her balance as her knees grow weak. Not five minutes ago, she couldn't sit down, too antsy to remain still. The second she heard him insert his key into the lock, she felt frozen in place—unable to do so much as *breathe*. Now, as she watches his eyes take her in from head to toe, her whole body feels like it's on fire simply from his perusal.

Her hair is loose, styled in big, wavy curls down her back. The lacey robe he'd gifted her a couple of nights prior seemed like an obvious choice. She wears it now over a matching, sheer, black panty and bra set. Remembering how much he liked her strappy sandals last time, she opted for the same heels. Her nails dig into the upholstery of the chair at the thought of his touch, and she can't help but wonder if he'll want her to keep her shoes on this time, too. When he doesn't cross the room right away, she searches his face, wondering what he might be thinking.

She doesn't have to wait long before he mutters, "I won't be taking you to bed this evening."

Jessica's lips part open, but the "*oh*" she breathes isn't audible—the sound strangled by a twisted sense of disappointment.

"It's no secret I have a reputation here at Clandestine's—a reputation I've marred given this is the fourth time I've requested you in my room."

Jessica drops her gaze to the floor, every word he speaks robbing her of the anticipation which ushered her into the room. For a moment, she's reminded of the shame that overwhelmed her Friday night. It starts to prickle at the back of her neck, and she wonders what's wrong with her—wonders why she allowed herself to get so excited or why she feels so disappointed now. She's so lost in her own thoughts, waiting for him to finish speaking, to put her out of her misery, she doesn't hear it as he crosses the room.

When Bryn robs him of her eyes, Khalohn comes unstuck from his position at the door. He crosses the room, all the while allowing his gaze to roam over the figure his entire body remembers. Upon coming to a stop, he extracts a hand from his pocket and curls the forefinger on his right hand beneath her chin, easing her face up. She gasps softly, as if she wasn't prepared for his touch—or, rather, the shock of need that shoots through her at his touch. He doesn't have to be inside her to recognize her need. He reads it in her eyes. Moreover, he feels it at his groin—in one touch.

"I'm not finished with you," he mutters, his voice low and gentle.

Bryn rocks toward him, as if she can't help herself, and he knows he needs to spit out what he's come to say before he does something he doesn't have time to see through to completion. He removes his finger from beneath her chin and reaches back into his pocket. At the last possible moment, he shifts his gaze down at the device and opens his contacts. That done, he turns the phone toward her and brings his eyes back up to meet hers.

"I've a business proposition for you. The specifics will be discussed tomorrow, one o'clock, at an address I will send you no later than tomorrow morning."

Jessica's eyebrows come together in confusion. She can't understand what he's saying. Instead of trying to interpret his meaning, all she can focus on is the statement, which sounded more like a *promise*.

I'm not finished with you.

"Bryn," Godrik calls, his voice both hard and soft.

It's as confounding as it is sexy.

"What?" she manages on a whisper.

"I need a way to contact you."

She jerks, suddenly aware he's inviting her to put her contact information into his cell phone. Hesitantly, she takes hold of the device. When it's in her grasp, she glances at it, then up at him, then back at the phone. She recalls Stefano's warning that *gifts* are forbidden. Something tells her exchanging personal information such as *phone numbers* is probably also frowned upon.

I'm not finished with you.

Jessica shakes her head, as if to clear it. The only thing that seems to rattle free in her mind is her apprehension. She lies, typing in *Bryn van Doren* into the appropriate name fields. Then she clings to the truth, offering him her real number before she hands the phone back to him. In one swift, smooth motion, Godrik accepts the device and slips it back into his pocket, his eyes on hers the entire time.

"Tomorrow," he states resolutely.

"Okay," she whispers.

He moves so fast, all Jessica can do is suck in a sharp intake of air when he reaches around her, pulling her hair away from her neck to create an opening. Her eyes fall closed and her head tilts to the side involuntarily when she feels his tongue and then his lips as he tastes and kisses her in the sensitive spot just behind her ear. He doesn't linger. When she opens her eyes once more, he's halfway across the room, yet she can still feel the tingling sensation of his beard against her skin.

Khalohn doesn't look back, taking up his key as quickly as possible when he reaches the door. He knows, given the state of his dick—standing at half-mast after a single *taste*—if he looks back, he won't leave.

Tomorrow, he reminds himself. *Tomorrow*.

Chapter Twenty

KHALOHN IS ON HIS WAY OUT, his calendar alerting anyone who may ask that he's heading for the airport for a quick trip to Tokyo. His latest deal is complete, another company under his name, but this is just the beginning. The changes he has in mind, he won't make them without sitting down with the team of people who will be at home base, handling the operation. While he only has time to get his feet on the ground for little more than a couple days, it's how he does things. It's a sign of respect. He is where he is because he understands how to treat the hands that put his plans into motion.

As he gathers what he needs from his office in order to take his leave, it's not just *Japan* on his mind. Before he gets on a plane, he has another important meeting to attend. With his laptop bag in hand, he strolls out of his office as Lorelai approaches.

"Shit. You're leaving," she says, stopping in her tracks.

"Walk me out," Khalohn replies, pausing to address Maribelle. "You know how to reach me."

"Of course, dear." She offers him a smile, as genuine as ever. "I do hope you have a safe flight. I'll see you Friday."

Khalohn dips his chin in a nod, signaling his agreement as well as his farewell. She winks at him, and a small smile tickles the corner of his mouth before he looks to Lorelai and continues toward the exit.

"You've got five minutes."

"Right. Well, I'm kind of getting shit on, here. Pier House was hemorrhaging money before, *Charlie* Winslow at the helm. I thought we were gaining traction after that dinner. Now, Christina Winslow is making her play."

"How so?"

"She's trying to sue her way into CEO. From what I can tell, it's ugly. No one will return my calls. Can't say I blame them. Any interest they had in Khalohn Morgan taking over ownership has now shifted to making sure there's ownership to sell to us in the first place. She's holding nothing back. Hired an outside guy to look into her brother, his management and accounting—Morgan, it's a shit show. Maybe we should drop out."

Khalohn presses the call button for an elevator. He doesn't need to be reminded he handed this deal to her, expecting her to handle it. Neither has he forgotten the way Maribelle teased him about finally letting some of his associates shoulder more of the weight he hired them to carry. Given the current week, the weekend behind him, and the promise of what could be the weekend ahead of him, he feels completely at liberty to give it to her straight.

"You took on this deal, it's your responsibility. We lose it, it's because you didn't have what it takes to get the job done. I believe it was you who told me there's blood in the water, which should make this a fairly simple catch. Find your way in and close the deal before we're left with a heaping pile of shit that holds no value."

By the time he's finished speaking, an elevator has arrived. He steps inside, but Lorelai is smart enough not to follow. She catches his eye as he presses the button for the ground floor and offers him a curt nod.

"Yes, sir," she mutters.

"Play it smart," Khalohn says as the doors begin to close. "I want another update a week from now."

She doesn't say anything in reply as he's shut in, but he doesn't miss her resolute sigh.

IT WAS IMPOSSIBLE for Jessica to process what happened with Godrik the previous night before Stefano barreled into the room. When she informed him of the very brief exchange she had with *Mr. Morgan*, they stared at each other in bewilderment. After the initial shock began to wear off, her best friend made her *swear* to tell him *where* she was going to meet the man and then swear again to not show up alone.

At ten o'clock the next morning, when she gets a text message from an unknown number, she relays the address to Stefano and then adds *Godrik Morgan* as a contact to her phone. A little after noon, Jessica is knocking on Stefano's door. He opens almost immediately, and they skip over *hello* in favor of staring at each other. Stefano appears apprehensive. Jessica wonders if he can tell her nerves are *strangling* her stomach.

"You can say no, Jess," he reminds her for what feels like the hundredth time.

Jessica shakes her head and reaches for his hand. "Remember when you told me you were interviewing to be Bea's *gatekeeper?*" she asks with raised eyebrows, knowing there's no way he could forget. Before he can argue this isn't the same thing, she insists, "Just come with me, Huey. Don't try to talk me out of it. I have to know."

Silently, he offers her a nod and then locks up his apartment. They hold hands out of his building, on their walk to the subway, and on the three trains they take before they arrive in Tribeca. Jessica tells herself to keep breathing deeply while simultaneously hoping she doesn't run into any familiar faces.

"Miah's is—"

"Yeah," interrupts Stefano. "You know I googled this place the second you sent it to me. She's practically right around the corner. I know where we are. I know where we're going. Jessica—"

"Stefano, I don't even know what he's going to—"

He cuts her off with a laugh void of any humor. "Dove, he doesn't even know your real name. Whatever this *business proposition* is, it involves you taking off all your clothes. You know it, I know it, the only difference is—"

"We won't know until he—"

"Okay, no bullshit." He stops, taking their conjoined hands and bringing them to his chest as he halts and turns to face her directly. "I'm not crazy about this idea. At least at Clandestine's, I'm just down the hall. You're part of Bea's collection. You're *protected*."

"He's not going to hurt me, Huey," says Jessica, stepping closer to him. Keeping her voice low, she goes on to say, "I know this is crazy. I know this isn't part of our deal. I didn't plan for this. But for reasons I can't really explain, I can't say no. Not yet. Not until I hear him out."

In truth, she *could* explain. Jessica just can't look Stefano in the eye and admit the thought of never touching Godrik again—of never having *him* touch *her*—makes her feel a desperation she's never felt before. Knowing he's not finished with her yet, knowing the possibility of *more* is likely waiting for her, her body won't let her say no. Two things in the world have made her feel more alive and attuned with her body than most people ever experience. Dance and Godrik. Shameful as it might be, she can't ignore it, and she can't say no. Not until she's heard him out.

Stefano stares at her for a minute, then presses his lips closed and continues to their destination. As soon as they reach the corner of Broadway and Warren Street, he stops, gives Jessica's hand a squeeze, and lets her go.

"I'm going to go grab a coffee. There's a place on Greenwich," he says, motioning to the next block over. "Meet me there or call me if you need me."

Jessica, suddenly aware she's about to be on her own, pulls in a deep breath and gives him a nod. She has no words to offer. They're trapped in the nerves which seem to be twisting her stomach and clawing their way up her throat. Stefano presses a kiss to her forehead and then crosses the street. She watches him go and then cranes her neck to look at the old, brick-faced building that stretches the length of street between Warren and Murray. Walking slowly, she notes the street level of the building is made up of a couple shops and a small bodega. On the corner is Wally's Market next to a dry cleaner and a souvenir place on the far end. When she looks up, it's not hard to ascertain what's above these places. Apartments. Five stories of them. Having memorized the address, Jessica knows she's heading for the sixth floor.

Sandwiched between the bodega and the dry cleaner is the front entrance to the lobby of the housing space. The stonework framing the door and the windows, well above it, is classic architecture—or, at least, as classic as one of the oldest cities in the United States can manage. When Jessica pushes through the revolving door, she's greeted by a doorman. He doesn't so much speak as he looks up from his newspaper, rakes his eyes up and down the length of her, then dips his chin in some sort of silent hello as she proceeds to make her way toward the elevator bay.

Jessica presses the call button, then catches her reflection in the worn gold covering of one of the closed elevators. Immediately, and anxiously, she reaches up and runs her fingers through her hair. Just as fast, it falls where it was, around her face and down her chest and back. Rather than curl it, like she's done all the other times she's met Godrik, she opted to leave it natural. Her maple tresses hang in loose, thick waves she hopes are acceptable. Also, given the time of day, she has kept her makeup fairly light. She took the time to apply a soft layer of shimmery, pale pink eyeshadow, a thin line of eyeliner, and a generous application of mascara. She had on lip gloss when she left her apartment, but she's nervously smeared her lips together enough it's all but gone now. She doesn't give it a thought as she takes in the rest of her outfit.

It's August, which means it's hot and sticky outside. She's dressed herself in a pale blue romper—the shorts cut high on her thigh, the material cinched at her waist, and the spaghetti strap top cut into a deep V neckline, edged with small diamond cut outs exposing a hint of cleavage. She's paired the outfit with a set of suede, nude, peep-toe, sling back, ankle booties with a thick heel. In short, she's comfortable yet leaning on the side of sexy. Even still, she's completely aware she's wearing double the amount of clothes she usually wears when in this man's presence. Even though she'll be entering the room as *Bryn van Doren*, who he'll see is more of *Jessica* than he's ever seen.

Well, sort of, she admits to herself as a small chime announces the arrival of an elevator. *Guess I can't be more me than me completely naked.*

Shoving that thought aside, she boards the lift car and presses the button to the top floor. She tries not to fidget during her ride but pulls out her phone to double check the apartment number and the time. It's 12:57. She's right on schedule. When she's reached the sixth floor, her heart beats faster and she wills herself to be brave. Stepping into the hallway, it takes her no longer than a moment to notice there are only four doors running the length of the hallway. Her breaths grow shallow. It doesn't take a genius to discern, only *four* doors mean the apartments are *huge*.

What am I doing here? Jessica wonders as she makes her way toward unit 601.

KHALOHN LEANS AGAINST one of the six, wooden support beams in the middle of the vast, empty space of the loft. His eyes trained on the beam about ten feet away from him, he imagines Bryn's legs wrapped around him, her back against the sleek maple, her arms above her head clinging to the edges for leverage as she arches into him and takes him—hard and fast.

He clears his throat, averting his gaze, willing his mind into submission, all the while hoping his half-mast dick will settle before the woman arrives. Shoving aside his fantasies, he shifts his focus around the room. He wonders what she'll do with the place.

He wonders if she'll accept his proposition.

When Khalohn stepped foot into the recently remodeled loft space in the old Tribeca building, he knew he'd found precisely what he was in the market for. The kitchen, located to the left of the front entryway, is bordered with walls made of exposed brick. The bedroom, on a raised platform across from the living space, and the living space itself—both to the right—also have the added charm of exposed brick walls. It's a smart, striking contrast to the off-white dry wall, the old, polished wood floors, and the uncovered, wood-beamed ceilings. The space is one, decent sized, open floorplan. The only rooms where privacy can be gained are the bathroom and utility room, to the right of the front entry. They share a rustic, sliding, steel farmhouse door. There's also the pantry, just off the kitchen, and a small walk-in closet in the bedroom corner—with another steel farmhouse door.

In the middle of the day, there's plenty of sunshine pouring into the flat. The six windows, stretching the length of the living space wall, plus the three in the bedroom corner, are enough to make overhead lights unnecessary, so long as the sun is shining. Not that it matters to him much. Khalohn knows with certainty, the majority of the time he intends to spend in the loft will not be during the hours in which the sun shines.

Other than the built-in shelves—spanning the length of the kitchen wall—along with the island—complete with a stove-top built into the butcherblock counter—the open space is empty. This is why, when a knock sounds at the front door, even Bryn's hesitant taps echo all around him. His eyes shift toward the entryway, then he pushes himself off the beam on which he's leaning and crosses the room. The heels of his dress shoes echo even louder than the knock. On his next visit, he expects there will be no echoes. When he opens the door and finds Bryn standing in the hallway, his expectation melts into *hope*.

As he takes her in from top to toe, he's reminded why he's here. Not that he needs the reminder. She's unforgettable. It's impossible to forget the ways in which *she* is *his*—his to ruin. Then again, given the contract he signed that morning, he understands his objective to *ruin* her for any other man at Clandestine's is all but forgotten.

"Hi," she whispers, pulling him from his thoughts.

"Come in," he replies, stepping aside to grant her entrance.

She does so, slowly, her heels against the wood floors filling the space with more *echoes*.

"What, um…" Bryn's voice trails off as he shuts the door, and he turns to see her peeking beyond the entryway, looking around in confusion. "What is this place?"

"It's yours, should you accept," Khalohn answers simply, following her into the empty room.

Bryn whirls around, her big, brown eyes growing wide as she breathes, "What?"

Slipping his hands into his pant pockets, he feels the second set of keys he dropped there as he closes the distance between them. He stops when they are almost toe-to-toe. He can smell her perfume, and it makes him want to taste her, but he refrains.

"As I informed you yesterday, I've invited you here to offer you a business proposition. I'll be straight with you. Your price at Clandestine's is not an investment I can continue to make wisely. However, I'm not through with you. I want you. Here. Exclusively."

Bryn opens her mouth to speak, but when no words come out, she clamps her lips closed and continues to stare at him with her doe eyes. Wishing to touch her, yet resigned to wait, Khalohn takes a step closer, causing her to crane her neck back when he continues to speak.

"If you agree, our arrangement will be as follows. When I want you, I'll make it known. I'll never give you less than an hour's notice; though, with the schedule I keep, I'm sure I can offer you much more than that. We'll meet here. Always here. When I come to you, I'm prepared to offer you a payment of two-thousand dollars.

"I don't have to know your arrangement with Beatrice to know my offer is likely well below your usual payment. To compensate for that, the loft is yours for as long as our arrangement holds. Should you agree, I'll have an interior designer meet you here tomorrow at nine a.m. Fill the space however you would like. It'll be on my tab. She'll know to make sure your selections are here no later than Friday. I'll be out of town until then. If you agree, I'll expect you here that evening."

Bryn continues to stare at him for a minute longer. Having made his proposal, Khalohn waits patiently for her response. Finally, with a shake of her head and after a long blink, she murmurs, "I don't—I don't know what to say."

This time, it's Khalohn who studies Bryn. Wanting to touch her, he doesn't deny himself. He lifts a hand from his pocket and slowly glides his fingers along the side of her neck, to her nape, and into her silky mane. He can feel it when she leans toward him, and he doesn't miss the way her lips part with her breath at his touch. Heat rushes to his groin as his fingers flinch in her hair, and he holds himself back a moment longer.

He doesn't know her story. He doesn't know why she walked into Clandestine's, or why she needed or wanted to offer her body in such a way. All he knows is that a decade ago, if anyone told him he'd be making such an offer, he would have laughed in their face. Now he's practically holding his breath for her reply. He's tasted her *value*, and he's not even close to being through with this treasure.

"This—what you're offering—it's—it's too much," she breathes.

"I'll be the judge of that."

The words are hardly out of his mouth before Godrik's tongue is tangled with Jessica's. One taste of him, and she can think of nothing else. Having not had his mouth in days, the memory of his kiss faded around the edges, she can't silence her whimper at the glorious reminder.

When he angles his head and kisses her deeper, her whole body responds. Without even thinking about it, she's pressed up against him, her arms around his middle as she pushes up on her tiptoes, wanting more. He growls—*growls*—and she can feel it vibrating from his chest as it pours into her mouth. A surge of wetness between her legs makes her squirm. When he extracts his other hand from his pocket and slides his arm around her waist, pulling her closer, she moans. In that moan, she acknowledges if he wanted to strip her naked and make her his on the bare, hard floor, she'd oblige. *Happily.*

When Godrik slows down their kiss and pulls away leisurely, it takes her a second to open her eyes. The moment she looks up into his perfectly blue gaze, she knows she can't deny him. Not with his taste on her lips. Not with his hand fisted in her hair. Not with his warmth all around her.

"Judging by that kiss, I'd say we're agreed."

"I—I have an apartment," she stammers, her voice still airy and breathless.

"Here the rent is paid for."

Swallowing hard, Jessica forces herself to think rationally, difficult as it seems in the moment. "I—I can't give up my apartment."

Godrik studies her for what feels like a long time. She sees it in his eyes—an understanding of sorts. Jessica isn't sure what it is he thinks he understands; but his hand moves in her hair, as if he's massaging her scalp, and she melts into him in response. The slightest smirk curls the corner of his mouth, and her gaze falls to stare at it as she unconsciously leans into him even more.

"Tomorrow morning," he murmurs, his voice low and gentle. "Nine a.m. Michelle will meet you here to discuss filling the place. I'll leave your set of keys with her, so she has access to the loft until it's done. I want it done by Friday. Keep your apartment if you must. You're still welcome here any time, day or night."

Jessica nods, still trapped in a daze.

Then he tells her something unexpected. Something that makes her gut wrench in guilt at the same time her stomach clenches in excitement.

"From now on, I'm Khalohn. Khalohn Morgan."

Wow, she sighs internally. *Now that's a name.*

Before Jessica can even *think* about offering him her real name in return, his lips are pressed to hers in a hard, closed-mouth kiss. He lingers only for a moment before he squeezes her hip and takes a step back. Mercifully, he holds on to her for a second longer—long enough for Jessica to take responsibility of her balance—and then he lets her go.

Chapter Twenty-One

JESSICA PULLS ON A SWEATSHIRT over her rehearsal clothes and then straps on her backpack. The other students call out their goodbyes and she waves, relieved for the end of the day. Since she started taking extra dance classes at a studio her mom found in Tribeca, dancing under the instruction of Edward Timson has lost its sparkle. Not that she'd ever speak such a thing out loud. She knows how hard it is to be a student at the Brooklyn High School of the Arts. She knows her mom fought to get her in; and while grumbling about Timson won't likely cause her to lose her scholarship, she won't take any chances. She's grateful for the opportunity to have advanced contemporary dance be on her schedule as one of her core classes.

Making her way out of the studio, she reaches up and tightens her ponytail, which started to droop during class. Her stomach rumbles and she smiles, thinking of her best friend, Hugh. When she reaches her locker, she pulls out her phone, certain he won't turn her down when she suggests homework and a salty snack. After she exchanges the books in her bag for the notebooks and textbooks she'll need to complete that night's assignments, she checks her phone *for a reply from Hugh. When she finds nothing, she heads toward the front entryway, wondering if he might already be waiting for her outside.*

She steps into the cool autumn air, and the breeze sends a bunch of dry, dead leaves skittering across the sidewalk. Grabbing hold of the straps of her backpack, she keeps her eyes peeled for Hugh. He's usually not hard to find, especially not since he died his shoulder-length hair dark blue. It still surprises her how much trouble he got into over that. One would think having an artist for a mother might give him a little rebellious leeway. However, given the rundown of his parent's reaction, it didn't take much to figure out Elsa Rockwell had had a little too much success and a few too many years married to Dr. Matthew Thompson—snooty psychologist and heir to whatever mommy and daddy leave behind.

Honestly, it's a wonder Huey's as normal as he is...blue hair and all, *she thinks, scanning the area a second time.*

A frown pulls at her brow when she spots him. He's across the street, his back pressed up against a tree, and some big bully in his face. Jessica barely stops to look for traffic before she races to him, yelling at the guy pegging him to the rigid bark of the trunk.

"What the hell? Get off him!" *She tugs at his arm and recognizes his face right away.* "Seriously, lay off, Duke."

Hugh does nothing to defend himself but merely glares at his aggressor.

Duke's lip curls as he gives Jessica a once over. "You want to take me on, Chapman?" *He shoves Hugh aside and reaches for his junk as he says,* "I'll wrestle with you any time you want, baby."

"Fuck off," *grumbles Hugh.*

At the same time, Jessica bites, "Ew. You're an asshole. Just leave us alone."

"Whatever," *he mumbles before taking his leave.*

Jessica watches him go and then heaves a sigh, turning to her friend. "Are you okay?"

"Yeah. Fine." *He reaches down for his messenger bag, draping it over his shoulder as he insists,* "Let's go."

She doesn't ask where they're going but follows his lead. "What did he say to you? Are you sure you're okay?"

Hugh ignores her question, running his fingers through his navy locks, pulling the strands away from his face.

"Huey, talk to me."

"Sick of this place," *he mutters, his voice so low she has to walk closer to him to hear it over the passing cars.* "High school is so fucked up. Whoever's idea it was to put a bunch of hormonal teenagers trying to figure out who the hell they are in one place—fuckin' morons."

Jessica forces a smile, still not completely satisfied with his response. "Well, year and three-quarters left to go. Hugh, you can't let people treat you like that. You didn't even fight back."

"He's a closet case," *he replies with a shrug.*

Jessica scrunches her face in confusion. Hiking her thumb over her shoulder, she blurts, "Duke?"

"He doesn't want to wrestle with you, dove, he wants to wrestle with me; but he won't admit it. He's too scared. And I won't fight him. I won't give him the satisfaction." *He pauses for a moment, staring down at the sidewalk that passes beneath their feet.* "Might sound cold, but he's got to come to grips with his sexuality on his own. I sure as hell did, and I didn't beat anyone up to figure it out, either."

Chuckling softly, Jessica takes hold of his hand, lacing their fingers together as she murmurs, "You've known since you were ten, Huey. Back then, you were even scrawnier than you are now—which is saying something."

"Hey," *he grunts, jabbing her with his elbow.*

"Just saying," *she giggles.* "Of course you weren't beating anyone up."

"And I'm saying, there's no winner if I fight back."

She gives his hand a squeeze. "You're a good guy, Hugh."

"Maybe. But I'm thinking, when we're free of this place, Hugh isn't who I want to be. Not anymore."

"Oh, yeah? Then who will you be?"

He shrugs. *"Myself. Someone not tied to the name Thompson and the ridiculous expectations that come along with my trust fund."*

"Well, whoever you are, I don't care—so long as you're front-row-center when I'm performing with whatever dance company will have me."

"You kid, but you'll get there. And when you do, I'll be there. Front-row-center."

Jessica slows her feet, forcing him to follow suit as she tugs on his arm. She then presses up on her tiptoes, reaching to kiss his cheek. Having the support of her best friend is everything. Sometimes, her dreams feel so big and scary; but when she sees them through the eyes of Hugh, when she sees what she's capable of through the perception of the two people in the world who love her most, it gives her the confidence to keep on dreaming—however big that may be.

"Okay, so," she starts to say as they continue on their way. *"Speaking of the future—where are we going? Your place?"*

His family lives in a brownstone in Cobble Hill, only a short walk from the school.

"No way," he insists. Veering left, he confirms his intentions to steer them in the opposite direction of his home. *"Duke just shoved me up against a tree. I need pie."*

A knowing grin spreads across Jessica's face. She understands right away they're headed for the subway, taking a ride to her neck of the woods.

"I'm in. Blueberry—for my guy."

He smiles down at her, she gives him a wink, and her stomach rumbles at the prospect of her favorite, flaky buttery crust.

Chapter Twenty-Two

JESSICA BLOWS OUT A QUIET breath as she leans forward, propping her forehead against the edge of the hospital bed. With her eyes closed, she listens to the monitor as it beeps, marking time with the beat of Beth's heart. Her stomach twists uncomfortably, and she seals her eyes closed tight, wondering how it's possible *this* is her life.

She'd made up her mind. For a moment, in unit 601, the taste of *Khalohn Morgan* on her lips—she was lost in the fantasy. The backdrop was different, but the man was still the same, the fire he ignited within her undeniable. Then she left the loft, she wandered back into the real world, the heat of the afternoon burning away the vestiges of the *lie* that is Bryn van Doren, and she knew.

She knew she couldn't go through with it. She knew she couldn't accept Khalohn's offer. She knew to do so would be like accepting a handout. A fully-furnished escape from the real world, nights of passion with a gorgeous man, and thousands of dollars offered in return—it wasn't right. She couldn't do it.

In the time it took her to reach the coffee shop on Greenwich, Jessica convinced herself she had taken too much from Godrik—from *Khalohn*—already. Her shame and guilt were one thing—but the idea of his *handouts* went against everything her mother taught her. That truth brought with it a different kind of shame; a shame she was sure she couldn't shoulder. In short, Khalohn Morgan had saved her, but now it was time for her to take a different route, to find a different way to support her and her mother.

And then her phone rang.

Jessica feels the knot of panic she felt earlier clog her throat, yet again, as she remembers the sound of Beth's wheezing attempt to speak between her coughing fits. She breathes deep, forcing herself to listen to the sound of the beeping monitor, proof her mother is being treated.

She'll be fine, she thinks, breathing deeply in order to combat her tears. *She'll be fine.*

Lifting her head, she props her chin against the mattress and looks up at Beth. In sleep, she seems peaceful, and Jessica is grateful for the oxygen that makes it easier for the woman to breathe. Just a few hours ago, her cough had been so bad she could hardly speak. Until a few hours ago, neither of them knew her *cold* had turned into pneumonia, a virus that is quite dangerous given her COPD and the state of her already compromised lungs. Now, drugged and sleeping, Beth is quiet; but according to her doctor and the X-rays taken shortly after she was admitted into the emergency room, it's pretty bad. She should expect to be in the hospital for at least a couple of weeks.

Jessica reaches for Beth's hand, and the warmth found in her touch soothes her. It soothes the stab of reality. Soothes the ache of fear. Soothes the bruises left by shame and guilt. Staring at her mother, she knows what she has to do. She knows how much she's needed—not just financially, but physically, emotionally. It's all she's been able to think about for the past several hours. With the Medicaid plan they'd chosen, most of Beth's medications are covered, but not an extended hospital stay. They'll have to pay for her first entire week before Medicaid will pick up the slack; even then, only a percentage of her hospital residency will be covered. They hadn't seen this coming. Even if they did, Jessica knows the policy they chose is barely in their price range as it is.

Isn't that how life goes?

Shaking off the thought, Jessica acknowledges they're not in a great place—but that very afternoon, she'd been offered a job. A job that will give her the flexibility to be at the hospital most days; that will help ease the financial blow of hospital bills. It's a job she's already agreed to. An opportunity she can walk away from as soon as her mother is better.

When Jessica's phone rings from within her purse, she jumps. Hoping not to wake Beth, she's quick to retrieve it. At the sight of his name lighting up the screen, she swipes her thumb to answer and gets up to make her way out of the room.

"Hello?" she murmurs in greeting. Jessica wraps her unoccupied arm around her middle as she props her shoulder against the large window looking into Beth's room. She stares at her mother, the distance between them reawakening the worry that's settled in her belly.

"Hey. How's your mom? How're you holding up? Sorry I can't be there with you," says Stefano, his tone laden in regret.

Remembering it was Stefano who had the presence of mind to hail a cab when she was a trembling mess outside of the coffee shop, and Stefano who held the cab when she raced inside their apartment to help her mom down the stairs, and Stefano who paid the fare upon arriving at the emergency room, Jessica is quite certain he has no reason to feel *regret*. He'd stayed with her while Beth was admitted. He waited with her when Beth was carted off for X-rays and testing. It wasn't until Beth was put into her own room that he gave her space. Hours later, night having fallen, Jessica knows he's in the decadent bowels of Clandestine's.

"I'm okay, Huey," she whispers. "Mom's sleeping. They tried to kick me out earlier, claiming visiting hours were over, but I refused."

"Jess…going home to get some sleep yourself isn't the worst idea."

"I'm fine," she insists, staring at her mother's body in bed. She's not sure if the bed is large or her mother has grown smaller in the last couple weeks; either way, she guesses if she gets tired, she can curl up next to Beth. That's the only thing that'll get her to tomorrow's dawn—the nearness of her mother. "I don't want her to be alone. Not tonight. Dr. Montgomery says she might be here for a couple weeks. I just—I don't want her to be alone."

A beat of silence passes between them. Jessica knows he wants to talk her out of her decision, but he's smart enough to bite his tongue. He can't change her mind, and they both accept it in the voiceless exchange they share.

Finally, he says, "The afternoon took a turn. We didn't get a chance to talk."

Jessica's eyes lose focus as her mind shifts away from her mother, taking her to unit 601. Walking into the space was so much like walking into Clandestine's. Godrik—*Khalohn*—took her to an alternate world. A fantasy so vivid her whole body *tasted* it. As she remembers the kiss they shared, she's aware, with the day's events, that fantasy has been cracked. Now it's not a promise of escape, it's a necessity tangled in a bed of lies she can't escape. The decision she made before her mother called, her choice to say no, Stefano will never know about it. Things are different, now. She only has one choice.

"He made me an offer I can't refuse," she admits, her voice barely louder than a whisper.

"Dove—"

She reads his tone right away, closing her eyes as she cuts him off. "I'm serious, Stefano. I need the money. Now more than ever. Besides, where else am I going to find work that allows me to be around for my mom? Hmm?"

"Jessica, I know you don't want to hear it, but if you need money—"

"I don't want *Hugh Thompson's* money," she insists.

There's no forgetting how much he hates his old name. The name of a boy he never was, from a family into which he never fit. The name he ditched as soon as he could afford it. Hugh Thompson is the one tied to his outrageous trust fund—the money he only touches if he has no other choice. For this reason, and a host of others, she hates it when he even implies he can help her out with said money. It's too much of a sacrifice for him. It's too much to ask, so she never does. And she never will. He isn't that boy. Not anymore. He's a man.

He's Stefano Neal, and she won't be responsible for allowing him to go back on that.

From now on, I'm Khalohn. Khalohn Morgan.

Her grip around her phone grows tighter as another name circles around her brain. Of all the things he offered, all the things he promised, his *name* was so real and honest an admission, it's almost enough for Jessica to imagine part of what they have can be real. Even if only a little. Even if it's only one sided. The longer she ponders it, the easier it is to convince herself—for her to make her decision palatable.

Khalohn is real. His desire for me is real.

She pulls her bottom lip between her teeth and bites down hard, shoving aside the thought that *her* desire for *him* is just as real. Deep down, she's aware she can't rely on his longing as a source of income forever. But for now, her mother is sick, the insurance they thought was enough a couple days ago feels like a joke, and it's time for her to be responsible. It's time she take care of her mother, like her mother did for her for so long.

"I have to do this, Huey. Okay? Until she's out of here, this is my best option."

Another round of silence is exchanged between them before Stefano murmurs, "I love you, you know that? You drive me fucking crazy sometimes, but I love you."

The truth of his statement is enough to cause a small smile to pull at the corner of her mouth. "I love you, too, Huey," she whispers.

"Call me if you need me?"

"I will."

They each mutter soft farewells and Jessica rests the side of her head against the window as she continues to stare in at her mother. She looks so fragile, so alone, Jessica can hardly stand it. When her vision grows blurry with tears, she forces in a deep breath and shakes her head clear. She blinks away the excess moisture in her eyes, steels herself, and then reenters the room. She returns to the seat she vacated a few minutes ago, wrapping her hand around her mother's once more. It's the steady beat of her heart mimicked by the monitor that lulls Jessica into listless sleep.

JESSICA WAKES WITH the sun, feeling as though she's hardly slept. When she moves to sit up, Beth opens her eyes, and they exchange *good mornings*, the words a feeble attempt to preserve any semblance of normalcy in an otherwise hard situation. They aren't alone for long before a nurse comes in to check on things. A half hour later, Dr. Montgomery makes his first round of the day. There's little change to Beth's condition, outside of the medication and oxygen helping to control her cough, but this comes as little surprise. Still, the doctor is able to leave with a hopeful smile on his face, which provides Jessica with a modicum of comfort. It's a comfort she clings to as she looks at the time, realizing she has to step out for a while.

"I'm sorry, mom, but I have to run an errand. I should probably head home and get a shower, too."

"Oh, go, baby," she wheezes with a wave of her hand. "I certainly don't expect you to stay here all day. Jackie told me she'd stop by if she could get someone to cover her. Anyway, one of us has to work."

"Yeah," Jessica replies, forcing a smile.

"I hate that I'm a burden to you. We were already struggling before I—"

"Mom, no, don't," Jessica insists with a scowl. She leans in close, kissing Beth's cheek before she props her forehead against hers. "You're not a burden to me any more than I've ever been a burden to you."

"This isn't how things are supposed to be," she breathes.

"We're going to be fine, mom. I'm going to make sure of it, okay?"

"You're twenty-four years old. This isn't the life I—"

"Mama, you're sick," Jessica states, righting herself. With a shake of her head, she goes on to say, "I'm not going to argue with you about how my life *should* or *shouldn't* be. I'm going to go. I'm going to grab a shower, I'm going to run my errand, and then I'll be back. I'll bring lunch. And you're not going to lecture me about what my life *should* look like. There's only one thing I know for sure, and it's that I can't live without you—so you're going to get better, and I'm going to handle the rest, get me?"

Beth hesitates, the expression in her eyes the only evidence Jessica needs to know emotions are high. She can feel her own ache in the form of pressure behind her eyes, threatening more tears. Rather than wait for her mother's reply, she starts for the door, waving as she crosses into the hallway.

"Love you. I'll be back as soon as I can."

It's the look on her mother's face which helps Jessica fully accept what she's about to do. Beth's worry is enough to feed her stubborn resolve to do whatever it takes to support them. As she makes her way out of the hospital, she does so with her head held high. Whatever reservations or doubts she had before are dried up now. Her shame is no longer, completely eradicated by her need to keep her promise. She's convinced, if she holds up her end of the deal, Beth will have no choice but to hold up her end, as well. All Jessica wants is for her mother to get better. For her mother to *live*—and she'll do whatever she has to, to ensure that happens.

It takes an hour for Jessica to make it home, shower, and get ready for her appointment. Before she leaves for the subway, she tosses a few of Beth's paperbacks into her purse. It's not much, but she hates to think of her mother away from the words that offer her the escape she loves the most. As she locks up their home behind her, she gets lost in her thoughts of Beth. It's not long before she realizes, in order to make her believe they really will be okay, she's going to have to come up with a lie that explains where her money is coming from and how she's spending her time when she's not at the hospital.

From now on, I'm Khalohn. Khalohn Morgan.

Boarding her first train to Tribeca, Jessica wonders what she might be able to find out about the man who, for all intents and purposes, is her employer.

A man with the kind of money he throws around can't be hard to find, right? she thinks as she pulls out her phone.

The nerves in her belly fire in alert as she types his name into the Google search bar. When she sees Khalohn's photograph appear with a Wikipedia page, her eyes widen in surprise. Her thumb hovers over the link, but the nerves in her belly twist into knots at the thought. There's something so *real* about the *facts* that define *Khalohn Morgan*—the business mogul. The thought of *reading* about the man she knows literally nothing about feels wrong. Still, she can't stop her eyes from glancing at the preview text:

Khalohn G. Morgan is an American businessman and financial executive. He's the founder, CEO and president of the Khalohn Morgan Group. His company is the fastest growing acquisition firm to hit New York City in the last decade.

Born: *February 2, 1984 (age 35) Philadelphia, PA*
Education: *New York University, Columbia University*

Before she can read any further, she blacks out her screen, suddenly a little short of breath.

He's thirty-five, she thinks, her mind immediately filtering through her memories of his solid, chiseled body. Her cheeks grow warm and her stomach drops in that weightless way it does at the recollection of his touch. She forces a swallow, her eyes darting around her in a desperate attempt to focus on something else. Anything else. As the train comes to a stop, passengers come and go, and she remembers why she even thought to look up Mr. Morgan in the first place.

It's another two stops before she can wrap her mind around the fact that Khalohn is the founder, CEO and president of a company that is his namesake. She doesn't think at all of his age. It's too personal. Too *real*. While she's not entirely sure the extent to which an *acquisition firm* operates, she's smart enough to figure out the man is rich, and business is noteworthy enough for him to have his own Wikipedia page. By the time she transfers trains, taking her further into the city, she knows what she'll tell Beth.

The idea of being a night shift assistant sounds like a stretch, but it'll have to do. Reminding herself the lie is only temporary, Jessica doesn't give it anymore thought. The closer she gets to Tribeca, the more aware she becomes that she's got other things to worry about—namely the task she's been assigned to have an entire loft decorated. A loft purchased for her use. An apartment offered as part of the transactional relationship she's agreed to. A residence with which she will not allow herself to become comfortable.

Unit 601 is just that.

The apartment on Broadway.

Chapter Twenty-Three

DAYS IN THE HOSPITAL ARE long. While the doctors say Beth's condition is improving, it's happening at such a slow rate Jessica can hardly tell. When Beth's not sleeping, she's reading, the television turned on with the volume low to help the time pass for Jessica. In order to have the excuse to get out, Jessica fetches their meals. Sometimes they settle for hospital cuisine, other times she ventures out of the building for something better. Their conversations are held in whispers and soft tones, as if they both fear speaking at a louder volume might ignite a coughing fit.

By Wednesday, Jessica feels guilty for her boredom—watching and waiting for her mother to be *better*. After leaving unit 601 on Monday afternoon, she swore to herself she wouldn't go back until it was finished and Michelle had surrendered her keys. She doesn't want to be invested in the space. She doesn't want to see it in various stages of completion. She doesn't want to get attached. Even still, she thinks of the apartment often, wondering about it, longing for a different space—someplace less sterile.

Wednesday afternoon, when she receives a text alert, reminding her of the contemporary dance class she'd signed up for the week prior, she jumps at the chance to go. She'd forgotten about it, and the reminder alone fills her with such a great measure of reprieve, she can't cancel. Just like it always does, dancing buoys her heart—so much so, it carries her through the next two days at the hospital. It's early Friday afternoon, after she and Beth finish lunch, when she gets another message that beckons her out of the hospital.

The apartment is finished. Michelle has left the keys with the doorman. When Jessica reads the text, her stomach drops in an eerie sense of anticipation. While she has no intention of moving into the space, she plans on packing her collection of lingerie and stowing it there. On Wednesday, after she left the dance studio glossy with sweat, the apartment hardly more than a block away, she also had the idea to purchase a few bathroom staples to keep there. It's impossible to ignore the convenience of having someplace to shower after dance before hopping on the subway to return to the hospital.

She hasn't heard from Khalohn at all since their meeting on Monday. With him out of town, and their arrangement hardly more than a promise sealed with a kiss, she doesn't know what to expect. He'll be back in town that day, but she has no idea how often he'll want to see her. Thinking back on their conversation, she wonders if he'll still want to see her that night. The possibility alone makes her skin break out in goosebumps.

"Hey, you okay?" asks Beth, reaching out to fidget with the ends of Jessica's wavy hair.

Jessica blacks out her phone, placing it face down on the side of the bed as she directs her attention onto her mother's pale brown eyes. Forcing a smile, she murmurs, "That's my question."

Beth only raises her eyebrows in response. Jessica is familiar that look. Her lips curl a little more, her expression more genuine as she reaches for her mom's hand. She laces their fingers together as she admits, "It was work."

"Don't you start tonight?" Beth is interrupted by a cough. She tries to suppress it, as her chest and back are sore, but it only makes it harder for her to breathe. Her face turns a shade of red in agitation. Jessica flexes her fingers, holding Beth's hand tighter, until she sucks in as deep a breath as she can manage. "I'll be fine, you know," she wheezes.

"My new boss—he might not need me long tonight. If he doesn't, I'll just come back."

"Jess, baby, I'm not alone here. There's an entire staff of people checking on me. And Jackie's coming for a little while after work. Sleep in your bed tonight. Please. It'll make me feel better."

"Mom—"

"Look, I might be the vulnerable one here, hooked up to these tubes and shit, but I'm still your mother. Stand down, baby. Spend the night stretched out in bed alone. For me."

It doesn't take long for Jessica to relent. There's not much she can do for Beth's ailing body. If sleeping in a bed will give her mother some peace of mind, she'll do it. After she agrees, she lingers at Beth's bedside for another few minutes. Knowing she's got a short to-do list she needs to see to, she takes her leave, promising to check in by phone after a while.

An hour later, a bag full of sexy underwear, silky nighties, and her floor-length lace robe over one shoulder, and her purse over the other, Jessica decides to hail a cab into the city. In spite of the heavy, Friday afternoon traffic, she steps out on the corner of Broadway and Warren a half hour later. Before she enters the lobby of the apartment building, she goes into Wally's Market, where she purchases a few necessities. Shampoo and conditioner. Face wash and moisturizer. Eyeliner and mascara. Toothbrush and toothpaste. Body wash and a loofa. It takes her no longer than ten minutes, and then she's at the check-out counter, trying not to think too hard about the strange, clandestine nature of her purchases.

She thanks the clerk behind the counter after she pays, then hurries next door. The man behind the front desk is the same guy she's seen the last two times she visited unit 601. Like every instance she sees him, his eyes do a body scan down her length. She tries not to roll her own. With no intention of impressing anyone, her outfit was chosen for comfort.

Jessica's feet are tucked into a pair of non-descript, gray tennis shoes, her toned, slender legs on display beneath her black, spandex shorts. The white tank top she has on is loose, draping over her gray sports bra and hanging around her hips. Her hair is down, the heat of the day, the burden of her bags, and the weight of her wavy locks against her neck making her hot.

"A set of keys were left for me. I'm Jes—I mean, my name is Bryn," she mutters with a shake of her head. "Bryn van Doren. Unit 601."

"Yeah," he grunts, turning in his chair for a lock box. He extracts her keys and hands them over without another word.

Jessica thanks him, in spite of his rudeness, then heads toward her final destination. All the while, she can't help but think of Stefano. A doorman and a gatekeeper aren't exactly the same thing, but it makes her miss him and his presence as he escorted her into *Godrik's* suite. As she rides the elevator to the sixth floor, she wonders what'll happen to the room—if he'll use it when he's not with her, or if it'll collect dust in his absence.

The elevator doors open with a chime, and she shoves the thought of Khalohn sleeping with other women out of her mind.

He bought this apartment so we could be together exclusively. Because he's not done with me. Besides, I'm his call girl. Even if he is sleeping around, can I be surprised? He's not mine.

Pausing in front of the door, she exhales with a huff and rakes her fingers through her hair, gripping the strands at the back of her head.

Fuck, she thinks, willing her mind, body, and soul to stay firmly rooted in *reality.*

When she feels like she's in control of her thoughts, she slides the key into the lock and twists it free. The door opens and, immediately, she can feel the place has changed. There's a coat rack just beyond the door, a small, round, wooden table with distressed metal legs nearby. On the wall to the left of the door, there's a large, framed photograph—the piece printed in sepia tone, the image that of a row of brownstones. Slowly, Jessica walks past the art and into the space, easing the door closed behind her. She stops, her eyes wide in awe when she reaches the end of the entryway, where the loft comes into full view.

Thinking back on her meeting with Michelle, Jessica recalls how uncertain she felt. Khalohn told her to fill the place however she wanted. Resigned to the truth it isn't *her* space, she couldn't figure out how to even begin. With a little nudge from the interior designer, who'd worked with Khalohn in the past, Jessica opted for cozy, yet masculine; upscale, but not pretentious. She picked items not seeing them as part of a whole, but as *pieces* chosen to simply fill the emptiness. Now that she's seeing the finished project, there's a warmth in her belly she can't ignore, no matter how hard she tries.

The French Victorian room beneath Clandestine's Closet—rich, elegant, and old fashioned—is a fantasy in which anyone who enters can get lost. But *this*—this is *their* space. Unit 601 is private. Cozy, yet masculine. Upscale, but far from pretentious.

And she likes it.

On the brick wall in the kitchen, the open shelves are filled with beige, porcelain plates, bowls, and mugs. There are tall, thick glasses, stemless wine glasses, and martini glasses—copper shot glasses and a matching shaker set included, as well. In the center of the kitchen, on the shelves beneath the butcher block island, are a collection of copper pots and pans. Just beyond the shelving, on the opposite side of the flat-top stove, there are four bar stools—two on either side of the counter—for casual seating.

To the right of the kitchen, on a printed, red rug, there's a dining room table, complete with eight black wire chairs. Draped over the backs of each are white faux lambskin throws for cushion and comfort. Above the table hangs an intricate, black iron, circular chandelier. Jessica knows they'll never have use for that many chairs. There are no dinner parties in their future, but it breaks up the space nicely, just like Michelle said it would.

Further into the room, in the large open space in front of the bedroom platform, is the *cozy* she was aiming for. The espresso-leather, L-shaped sectional faces the windows and is made into a U with the addition of two chestnut leather armchairs. The side table between them completes the semi-circle of furniture that frames the square trunk serving as the coffee table. All of it is situated on a furry, white rug she can tell is heaven to the touch.

After taking this all in, Jessica inches her way further into the loft. When she reaches the step leading up to the raised platform where the bed is, she lets her bags slide from her shoulders and onto the floor. The king-sized bed is situated against the wall on a simple, raised frame, atop a dark, teal printed rug. The duvet cover is white, as are the four large pillows piled at the head. There's one accent pillow, its cover a shade of mustard yellow with teal accents printed diagonally across the bottom. There are two, basic, retro designed wooden nightstands on either side of the bed—a golden lamp on the right side and a pot of succulents on the left. By the window, beside the nightstand with the plant, is a full-length mirror propped on the floor—the triangle cut of the class allowing it to fit perfectly in the corner.

Jessica notices little knickknacks everywhere. These are Michelle's doing, just like the large framed photographs she's hung. Each piece is a little touch that completes the space without making it cluttered in any way. It's perfect. It's more than Jessica imagined. Even with all the furniture in place, there's still a lot of empty space, but she likes it that way. Living in a tiny apartment with her mother, every corner stuffed full of belongings to accommodate two people in a residence meant for one, she feels like she can *breathe* here. There's so much extra room, she could dance in it if she wants.

As soon as the thought crosses her mind, she pulls her bottom lip between her teeth and looks around. A smile fights against her captured lip, and she's quick to pull her hair up into a ponytail. She then reaches for her phone, opening up her music app as she kicks off her shoes. In bare feet, she slowly makes her way to the dining room table as she finds the song she's looking for. The choreography she learned in Miah's class, just a couple days before, still lingers beneath her skin. The thought of dancing it out right here and now brings her a sort of peace she's only ever granted in movement.

As soon as the beat drops to "Movement" by Hozier, her hips sway from side to side and she feels herself being pulled under. She turns up the volume on her phone until it's maxed out, then tosses it on the dining room table before she completely loses herself in the dance.

KHALOHN POWERS ON his phone as the plane taxies to the gate, already impatient to be back in the city. It's been a packed couple of days sandwiched between two long, transcontinental flights. He wants to get to the office, take care of his urgent tasks, then indulge in his latest investment. He allows his thoughts to conjure the memory of Bryn, as he's done a dozen times throughout the week. Then he shuts his daydreams down in an effort to focus his mind on his present needs.

He sends a text to Atzel, alerting him to his status, and then scrolls through the emails he received since he powered down his computer a few hours into the flight. The sleep he caught in the air wasn't much, but it'll get him through the rest of the day. When the plane finally comes to a halt and the seatbelt sign goes dark, Khalohn is quick to stand from his seat. He gathers his suit jacket from the hanger it hung on for the journey, slipping his arms into it before he reaches for his bag in the overhead compartment. He's one of the first off the plane, and he weaves his way through JFK Airport as quickly as the crowds allow. When he spots Atzel climbing out of the front seat of the Maybach at his approach, Khalohn feels at home—the familiarity of routine making it so.

"Good afternoon, Mr. Morgan," greets the man, reaching for Khalohn's bag.

"Atzel," replies Khalohn with a dip of his chin.

The Honduran opens the backseat door, and Khalohn folds himself inside. His bag is stowed in the trunk, then Atzel returns to his spot behind the wheel and eases into the traffic leading out of the airport.

"To the office, sir?"

It isn't until the question is posed that Khalohn considers an alternative. He checks the time, noting it's nearly two in the afternoon. His stomach growls, alerting him to his need of a decent meal, but it's his curiosity which has him going off course.

Pulling out his phone, he brings up Maribelle's contact information and opens their thread of messages. "Tribeca," he mutters, typing out his late lunch order to his secretary.

"Right away, sir."

After he's certain his lunch will be waiting for him upon his arrival at the office, he mulls over the business he must see to before he can call it quits for the day. He returns a few emails and takes a couple incoming calls during the forty-five-minute drive to the apartment on Broadway. As Atzel comes to a stop right in front of the building, Khalohn looks up the length of it, a mild sense of anticipation mingling with his curiosity. He wonders what the space looks like. He knows it's complete. He knows because that's the arrangement he made with Bryn; but also because that's what he paid Michelle to make happen, and he saw the charges that hit his account as necessary purchases were made throughout the week. Now he's impatient to see another side of Bryn by way of her tastes.

Atzel opens his door, and Khalohn steps out, buttoning his jacket as he addresses his driver. "I won't be but a few minutes. I need to return to the office."

"Of course. I'll keep the car running."

Khalohn strides into the building, passing the doorman without even a glance. He pushes the call button for an elevator, and one opens right away. As he rides to the sixth floor, he does so remembering Bryn's declaration that she wouldn't give up her apartment. With this in mind, he doesn't expect to find her inside. Moreover, as he steps off the elevator, he reaches for his phone with every intention of sending her a message—beckoning her to 601 that night.

He's barely got her contact information pulled up when he arrives at the door. He pauses, the sound of music coming from the other side indisputable. When he reaches for the knob, he frowns when he finds it unlocked.

Quietly, he grants himself entrance. He shuts the door behind him, then steps out of the front entryway and into the mouth of the loft, where he stops dead in his tracks. His eyes find Bryn immediately. He doesn't see the décor of the space. He doesn't notice the colors of the furniture, the accents of the rugs, or the way his footsteps don't echo as loudly as they did the last time he was here. All he sees is Bryn, her body moving in such a way he's never seen before. Each movement is synced with the beat of the song; but it's more than that. She *is* the music.

He's so transfixed, he can't decipher the lyrics. But he doesn't need to hear the words. He can *see* them—with every dip, twist, turn, leap and lunge Bryn makes. In the span of a single verse, something inside his mind recognizes *this* is Bryn. The woman in front of him isn't just dancing, she's a dancer. The way she moves her body, it's outrageously sexy. Not because her movements are sensual, but because she's so completely in control of her body. Never before has he seen someone so *at home* in their skin. Without being able to put it into words, he understands while he's seen her stripped naked—it isn't until this moment that he's really *seen* her.

She's dancing in the space in front of the windows across from him, her back to him at first. Yet, even as she moves and spins, she doesn't notice him, too lost in the song. Just as lost as she is to the melody which fills the room, he is as lost in her. He can't take his eyes away from her. The first time she danced for him, it turned him on. Now, watching her, it doesn't arouse him. It's more than that. More arresting than the base urge brought about by his carnal nature. To him, she's mesmerizing—the glimpses of her face he catches are evidence of a peace he's sure he's never known.

As soon as the song ends, it starts up again. Except, as Bryn stands to reposition herself—breathless from her efforts—she finally spots him. A yelp erupts from her mouth, and she jumps back. She almost collides into one of the wooden beams in the middle of the room as she claps her hands over her lips. Realizing its him, her hands drop to her chest, still rising and falling in rapid succession as she stares at him.

"I didn't—didn't hear you come in," she breathes unnecessarily.

Khalohn doesn't speak right away. He takes her in from top to toe. Her thick mane is hardly contained in a ponytail, the hair tie drooping at her nape, loose strands framing her face, now glowing in a thin layer of sweat. She's dressed down, her face void of makeup, her outfit functional—her clothes made to give her the complete freedom of uninhibited movement.

This is Bryn.

His dick comes to life in his slacks, reminding him of his desire.

He doesn't realize the length of time that passes as he stares at her. When she straightens, quickly tugging her hair tie off, her long mane falls around her shoulders. Self-consciously, she runs her fingers through the strands, tossing a bit to the side, creating a voluminous effect he finds appealing.

"Come here," he finally speaks.

She nods but doesn't move immediately. He watches her swallow nervously before she slowly crosses the room. The closer she gets, the more defined her features become. Without her makeup, she appears younger. Purer. Natural, in the most beautiful and appealing way. Her cheeks are tinted pink, the residue of her exertion lingering on her face. He wants to touch her, to slide his hand beneath her tank top in search of the damp skin at the small of her back. He wants to *taste* her skin, perspiring with her very essence. He shoves his hands into his pockets instead, curling his fingers into fists in an effort to restrain himself.

Tonight.

In spite of his self-assurance, when she stops a foot away from him, it's too far.

"Closer," he demands.

Peeking at him from beneath her lashes, she steps even closer, until there are mere inches separating her chest from his. He can smell the musk of her sweat as it mingles with the remnants of her perfume, and he can't resist. With his hands still buried in his pockets, he leans down and presses his lips to hers. The song starts over again, and she leans into the kiss. He traces the seam of her mouth open with his tongue, and she steps closer. In the same moment she sneaks her tongue out to meet his, she delicately slips her fingers under the lapels of his suit jacket. He tilts his head, opening his mouth wider, kissing her deeper, longing to gulp from her well.

His fists clench at the sound of her soft moan, but he can't touch her. If he does, he won't be able to stop. So, he drinks. He drinks from her like the parched man he is. When she presses up onto her tiptoes, circling her arms around his neck, he knows he needs to stop. When he lifts his head abruptly, her arms around his neck tighten, as if he's thrown her off balance simply by severing their connection. Looking down at her, another rush of blood heads straight for his groin at the sight of her pink, swollen lips.

The song starts over a third time.

"I've got to go," he mutters, his gaze still aimed at her mouth.

"Oh," Bryn replies on a sigh.

She unlocks her arms and takes a step back. There's something in the act accompanied by the sound of her voice that causes him to extract a hand from his pocket. He wraps an arm around her waist, pressing her against him. Bryn gasps, her hands flying up to grip his lapels a second time, and his eyes dance around her face. He studies her, realizing that when she's in his arms, the control he saw in her while she was dancing, it's not as prominent. He curses under his breath, aroused by the idea he can make her lose control—and now, he understands just how much control she's capable of.

"I'll be here by nine. I expect you here until morning. Understood?"

She nods her head without hesitation, and he allows his hand to slide down over her backside. He lingers only a second, then forces himself to pull away from her.

In an attempt to center himself, he breathes deeply as he takes his leave. For the duration of his elevator ride, he tries to think on things that will ease his state of arousal. As he makes his way through the lobby, he realizes he didn't take in a single detail of the fully furnished loft.

Chapter Twenty-Four

J ESSICA LEANS PROPPED UP against one of the large windows on the far side of the apartment, her eyes taking in the view of the city street below. She can hear the sounds of traffic—honking horns, bus engines, even a subway train in the distance—the night's soundtrack seeping through the glass behind which she stands. She pulls her short, silk robe around her tighter, wondering what time it is and how long she's been waiting, but not at all interested in checking the time. If she does, it'll only make her anxious. It'll only make her think of the kiss Khalohn planted on her lips a few hours ago.

That kiss was a reminder.

That kiss was a promise.

When he slipped his tongue into her mouth, she was able to fully admit how much she's missed his touch. She longs for it. Staring out the window, looking past her reflection, she wonders in an effort not to count down the minutes. Filling the hours of the evening has been a challenge, her anticipation making every activity feel menial.

After Khalohn left, she was in too much of a daze to find the focus to keep dancing. She couldn't be sure how long he had watched her. She didn't ask. But the thought of him standing there, staring, not saying a word to interrupt her—the memory makes her belly tingle even still. Unintentionally, he'd stumbled upon something *real*. People watching her dance never makes Jessica uncomfortable or embarrassed, and this instance wasn't an exception. Except, it wasn't simply because he was watching her do something she loved, but because she wanted him to have that. Something *real*.

I know his name. I know his age and how he makes his money. They're just pieces of him—but he should have a piece of me, too. It's only fair.

Jessica blows out a sigh, reaching up to tuck a bit of hair behind her ears. Earlier, after she came unstuck from where Khalohn left her, after she unpacked her things, left the apartment to walk down to the market, and stopped at a deli to pick up something for dinner, she came back to 601 to prepare for her night. She showered, then ate standing in the kitchen, wrapped in only a towel at the island. While she applied her makeup, she spoke with her mother on the phone, and then she took the time to blow her hair dry before she curled it. That done, she lathered her skin in lotion and spritzed on her favorite perfume.

Wearing a fitted, dusty rose, silk nightie underneath her robe, her face done up and her hair falling down her back, she's ready, and she's waiting. In spite of her acceptance of the situation, of their arrangement, the thought of being with Khalohn—of having him between her thighs for a second night—it ignites an excitement that makes her feel slutty. She can't help it. He's *that* good.

When she hears him insert the key into the lock, she sucks in a breath and turns slightly from the window. Her heart beats faster, that familiar feeling associated with his arrival sending a shot of desire from her belly down to her core. She can't see him from where she stands as he enters the apartment, but she listens as he does what he's always done.

He locks them inside, discarding his key on the side table. As his movements become silent, she imagines him stripping out of his suit jacket

246 | R.C. MARTIN

and hanging it on the coat rack. Finally, the heel of his shoes clicks against the hardwood floor, his steps bringing him through the entryway and into the loft space. Her breath catches in her throat at the sight of him. It doesn't matter that she saw him a few hours ago. As her gaze settles on his perfectly blue eyes, she can barely catch her breath. The promise of his touch is imminent.

Khalohn hesitates a moment at the sight of her. He takes her in, noting the changes she's made since he stopped by earlier that afternoon. Her hair falls in big, soft curls down her chest and back, the way he likes it best. Her big, brown eyes are darkened with makeup, and her casual attire is gone, replaced by a robe he intends to remove as soon as possible.

The thought of touching her reminds him his hands are full. Reluctantly, he takes his eyes away from her as he makes his way toward the kitchen. Raising the bottle in his left hand and setting it on the island, he says, "I don't know your preference, but this is merlot." Without waiting for her reply, he takes the paper sack in his right hand and announces, "I brought a charcuterie board as well, in case we get hungry." He opens the fridge to stow the meat, cheese, and olive filled board, noticing she, too, purchased a few things stowed in the ice box.

As if she notices his observation, she murmurs, "I got stuff for breakfast."

"Good," he replies, turning to face her once more. "Moving forward, I'll arrange for someone else to keep the fridge stocked."

Something about their exchange gives him pause. Khalohn leans his backside against the counter beside the fridge, slipping his hands into his pant pockets as he stares at Bryn. It's been a long time since he's so much as thought about sharing a meal or even a drink with a woman he intends to take to bed. While it makes sense that their arrangement would lead to such a reality, it's an aspect around which he's just now wrapping his head. When Bryn slowly starts to cross the room, her eyes pinned to his, anticipation causes his penis to stiffen, and it's enough to remind him *why* he's here.

It's her.

It's all her.

When she's within reaching distance, he widens the space between his legs and takes hold of her waist, pulling her closer. Without a word, he loosens the tie of her silk robe, allowing the belt to fall to her sides as the flaps open to reveal her short, pink nightgown. The fabric clings to her breasts, molding her narrow waist and the slight flare of her hips. Readjusting his grip around her waist, so his hand is now inside the robe, he uses his other hand to shape her body—skimming his fingers up her stomach and around her ribs, until his thumb is grazing the underside of her breast. He watches as her nipples harden, and his erection presses against the seam of his pants.

Hesitantly, Jessica reaches for his tie, keeping her eyes on his face in order to assess how she's doing. His gaze collides with hers as she loosens the accessory and slips it off, allowing it to fall to the floor. As she begins to unbutton his shirt, he sweeps his thumb over her pebbled nipple, and her stomach dips, taking her breath with it. She works her fingers faster, her longing to touch him making her brave.

With his shirt undone and pulled free from his slacks, his hands slide down and around her rear, pulling her flush against him. She gasps in the same instant he closes his mouth around hers, and the moan that crawls up her throat won't be silenced. She returns his kiss, smoothing her hands up his hard abs and over his solid pectorals, covered in a thin layer of fine chest hair. His grip around her intensifies, and the feel of his hard length pressing against her hip causes a rush of desire to pool between her legs.

They've barely exchanged two sentences with one another since he walked through the door, but Jessica doesn't care. At the mercy of his hands, she wants only one thing. *More.*

With a grunt, Khalohn takes hold of Bryn's hips, pushing her away from him. Rather than letting her go, he lifts her from her feet and carries her the short distance to the island. No sooner does he set her on the counter than he's ripping her panties down her legs. She shrugs the sleeves of her robe off as he discards his shirt, and then his mouth is on hers again. He swallows her whimper as she hooks her legs around his hips, her hands clasping the back of his neck. He holds her tightly at her waist with one arm, using his free hand to feel his way along her smooth thigh. When he reaches her hip, his fingers find their way to her center, and her back arches, causing her chest to press into his as he grazes over her entrance.

Fucking hell, he thinks as he groans. *Sopping wet.*

He ends their kiss, nibbling on her lip before he dips down, spreading her legs and hooking them over his shoulders. She quivers at the first swipe of his tongue, and he's so hard he can feel his pulse in his dick. The second her fingers are in his hair, he knows he won't stop until she's trembling with her release.

Jessica can't think straight, she's too busy *feeling*. Throwing her head back, she holds herself upright with one hand propped behind her, the other holding tight to Khalohn's thick mane. She's entirely unaware of how fierce her grip is, and completely oblivious of the fact that she doesn't have to worry he'll stop. All she knows is a tongue has never felt so good. It's like she's a delicacy, and he intends to savor every bite.

"*Khalohn,*" she mewls as the fuse he's lit deep inside of her starts to burn. She seals her eyes closed tight, gasping and moaning as her orgasm draws closer and closer. He slips a finger inside of her, sucking on her bundle of nerves, and she detonates. "Oh, god!" she cries as her legs shake, the heels of her feet digging into his back.

He draws out her pleasure, adding another finger as he lifts up, grabbing the back of her neck. Humming in satisfaction, she rights her head and happily offers him her mouth. When the walls of her sex begin to relax, he removes his hand from between her legs, taking hold of the back of her knee to keep her close. Their kiss is hard and greedy, and he likes how much she appreciates the taste of herself on his tongue. It's not long before Bryn's reaching for his belt, silently begging for more. When her hand finds its way into his pants, grabbing him through his briefs, he grunts and pulls up for air.

"Let me," she pants, pressing her forehead to his. "Please?"

He considers it only for a moment. He doesn't need longer. If there's one thing he's sure of, it's that it's been a week since his dick has been inside of this woman. Her mouth won't be enough. Her mouth isn't what he craves.

Reaching for the hem of her nightie, he looks her straight in the eye and then grumbles, "No."

Before she can react, he's pulling off her last item of clothing, forcing her to let him go. He tosses her garment aside and then gathers her into his arms. She clings to him as he lifts her from the counter and carries her through the apartment to the bed. Upon arrival, he eases her atop the white comforter and then stands to remove the rest of his clothing. The hungry look in her eye at the sight of his stiff penis doesn't go unnoticed, and Khalohn almost gives in to her previous request. Before he can change his mind, he strokes himself once and then settles his body between her hips.

Dragging his heavy length across her center, he brings his lips to hers and inquires, "You on the pill?"

"Yeah," she breathes with a nod, spreading her legs wider.

Somewhere, in the back of her mind, Jessica knows whatever conversation they're having in that moment should probably include more words. More explanations. More assurances. But she wants him too badly. She's been here before—on the brink of having him inside of her. Even though she came just a few minutes ago, the anticipation of having *all* of him makes it impossible for her to listen, let alone interpret, her own thoughts.

"*Khalohn!*" she cries as he fully buries himself inside of her.

His eyes are completely dilated as he gazes down at her, pausing when he's perfectly seated.

God, how is this possible, Jessica thinks, clinging to him with all her limbs. *It's better—holy hell, it's better than I remember.*

Khalohn pulls out of her slowly and then pounds into her again, never taking his eyes from hers. On his third pass, he tucks his face into her neck, gripping her waist tightly in an effort to remain in control. Needing to taste her, he licks his way up her neck before kissing the spot just behind her ear. He pulls out and then returns as he mutters, "Absolutely precious."

Keeping his hold on her waist, he slips his other arm beneath her before flipping them over, until he's on his back. Bryn rights herself, her eyes widening as she glances down at their connection. Khalohn simply stares up at her, waiting to see what she'll do next. He doesn't have to wait long before she plants her hands on his abs—her contact making his muscles flex. They keep their eyes on one another as she lifts her hips, until only the tip of him is inside of her. Then she slowly takes him inside of her again. Her jaw falls open and she squeaks in desperation before she repeats the act. She goes slow for three strokes as she grows comfortable, confident, *greedy*.

Jessica has never been so turned on in her life. The gorgeous man underneath her—*inside of her*—deeper than anyone has ever been—she can't get enough. She rides him faster, harder, needing more. *Desperate* for it.

"More," she mewls unabashedly. "*More.*"

Smoothing his hands up her thighs, Khalohn takes hold of her hips, syncing his movements with hers. Every time she works her way down, he charges up. Soon, they're both chasing the tingling sensation that grows stronger and stronger between them.

"Khal—" she breathes before she's cut off by a gasp. "Khal—don't—oh, god—don't—don't stop!"

Her nails dig into his chest as her body locks up around his. Her sex strangles his so tightly—Bryn's hot, slick, tight walls demanding his seed—he can't hold back. Thrusting his shaft into her relentlessly, he rides the wave of her orgasm as it pushes him into oblivion right along with her.

IT'S NEARLY MIDNIGHT, and Jessica's body is so loose and sated, it's as if she's had a full body massage. She doesn't close her eyes, too afraid if she does, she'll sink into a deep sleep. Given that sleep would hinder the possibility of having Khalohn inside of her again, she stubbornly clings to her current state of consciousness. She's stretched out in the middle of the bed, the top sheet pulled up to her waist, her hands pressed together and tucked underneath her cheek as she stares at the man responsible for her last four orgasms. He lays in the mirrored position of hers, only his eyes are closed.

She misses the blue of his irises, but she doesn't dwell on it. It's pointless to do so. As good as she feels, as many times as he's owned her body in the most splendid ways, she reminds herself she doesn't belong to him. She barely knows him. More than that, he doesn't know her. Not even so much as her name.

Except, the longer she lays beside him, the longer she admires the lines of his face, the more she *wants* to know him. Jessica wants to know the man who cares more about getting her off than letting her take care of him. She wants to know the man who kisses her like she's the last woman he'll ever have the chance to kiss. He could have his pick of women in all of New York City, and yet he's chosen to *pay* for her. Most of all, she wants to slip under the skin of the man who thinks her *precious* and stay a while.

Knowing this'll likely never happen, she continues to lay still in the silence, taking what he'll give her. When she hesitantly extracts a hand from beneath her cheek, she holds her breath as she reaches for his face. Her fingertips graze through the soft hairs of his thick beard along his jaw. She likes the feel of his whiskers, especially against the sensitive skin of her inner thigh. Jessica freezes when Khalohn moves. He doesn't open his eyes as he frees one of his hands and reaches for her. Her belly flips in excitement when he presses a hand to the small of her back, pulling her closer. She fights a smile, tracing her fingers from his jaw, to the hairline around his ear. When she submerges her fingers in his thick strands of mussed hair, he grazes his fingers back and forth across the top of her backside.

"Do you like the apartment?"

Jessica isn't sure why she asks. She can't explain her desire for pillow talk, only that she's not ready to go to sleep yet. There's something about the moment, about the quiet, content nature of it that begs for more.

When a smirk pulls at the corner of Khalohn's mouth, she stares at his lips, watching as he murmurs, "Honestly, I hadn't noticed." His voice is sexy—his tone soft and rough, as if held in the clutches of a battle between exhaustion and resilience. "The two times I walked through the door today, something else had my attention."

Jessica now bites her lower lip in a last-ditch effort to conceal her grin. Khalohn opens his eyes, his gaze immediately pinned to her mouth. She can tell he appreciates what he sees when his hand slides down over one of her butt cheeks, pulling her closer still.

"Do you like the apartment?" he asks, lifting his eyes to find hers.

She nods, he squeezes her ass and then closes his eyes again.

"Good," he breathes.

"Are you going to sleep?" she whispers.

He grunts then blindly reaches for a kiss. His lips still grazing hers, he replies, "Not done with you yet."

Relieved to hear their night is not yet finished, she slips one of her legs up over his hip, touching her forehead to his as she murmurs, "Are you hungry? I could make us some bacon and eggs. Or we could open the wine and eat what you brought."

"Both," he grunts.

"'Kay."

Before Jessica can move, Khalohn slides his hand further down her rear, until it's between her thighs. She sucks in a spurt of air as he teases her entrance with his fingertips, instantly aroused at his touch.

"Khalohn?" she calls softly.

"After."

It's all he says before he owns her body yet again, beckoning her fifth orgasm of the night.

KHALOHN WAKES, FULLY immersed in a daze. He squints his eyes open, the sun shining brightly through the windows beside the bed. He's on his side, and the first thing he's aware of are the bare breasts of the woman at his back. He looks down and see's Bryn's arm draped over his waist, her hand anchoring them together pressed against his abs. It's been a while since he's woken in the morning with a woman. Even longer since he didn't mind. He has no idea what time it is, only that he can't stay. It was after two a.m. before he was ready to let Bryn sleep. It's only the awareness that she's his when he wants her which makes him not regret slipping out of her grasp.

Gently, he lifts her arm from around him and climbs out of bed. He pauses when she stirs. As she settles, he starts to gather his clothing from around the apartment. Picking up his shirt from the foot of the bed, he remembers Bryn slipping into it after midnight—rolling up the sleeves before she made them scrambled eggs. The memory slows down his movements until he shakes it away. Looking down at himself, wrinkled and in need of a shower, he makes a mental note to bring a couple suits and a few bathroom necessities to prevent him leaving the apartment looking like a slob in the future.

Before he dons his shoes, he sends a text to Atzel and then returns to the door to grab the cash he brought with him for Bryn. He sets the two thousand dollars on the dining room table and then returns to the bed. Sitting on the edge, he does up his shoes and takes a moment to absorb the details of the apartment he was too distracted to notice the day before. The décor is simple. Clean. Warm. Neither feminine nor entirely masculine. He wonders if he's seeing Bryn's tastes or what she thought he might like. Either way, after last night, there's no question that it's *their* space; and if she likes it, so does he.

Khalohn turns and takes in the sleeping figure beside him. He thinks of the work he has to catch up on, having been out of town with only a few hours in the office the night before. It's not realistic to think he'll have time to come back that night, but he can't ignore his desire to prioritize a return as soon as possible. All night, she'd called his name over and over— *Khalohn*. He didn't realize how much he missed hearing his name on a woman's lips in the throes of passion until he had it again.

He wants more, and he's not too proud to admit it.

Knowing Atzel will likely arrive any minute, Khalohn reaches out and grazes his hand down Bryn's back. When he reaches her naked waist, he gives her a squeeze. She pulls in a startled breath before turning to face him.

Her eyes take in his present state before a frown tugs at her brow. She washed away her makeup when she freshened up, prior to their midnight snack. The sight of her bare face is just as alluring as it is when she's all made up.

"Hi," she mumbles, clearly still half sleep.

"Hi."

"You're dressed."

"Time for me to go. Your payment is on the table."

The slight crease between her eyebrows vanishes, her face falling at his declaration. Instantly, he understands what he's done. Never before has he mentioned payment with a woman while she's still naked. Their arrangement is business, and they both know it. But as a man determined to provide pleasure, it's impossible to ignore—whatever fantasy they'd created since he walked through the door the night before, his announcement of *payment* has shattered it.

In that moment, he vows never to ruin another morning like he feels he just has. Never again does he wish to see disappointment rob him of the cute way she looks upon first waking.

"On Monday, I'll have my accountant contact you. From here on out, I won't leave cash. The funds will be wired to you."

"Okay," she murmurs with a small nod.

He reaches out, sweeping her wild hair away from her neck before leaning over her. He presses a soft kiss just behind her ear and then whispers, "Bryn?"

"Hmm?" she hums.

"I like the apartment."

As soon as the words escape his mouth, he darts out his tongue, tasting her skin before delivering a final kiss. He feels her shiver, and this is all the sign he needs to know his unspoken apology has been accepted.

Without another word, he takes his leave.

Chapter Twenty-Five

WHEN JESSICA WAKES ON Sunday morning, it's the cold sheets beside her she notices first. Glancing out the windows, she notes how bright the sun is, cluing her into the fact that she's slept through dawn. On a deep inhale, she lifts her head, turning her face the opposite direction. With her cheek resting on her pillow, she looks into the apartment and listens for movement. She hears and sees no sign of Khalohn, causing a slight frown of confusion to tug at her brow.

It's been more than a week since Khalohn returned home from his business trip and they began their clandestine affair in unit 601. While he doesn't call on her every night, it's safe to say they've fallen into a routine of sorts. They've met five times since that first night. As promised, he gives her at least an hour's notice—but it's usually more. If he arranges for them to meet on a weeknight, he'll stay until around midnight before he heads home. Wherever that is. She convinces herself she doesn't mind. It's the nature of their relationship. Anyway, he tends to leave her sated and exhausted, and she has no trouble slipping into slumber shortly after he locks the door behind him. Still, she can't deny she prefers their weekend rendezvous.

She likes falling asleep with his warmth at her back, his heavy arm draped around her and their legs tangled beneath the sheets. Even more, she likes to wake to the smell of coffee, or the sound of him in the shower. It's all a fantasy, a truth she repeats to herself often, but she allows herself to enjoy it just the same.

So long as she's in Tribeca, her life is more. So long as she's in Tribeca, she can be the woman who lives in a beautiful loft; a woman who's sleeping with a handsome, wealthy, generous lover. Moreover, she can afford to sneak away two times a week for dance class at Miah's.

In the world of unit 601, she doesn't have to be the daughter who sleeps on a pull-out couch; she doesn't have to be worried about a job or how she's going to pay the bills. Because of Khalohn, because of the *fantasy*, she can spend her days sitting with her mom at the hospital, concerned only with when she'll finally get to return home.

Though now, in the quiet apartment, the sheets cold where Khalohn fell asleep, she realizes this is the first Sunday morning she's woken in unit 601. Even though Khalohn has never left without saying goodbye, she begins to question what could make Sunday different. Given the nature of their relationship, they don't spend a whole lot of time talking. When they do, it's usually about food. He's always thoughtful enough to take note of what she likes. When they need sustenance, it's merely another round of satisfaction.

Jessica hides her smile in her pillow when she thinks back to Friday night, when Khalohn had apple pie delivered at eleven o'clock. They each had a slice, and then he fucked her on the dining room table. It was marvelous. Nonetheless, the memory doesn't completely quell the disappointment of sleeping through his departure.

She pushes herself up into a seated position, holding the top sheet against her naked chest as she searches the floor for a piece of clothing. When she spots the button-up shirt Khalohn was wearing the night before, she turns her face to look across the bedroom platform to the open closet. It isn't a huge space, but his interior designer made sure it was outfitted with cubbies and drawers where Jessica stashes her lingerie and the couple outfits she keeps around, just in case. Khalohn, too, has brought three garment bags that hang there, in the event he needs something fresh to wear in the morning. She thinks back to the previous day, when Khalohn donned a fresh pair of slacks and a dress shirt before hanging his discarded clothes in the empty garment bag. When he left, he took it with him. There are two garment bags remaining—only one of them is empty, and the clothes he wore the night before are still strewn across the floor.

Hopeful wherever he is he'll be back, Jessica slips out of bed and reaches for his shirt. She pulls it over her shoulders, fastening a few buttons, all the while appreciating the scent of him, which still clings to the fabric. She then snatches up her previously discarded panties and shimmies them up her legs. On her way to the bathroom, she rolls up the cuffs of his sleeves, leaving her forearms exposed. After she handles her business, she washes her hands, tugs her hair back into a high ponytail, and then brushes her teeth. It's just after she's washed her face when she hears the front door open and close. She catches her own eyes in the mirror, and she doesn't even bother to hide her smile.

As Khalohn enters the apartment, he heads straight for the kitchen. At the sound of the bathroom door sliding open, he glances over at Bryn. Something about the sight of her in his shirt makes him stop. It's not that he's never seen it before. It's the level at which he likes seeing it—likes seeing her bare, toned legs stretching out from beneath the hem; likes knowing what's beneath the fabric is his to touch and taste. In the space they occupy, there's a familiarity he hasn't had in a long time—a comfort that gives her the boldness to don his shirt as casually as if it belonged to her.

"Hi," she greets him softly, a small smile brightening her clean face. "Morning."

Slowly crossing the room, she says, "I thought—I thought you left."

Dislodging the two piping hot coffees he picked up at the corner market from the cardboard carrier, he remembers how she slept through him waking, showering, and getting dressed. He doesn't admit to her he's pleasantly surprised to have found her awake upon his return.

He tips his chin down at the coffees and lifts a white paper sack as he informs her, "Bagels."

Her smile grows, and he doesn't deny himself the pleasure of admiring it before he takes the paper from underneath his arm and tosses it by a stool at the end of the island. He unpacks his whole wheat bagel, already filled with cream cheese, grabs his coffee, and takes a seat. He sips his beverage, vaguely aware of Bryn moving about the kitchen as he opens the *Sunday New York Times* in search of the crossword puzzle. Folding the paper back, he extracts the pen he borrowed from the doorman out of his shirt pocket, takes a bite of his bagel, and reads the first clue.

Khalohn is accustomed to working on his puzzle at home. Alone. When he woke up nearly an hour ago, he acknowledged he was exactly where he wanted to be. As he listens to Bryn doctoring her coffee, extracting her bagel, and pulling out a stool on the opposite side of the counter from him, he's still certain he's precisely where he wants to be.

His loft—*Bryn's loft*—it's vastly different than his penthouse on the Upper East Side. There's no television. No computer. No empty rooms filled with furniture that goes unused for months at a time. What he and Bryn have is just sex—just a business arrangement to which they've both consented; but it doesn't make void the intimacy of sharing a space with someone. The routine that links their lives together—however minor—is more than he's had with a woman in years. *Bryn's body* is more familiar than any woman's body he's had since he called another his wife. He likes it. He's paying for it, so he sees no reason not to indulge in it.

He's halfway through his bagel, Bryn a couple bites into hers, when she murmurs, "Is this your Sunday morning ritual? Coffee, bagel, and the crossword puzzle?"

Khalohn lifts his eyes to find hers, noting the curiosity he spies in her gaze. "The puzzle, yes."

"So, the coffee and bagel...?"

Her sentence trails off, her question implied. "Breakfast," he replies, minimizing the fact that he's never stayed for breakfast before.

Jessica nods, but he doesn't see it as he shifts his focus back onto the paper. She takes another bite of bagel, chewing it slowly as she admires him. She's never even so much as attempted to tackle *The Time's* Sunday crossword. As she watches him fill in his third answer, she decides the man across from her must be outrageously smart. It makes sense, given his success; but there are businessmen and then there are *businessmen*. She recognizes he's the latter. As illogical as it might seem, watching him in that single moment, she's sure he's not manipulative or shady. He's wise and intelligent. Even more, he's the kind of man who leaves early on Saturday morning, but takes his time on Sunday—takes his time working on a puzzle.

She draws a long sip from her coffee, a small voice in the back of her head suggesting she stay quiet and leave him be. She ignores it, her nerves alerting her what she really wants is to *talk* to him. To know him—the man across from her, sitting in the light of the morning sun—even if just a little bit.

"You work a lot, right?" she asks hesitantly. He peeks up at her, but he doesn't reply. His silence doesn't deter her, his blue eyes soft and his gaze seemingly open. "I mean, it's just a guess, but you're almost always in a suit, and you keep a pretty strict schedule. We never meet before nine, you don't stay out all night during the week, and even Saturdays you leave pretty early."

Khalohn merely nods his head, and Jessica licks her lips, contemplating her next question. It's one she's found herself wondering over and over as time slips by. "Why don't you have a girlfriend? Or a wife? I—" She cuts herself off, reconsidering all she's said and her awareness of his schedule. Suddenly, something she never considered flares to life in her mind—because there are businessmen, and then there are *businessmen*. Her eyebrows knit together in concern, she swallows and then inquires, "You don't, right? You don't have a wife?"

Amused by the cute expression tugging at the features of her face, Khalohn breathes a quiet chuckle, smirking at her as he shakes his head. "No."

He watches as Bryn's face relaxes in relief. It lasts only a moment, and then she tugs her bottom lip between her teeth, eyeing him apprehensively. He keeps his gaze trained on her, waiting for her next question. They've never talked about anything so personal before, but he doesn't mind. Something about the way she's looking at him, her eyes hesitant and yet wanting, he finds himself willing to give a little.

"What?" he prompts when she doesn't speak.

"It's just—you're really nice," she says softly. He raises an eyebrow at her, and she breathes a giggle. "Nice might not be the word I'm looking for. Generous. Kind. I don't know. What I *do* know is, you're really good looking and great in bed—I just—I don't get it."

"I could say the same of you."

At his comment, he loses her eyes. Bryn drops her chin, reaching for her coffee cup, but she doesn't lift it to her lips. "It's complicated," she admits.

Khalohn nods, but Bryn doesn't see it. Silence passes between them. Silence passes between them often, but this time feels different. This time, his own curiosity is stirred within him. For the first time since he met her, he wonders what details make up her complicated story. Rather than entertain his questions, he discards them. Whatever her story is, it brought her to him. The precious treasure he continues to unearth. After more than half a dozen times in bed, he's still nowhere near done with her.

"It's exactly the opposite for me," he says. She lifts her eyes to find his once more, and he suddenly realizes why he's spoken. Holding her gaze, what he was after all along, he confesses, "I was married once before. Didn't work out. This is less complicated."

"I'm sorry…"

"Don't be."

Reaching up to tuck a loose strand of hair behind her ear, she's bold enough to ask, "What happened?"

Ready to put an end to her questions, Khalohn directs his gaze back down at the paper and mutters, "I wasn't enough."

Jessica's mouth falls open as she gapes at Khalohn. She sucks in a breath, but she has no words on which to accompany her exhale. She can barely make sense of what he said. But it's more than that. It's the *way* he said it. The tone in which he wrapped his words. It wasn't melancholy or regretful. Worse, it was matter of fact. Like he not only knows why his marriage didn't work, but he believes it himself—that he's not enough.

It's not complicated. That's what he said, she thinks, forcing her lips closed. *I think he thinks this is safe. That I'm safe.*

Taking another bite of her breakfast, Jessica chews absentmindedly, studying Khalohn all the while. He doesn't notice, too focused on his task, but she doesn't mind. His comment is on repeat in her thoughts. As stupid and reckless as it might be, she tucks away his admission for safe keeping. She holds on to it, hoping, in some way, she can prove him wrong. It's a foolhardy and ridiculous endeavor to take on. She's his call girl. However, Jessica can't help it. The truth of the matter is, she's *more* than Bryn van Doren, and she likes Khalohn Morgan—as much of the man she knows. All he's shown her is that he's *more* than enough. The way he touches her, kisses her, *fucks* her. Unless he's a monster in disguise, she can't imagine a woman having him and then choosing to give him up.

He bought me apple pie, and I'm not even his girlfriend, she thinks, as if justifying her feelings.

Maybe it's all part of the fantasy...

Even so, she makes up her mind to indulge it to the fullest.

She finishes the rest of her bagel in silence and then gathers up both of their trash. Khalohn murmurs his thanks, not lifting his head. Having never had such a long morning with him, she's not sure how long he'll stay. Jessica doesn't want to wait too long before she heads out herself.

She doesn't like for Beth to be alone for longer than she has to be in her hospital room. With this in mind, she doesn't waste time before she puts into motion her first attempt to show Khalohn he's definitely enough.

After she discards their trash, Bryn doesn't head back to her stool. She makes her way behind him, slipping her arms around his waist as she presses her chest to his back. He feels it as she pushes herself up on her tiptoes, in order to prop her chin on his shoulder. He turns his head as she begins to speak.

"You showered. I can smell it," she whispers, her warm breath tickling his ear. "But since you're here, I thought you'd appreciate the invitation to join me anyway."

Khalohn doesn't even stop to think about it. He turns his head a little more, until his lips are grazing hers. He kisses her, barely pulling away before he replies, "Right behind you."

Her face lights up, and from his vantage point, he's sure he's never seen anything so beautiful.

WHEN JESSICA ARRIVES at the hospital, she finds Beth sleeping. After nearly two weeks hooked up to IVs pumping her with meds, and tubes that give her plenty of oxygen, she's still not in any condition to be released. By Jessica's assessment, her mother has good days and bad days; moments where her energy seems to be up, and others where it seems like it's taking everything she's got to fight off the virus. As Jessica takes her seat beside the bed, she pulls her legs into her chest, resting the heels of her feet on the edge of the chair, all the while debating with herself. She's not sure if sleep is a good sign or a bad one. While she's no doctor, she knows sleep leads to rejuvenation. However, she can't help but argue, sleep so late in the morning means Beth is far from out of the woods.

Dr. Montgomery has informed her, more than once, even someone with a healthy set of lungs could battle pneumonia for a few weeks. Given Beth's lungs are far from healthy, it's not abnormal her body is having a harder time getting to the other side of this sickness. In spite of the hopeful look in his eye or the optimistic tone in his voice, Jessica is growing impatient. Not because she's tired of spending her days in the hospital, or because she's worried about the cost of the hospital stay, but because the moment they discharge Beth will be the moment Jessica feels like she can worry a little less.

Freeing a sigh, Jessica closes her eyes and tries to relax. In the darkness, behind her lids, she pictures Khalohn. Her belly flutters in a giddy sort of excitement she *should* ignore. She doesn't. Memories from just an hour ago are hard for her to shove aside. They'd teased each other in the shower, making out until neither of them could stand it any longer. Then he'd turned her away from him, pushed her up against the wall, and took her from behind. The memory alone causes an ache between her legs, and she can feel a blush of desire crawl up her neck. She shoves the elicit thoughts aside, settling on something less intense.

For the first time ever, it was Jessica who left the apartment first. While she got dressed, he settled himself at the dining room table, where he resumed his crossword puzzle. She wanted to get to the hospital, so she told him she had someplace to be. Jessica was hesitant to leave, even after he told her he'd lock up on his way out. It felt odd, being the one to initiate goodbye. She didn't know how to leave. He's the one with the signature move—always kissing her behind the ear. It's an act that says so much without him having to say anything at all. It reminds her he isn't finished. That he still wants her.

After the conversation they shared over breakfast, she felt responsible to depart with the same message. Mustering her courage, she stood behind him, slid her hands over his shoulders and down his chest before leaning in close. She then pressed her lips against his neck—covered in a thin layer of stubble she knew he'd shave later—and whispered her farewell. Then, just as he always does, she snuck a taste, pressed another lingering kiss to his skin and left without another word.

She wore a smile on her face until she reached the lobby.

"You having sweet dreams over there?" mutters Beth, her voice mild and weak.

Jessica's eyes snap open and her spine straightens as she looks over at her mother. "What? Hi."

"Don't *hi* me," Beth teases, a small smile playing at her lips. "What's got you smilin' pretty?"

She shrugs, feigning ignorance. As much as she wants to tell her mom about the hot guy who bought her breakfast that morning, she can't. It fills her with regret. Under different circumstances, she knows her mom would love to hear it. For now, she's forced to shove aside all thoughts of Khalohn as she replies, "Just a good morning, I guess. How are you feeling?" she asks, hoping to change the subject.

Beth studies her for a second, clearly dissatisfied with her daughter's remark, but she doesn't voice her thoughts. "Sick of this bed," she answers.

"How about we go for a stroll?" Jessica doesn't even wait for Beth to agree before she's up on her feet. "I'll get your slippers and your robe."

The two of them walk around the halls of Beth's floor until she gets hungry. Her appetite comes and goes, so when she mentions she might want some food, Jessica is quick to take her back to her room so she can run down to the cafeteria and get her something to eat. They watch a movie on the Lifetime channel as Beth slowly eats a bowl of soup with crackers and Jessica munches on an apple. When a knock sounds at the door a little while later, both women smile at the sight of their visitor.

"Hey, Ms. Chapman," greets Stefano with a fresh bouquet of flowers.

"All these years, and I still can't get you to call me Beth," she teases.

Laughing, Jessica grins at her best friend as she says, "You're the only one who knows he has manners, mom."

Stefano flips her off, not hiding the gesture in the slightest, and they all laugh. That is, until Beth is interrupted by a cough. Everyone's amusement dies instantly. Beth waves away their worried expressions and then points to the withering flower arrangement Stefano brought with him the last time he was able to drop in.

"'Bout time you refreshed my stash."

"I'm sorry I haven't stopped by more often," he says, setting the fresh flowers closest to Beth.

"Nonsense. I've been trying to convince this one there's not much going on around here, and she doesn't have to spend all her free time stuck in this room."

Standing beside Jessica's chair, Stefano reaches over and gives her shoulder a squeeze as he proclaims, "Stubborn as a mule, this one."

"And you both love me for it," says Jessica in her defense.

"How you feelin', Ms. C?"

"As expected," she answers, clearly uninterested in talking about her condition. "What have you been up to this weekend? All my girl ever does is work, sleep, and dote on me. I do hope your life has got more color in it than that."

"Mom," chides Jessica.

"Can't say things are a lot different on my end," Stefano admits mercifully. "Though, I was hoping to steal this one for a little while. Early dinner?" he asks, looking down at Jessica. "I've got to work tonight. You?"

Jessica forces a smile in an effort to look natural. What she really feels is anxious at his simple question. With Beth in the hospital, she's managed to avoid talking to Stefano directly about the arrangement she has with Khalohn. While it's obviously no secret what she's doing, she hasn't been forced to discuss it. As much as she would like to keep that streak going, there's no way out of the conversation that's always been inevitable.

"On call," she murmurs honestly. "But I don't expect I'll be needed tonight."

"It's a date, then," chimes in Beth. "Get her out of here," she insists, eyeing Stefano expectantly. "She'll be sleeping in that chair tonight if she doesn't get called in. It'll make me feel better knowing she at least got a decent meal."

Jessica fights the urge to glare at her mother. Her *make me feel better* slogan is becoming a tactic she uses often. Deep down, Jessica recognizes it's just a ploy. Beth feels guilty. No matter how hard she wishes to convince her mother she's not the burden she thinks she is, Jessica is all too aware she'll never win that fight. It's not the woman or the mother Beth is. Never has been, and never will be.

"Fine. I can take a hint," mutters Jessica in jest. She stands, reaching for her purse before looping her arm around Stefano's. "I'll be back."

"I know you will."

"It was good seeing you, Ms. C," calls out Stefano as they make their way out the door.

"Thanks for the flowers," murmurs Beth sincerely. "They're beautiful."

As Jessica and Stefano walk to the elevator, they don't speak. On their ride down to the first floor, the lift car is full of other visitors, nurses, and doctors. This gives Jessica even more of an excuse to let a few more moments of silence pass before she's forced into the inevitable conversation from which there's no escape.

She and Stefano step out into the lingering heat of the early evening August air. He tilts his head to the corner and merely says, "We'll hit the Fifth Ave Diner."

Nodding, Jessica follows his lead.

"How are you holding up?" he asks, glancing at her as they walk shoulder to shoulder, maneuvering their way through the other pedestrians. "I know it's not easy, her being here for so long."

"You're right. It's not. I hate seeing her sick like this."

"I know you do." They arrive at the corner and stop at the traffic light. He reaches over and takes hold of the back of her neck, massaging her muscles as he goes on to press, "So, how *are* you holding up?"

Jessica furrows her brow, suddenly aware this is the first time she's stopped to really think about it. Life has been coming at her too quickly, too forcefully. She's simply been trying to handle it without overthinking it. Considering her answer, she doesn't think of money or her obligations; she ponders the physical existence of her mother, in the same hospital bed she's occupied for the last almost two weeks—no end date in sight. Her heart seems to swell as she draws in a breath, the ache that accompanies her exhale weighing the organ down in her chest.

Concentrating on the feel of Stefano's fingers working her neck, she tries to keep her emotions in check as she admits, "I'm scared." Saying the words out loud triggers the burning sensation behind her eyes, but she blinks to prevent herself from crying. "I remember when she first got diagnosed with COPD. I remember how terrified I was, not knowing what it would mean for her. The uncertainty of it was daunting. But we got used to it. We were handling it. Now—her in that hospital—it's my worst nightmare. The waiting. The uncertainty..."

Her voice trails off as Stefano's hand disappears. He slides it down to the small of her back and applies the necessary pressure to make her legs start moving. She sees the walking man lit up and the crowd of people crossing both ways only after they step into the street. As if the movement pulls her out of her vulnerable frame of mind, she shakes off her previous thoughts and rakes her fingers through her hair.

"I'm dealing," she declares, squaring her shoulders. "Most afternoons I'm with her. I've been dancing. Not much, but I've been to three classes in the last couple of weeks. I justify the time away from mom and the investment because I think it's helping to keep me sane. It's something for me. Something I haven't had in a long time."

"Jess, it's not selfish to spend a little time doing what you were born to do. You heard your mom. She doesn't want you to stop living."

"Yeah," she murmurs, certain he's right. Just the same, she clings to the excuse.

"And—what about your deal with Morgan?"

Jessica doesn't realize that at the sound of his name, she pulls her bottom lip between her teeth. She remembers the scent of him; the feel of his morning stubble against her lips; the way he smoothed his hands around her wet body, like he couldn't get enough of her. She's so distracted by her thoughts she doesn't hear Stefano when he calls her name. It isn't until he steps in front of her and she almost collides into his chest that she looks up at him, remembering his question. Rather than answer him, her breath gets caught in her throat at the expression she finds in his hazel eyes. She recognizes the guilt and the concern that warms his gaze as he studies her, forcing her back into reality. A reality that seems more complicated now than it was upon first waking—or the day before—or the day before that.

"Are you falling for him?" he asks bluntly.

"What?" Jessica jerks her head back in surprise. "No. I—no. I barely know him."

I wasn't enough.

She hears Khalohn's voice, and her heart rate picks up speed.

"You forget, he's got a reputation. A long standing one. There's a reason he only ever beds a woman twice. There's a reason every one of them hopes to be the exception to his rule."

"What, you think his dick is magic?" she scoffs. Even as she says the words, she knows—in a way—it definitely is. At least, his ability to use it is. Nevertheless, she shakes her head at her friend and continues, "You think sleeping with him will make me fall under some spell?"

Stefano works his jaw left to right before he says, "I think when I brought him up, your head took you someplace else. I think I'm your fucking best friend, I know you better than anyone, and this whole fucked up scenario is changing you."

"Huey," she begins with a frown. Taking a step closer, she insists, "I'm still me."

"Yeah, well, how do you explain the way your face went soft when I mentioned his name?"

She blows out a sigh, tearing her gaze away from his as she tucks a bit of hair behind her ear. "Huey, I…" Looking down at their feet, it only takes her a moment to come to grips with the fact that she can't lie to him. He's right. He knows her better than anyone. Besides, it does neither of them any good to lie. In fact, he's the *only* person in her life she's not lying to, and she can't start now. It would only prolong the conversation from which she'd rather be free.

She looks at him through her lashes and confesses, "He makes me feel good. And he's nice to me."

"You say that like you're some desperate woman who's only known dipshit men."

Coughing out a laugh, Jessica quirks an eyebrow and challenges, "Are you saying my ex's are saints? Because I'm pretty sure any guy I've screwed since high school would be accurately categorized as a *dipshit*. Especially the last one."

Speaking in a harsh whisper, Stefano reminds her, "He's *paying* you for sex."

Unappreciative of the way he's thrown it in her face, Jessica bites her tongue in an attempt to reign in her frustration. The last thing she needs is a fight with her confidant. She takes a deep breath, willing herself not to say something she'll regret.

"Stefano—I'm well aware of what I'm doing. I know how much you hate it, but it is what it is. It's done. It's happening. And you know what? I don't regret it. It's like I said. He makes me feel good. There are worse things than getting paid for the most mind-blowing orgasms I've ever had in my life." She starts to step around him but then changes her mind. Glaring up at him, she goes on to say, "And you know what? You may have heard *rumors* about him, but you've never been with him. And something *I* know that none of the women in Bea's collection know, is that he's more than a good lay. He's a man. A successful, intelligent, thoughtful man. It's— it's complicated."

Khalohn said that very morning what they have is exactly the opposite, but she's convinced it's only what he wants to believe. He said as much when he explained why his wife left him. While she doesn't imagine she can fix him—even more, she's not entirely sure he needs fixing—she's still determined to be everything he wants. She endeavors to live up to what he's paying for. Whatever Stefano believes, she *is* the exception. Whatever that means.

When the man in front of her doesn't respond but merely stares down at her, Jessica returns the favor. After a minute, he breaks. His hands tucked into his jean pockets, Stefano leans down, pressing his forehead to hers before he shakes his head.

"I need you to be careful. This can't end well. I'm worried."

Her defenses fall immediately. Pushing up on her tiptoes, Jessica wraps her arms around his shoulders, pulling him into her. He returns her embrace, and she tucks her chin into the space between his neck and shoulder. "I love you," she whispers. "Thanks for always having my back. Always." He tightens his grip around her, and a small smile helps ease the tension now rolling off her shoulders. "I'll be fine. I promise."

She doesn't know how it'll end. The thought of it ending poorly is enough for her to shove the thought aside, putting it out of her mind for whenever she's forced to deal with it.

Chapter Twenty-Six

A T SEVEN-THIRTY MONDAY morning, there are two taps at Khalohn's office door before he hears the latch give way. Khalohn looks away from his computer not at the sound of Maribelle's heels *clunking* across the carpeted floor, but at the mischievous chuckle which accompanies a second set of shoes.

"Good morning, dear," Maribelle greets, her ruby painted lips pulled tight in a forced smile. "I do hope you had your swim this morning. It'll be your only saving grace if this is your first cup of coffee." She sets his usual tray of breakfast on his desk, but Khalohn ignores the food as his gaze shifts to Porter. Unlike Maribelle, the grin he wears is far from forced.

"I don't know how she forgets I'm your best friend," he teases, pointing at the woman. She rolls her eyes as he says, "Seeing my face first thing Monday morning is a gift, not an intrusion."

Ignoring his broker, Maribelle looks Khalohn in the eye. "You've got a conference call with Oceana in a half hour," she reminds him.

He dips his head in a nod. The agenda for his call with the Italian based yacht company he intends to partner with is pulled up on his computer screen.

"You're to meet with your executive team right after."

"Thank you, Maribelle." Squelching a smirk, he offers her a subtle nod toward the door and assures her, "I require nothing further."

"All right, dear."

As she takes her leave, she offers what Khalohn is sure is a glare to Porter. He doesn't have to see the expression to know it doesn't faze the man in the slightest. Khalohn watches Porter wink at his secretary, his grin growing wider as she hurries from the room.

"She's barely had a chance to check her messages, and already you've irritated her," mutters Khalohn, reaching for the nob on top of his French press. Porter makes his way to the window, gazing out at the view while Khalohn pushes down the coffee grounds.

"Oceana?" he inquires, completely brushing off any mention of Maribelle. "Khalohn Morgan is going to have yachts sailing from Tokyo by year's end. Dibs on the first one ready to set sail."

"What are you doing here, Porter?"

He turns away from the window, shoving one hand into his pant pocket, using the other to smooth his already clipped down tie. "Thought I should check on you. Tried to reach you yesterday morning. I was going to convince you to let me take the Monte Carlo for a spin, but you never picked up."

"This is about the Monte Carlo?" Khalohn pours a serving of coffee, ready for their conversation to be over.

"This is about *you* not answering my calls. You always take my calls." He pauses, as if reconsidering. "Strike that. You can be a pain in the ass to reach during the week, but never the weekend."

"I was busy. Kind of like I am now. Sorry to ruin whatever grand plans you had for my yacht."

"Busy? On Sunday morning?"

Khalohn doesn't bother with a response. He reaches for his bagel, glancing at his friend before taking a bite. Porter merely studies him, his eyes narrowing the longer he stares.

"You know what?" He shakes his finger, as if he's on to something. "Only one reason a man like you doesn't answer his phone on a Sunday morning."

"Yeah. Because I'm busy," mutters Khalohn.

"Yeah, with pussy."

Again, Khalohn doesn't bother with a response. He takes another bite of his breakfast, the taste of the whole wheat bagel taking him back to the morning before. He remembers the feel of Bryn at his back, her arms wrapped around him, her lips near his ear, inviting him for a shower.

"Shit. I'm right, aren't I?"

Before Khalohn has a chance to answer, the phone on his desk sounds. He doesn't hesitate to pick up the call.

"Lorelai would like a word. I presume you wouldn't mind the interruption," says Maribelle.

"Not at all."

They both disconnect without further prompting, and Lorelai comes strutting into the office not a second later. Porter's attention shifts toward the woman, instantly distracted as his eyes scan her from head to toe. The dress she has on makes it impossible not to see every curve of her lithe body. Khalohn is grateful for the determined look in her eye that makes her all but overlook his incorrigible broker.

"Morning, sir," she says, coming to a stop in front of his desk.

"*Sir?*" Porter murmurs incredulously. "You've trained this one well."

Lorelai turns to glance at Porter, but Khalohn is quick to demand, "Ignore him. What is it?"

"Had a message in my inbox this morning. Charlie Winslow and his lawyer are willing to move forward with negotiations, but we have to move fast. Pier House is on life support, but there's enough red tape preventing his sister from getting her hands on it."

"Okay," he replies, lifting his eyebrows expectantly. He doesn't ask why this has brought her to his door. He doesn't need to, and they both know it.

Lorelai blows out a sigh and then admits, "I need to pull you in. I think the safest way to play this is casual. Another dinner. In the next couple days, if you can manage it."

Khalohn leans back in his chair, mourning the dropping temperature of his coffee as he deals with the first interruptions of his day. He jerks his chin in acknowledgement and then instructs, "Speak with Maribelle. She'll set the time and place."

"Thank you, Mr. Morgan," she says, sounding relieved.

"Lorelai," Khalohn stops her before she's out of sight. "Be prepared to ride along with me to that dinner. I'll want up to speed along the way."

"Certainly."

When she's gone, Khalohn shifts his attention across the room to Porter. He grins, pointing after Lorelai as he inquires, "Is it her?"

Khalohn fights the urge to roll his eyes. "I'm busy," he replies. "Just like I was yesterday morning. Now, if you'll excuse me, I've got a meeting to prepare for. Don't you have something to do this morning?"

"Money never sleeps, my friend," he replies with a shrug. He starts to take his leave, turning to walk out the door backwards as he warns, "I've got my eye on you, boss man. I'll call you later. Drinks this week. Unless you're too...*busy*."

He waggles his eyebrows and then he's gone.

THE FIRST THING Jessica does when she steps out of the studio Wednesday afternoon is check her phone. With her heart and mind wide open, the way it always is after a couple hours working her body on the dance floor, she doesn't even try to ward off her disappointment when she doesn't find a message from Khalohn. She hasn't seen him since Sunday. Since he'd wired ten grand into her bank account over the course of the previous week, it isn't money she's worried about. While her mother's hospital bills are mounting by the day, they won't come due until her stay is over. Dropping her phone back inside her purse, Jessica allows herself to embrace what her disappointment really means.

I miss him.

Summer heat still hanging on to the tail end of August, Jessica barely thinks twice about walking the short distance to the Broadway apartment. Her skin, slick and sticky from class, is begging her for a shower. By the time she reaches the lobby of the building, there's a new trail of sweat tracing a line from the base of her neck down to the small of her back. She hurries to the elevator and watches as the numbers climb while she rides to the top floor. When she lets herself into 601, she remembers the last time she let herself *out* of the loft, and her belly twists in longing. Again, she doesn't deny herself the feeling. She hopes she'll have a reason to spend the night in a bed tonight.

Much to Beth's annoyance, Jessica has refused to spend the previous few nights at home. She doesn't like sleeping on the pull-out so long as her mother is confined to the hospital. Even still, when she woke up that morning, she knew if she didn't get out of the room for a while, Beth might use what little strength she's got to throttle her. Not wanting to miss a dance class anyway, she left with no argument.

After a shower and another glance at her phone, Jessica wonders if she'll have no choice but to spend the night at home—if for no other reason than to pretend she's got an employer who makes her work every once in a while. Even though she has permission to sleep in the very space she occupies, to stay for the night without even a single touch from Khalohn would only make her miss him more.

She's just getting ready to leave the apartment when her phone sounds with an alert. She's quick to check her message, and she sighs when she spots it's only a text from Kierra. Raking her fingers through her damp hair, she opens it and finds an invitation.

Loca! Tonight – 7pm. You're coming. You're dancing.

All at once, Jessica's disappointment is dulled at the prospect of spending her evening at one of the hottest clubs in Hell's Kitchen. A night at Loca always includes amazing Tex Mex, strong margaritas, and men tossing her around the dance floor with their salsa-swaying hips.

Well, the brave ones, at least.

Before she has a chance to type out her reply, another message comes through.

Missed you Sunday at Miah's. It'll be a group of us tonight. You won't regret it...

The five o'clock hour is drawing near, and Jessica can't think of a reason to say no. Khalohn hasn't called on her yet, Beth has been begging her to do something besides work and sleep at the hospital, and with two hours before the group gets together, she has time to drop dinner off for her mom before heading home to change into club attire. Her feet carrying her to the door, she gives in and constructs her reply.

I'll be there.

Lorelai and Khalohn arrive at the steak restaurant, on the edge of Hell's Kitchen, five minutes before eight. As Khalohn steps out of the Maybach, fastening his suit jacket closed, he reminds his associate, "I'm the closer, not the dealer."

"Yes, sir."

She smooths her hands down the front of her skirt, the only sign of her nerves, and then they make their way into the establishment. They're seated at their reserved table a few minutes before Charles Winslow and his lawyer arrive. As he stands to greet them, Khalohn takes note of the Winslow heir. He's a tall, lean man, tucked into a suit Khalohn knows is tailored. His dirty blond hair is in need of a trim, and the pale green eyes which meet his are dull, no doubt from countless restless nights. His lawyer, Barry Shephard, is an older man—soft around the middle, hair graying at his temples, the rest of his thinning mane combed over to one side. Khalohn's been in business long enough to know, if it were up to him, the deal would be closed before second-round drinks. As things stand, he takes his seat with the rest of the table and looks to Lorelai to get the meal started.

Lorelai skips over idle chitchat in favor of rehashing the state of Pier House Resorts. The truth hurts, and Charles proves this to be true when he takes a big gulp of his drink upon its arrival. Soon after their dinner orders are taken, Lorelai outlines the deal she's been working on for weeks. There's no question, if Khalohn Morgan steps in, it'll take over full ownership; but she leaves the option open for a single Winslow to have a spot on the board. Charles and Barry attempt to negotiate. As Khalohn instructed her on the way over, Lorelai doesn't budge. Khalohn's halfway through his steak when he cuts in, eliminating any and all nonsense.

"This offer expires in twenty-four hours. After that, I suppose your best option is to see how you fair with your sister at the helm. Sounds like you've got a battle on your hands if she makes it through that red tape."

"No shit," grumbles Charles. He glances at his lawyer and then takes another swig of his second scotch. Setting down the glass, he looks between Lorelai and Khalohn and announces, "Send the paperwork tonight. Barry and his guys will go over it first thing in the morning."

"I will," Lorelai agrees with a nod.

It's nearing ten when Khalohn settles the bill. As he signs the check, he thinks back over the last couple of nights. This week is shaping up to be all work and no play. He regrets this fact more than he has in a long time. It's within the terms of their agreement that he can call Bryn right then and arrange for them to meet at eleven, but he can't bring himself to entertain the thought for long. She won't be at the apartment without him. She rarely is. Furthermore, there's something about her—something about what they have. As transactional as the relationship may be, she's more than a woman he can call upon at Clandestine's. He respects her too much to call her at ten o'clock on a Wednesday night. He doesn't know much about her, but whatever she's doing with her evening, he doesn't feel inclined to interrupt.

Charles and Barry leave after a round of handshakes while Lorelai and Khalohn terry at the table a moment longer. Khalohn finishes the last bit of his drink, and Lorelai takes out her phone to send the necessary paperwork to Barry Shephard, as Charles Winslow instructed. When they finally make their exit, Lorelai breathes a happy sigh and turns her smile on Khalohn.

"Thank you. For tonight. For giving me this chance. For pushing me."

"Won't be the last time," he assures her.

He's on the verge of offering her a lift home when his phone sounds from within his jacket pocket. He doesn't hide his frown as he pulls the device out to take a look at the screen. At the sight of her name, his frown clears as he glances at Lorelai.

"I have to take this."

"Of course. Don't let me keep you. I'm going to grab a cab. See you tomorrow, Mr. Morgan."

He lifts his fingers and flicks a half-hearted wave, his attention completely captivated before his thumb makes it across the screen to pick up the call.

AFTER FOUR MARGARITAS and more than an hour on the dance floor, Jessica can't stop thinking about him. It doesn't matter how much fun she's having, or how breathless a single partner can make her after yet another salsa dance, there's only one man's hands she wants. Even more, there's only one kind of dance that can satisfy her craving, and it's enjoyed best fully naked and horizontal.

When the clock strikes ten, the energy in the club goes up, but Jessica steps away from her group, insisting she needs some air. She makes her way through the crowd, climbing from the ground level to the rooftop bar. Even though it's still warm out, the breeze against her damp skin feels good. In spite of the fresh city-night air, her alcohol induced bravery doesn't lose a bit of its bravado—which is why she doesn't hesitate to extract her phone from her clutch. She dials him without second guessing herself, holding her breath until he answers.

"Hello?"

The sound of his voice is like taking a hit. Her heart beats faster and she presses her thighs together, embracing the high he evokes simply by saying *hello*.

"You haven't called," she murmurs.

"I've been busy."

"Right." She seals her eyes closed tight, shaking her head once. The last thing she wants is to sound *needy*, even if that's exactly how she feels. "You—you don't have to explain. You don't owe me anything. I just…"

"You just what?" he inquires, his tone soft and low.

With her eyes still closed, his timbre a reminder of all the power and confidence he exudes—power and confidence she finds incredibly sexy—she can't hold back any longer.

"I want you," she breathes. Her cheeks grow warm at her admission, but she's drunk enough to keep going. "I know this is backwards. You beckon me, not the other way around—but I don't care. I want a freebie. Am I—am I allowed to ask for that?"

Standing out on the curb of a restaurant no more than five city blocks away, Khalohn glances down at his shoes as he allows her request to wash over him. A satisfied smirk curls the corner of his mouth at the same time that his dick pulses with a rush of blood. He's not fully aware, too distracted by desire to contemplate it, but it turns him on knowing at the same time, in the same city, he wanted her, and she wanted him.

"I'm on my way."

He hangs up before she can say another word, but she doesn't care.

Neither does Jessica take her time before making her way to the street in order to hail a taxi. As soon as she snags one, she rattles off her destination and shoots a text to Kierra, letting her know she had to run, with a promise to explain later. There's a tiny, coherent voice in the back of Jessica's mind that warns her, when she isn't in a margarita and lust-filled haze, she won't know how to explain Khalohn—but she's too elated to think about that right now.

She called.

He answered.

And he's on his way.

KHALOHN ENTERS THE apartment, pausing just beyond the door when he realizes he's alone. He lays his keys on the entryway table and shrugs out of his suit jacket, blindly hanging it on the coat rack, which becomes more and more familiar as the days pass. Slowly, he strolls into the open floor plan, guided by city lights casting shadows throughout the room. His hands in his pockets, he makes his way to one of the windows, staring out at the street below, wondering if he'll spot Bryn as she arrives. His thoughts wander, his gaze drifting as he remembers the sound of her voice slipping into his ear.

I want you.

He remembers over and over again, his hardening length trying the seam of his pants as he waits. He's unaware of how many minutes pass, only that he grows a little more impatient with each one. He wants her, too—in ways he hasn't wanted another in as long as he can remember. While he waits, he doesn't think about the dinner he just left. He doesn't think of his schedule the next morning—all he thinks about is *her*.

As Khalohn stands alone in the apartment, Jessica deep breathes on her trip up the elevator. Her cab ride over did little to sober her mind. Whether it's tequila tainting her bloodstream or her lust for the man capable of making her lose herself completely, she's not sure. Either way, when the lift car chimes, announcing her arrival, she licks her lips, straightens her spine, and takes herself to the door of 601.

She tries the nob, and her belly flips in excitement when she finds it unlocked. She slips through the door, unable to hide her smile when she turns to lock them inside. Biting her lip, she tries to control her desire as she becomes aware of the extent of their role reversal.

Tonight—I'm not his. He's mine.

Jessica doesn't turn on any lights as she struts out of the narrow entryway and into the main room. Khalohn is standing where she stood the first night he came to her in their space. He doesn't move as she closes the distance between them, dropping her clutch on the kitchen island as she passes. She can't take her eyes off of him. His tie is undone, draped around his neck and down each side of his chest. He's unfastened his collar, and his sleeves are rolled up his forearms.

Jessica doesn't notice how her breath has increased in speed.

Him, standing there, waiting for her, making her chest ache and her core pulse with need—it must be how he feels when he walks in to find her waiting for him. Breathless as she may be, she also feels powerful. Powerful and confident. Confident enough to act without second guessing herself.

Tonight—I'm not his. He's mine.

In the dim light crawling through the window, Khalohn can see the dress Bryn is wearing is white. Her shoulders are bare, the sleeves of the garment pushed down around her upper arms. It molds her perky breasts, clinging to her small waist before it loosens up and dances around her hips and upper thighs. She makes her way toward him slowly. Intentionally. His eyes devour her in the same manner.

He admires her legs, his penis growing harder when his eyes make it down to the strappy, black sandal heels wrapped around her feet. Neither of them speaks a word, as if all that needed to be said was muttered through the airwaves before either of them stepped foot into the apartment. When she's within reaching distance, Khalohn stretches out his arm, taking hold of her waist in order to pull her closer. She follows his lead only until her heaving chest is pressed against his.

Taking him by surprise, she shoves his hand away from her with her left hand, pressing her right fingertips against his lips. Tracing his mouth delicately, she stares into his eyes and shakes her head. He doesn't get her meaning until she starts to drag her hand down over his bearded chin, along his neck, grazing his chest, until she's reached the belt at his hips.

His breaths are harder to come by at the feel of her unfastening his buckle. She doesn't take her eyes off his as she slides the accessory off entirely, dropping it onto the floor. When she unbuttons his pants, he leans down to kiss her, but she jerks her head back and forces his zipper out of her way. A low growl tickles the base of his throat, but he doesn't fight her as she yanks the hem of his button-up out of his pants. Her hands fist the fabric, as if she's fighting for control, and he can't take his eyes off of her.

Bryn pulls her bottom lip between her teeth and makes quick work of the buttons on his shirt. He helps her rid his body of the fabric only after she forces it over his shoulders. As the garment hits the floor, she flattens her palms against his chest, feeling her way over his pecs, across his abs, down his hips, until she slips a hand beneath the waistband of his boxer briefs and wraps her fingers around his long length. Khalohn clenches his jaw closed tight and reaches for Bryn's hips. When she lets him go only to push his hands off of her a second time, his nostrils flare, the side of his mouth lifts, and he coughs out a clipped laugh that dissolves into a grunt.

Jessica is so wet, aroused by the gorgeous man in front of her just as much as she is by the upper hand she's got—the dominance she's taking. When Khalohn doesn't fight her, it makes her impatient, but she tries to take her time. She wants to savor this moment. Leaning toward him, she licks his chest, starting just below his collar bone and working her way up his neck, until she meets his beard. She can feel him practically *vibrating*, his lack of control driving him crazy and turning her on even more. She licks and kisses his neck, sliding her hands around his waist before submerging them into his briefs and over the bare skin of his ass. He jerks his hips, pressing his erection against her lower belly, and they both moan together.

Her soaked panties make it impossible for her to hold back a second longer. Jessica drops to her knees, shoving Khalohn's clothes out of her way as she descends. His shaft springs free, jutting straight at her, and her mouth waters at the sight. She's wanted to take him in her mouth since their first night in 601, but he's always denied her. Now she wonders if she'll come at her first taste.

Bryn wraps her mouth around the tip of his painfully hard length, and Khalohn clenches his fingers into fists. She feels so good, he can hardly stand it. She sucks, swirling her tongue around him greedily, and it takes everything in him not to thrust himself further into her mouth. As if she can read his mind, she slowly swallows more of him, humming as she does so. Her eyes are closed, her hands pressed against the front of his thighs, as if she's savoring him. After a couple strokes, she starts to set a steady rhythm. When she lifts her hands, wrapping both around the base of his length, working him in tandem with her mouth, he knows he'll come before he's ready if he doesn't stop her soon.

He buries his fingers in her hair with every intention of pulling her away. Then she hollows out her cheeks, and his hands only end up helping to guide her back and forth along his erection.

"Fuck, precious," he mutters, willing himself to reign in his desire.

She moans in response, and he can't take it anymore.

Khalohn yanks on her hair, forcing Jessica off of him. She pants, her eyes flying open as her gaze goes straight for his dick. She wants more, but before she can take what she wants, he shoves his hands underneath her arms and brings her to her feet. She blinks, and suddenly her dress is being pulled over her head. Then his hands are at her hips, gripping her so tightly she wonders if he'll leave bruises. She doesn't dwell on it long as he lifts her from her feet. Just as her body reacts, her legs and arms stretching out to encircle him, her back is pushed up against one of the smooth, wooden beams in the room. A second later, Khalohn is shoving aside her panties.

He buries his face in her neck, growling deep as he sweeps his fingers along her seam, drenched in her arousal.

"Precious," he whispers before slamming his hard length inside of her.

"*Khal*," she mewls, her legs tensing around his hips.

He rams into her twice, and that's all it takes. Her back arched, her hands reaching for the beam above her head, she holds on tight as her orgasm barrels through her, setting her whole body on fire.

"That's it, baby," he mutters, his lips grazing the skin just beneath her ear.

He rides her through her climax, his thrusts coming faster as he races to find his. When it hits him, it crashes over him like a wave, euphoria sweeping through him from his head down to his toes. He buries himself deep once, then twice, going as far as he can go, fusing their bodies together as he spills his seed inside of her.

When he's finished, he lifts his head in search of one thing. Closing his mouth around hers, he plunges his tongue between her lips, groaning when she drops her arms and submerges her fingers into his hair. She kisses him back hungrily and without restraint, and Khalohn can already feel his semi-hard length—still inside of her—gearing up for another round.

"You had your turn, precious," he pants against her mouth. Slipping out of her, he reaches down to grab her ass and keeps hold of her as he steps away from the beam. "Now it's mine."

"'Kay," she whispers.

WHEN JESSICA SUCCUMBS to the unrelenting pull of sleep, she's cognizant of only one thing—the warm, hard man at her back, his arm draped heavily around her middle, his thigh wedged between hers. She doesn't know what time it is, and she doesn't care.

She called.

He answered.

And the hours that followed were better than she could have ever imagined.

Three hours later, when Khalohn's phone pulls him from what little slumber he was able to find, she barely stirs. He reaches behind him, silencing the device, regretful of only one thing—that he has to leave. He sends a message to Atzel and then tosses aside his phone with a sigh. Gazing down at the sleeping beauty curled into his side, Khalohn doesn't know what to make of her. He's known for a while she's valuable; that she's a treasure he's wanted to unearth. It's indisputable how precious a find she really is—but she does things to him he can't comprehend.

Upon first learning of her, he had a mission: to ruin her for all others. After her call last night, beckoning him to her, he's certain his mission has been accomplished. She's his. But the pull that has him lingering in bed, the pull that made him stay all night and break his usual routine, it says it all.

She has ruined him, too.

Reluctantly, Khalohn climbs out of bed, carefully tucking the sheets around Bryn's body before he starts to collect his clothing. He doesn't bother showering or donning a new suit. Exhausted as he is, he has every intention of heading home for a swim. He needs to get his head on straight in order to find the focus he'll need to get through his day. He's fully dressed by the time his phone alerts him to a new message, and he knows this means his driver is waiting.

Jessica feels it when he sweeps a bit of hair behind her ear before pressing a kiss against her temple. He lingers for a moment, and she forces her heavy eyes open. She only manages to crack her lids a sliver when he turns to walk away from her. Dawn's early light illuminates his retreating figure. Before she surrenders to her body's demand for more sleep, she grants her heart its desire—to catch whatever glimpse of him she can before he's gone.

Chapter Twenty-Seven

Sunday morning, Jessica wakes at the sound of a low voice. She frowns in confusion, slowly blinking her eyes open, wondering if she's in a dream. Her gaze sees hardly beyond the white plane of sheets on the bed in which she's resting. At the sound of the door opening and closing, she gasps softly, clutching the comforter around her nakedness as she freezes and listens. When she hears movement in the kitchen, plates being pulled from the shelf and laid on the counter, she pushes herself up to a seated position, still careful to keep herself covered. She reaches up with her free hand and rakes her fingers through her messy hair, tossing it down her back.

Hearing no other voices, she searches the floor and finds the black nightie she had on last night. She slips it over her head and shimmies her way into her lacy thong before tiptoeing her way off the platform in search of Khalohn. She stops short when she sees him behind the kitchen island, wearing no more than the fitted pair of jeans he had on when he arrived the previous evening.

I love the man in a suit, she thinks to herself as she allows her eyes to drink him in. *But those legs in a pair of jeans…*

Her nipples tighten as she admires the hard lines of his defined chest, the way his muscles jump and ripple in his arms at the slightest movement, and his thick hair, disheveled and out of place at the command of her very own hands.

"Hungry?"

Jessica is startled out of her stupor at the sound of his voice. She blinks, and when her eyes open once more, she notices the breakfast he's obviously had delivered. A bowl of mixed fruit, a container of piping hot omelets, and two whole wheat bagels. As she nods, she begins to make her way toward him, hiding her smile. A warm feeling pools in the bottom of her belly, easing her hunger as she thinks of the man who has seen to eradicating it. There's food in the fridge. There always is. Even if she doesn't see to filling it, he makes sure it's taken care of. But just like the previous Sunday they shared together, he makes sure she doesn't have to lift a finger for breakfast.

By the time she's reached the kitchen, he's filled both of their plates. She sidles up next to him, wrapping her arms around his middle and tipping her head back expectantly. He doesn't disappoint her. Far from it. He wraps an arm around her shoulders and buries one of his hands in her hair as he leans down for a kiss. It's doesn't last long, but it's sweet and wet enough to satisfy her before he pulls away.

"Smells good," she says softly, leaning into him a little more.

His only response is to press his lips against her forehead before taking his plate and heading for a bar stool. Taking her own plate, she watches him as he opens his paper, folding it to the crossword puzzle. Her smile returns. She likes this. The familiarity of what is obviously becoming their routine.

Sitting on the bar stool across from him, she dives into her eggs and then asks, "Do you cook?"

A sly smile plays at his lips, but he doesn't look up at her as he answers, "I can preheat an oven and operate a microwave."

This makes Jessica grin. "Your mom never tried to teach you?"

His smile falls and his blue eyes shift to find hers. "No," he answers matter-of-factly. "She didn't stick around long enough."

"Oh," she breathes in response.

I should really stop asking about the women in his life, she muses with a heavy heart. *Or, I guess, the women who* left *his life.*

Wanting to know more but not wishing to pry, she steers clear of any further questions about his mother and carefully inquires, "What about your dad?"

Khalohn stares at Bryn for a long moment, not entirely sure why he feels compelled to answer her, but unable to combat the desire. Whatever it is about their quiet Sunday mornings together, he doesn't want to be the ass who tarnishes its sacredness.

"Remarried when I was seven. Had another son when I was eight. Prodigy. By the time I would have been old enough to be trusted in the kitchen, they were spending all their free time out in the snow."

Bryn takes a bite of her bagel, chewing slowly, her brown eyes staring at him, silently asking for more. He doesn't give it, content to see her curiosity reflected at him. Her big eyes, void of any makeup, a little swollen from sleep, and alight with interest makes her even prettier than usual.

Finally, swallowing her bite, she asks, "The...snow?"

"Blair is an Olympic snowboarder. He's been competing with the biggest names in the sport since he was fourteen."

He watches as her eyes widen at his admission, and he waits for it. Waits for the truth about his brother and his celebrity status to sweep her away. He doesn't speak of his brother often, out of habit more than anything else. They've never been particularly close; yet, while his relationship with their father has been strained for nearly three decades, he respects Blair. Admires him, even. When people get star struck at the mention of him, he doesn't blame them. That's why Bryn's response takes him by surprise.

"Wow. A son ranking among the elite on Wall Street, and another an Olympic athlete. Your dad must be incredibly proud."

Taken aback, Khalohn searches her expression for a hint of amusement. It doesn't take long for him to acknowledge she's completely serious. In Bryn's eyes, his brother is no better than he is.

"Yeah," he manages to speak before returning his attention to his breakfast.

Jessica hears so much in that one syllable. It's obvious he doesn't agree. Or perhaps what she's said isn't the truth. She thinks back to what he said earlier, about his father spending all his free time in the snow, and she wonders what that really means. Not for his father or his brother, but for him—for Khalohn. She watches as the man across from her takes a bite of his omelet, all the while trying to piece together the parts of him he's given. She doesn't have long to ponder anything before she hears her phone.

Glancing behind her, she tries to remember where she put it. Spotting her purse in one of the chairs tucked beneath the dining room table, she slips from her seat and hurries to see who it is. It's unusual for her to answer a call when she's with Khalohn. Then again, it's just as unusual for anyone to call her in the hours they spend together. When she sees it's the hospital trying to reach her, her stomach drops. Immediately, she swipes her thumb across the screen, lifting the device to her ear with both hands.

"Hello?" she asks, unable to hide the anxiety from her voice.

"Hi, is this Jessica Chapman?"

"Yes, yes. What's wrong?"

"Dr. Montgomery wanted me to reach you. Beth is having difficulty breathing this morning. We've increased her oxygen, and she's stable, but—"

"I'm on my way."

She hangs up, unable to hear another word. Tossing her phone aside, she forgets about her breakfast and doesn't feel Khalohn's eyes staring at her back as she digs through her purse for the change of clothes she packed. Without sparing a glance over her shoulder, she rushes to the bathroom to freshen up as quickly as possible. Fear courses through her body, her adrenaline spiking, causing her hands to tremble.

"*Oh, my god, mama,*" she whimpers as she splashes cool water onto her face.

It doesn't matter that the nurse who phoned her made sure to inform her Beth is stable. Such assurances mean nothing given the situation is serious enough to phone her *at all.* After nearly three weeks in the hospital, news of her mother's condition deteriorating rather than improving makes her sick to her stomach.

Jessica grabs hold of either side of the sink, forcing in deep, calming breaths. Calm seems like a state of being she won't be able to manage closed in a bathroom that seems to be shrinking by the second, so she keeps moving. She tosses her hair into a messy bun on top of her head, ripping off her nightie in exchange for the sports bra, tank top, leggings, and tennis shoes she grabbed. When she packed the clothes, when there was no news from the hospital, and her mother still had enough energy to argue with Jessica about sitting at her bedside too much, Jessica thought she might squeeze in a dance class that afternoon. Now, regardless of what her outfit might imply, dance is so far outside the realm of possibility.

Beth is having difficulty breathing this morning.

She swallows the knot in her throat, shoving aside the bathroom door and returning to her purse. This time, as she grabs her phone, she notices Khalohn staring.

"I'm sorry," she whispers, making her way toward him. "I have to—I have to go. I'm sorry."

"Okay," he says simply, his eyebrows knit together in confusion.

Her mind still racing, she doesn't think about kissing him goodbye, she just does it. The moment her lips are smashed against his, a spark of calm flickers in her chest. Needing that feeling like she needs air to breathe, she doesn't pull away. Lifting one of her hands, she molds it around his bearded cheek, opening her mouth just a little. He does the same, teasing her with the tip of his tongue before she pulls away. She touches her forehead to his, closing her eyes as she draws in a deep breath. She inhales his scent, clinging to a comfort she can't explain.

Afraid she can't afford to waste another second, she whispers, "I have to go," and then she's gone.

THE NEXT MORNING, as Khalohn folds himself into the backseat of the Maybach, Atzel closing him in, he's still thinking about that kiss goodbye. All the way to the Financial District, he stares out of the window, wondering what it was that made Bryn kiss him like that. Like she needed it. Like she knows something he's only just begun to question—that what they have is far greater than what it seems.

Upon arriving at his office building, he wishes Atzel a good day, fastening his suit jacket closed as he walks to the front entrance. The lobby is quiet, as it usually is at such an early hour, and his elevator ride into the sky is a solitary one. By the time he's granted himself entrance into his company's suite, he's made up his mind. He wants to see her again. Their Sunday morning was cut short. More importantly, when he has her in his arms again, it'll be all the assurance he needs to know that whatever it is that called her away in such a hurry is all right.

I won't ask after the details, he thinks to himself, shrugging his way out of his jacket as he crosses into his office. *It's not my business unless she makes it my business.*

He pauses as he hangs his jacket, suddenly wholly aware she's never asked him for anything.

Except once...

The only thing she's ever wanted from him is *him*.

He doesn't know what to make of this realization, and he chooses not to dwell on it. The matter at hand is simply that he wants to see her. He can make that happen, and so he will. Whatever she decides to share with him is up to her, but her presence will be enough for him.

He goes about his usual Monday morning routine, letting the day begin and allowing his office to fill before he sends his message. He's in between meetings when he pulls out his phone and shoots off his text.

Tonight. 8:00.

He enters a conference room, the table already occupied by the participants of his next obligatory hour. He barely has his seat in a chair when he gets a response. Casually, he glances down at his phone and opens the message.

I can't. I'm sorry.

Khalohn's brow furrows. She's never denied him. It's not the way their arrangement works. With no choice but to let the matter lie, he blacks out his screen and turns his attention to the people in front of him. A little more than an hour later, when the meeting comes to a close, he's immediately pulled aside by one of his analysts. That conversation is interrupted by a phone call he can't refuse. Before he knows it, Maribelle is announcing her lunch break.

The instant he has a chance to think on it, the irritation he feels at Bryn's refusal creates a dull burn in the center of his chest. His annoyance at the sensation of being out of control is compounded by the way his day continues to bombard him. Before he can manage to get through one thing, another arises. Now that he has a second to himself, rather than dissect and stew over what he's feeling and why, he charges straight ahead.

Khalohn stands in front of the window in his office, staring out at the Brooklyn Bridge as the line rings. The longer he waits, the further his mind retreats, until he doesn't see the bridge at all. Finally, at the sound of her voice in his ear, his clarity returns.

"Hello?"

"Bryn, do you have a moment?"

He hears her soft sigh before she replies, "Not really. Khalohn, I'm sorry. I can't do this right now."

"When then?"

"I don't—I don't know."

He shoves his freehand into his pocket, balling his fingers into a fist as he tries to make sense of his frustration. If he's honest with himself, he'd acknowledge what he wants more than sex are answers—answers to questions he won't ask. Questions which would shift the dynamic of their relationship into something more. But he isn't honest with himself. Neither is he patient. He decides to use his power in order to get what he wants. It's a business tactic he's used before, and he isn't afraid to use it now.

"Your refusal is not part of our agreement. Meet me at eight, or I'll be forced to reconsider our deal. The choice is yours."

He hangs up, and Jessica sucks in a startled breath. She yanks her phone away from her ear, staring down at the screen, in need of confirmation that he's really gone. She tightens her grip around the phone and seals her eyes closed, in an attempt to keep her emotions in check. For more than twenty-four hours, she's been on edge. Khalohn's threat has her teetering. On her next inhale, her breath sputters into her chest. Pressing her head against the wall beside her mother's hospital room door, she tries to calm down enough to gather her thoughts. As much as Jessica can't imagine leaving her mother's side for any length of time, she can't see a way around it.

If I stay, what then? she asks, reasoning with herself. *Khalohn ends it, the money stops, and then what?*

"Shit, shit, shit," she hisses, her fear and worry billowing up inside of her. She can feel the prickling sensation of tears behind her eyes as the possibility of the unthinkable crosses her mind. She can't put it into words, but there's a cold, dark, rational part of her mind emitting an ugly cloud of truth. If Beth doesn't pull through, Jessica won't have to worry about paying for what now feels like a never-ending hospital stay.

No, I have to go, she demands of herself. *I have to go because I have to hope—I have to believe I need this, for mom. How can you possibly ask her to hold on and keep fighting if you won't?*

She hates the position in which she finds herself. Even more, she's angry with Khalohn for forcing her hand. Though, just as soon as she admits it, she lifts her head and thumps it against the wall. Defeat deflates her anger as she acknowledges he can't possibly know what she's dealing with because she's never told him. He doesn't know Jessica's struggles because he doesn't know *Jessica*—he knows *Bryn*, and Bryn is no one.

Bryn comes when beckoned because she is no one. She has no one. She's a fantasy.

A single tear breaks free of her closed eyes, and she scrunches her face in irritation. Righting herself, she steps away from the wall and quickly sweeps away the drop of helplessness racing down her cheek. She sucks in a breath and blows it out in a huff, knowing there's no way she can return to Beth's side looking like the emotional wreck she is. She has to be brave. There's no other choice.

Rolling her shoulders back, she reaches for the door and steps into the room. The simple oxygen tube her mother wore for days has been replaced by an entire mask. She's barely awake, her eyes fluttering open as Jessica takes her seat beside the bed. Her skin seems to be growing paler by the hour. Every time Jessica takes hold of Beth's hand, she's startled by how cool she is to the touch.

She's still here. She's still breathing, if not well—but Dr. Montgomery doesn't leave the room with a hopeful smile anymore. He's afraid Beth's lungs might be failing. In spite of the treatment she's been receiving to fight the virus, the damage done to her already weakened organs has granted her no favors. With her inability to breathe properly, the rest of her body is having trouble functioning. To Jessica, everything seems to be happening so fast, and her brain can hardly keep up with the updates or the rate at which Beth's increasing fatigue is changing her.

Beth slowly reaches up for the mask she hates to wear, shoving it down her chin as she looks into Jessica's eyes. "Everything okay?" she wheezes.

"Mom, you have to keep your oxygen on."

When Jessica reaches up to readjust the mask, Beth flinches just enough to make her daughter pause. She then scowls and asks again, "Is everything okay?"

"It was—it was work. I have to go in tonight. But I won't stay. I'll be back as soon as I can."

Beth studies Jessica for a long moment. An insufficient amount of oxygen makes her cough, and both women react. Jessica is faster, standing to her feet as she reaches for her mother's mask and puts it back in place.

"Mom, please," she begs, sitting on the edge of the bed.

Stubbornly, Beth takes only a couple gulps of air before she grabs hold of the mask again, lowering it so she can speak. "You're my beautiful girl. And I love you. More than I can say—I love you."

A dry cough crawls up her throat, but she swallows it down, a determined look in her eye as she continues. "I'm so proud of you. Of the woman you've become. You're so strong. So strong."

"Mama, you don't have to—"

"No matter what happens to me, you'll be okay. I know you will. It's who you are, and I'm *so* proud."

Jessica's throat constricts, and she can hardly swallow as her eyes fill with tears. She shakes her head, blinking furiously, trying with all she's got not to cry. "Nothing's going to happen to you. You're not going anywhere," she declares. "Okay?" She brushes Beth's hand away from the mask and puts it back over her mouth. "Stop talking like that. You need to rest, okay?"

This time, when Beth lifts her hand, it's to take hold of Jessica's. They both hold on tight, and as she loses the battle against her tears, Jessica doesn't bother wiping them away. She just holds onto her mother, hoping with all her might that whatever strength she possesses will seep into the woman who gave her life.

They hold on to one another until Beth drifts to sleep. When a nurse comes in to check on her a little while later, Jessica pesters her with questions until she feels assured she can leave the room for a couple of hours. At seven o'clock, in spite of how much she doesn't want to, she makes her way out of the hospital. Hoping to be gone for the least amount of time possible, she hails a cab to take her home. After a quick shower, she doesn't bother with makeup, and she twists her wet hair into a low bun at the nape of her neck. She dresses in another pair of leggings, a sports bra, and a sweatshirt, more concerned about the temperature of the hospital than whether or not Khalohn will be turned on by her appearance.

By seven-thirty, she's in a taxi and on her way to Tribeca. Traffic makes her late, but she can't find it in herself to care. She's doing the best she can. Somewhere between Brooklyn and Manhattan, she decides she'll say what she needs to say to keep their arrangement intact. She'll give him as much of the truth as she can bring herself to share, but she won't stay. She can't stay. Surely, he'll understand. As little as she knows him, she trusts he cares about her in some capacity. She's spent enough nights in his arms to know that.

Stepping out of the cab, Jessica hurries onto the sidewalk and then pauses. She glances up the length of the building and steels herself for the conversation ahead. She enters the lobby, catching the elevator with another tenant. After stopping on the fourth floor, she endures the ride to the sixth and wastes no time approaching 601. Much like the last time she arrived at the loft after Khalohn, she finds the door unlocked. In contrast, when she walks inside, the room is lit. She finds the man with his back leaned casually against one of the exposed beams nearest to the small entryway. He's still wearing his jacket, the front buttoned closed, his forearms lifting the bottom, where his hands are shoved into his pant pockets.

Jessica doesn't approach him. She doesn't want to be within reaching distance. She doesn't want to be touched. Staring at him, even with the blank expression on his face, cooling his blue eyes, she's afraid she'll break at his touch. Her chest tightens, memories of the previous morning flashing before her eyes against her will. Her gaze drops to his lips, and she remembers the tickle of his mustache against her mouth as she pressed hers to his. For a second, she can't ignore the ache she feels, longing for the unexplainable sense of calm and comfort she felt.

"You're late," mutters Khalohn, breaking her away from her thoughts.

Her spine straightens, and she clutches the strap of her purse over her shoulder as she lifts her gaze to meet his. Khalohn spots the dark circles beneath her dull brown eyes. He surmises, whatever is troubling her, it's more than lack of sleep which has painted her pretty, fresh face with what he can only describe as pain.

He's not one to be left waiting. Not for years. Something his net worth has garnered him. Nevertheless, he's not upset with her for being late. All he wants is Bryn. All he wants is *this*—to see her. To touch her, in search of the answers he seeks.

Khalohn pushes himself away from the wooden beam and takes a step toward her, but Bryn shakes her head and replies, "I can't stay. I'm here because you didn't give me a choice."

Her words stop him in his tracks. He wants to go to her, to hold her, but what she's said is like a reality check. She's not there because she wants him. He can't interpret how this makes him feel. It's a sensation that registers as foreign. All he can be sure of is, whatever's happening is out of his control. Not merely his reaction to Bryn, but also her reaction to him.

His frustration speaking on his behalf, he says, "You're here because that was the deal."

Jessica shakes her head involuntarily, her body's warning that she's on the verge of losing it. The weight she's carrying—her worry, exhaustion, fear, and sadness—it can't withstand the pressure of another thing.

"Khalohn, I can't handle this right now, okay? I have to go."

"You want out?" he asks, lifting an accusatory eyebrow at her.

"No. I'm here, aren't I?" she bites back.

He extracts a hand from his pocket, reaching up to run it over his mouth and down his chin. When he drops his hand, he spreads his arm out wide and grumbles, "I don't pay for this place so you can stand there and tell me no."

Khalohn regrets what he's said the instant Bryn's face falls. He doesn't have a chance to take it back before she begins to crumble right in front of him. All he can do is watch.

Her brown eyes grow dark in anger at the same time they fill with tears. She sucks in a breath so desperate it sounds like a shriek. Bryn takes a step toward him and cries, "Fuck you. Just—fuck you! You wanted *me*, remember? You don't *own* me." She turns to storm out the door, but she only gets two steps before she whirls back around to face him. Tears streak her cheeks, her anger cooling into something else. Something he can't understand. Her voice sad and resigned, she tells him, "Actually—the truth is, you might own *Bryn van Doren*, but you don't own me. Goodbye, Khalohn."

When she turns away from him a second time, she doesn't look back.

Chapter Twenty-Eight

KHALOHN SITS IN HIS HOME office, staring blankly across the room. His laptop has gone to sleep, but he doesn't notice, his mind in an apartment across the city. It's been nearly two hours since Bryn walked away from him, and the *mess* that defines the five minutes they spent in each other's company seems to be keeping him captive.

How he felt.

How she felt.

Where they stand.

It's all unclear.

She said she didn't want out, he tells himself. *Yeah, she also said* fuck you.

Khalohn scrubs both of his hands over his face. He can't figure out why he's so bothered. Or, rather, he doesn't want to go to the place inside of him that holds the answers he's avoiding. What he has with Bryn, it was working. It was working better than he could have planned. Thinking back over the last few weeks, it's quite obvious he was satisfied. But it was more than his sexual appetite being fed. He spent more nights falling asleep wrapped around her or her wrapped around him than he had with any other woman in years.

I'm here because you didn't give me a choice.

As her words circle through his mind again, Khalohn props his elbows on top of his desk, dropping his face into his hands. She was right. He didn't give her a choice. He needed to see her, so he forced his hand the best way he knew how. In doing so, he pushed her too far. He'd taken a risk, but for what?

He scowls, irritated he can't shake her; resigned to the fact that he doesn't want to. Rubbing his temples, he forces himself to dig deeper, to search for that vulnerable place inside of him he's kept under lock and key for ages. He's been a man about business for so long, he's amazed there's still a part of him that could even contemplate wanting more. Building the name Khalohn Morgan has been enough. The prestige, the money—that comes with the job, but it's always been the challenge of seeking and finding something of value, something worth salvaging, worth fixing, worth *resurrecting* that has driven him. It gives him purpose and focus. A focus he had a firm grip on until Bryn.

He doesn't know her. Not really. But he sees her. He sees her for the treasure she is. He's tasted it. Even his own logic questions the validity of his feelings, but he reasons his way through the doubt. He's been with enough women to know. Whatever it is Bryn gives him, it's pure. It's precious. It's more than what's between her legs. The idea of giving her up and returning to his old routine—just thinking about walking through the dimly lit halls of Clandestine's—he knows it won't be enough. Not anymore.

You don't own me.

I'm here, aren't I?

Fuck you. Just—fuck you!

Over and over, he replays their argument.

With a sigh, he sees the scene not from his perspective, but from the vantage point of someone else. He was a dick, saying all the wrong things, evoking all the wrong reactions. For the first time since she left him in a rush on Sunday morning, he acknowledges he's worried about her. The way she was earlier, her long hair contained, her face clean, preventing her from hiding the truth that something's wrong—she was a picture of someone on the cusp of breaking. Khalohn wants answers, but he doesn't have a right to them. Not the way things are. This fact frustrates him. It binds him, the truth that he can't fix what he doesn't know. He can't help a woman who isn't his.

You don't own me.

Actually—the truth is, you might own Bryn van Doren, but you don't own me.

Khalohn's spine straightens as he recalls the last thing she said to him. He repeats it, wondering what she meant.

"Damnit," he grumbles, reaching for his phone.

He's spent too much time thinking about her, and he hasn't gotten anywhere. Sick of wandering in circles, he decides to take the easy way out.

"Morgan?" asks Adams on the fourth ring.

"Sorry for calling you so late. I need a favor."

"All right. What can I do for you?"

"It's a personal matter."

A low chuckle sounds over the line before he mutters, "Khalohn, I said okay. What do you need?"

"I need you to look into someone for me. Her name is Bryn van Doren. I don't have a picture, I don't know how old she is—mid-twenties, maybe. I have her phone number, that's it. Oh, and my accountant has her bank information."

"I can work with that. What do you need to know?"

"Who she is. Where she lives. How she spends her days."

Brett Adams is silent for a moment, and Khalohn is certain his private investigator wants to ask him questions. Adams has been on Khalohn's payroll for a few years now, but only for business deals. This is certainly outside the norm. When Adams doesn't ask anything further, Khalohn is reminded why he called this man in the first place.

"Shoot me her number then give me a couple days."

"Appreciate it."

"Don't mention it."

As soon as Adams disconnects, Khalohn forwards along Bryn's contact information. That done, he closes his computer and exits the office. If he wants even a slim chance at sleep, he'll only get it one way; so, he suits up for a hundred laps in the pool before bed.

KHALOHN WAITS FOR two days to hear from his PI. He does his best to concentrate on his work, and he manages just fine. That doesn't mean he's not quick to pick up Adams' call when his phone rings late Wednesday evening. He's in the back of the Maybach, heading home for the night, when he answers.

"I don't have much, but I didn't want to keep you waiting. Seems you sent me after two women, not one."

With a furrowed brow, Khalohn mutters, "Excuse me?"

"Bryn van Doren—mid-twenties, can't hold a job to save her life, trying to make it on Broadway; from the looks of things, she should hang it up. She's got the face but not the talent, and she'll likely be out on her ass after she's evicted from her spot in Greenwich Village."

"What? What does she do with her money?"

"Morgan, she's got none. I don't know what your connection with her is—or what you *think* your connection with her is—but the information *you* provided pointed me to a Jessica Chapman. The two are tied to each other because they both graduated from Brooklyn School of the Arts. Chapman is twenty-four, born and raised in Bay Ridge, and still lives with her mother. Can't tell you what she does with her days, but I know her bank account is *stacked*." He pauses, as if giving room for Khalohn to contribute to the conversation. When he doesn't, Adams continues. "Her last job was at a dive bar, but she got let go more than a month ago. Sat on her place last night into this morning, but she neither came nor went. If she's who you're after, I can sit on her a little longer. Just say the word."

"No," mutters Khalohn distractedly. "That won't be necessary. Send me the address you have for Jessica."

Saying her name out loud is strange. It makes him feel unsettled, but he shoves aside the weirdness long enough to wrap up his phone call. When the two men disconnect, he stares down at his device, lost in thought until Adams sends over the address he has for one *Jessica Chapman*.

Glancing out the window, he tries to piece together the fragments of information he knows, but he falls short. As the city of Manhattan passes by him, the thought of going home is off-putting. He won't find anything there. Sick of his head being crowded with questions he can't answer, he decides to shift course.

"Atzel, I change my mind. I need to make a stop. Tribeca, please."

"Certainly, Mr. Morgan."

After his driver turns around, heading back in the direction from which they came, it takes just over twenty minutes before they've reached his destination. As he steps out of the backseat, he waves his hand, signaling to Atzel he has no need for the suit jacket he abandoned after leaving the office.

"I don't know how long I'll be," he says, staring at the front entrance of the building. "Stay close."

Atzel offers him a silent nod, and then Khalohn makes his way inside. When he reaches the door of 601, he hesitates, acclimating himself to the regret which lingers in his chest, knowing Bryn—*Jessica*—won't be inside. The truth found in her name, the fact that she lied to him about who she is, is enough to get him through the door. He stops at the threshold between the entryway and the main room, the loft as spotless as he should expect. The cleaning staff he hired to see to the place comes on Mondays, and the loft hasn't been used since.

Sat on her place last night into this morning, but she neither came nor went.

The first time he ever met her at their place, she told him she couldn't give up her apartment. Taking a few steps forward, Khalohn powers on the overhead lights, looking around for any trace of her. Nothing is out of place, and this irks him even more.

If she's not sleeping at home and she's not sleeping here, where the hell is she?

His first thought is to wonder if there's someone else. It sounds implausible, but he can't think of another explanation. As far as he's concerned, they're exclusive. That was part of their arrangement. But if she lied about her name, what else is she lying about?

Khalohn stomps to the kitchen and starts pulling out drawers, blindly looking for clues—for *evidence* of the woman he's been taking to bed for the last few weeks. He doesn't know what he's looking for, but he can't think clearly enough to search efficiently. After tearing through the kitchen, he hurries toward the bedroom closet. On his way there, it dawns on him— he, too, gave her a different name when they first met. Stepping up on the platform, he pauses for a second, looking over his shoulder at the bed.

Godrik. I gave her a third of my name, hiding my identify for a reason. What's her excuse?

Ripping his gaze away from the neatly made bed, he stifles a growl of frustration at how many times he stayed there all night. *As Khalohn.*

She had every chance to tell me who she really is, he thinks to himself, sliding the closet door open. He starts to rifle through it, tossing lacy panties, matching bras, and silk nighties onto the floor. *She chose to lie. She had the audacity to ask about me, about my past, and she wouldn't even give me her fucking name?*

When the closet is empty, ransacked by his own hands, he realizes he's so upset he's out of breath. Even more, he's found nothing. There's not a trace of Jessica in the place. Reaching up to sink his fingers into his hair, he pulls in a deep breath, suddenly aware of how reckless he's been. He let himself get swept up in the fantasy. He called it a business arrangement, but he entered into it ignorantly. He wanted her, he craved her, and he let himself be led by his dick. He didn't investigate. He didn't draw up a contract. He didn't even check in with his accountant after he put the two of them in touch. He did *nothing* but seal their agreement with a kiss.

A fucking kiss.

He blames himself for getting played. But as he drops his hands to his sides and glances around the apartment, all he sees is *her.* Bryn. *Jessica*—whoever she is. Or, at least, he sees the woman his body knows; the woman who made him want more.

Do you like the apartment?

His eyes fall closed at the memory of her question. Now he doesn't know. Now he's got more questions than answers. He wonders if any of it was real, or if it was all just a lie.

Chapter Twenty-Nine

K<small>HALOHN LETS HIMSELF INTO THE</small> *apartment, the bottle of bourbon he picked up on his way home firmly within his grasp. It was his first stop after he got the call from his lawyer. It's done. She signed the papers. Three months. That's all it took to dissolve a relationship he thought would last a lifetime. On his way to the kitchen, he doesn't deny himself the feeling of self-pity, which settles heavily in his gut. Taking down a tumbler from the cabinet, he wonders how he managed to be so naïve for so long; how he managed to trick himself into thinking he'd finally found someone who wouldn't abandon him.*

Gripping his fingers around the glass, he resists the urge to throw it across the room. He's had weeks to wrap his mind around the situation. He's more frustrated he's still hurting than anything else. It should come as no surprise that what he had to offer wasn't enough for her. He's never been enough for anyone. Not as a child. Not as an adolescent. Now, as a grown man, on the verge of seeing the first fruits of a business with bottomless potential, life has ripped the blinders from over his eyes, revealing what he was stupid enough to forget.

He walks through the silent apartment and sinks down onto the couch. Uncorking the bottle, he surrenders to the loneliness he now feels in his home.

The home he used to share with Hollie. Pouring his first glass, he thinks of his ex-wife. She moved out a week after admitting to the affair. When he told her she could stay and he would go, she argued that unlike her, he had nowhere else to go. She wasn't wrong. She told him she'd stay with her parents for a while, but as Khalohn downs a healthy swig of the brown liquor, he wonders if that's even the truth. Lifting his tumbler to his lips once more, he finishes off his first pour, imagining a likely scenario in which she's with him. *The best friend he thought he could trust. The bastard who stole his wife right from under his nose.*

Khalohn scoffs at himself, twisting the truth into the gnarled version of reality he recognizes and understands far better than any other. In his own mind, he knows he's not perfect, but he never claimed to be. It was never a promise he gave anyone. What he'd promised Hollie—his wife—was a life. A partnership. A place at his side as he worked tirelessly to be who he is, to chase after what gives him purpose, and to share every ounce of it with her. Somewhere along the way, she forgot what that meant. She forgot what it meant for him to want to build something for them.

Khalohn fills his tumbler without delay, anxious for the haze of obliviousness to overtake him. He just wants one night. One night to wallow. One night to grieve. One night to drown the man silly enough to share his dreams and ambitions with another. When he met her, he had no intention of losing his way. And then he fell in love. He fell in love, and the vow he made to himself at eighteen—to find what he was good at, to work hard, to thrive and succeed, to do it for himself, to prove to himself *he could do it alone and he didn't need anyone to support him—he let that vow slip out of his grasp as he took hold of another. A vow to share himself with his wife.*

"Fuck," he grumbles, gulping down his third glass all at once.

The burn of alcohol ignites in his throat, and he winces, welcoming the sensation. He can feel the bourbon starting to warm him from the inside out, his head buzzing with the promise of intoxication. He pours himself some more and then leans against the back of the couch. His sips the drink down slowly this round, looking around the apartment. As he swivels his head left and right and back again, his vision begins to blur around the edges, along with the memories that filter through his mind.

Everything he was sure of just a few months ago is rimmed with doubt. He questions when Hollie left him. Not physically, but mentally. Emotionally. Was it the first time Timothy was brave enough to touch her? Or before?

Was any of it real? he wonders. Or was it all a lie?

Swirling the contents of his glass around with a flick of his wrist, he frowns, his muddled thoughts proposing another possibility—that they'd both been lying. She to him. He to himself. And maybe, just maybe, if he is merciful, he could believe she lied to herself, too.

No matter how he slices it, it all comes down to one undeniable truth.

Doesn't matter what I do.

Doesn't matter who I am.

Doesn't matter what I accomplish.

It's not enough. It's never enough.

Khalohn finishes the last bit of bourbon in his glass, then stares at the bottom. The sluggishness that accompanies a bloodstream diluted with alcohol seems to hit him all at once. Still, as he gazes into nothing at the bottom of his glass, he makes himself a promise. From now on, he will give himself to his work. He will sail into the unknown alone—the captain of his own ship— seeking and finding treasure wherever he can. He will take from life and enjoy the spoils. But his heart—his heart he will store in the deepest bowels of the ship. His mind, his most valuable asset, will be his guide, and solitude will be his constant, faithful companion.

He jerks his head in a decisive nod and the room spins a little. Knowing he's on the cusp of drowning the weakest part of himself—the man who used to be someone's husband—he pours himself another glass.

Chapter Thirty

It happened so slowly. From where she wedged herself on the mattress, her body squeezed between the bed rail and her mother, Jessica felt the achingly slow rise and fall of Beth's chest for one hour. And then another. And another.

It happened so fast. Her last breath. Jessica didn't realize she had synced her own breath with her mother's until she found herself holding hers. When it registered that Beth no longer needed to inhale, Jessica held her breath until she felt the squeeze of Stefano's hand.

Now she can't stop weeping. She clings to Beth's lifeless body, wondering how it's possible she's gone. Wondering how it could have possibly happened so fast. Only a week ago, there was still hope, and now there's nothing. Her heart is broken, shattered into a million little pieces she doesn't want to pick up. She's not ready. She's not ready to face a world where her mother no longer resides. She's not ready to wake up in a place where the only family she's ever known is gone. She's not ready.

Mama, I'm not ready. I'm not ready. I'm not ready.

"Jess?" It's Jackie who speaks, but Jessica ignores her.

She can barely feel it as Stefano combs his fingers through her hair. He presses a gentle kiss against her temple before reaching for her hand, still wrapped around Beth's waist.

"I'm so sorry, dove. I'm so sorry, but we've got to go, sweetie. We've got to go."

Jessica shakes her head, squeezing her mother tighter, terrified of leaving her side for the last time.

"I can't. I can't. Huey, I can't," she cries. "Oh, my *god!*"

There's a loud hiccup followed by a sob, and then Jackie rushes from the room with a feeble, "Excuse me."

"It's okay. I'm right here. You're not alone," Stefano speaks softly into her ear, not losing his focus. "I've got you, dove. I've got you."

Stefano pries her arm away from Beth, lifting it until its draped over his shoulders. Sliding his own arm under her, he lifts her from the place she's been laying for hours.

"It's time, Jess. They've got to take her," he insists as she twists to catch another glimpse of Beth.

He tightens his hold around her middle, and she stumbles over the side of the bed and onto her feet. As soon as her feet hit the ground, her knees give way. Stefano catches her, folding her into a clumsy embrace.

"Let's get you home, okay? Can you stand for me, dove? I've got you."

By the time Jessica is able to command the muscles in her legs, her wracking sobs have quieted. One arm snaked around Stefano's waist, the other clinging to the front of his thin sweater, she allows herself to be guided out of the hospital. She sees nothing and hears even less, silent tears soaking her cheeks unceasingly.

Stefano manages to get her into a taxi. It isn't until they pull up in front of her apartment that she notices it's nighttime. With her best friend's support, she's escorted to her unit. The second the door swings open, her grief becomes so much that her body goes numb.

"What do you need?" asks Stefano, closing them inside.

She shakes her head, offering him nothing more before she turns out of his hold and walks straight for her mother's room. The scent of Beth is overwhelming, and she closes her eyes as she breathes it in. From where she's standing, the scent is untarnished. It isn't mingled with the sterile smell of a hospital. Wishing to drown in it, Jessica slides out of her shoes and buries herself under the covers on her mother's bed. As she hugs the sheets close to her chest, the awareness that she'll never hug Beth again causes a crack in her body's numbness. As her eyes well up with fresh tears, she clenches her fists tight beneath her chin, afraid if she starts crying again, she won't be able to stop. But she can't help it.

Fortunately, mercifully, her sobs wring her completely dry, until sleep pulls her under.

KHALOHN PACES AROUND his office, the Bluetooth headset in his ear tuning him in to a conference call on which he's too distracted to focus. As a voice drones on, he stops in front of the floor-to-ceiling windows, his eyes catching sight of the Brooklyn Bridge. Like he's been doing since the previous night, he surrenders to the pull Jessica has on his thoughts. He told Adams he didn't want him watching for her any longer, but that doesn't stop him from wondering about the woman who was born and raised across the bridge.

"Listen, I've got to hop on another meeting." Khalohn refocuses on the conversation in his ear, shifting his gaze back into his office. "We're scheduled for a follow-up next week. We should have the loose ends tied up by then, and we'll go from there."

As the call comes to an end, Khalohn knows he should be more concerned with the business he was too distracted to digest. Trouble is, he's not concerned. He's curious. He's frustrated. He's annoyed. Worst of all, he's restless. It's uncharacteristic of him to pace around his office, but he can't shake the unsettled feeling that's been pestering him at an increasing rate as the week drags on.

He hasn't seen or heard from Bryn—*Jessica*—since their argument. He was too stubborn to admit his concern then. Looking back, it's obvious his stubbornness is something he's been holding onto for a lot longer than a few days. Since the first time he sank himself inside of her, she's been more than his beck-and-call girl, but he arranged it so it was impossible for her to be anything else. He took what he wanted, clung to the fantasy, and ignored what was real.

Now he has no one to blame but himself for believing the lie—but he blames her anyway. He blames her for being the most genuine woman he's ever had, wrapped in the guise of someone else's identity. He blames her for the desire that still stirs deep within him. He blames her for the questions which plague his mind. He wants answers; and he won't be able to get her out of his head until he has them.

I let her get under my skin.

No one gets under my skin...

"Khalohn," Maribelle calls from across the room.

When he jerks his gaze in her direction, he finds her studying him with a furrowed brow.

"Is everything all right?"

"Fine," he mutters. "Why?"

"I've been trying to reach you," she says, pointing toward his desk phone. "When I came in, I called your name twice." Lifting a single eyebrow inquisitively, she stares while she waits for him to amend his answer.

He doesn't. He simply returns her stare with his own. Then he looks back over his shoulder, eying the Brooklyn Bridge as he mutters, "I need you to clear my calendar for the next couple of hours."

"I'll do you one better," she says suspiciously. "I'll clear your afternoon, dear."

"Thank you."

He listens to the sound of her footfalls as she takes her leave, and then he reaches for his phone. He alerts Atzel of his impending departure and then returns to his computer to wrap up a couple tasks that can't wait. It takes him no longer than ten minutes, and then he's out the door. Atzel is ready for him when he exits the building, and he finds he can't look his driver in the eye as he announces his intended destination. He doesn't journey into Brooklyn often, and certainly not in the middle of his workday. Even still, Atzel doesn't miss a beat.

It takes them nearly forty minutes to get to the address in Bay Ridge Adams has for Jessica. Atzel parks along the neighborhood street in front of the small apartment building, and Khalohn's heart rate spikes as evidence of Jessica becomes tangible. He doesn't offer Atzel any instruction as he exits the back of the Maybach, too focused on what he'll say if the woman he's after is home.

Tuesday night, she neither came nor went. What about last night?

He makes his way up the front steps the same time a tenant is exiting the building. The businessman inside of him can argue the case that he has every right to be possessive, to be irritated at the possibility of her sleeping anywhere other than the building he just entered or the loft for which he pays. But he's more than that man. Much as he'd like to deny it, there's a part of him that acknowledges he has no claim over her. Be that as it may, when he reaches her door, he doesn't care whether or not he has any right to be there—he's not going anywhere until he talks to her.

STEFANO IS IN THE kitchen, making a sandwich he assumes Jessica won't eat. He can't remember the last time he saw her eat anything. It's been two days since she called him, begging him to come to the hospital as her mother's condition got worse. He came immediately. She didn't need to beg. He's dropped everything to be with her for at least a few days. Today, if he can get her to take even a single bite of this sandwich, he'll count it as a win.

When a loud knock sounds at the door, Stefano's hands go still. Even though he can't see through walls, he leans to the right, peering through the kitchen opening and across the living room to the front door. He has no idea who could be knocking. Jessica isn't exactly in the mood to entertain guests, and Stefano hasn't called in any reinforcements. He knows better than that. She's got more friends than just him, but she's too fragile to see anyone else. Beth hasn't even been gone for a full twenty-four hours yet.

Whoever stands in the hallway grows impatient and knocks again, louder this time. Muttering a curse under his breath, Stefano hurries across the small apartment. Last he checked, Jessica was still sleeping. Given all she's been doing is sleeping and crying since he brought her home, he'd rather she be resting than roused by an intruder.

As soon as he reaches the door, Stefano peeks through the peephole. He jerks his head back after he catches sight of who's knocking. His hand resting on the doorknob, he looks down at himself, wishing he could make the man go away without opening the barrier between them. Aside from the fact that he's in no state to see a client from Clandestine's—dressed down, in a pair of gray joggers and the fitted tank top he slept in, his hair loose and around his shoulders—he's without a doubt the man wasn't invited.

How the hell does he know where she lives?

Stefano seals his eyes closed tight, muttering another curse as he reluctantly unlocks the door. He blows out a sigh and opens his eyes as he swings the barrier open. When Mr. Morgan first looks at him, he can tell he doesn't recognize Stefano right away. He opens his mouth to say something; but when he immediately closes his mouth instead, Stefano sees the recognition in his blue eyes.

"What are you doing here?" asks Mr. Morgan.

"You stole my line."

It's not normally how Stefano would speak to a client, but they aren't underground—they're above it. In the present moment, he's not a gatekeeper, he's a best friend. With this in mind, he holds Mr. Morgan's gaze unflinchingly.

KHALOHN STRUGGLES TO find his words. The juxtaposition between fantasy and reality is uncanny. It's not lost on him how the first time he met *Bryn*, it was the man in front of him who granted him access. Now, in a very different place, at a very different time, with very different intentions, it's the same man through whom he must pass. The same man who stands between him and *Jessica*.

"I need to speak to her," he finally manages.

"You shouldn't be here."

"As far as I understand, you don't live here. I'm not leaving until I speak with her."

"Look…" Stefano heaves a sigh, reaching up to run his fingers through his hair. He tosses the long, silky looking strands down his back, holding a handful at the nape of his neck as he explains, "I don't know what you're doing here, I don't know how you found her, but I don't care. It's not a good time. You need to go."

Khalohn studies the man more carefully, the same feeling he had Monday morning returning with a vengeance. His irritation takes a backseat to his concern as he steps forward and declares, "Like I said, I'm not leaving until I speak with her."

"Fuck, man," Stefano hisses, losing his composure. "When I tell you it's not a good time, I'm not bullshitting you. Her mom just died. Please, just—get lost."

In the blink of an eye, he sees Jessica the moment she got the phone call on Sunday morning. He sees the pain in her eyes when she came to meet him on Monday night. He hears Adams telling him, Jessica Chapman lives in an apartment with her mother in Brooklyn; that he sat on it Tuesday night and she neither came nor went.

He acts instinctively, not bothering to question Stefano or himself. Placing a hand on the man's bony shoulder, Khalohn pushes his way into the apartment. Stefano protests, but he doesn't lift a hand to stop Khalohn. The one-bedroom unit is small enough that it doesn't take him but a second to realize, if she's not in the little living room he barged into, there are only a couple other places she can be.

He veers right, steps into the narrow hallway, and sees her instantly. She's curled up on the bed, her beautiful, dark eyes swollen and red rimmed, staring straight at him. Her face is pale, and her hair is a mess—like she hasn't even thought about leaving that bed all day. She doesn't move or speak; but when she blinks, silent tears crawl across the bridge of her nose and seep into the pillow underneath her cheek.

Khalohn's chest tightens as he stares at her. He acknowledges the ache he feels at the sight of her brokenness. But it's not just *her* he sees. In her devastated eyes, he sees a version of himself he hasn't seen in a really long time. A version of himself he thought he'd drowned in a bottle of bourbon nine years ago. He sees a heart—vulnerable, exposed, and completely raw. He sees someone who chose to love wholeheartedly; someone who lost that love and is crushed because of it.

Staring at the grieving woman in front of him, he also sees a choice. He understands that right here, right now, he can turn around and walk away. He can leave Jessica Chapman behind, believing the lie of Bryn van Doren. Or—he can choose Jessica. He can forget the fantasy, forget the concept of taking her body without accepting responsibility of her heart. He can allow himself to want her, all of her, because that's the kind of man he is, no matter how hard he tries to deny it.

Jessica's eyes follow him as he crosses the threshold, stepping into the bedroom. Without a word, he removes the covers from over her body and finds her fully clothed underneath them. His eyes connect with hers again as he leans down and scoops her up into his arms and against his chest. She doesn't resist. She doesn't speak a word. She merely rests her head on his shoulder, reaches up to grip hold of the lapel of his suit jacket, curls into him, and sobs quietly.

"What—what are you doing? Where are you going?" Stefano demands to know as Khalohn carries Jessica into the living room. She's shaking, and all he wants is to get her out of there.

"Her purse. Where is it?"

"Mr. Morgan—"

"I'm not leaving her here," he insists. "Her bag. Either it comes with us and she'll call you when she's ready, or I walk out of here without it."

He hesitates, his eyes darting between Jessica and Khalohn. When he relents, his whole body deflates before he goes to retrieve Jessica's purse.

When he's got everything he needs, Khalohn meets Stefano's eyes and assures him, "I've got her."

He carries her out of the building, not the least bit worried at the sight they must be as he makes his way to the Maybach. Atzel climbs out of the driver's seat, his eyes widening when he spots the woman in Khalohn's arms, but he speaks not a word. He simply opens the door to the backseat, allowing Khalohn to fold himself inside. He manages to do so without letting go of Jessica.

As soon as Atzel is behind the wheel, he clears his throat and then inquires, "Uh, will we be on our way to Tribeca, sir?"

"No. The penthouse."

Chapter Thirty-One

J ESSICA WAKES IN A FOG. She doesn't know how long she's been asleep, but she's still weighed down by an exhaustion so heavy, it's as if her limbs have been filled with sand. As she blinks her eyes open, she fights a groan. It takes her a moment to get used to the painful sensation of using her sight. She feels how her eyelids are swollen and raw, like she rubbed salt into her eyes. As easy as it would be to simply sink back into the darkness of slumber, to escape to a place where her agony is a little more manageable, her whole body seems to protest even the idea of more sleep.

Tuning into her body, the first thing she notices is she's extremely comfortable. This doesn't make sense to her. Still not entirely cognizant of where or *when* she is, she forces herself to focus on her surroundings. The bed she's in molds around her body perfectly, the sheets tangled around her bare legs incredibly soft. She tries to remember taking off her pants, but she can't. To confirm she really isn't wearing any, she lifts the sheet and blanket under which she lays. That's when she smells him.

Khalohn.

An ache she can't quite identify threatens to drag her back into the darkness, but she seals her eyes shut and forces the feeling away. When she sucks in a breath through her nose, she not only smells Khalohn, she remembers him lifting her into his arms and carrying her away from her apartment. Away from her mother's bed. She still doesn't understand how he could have been there; but rather than question what was, she decides to save what little energy she has to figure out what *is*.

When she pushes herself up into a seated position, her head spins. She buries her fingers in her hair and waits for the room to settle before she drops her hands into her lap. Glancing down at her chest, she sees part of the reason she still feels so comfortable. She's wearing a NYU hoodie, the material worn thin from years of use. It doesn't take her but a moment to realize this is about all she's wearing, along with her panties. The thought of Khalohn changing her out of the clothes she'd had on since she was at the hospital causes that ache in her chest to return. Again, she shakes it off and tries to focus on something else.

She can tell, by the sheer size of the room, she's in a master suite. Aside from the king size bed she's in, flanked by a couple of nightstands, there's what appears to be a sleek, modern looking, gray suede, armless couch angled in the corner nearest her, complete with a coordinating coffee table. On the opposite side of the room, there's a fireplace built into the wall and an entirely separate seating arrangement. There are windows all around her, but he's drawn all the drapes closed, so the room is almost dark. Jessica has no idea what time it is, but she knows the sun is up by the way light is fighting its way into the room.

A single swallow brings her mental focus back to her body. Her throat is dry, and simply acknowledging how that feels triggers an all-consuming need for water. She can tell her legs are unsteady before her feet even meet the rug beneath the bed, but she curls her fingers around the edge of the mattress and eases her way to standing. As soon as she's upright, she sees the glass of water on the nightstand and her knees act of their own accord. Her backside resting against the bed, she reaches for the water and guzzles it until its gone. When she puts the glass back where she found it, she spots her phone. With no interest in contacting the outside world—the world where her mother no longer exists—she stands to her feet again and goes in search of the door.

She finds three closets, one of which appears empty, before she finds the door that leads out of the room. The minute she passes into the hallway, she squints. The light of day, pouring in through the windows at the end of the galley, hurts her already aching eyes. It's not bright, hinting at either dusk, dawn, or merely a cloudy day. She's not sure which. Slowly, Jessica ventures down the hall. Khalohn's place is so quiet, she wonders if he's left her all alone. She walks by what appears to be two separate guest rooms and then finds the stairwell. Holding on to the handrail, she descends a flight of stairs, overwhelmed by what she sees when she reaches the bottom.

Jessica knows Khalohn is wealthy. She's seen the designer brands sewn into his suits. She's slept in an apartment paid for and furnished by him. Moreover, just about every dime she has to her name is because he gave it to her—but seeing his home adds a whole new dimension to his status. When she hears the sound of his voice, the deep tone barely audible as he talks softly, she clings to the distraction. She doesn't want to get lost in his penthouse. She doesn't want to think about his wealth. She can't handle that right now.

"I'll take it from home," she hears him say as she practically hugs the wall, following the sound of his voice. "Just the one call, and then I'll be unavailable for the rest of the day." He pauses and then informs the person on the opposite side of the line, "It's likely I'll be working from home for the next week. Please adjust my schedule accordingly." Another pause. "One more thing. In a couple hours, you'll receive an email from Brett Adams. In it, you'll find the information required to make arrangements for a funeral." He pauses and then, "Bethany Chapman."

Jessica's breath catches in her throat at his words just as she reaches the open doorway of what is obviously his home office. Khalohn is standing with his back to her, his gaze trained out the tall window. When the ache she felt a few minutes ago returns, she can't shove it aside. It invades her chest, making it difficult for her to pull in a deep breath. She wraps her hands around the doorjamb, clinging to it as her legs start to tremble.

"I trust your taste, Maribelle. Spare no expense."

Jessica tries again to fill her lungs as her eyes fill with fresh tears. Khalohn notices, and he turns to face her directly, but she can't make out the expression on his face—her watery eyes making it nearly impossible.

"As soon as you have an update, I want to know. I have to go."

He ends the call, sliding his phone into the pocket of his athletic shorts. Jessica blinks, and the image of Khalohn—in a plain white t-shirt, a pair of shorts, his hair disheveled, as if he'd been running his fingers through it—becomes overwhelmingly clear. As he begins to close the distance between them, the ache in Jessica's chest expands, and a knot of emotion clogs her throat.

When he's standing right in front of her, he slips a hand underneath her hair and around the back of her neck. Tenderly grazing his thumb along her jaw, he murmurs, "What do you need, precious?"

His touch and his inquiry are all it takes. The ache splits Jessica's chest wide open. As she reaches out to grab a fist full of Khalohn's t-shirt, a warmth the likes of which she's never known spreads like wildfire through her veins. She pulls herself away from the doorjamb and into his chest. When she buries her face beneath his chin, he folds her in his arms, and she melts into his hold.

Instantly, she knows one thing with absolute certainty. More than ever before, she needs this. Wrapping her arms around Khalohn, she holds on for dear life, giving him her weight, surrendering to him completely. She doesn't care how he found her. What matters is he did—and when he did, he didn't ask her any questions. He picked her up and carried her away.

He picked me up, and he hasn't put me down.

He hasn't put me down.

"Khal," she whimpers.

"Right here, Jessica."

Hearing her name pass his lips makes the warmth spreading from her chest burn hotter. Knowing the lie is over, standing in the fullness of truth, she can hardly believe it. The devastation of her loss is rooted so deep, she can't see the end of it. Yet, the feel of Khalohn's arms around her—around Jessica—it makes her want to hold on tight.

He picked me up, and he hasn't put me down.

Me. Jessica.

He hasn't put me down.

He holds her as they are for a few minutes. When she shows no sign of letting him go, he adjusts his grip, scoops her up into his arms, and carries her out of his office. As he reaches the sectional in his open living room space, he eases the both of them down into the corner, cradling her until she begins to relax.

"Precious," he mumbles softly, touching his lips to her forehead. "We should get some food in you."

"I'm not—I'm not hungry," she whispers, curling into him further.

Gently rubbing his hand along her exposed thigh, he replies, "Something tells me it's been more than a couple days since you've eaten anything. Please. Just a little something."

She hesitates for a long moment, but Khalohn lets out a sigh of relief when she nods her head in agreement. He then presses another kiss against her forehead before slipping out from beneath her. Walking to the opposite end of the couch, he grabs the microfiber throw blanket, which has always been merely a decoration, and unfolds it. Jessica peeks up at him through her lashes as he lays it over her, and he catches himself staring.

There's so much he wants to say. Even more he wishes to know.

But she's here, he reminds himself. *Everything's different now.*

For the time being, it's all there is. This doesn't stop him from leaning down to brush his lips against hers. It's no more than a whisper of a kiss, but she doesn't deny him, and that's enough.

In spite of the fact that Khalohn told her he doesn't cook, he makes her a small plate of scrambled eggs. After he brings it to her, he watches her eat them until they are gone. She doesn't want to admit it, but her body is relieved to have some sort of sustenance in her belly. He said he guessed it had been a couple days since she's eaten. The truth is, until the eggs, Jessica can't remember the last time she had food. She'd lost her appetite right around the time Dr. Montgomery told her Beth's lungs were too far gone, they were losing her, and there was nothing that could be done.

"I've got a meeting I can't miss," Khalohn starts to say, rescuing her from her thoughts.

Jessica shifts her gaze from her lap, locking in on his steady, blue eyes.

"I'll just be in my office. You're welcome to stay here or wander around. Make yourself at home. We'll talk when I'm through."

She offers him the tiniest nod, he stares at her for a second, and then he takes her empty plate to the kitchen and closes himself into his office. Jessica looks around the room, more than a little uncomfortable at the prospect of *wandering* around. It isn't that she expects him to give her a tour or anything; she simply doesn't wish to get caught up in another fantasy. In the midst of her grief, something tells her becoming acquainted with his home won't make him hers. Turning her neck, she looks at his closed office door, replaying what she felt when he wrapped her in his arms. It confuses her—the depth of her longing for a man she hardly knows.

Closing her eyes, the vague memory of the argument they had, what feels like a lifetime ago, flashes through her mind. In that moment, she felt so used. Frowning, she reaches for that anger, simply to examine it. Mentally grabbing hold of it, she remembers how his words made her feel like his property. Until that argument, regardless of their arrangement, he'd *never* made her feel any less than a woman. That night, she hated Bryn van Doren. That night, she was angry with Khalohn for being the man who *owned* her. She was angry with herself for creating the persona he possessed.

I was angry, because I didn't want to be owned by him. I wanted...more. I wanted to mean more.

Jessica emits a soft sigh, opening her eyes to look down into her lap. Bryn is gone, and she's in Khalohn's home, sitting beneath a blanket he draped over her. She doesn't know what it means. She doesn't understand how he found her or what it signifies for him to rearrange his schedule for her. She doesn't know why he stepped in to take care of her mother's funeral, or why he's being so gentle with her. All she's sure of is she doesn't have the strength to shoulder the world; she doesn't have the fight to reject his handouts. This is the *more* she wanted. Not the money. Not the penthouse. Just the man—the man who causes that warm ache in her chest whenever he's near.

She isn't sure if she can trust if what's happening is real. Maybe he feels sorry for her. Perhaps he feels guilty. In all honesty, she doesn't have the strength to guess. Neither does she have the energy to figure it out. So, she sits curled up on his couch, with no interest in *wandering* around, until nature calls.

Rather than searching for a bathroom on what she assumes is the first level of his home, she gets up and makes her way back to his bedroom. Bypassing an elaborately spacious and decked out closet, across the way from an empty closet, she spots another full walk-in closet—albeit *less* elaborate than the first—across from her final destination. She's not the least bit surprised by his extravagantly beautiful bathroom. The countertop and the floors are dark marble—except for the surface of the platform on which his standalone bathtub sits, beneath one of the windows. The surface of the platform, along with the entire shower, is white marble.

The toilet is nestled between the enormous shower—with more nobs and spouts than she's ever seen—and the double sink vanity. As she relieves herself, she can't help but to stare at the huge, gorgeous tub across the room. Much like she can't remember the last time she ate before Khalohn's eggs, she can't remember the last time she bathed. This is why, after she flushes and washes her hands, she strips herself naked and runs herself a tub of piping hot water.

When it's full, she submerges herself completely, soaking her hair before she resurfaces. The water feels refreshing, but as she reclines in the tub and stares out the window into the sky, the promise of clean skin is swallowed up by sadness. As the minutes pass and the water cools, she acknowledges how life must go on; yet the thought of resuming life as normal hurts worse than she can explain.

She doesn't notice Khalohn when he fills the doorway. When he glides his hand through the water, she realizes he's there. Without saying a word, he unstops the tub, allowing the cool water to drain away as he refills her bath with heat. It's a simple gesture, but she stares at him with tear filled eyes all the same.

"Why are you doing this?" she whispers.

He knows what she's asking, but he takes the easy way out and replies, "You'll catch a chill."

She blinks, causing a couple tears to cascade down her cheeks before she murmurs, "Why?"

Khalohn sits on the edge of the tub, staring down at her naked body until he's satisfied with the temperature of the water. He then stops up the tub, shuts off the faucet, and lifts his eyes to find hers once more. The pain he sees encircling her brown irises reminds him who he is and what he wants. He admits now's not the time to play games.

"I think we both know this—you and me—it's more complicated than a business deal."

She stares at him, and he can read it in her eyes. Her doubt. Doubt he blames on himself. Doubt he planted four days ago, when he leveraged his position of power like an asshole. He regretted it then, just as he does now. He wants nothing more than to right that wrong. He owes her the truth. He owes it to the both of them.

"After our first night, I never should have paid a dime for you."

Her lips part at his declaration, and the anguish on her face is only proof of how right he is.

"I knew then," he goes on to say. "One dance, and I knew you were different. Then I tasted you." He pauses, staring at her intently. "On our third night, when I finally sank inside of you—it was unquestionable."

Jessica stares at him, more tears dripping from her chin into the water.

Khalohn stands from the side of the tub, reaching for the back of his t-shirt as he does. He yanks the garment off, then rids himself of his shorts and his underwear before he reaches into the water for her hand. He tugs her until she's sitting upright, then eases his way into the tub, situating himself behind her. When he wraps his arms around her waist, she doesn't resist him, but reclines against his chest, turning her head until her forehead is resting against the base of his neck.

Giving her a squeeze, he tells her, "You're priceless. Undeniably priceless. Never should have paid a dime for you, Jessica. I know that now."

Her shoulders jerk with her silent sob, and he tightens his grip around her. It takes her a few minutes to calm down. When she does, Khalohn asks, "Will you tell me about her?"

Jessica seals her eyes closed tight, squeezing out a few more tears as she swallows the knot in her throat. All the while, she focuses on the warmth burning in her chest. This is the first personal question he's ever asked her—and it's the perfect question.

She tilts her head back, until her lips are grazing the skin beneath his jaw, along the edge of his beard, hoping to memorize every detail of this moment. For in this moment, it's confirmed that whatever it is they have—the weeks they've spent together—it wasn't all fantasy. Parts of it were real. Real enough to lead to this moment. Real enough that at his question, she knows she can trust him with the truth. So, she gives it to him. All of it, sparing not one ounce of love for the woman she'll carry in her heart forever.

"She was the best—" A knot lodges itself in her throat, and she presses into Khalohn as she fights a sob. His arms circle around her tighter, and through her tears she manages to begin again. "She was the best woman I've ever known. Strong. Determined. So damn beautiful…" As the words pour from her lips, she begins to relax in Khalohn's hold, a couple pieces of her shattered heart finding their way back home.

"Didn't know her, precious," he whispers when she goes quiet, "but I owe her a debt."

"What?"

"Without her—everything she was, everything she taught you—I'd never have met you."

Jessica sucks in a breath, startled by his words.

Before she can fully sink into the truth of his statement, he starts to stand, bringing her with him. "Shower," he insists, holding her hand as he encourages her out of the tub. "When we're done, I'll order lunch."

"I'm not—"

"Lunch, precious," he says, his lips pressed to her temple. "Whatever you want."

She doesn't know if it's the gentle way he delivers his nonnegotiable command, the tender way he kisses her head, or the way he squeezes her waist while he does both—but the warmth in her chest continues to funnel through her veins, and she can't find it in herself to refuse him.

Chapter Thirty-Two

BETH'S MEMORIAL SERVICE WAS beautiful. It was held at a Catholic church in Brooklyn, not too far from where she was laid to rest. The alter was adorned in an array of flowers, Jackie read the perfect eulogy, and when she was finished, the choir sang from the balcony. Jessica and Beth weren't particularly religious. When Khalohn asked her—one of only three questions he asked in order to pull off the service—she told him the truth. They were Catholic on Christmas and Easter, which meant she'd been to a handful of masses throughout the course of her life; but none as perfect as this one.

Khalohn's driver brought them to the church. Jessica, wearing the black dress Stefano brought with the bag of clothes he dropped by on Sunday, held Khalohn's hand as he escorted her inside to the front pew. He didn't sit with her. He took a seat a few rows back, leaving her sandwiched between Stefano and Jackie, who each held one of her hands throughout the service. It wasn't until after it was all over; after the silent tears, the long hugs goodbye, and the promises to speak soon, that it hit her.

As she sits silently in the back of his Maybach, staring out the window unseeingly, Jessica thinks back over the last few days. She's barely had to lift a finger. Khalohn has seen to just about everything. Even the things she didn't know needed to be handled were handled. Then, rather than sit by her side during the service—rather than being front and center at the funeral he arranged and paid for—he gave her what she needed.

I needed my best friend. I needed my mom's best friend. I needed her life to be celebrated in the most beautiful way imaginable because she deserved it— and he gave that to me. He gave that to mom.

Without looking at him, she reaches over in search of his hand. He offers it willingly, gripping hers tightly.

Didn't know her, precious, but I owe her a debt.

Jessica blinks her eyes closed slowly, freeing a single tear in the process, as she replays his words from a few days ago. In so many ways, it's been the longest week of her life. Paradoxically, it's also been the fastest. Every day, she wakes up with a heavy heart, not entirely sure how to proceed. In ways she can't even begin to understand, she lost her mother in one agonizing moment that crushed her so fiercely, she couldn't breathe; and before she could even attempt to catch her breath, the man at her side swooped in and gave her what she needed.

As they pull up in front of his home, as he climbs out of the car without letting go of her hand, she wonders what will happen next. A small voice in the back of her head whispers that she can't hide in his penthouse forever. It's not who she is. It's not how her mother raised her. And yet, an even louder voice at the forefront of her mind declares she's not ready to let go of Khalohn's hand. Her whole body aches for him. To be touched by him. To get *lost* in him—even if only for a little while.

As they ride up in the private elevator, she squeezes his hand and steps closer to him. He looks down at her as she presses her chest to his. Jessica can see it when his blue eyes turn dark in hunger, but he doesn't make a move—just like he hasn't tried to make a move the last five nights she's been in his bed. Only now, she wants him. She needs him. And as she pushes herself up onto her tiptoes, reaching for a kiss, she aims to tell him as much.

The instant Jessica touches her mouth to his, Khalohn loses a bit of his restraint. As the days have gone by, the thread by which he's holding on has grown thinner as it's been pulled taut. Inappropriate as it may be, after sleeping next to her warm, soft body for nearly a week without tasting her—the sight of her body tucked into her fitted, sleeveless, knee-length, black lace dress along with her four-inch black stiletto heels has had him on edge all afternoon. When she flicks her tongue out, teasing his lips open, he can't silence the groan that crawls up his throat. By the time the elevator chimes on the fifteenth floor, he's got her locked in his arms, his tongue tangled with hers, and her fingers holding tight to the back of his head. Jessica moans, and one of his hands slips down over her backside. At his touch, she arches into him further, kissing him harder, and the thread he was holding on by snaps.

"Jessica," he growls into her mouth.

His voice is so low and husky in warning, even he barely recognizes it.

"Please," is all she says.

It's all she needs to say.

Khalohn angles his head, plunging his tongue into her mouth. She returns his kiss, oblivious to the elevator doors as they open and then close. They're both breathless when Khalohn finally lifts his face from hers, glances over her shoulder, smacks the button to command the doors open, and tugs her into his foyer. The sound of her heels against the hard floors as she hurries behind him only serves as a reminder of how fantastic her legs look. That one thought is all it takes for Khalohn to fantasize about those same legs wrapped around his hips.

Upon reaching the landing at the top of the stairs, he whirls her around, until her back is against the wall. She gasps, dropping her purse at their feet before he finds her mouth once more. The taste of her soft moan is sweet. Her hands tugging at the lapels of his suit jacket is sweeter. Khalohn is so hard, he wonders if he has it in him to be patient—to shower her in affection, bringing her to the height of her pleasure before indulging in his own. Then Jessica thrusts her hips, in search of the friction she craves, and he decides to merely give the woman what she wants.

The grip she has on his jacket changes as she moves to rid his body of the garment. It hits the ground, and then they're on the move. By the time they cross over the threshold of Khalohn's bedroom, they're clinging to one another—skin to skin. When he reaches down to assess the state of her sex, his stiff length grows painfully hard.

The simple tease of his fingers isn't nearly enough. Jessica says as much as she pulls away from him and climbs into the middle of the bed. Silently, she reaches for him, but there's hardly a need. He's right behind her. Then he's on top of her, the weight of his body between her legs incredibly welcome. Jessica spreads her knees wide as he grazes the head of his shaft along her seam, nudging her sensitive bundle of nerves before he eases back down. When he penetrates her entrance, his perfectly blue eyes staring down at her, her whole body shudders in anticipation. He pauses, barely inside of her, and she's certain there's nowhere else she'd rather be. It's been over a week since she's had this. Now, she doesn't want to be without it.

I'm his, she says to herself, her hands sliding around his waist and onto his back, silently begging him for more. *For as long as he wants me, I'm his.*

When Khalohn finally buries himself inside of her, he does it hard and he does it deep. Jessica gasps, her nails biting into his skin as she arches her back completely off the bed.

"*Khalohn,*" she mewls.

He freezes, entirely captivated by her face—her eyes closed, her lips parted, her pain forgotten in one single moment of bliss. It's then he understands. It's then he acknowledges just how much of an idiot he's been. Now, with his eyes wide open, he sees how precious she really is.

Jessica—my Jessica.

With no more lies between them, he takes her slow and makes it last.

When dusk begins to settle, casting the room in shadows, Khalohn and Jessica are still lying naked together in bed. Each of them on their sides, his leg wedged between hers, her thigh hooked around his hip, his arm draped around her waist—they lay sated in a comfortable silence, simply admiring one another. Jessica memorizes the color of his eyes in the current light, her fingers delicately tracing his cheek along the clean line of his beard. She used to think the silence between them after sex was about pretending; like if they didn't say anything, they could pretend what they had was real. Now it doesn't feel like pretend. It feels like pure intimacy. So much so, she's almost afraid to ruin it.

Unable to hold her tongue a minute longer, she finally whispers, "Who are you?"

Khalohn doesn't answer. He looks her straight in the eye, as if he's inviting her into his soul. This makes Jessica almost smile. The temptation to do so feels good. She's barely smiled in a week.

Still, hoping for more, she amends her question. "Who are you beneath *this?*" she asks, dragging her fingers through his beard.

"Just a man," he murmurs, his voice deep and tender.

"I don't believe that," she replies, resting a hand against the side of his neck.

"I loved my wife," Khalohn confesses. As soon as the words are out of his mouth, he can feel Jessica flinch. He tightens his grip around her waist and goes on to say, "I'm not a perfect man. Never claimed to be. Still, I loved her. I was loyal to her. I thought I could trust her to do the same. I was wrong."

He pauses, never taking his eyes off Jessica. His hand at the small of her back dips down lower, cupping her backside as he pulls her even closer. Her breath catches in her throat, her eyes widening for a fraction of a second before she melts into him. Her hand travels to the back of his neck, her arm wrapping around him as she submerges her fingers in his hair.

"When she left, I promised myself I wouldn't go there again. I'm a businessman. I make smart investments. I take calculated risks. Matters of the heart are unpredictable. Unreliable. So, I took mine out of the equation. I convinced myself I didn't need love."

"Everybody needs love."

Khalohn doesn't know why he does it, why he gives her a part of himself he's not given anyone in a long time. He's confident of only this, as he looks into Jessica's brown eyes, wet with fresh tears he's unsure if she's even noticed yet, he can trust her with it.

She's entrusted me with her pain. Seems only right I do the same.

"My mother left when I was five years old. I didn't understand it then, but I felt it. Felt the weight of that loss; the meaning of it. When I hear about mother's like yours, it's only further proof my mother didn't love me. Or, if I'm merciful, maybe she couldn't.

"My father raised me. Maybe that's love. It's possible it's all the love he could give me. When my mother left, maybe she took some of my father, too. Then he met Cheryl. When Blair was born..." He stops himself, hesitating for a long moment before he explains, "The only reason I didn't grow up in his shadow is because I was eight years older than him. I was too tall to be dwarfed by it.

"I guess what I'm saying is—Hollie was different. I thought she was different. In a lot of ways, I suppose she was. But she still left. And when she did, I felt like an idiot for feeling so surprised."

"Not an idiot," Jessica breathes, her voice so soft it's hardly audible. She blinks, freeing a couple tears she doesn't bother to wipe away and then says, "You can't just shut your heart off. It doesn't come with a switch."

"Yeah," says Khalohn on a sigh. He slides his hand up Jessica's back, stroking her spine lazily as he continues, "I would have argued otherwise. Then I met you."

"Khalohn?"

"Right here, precious."

Licking her lips anxiously, she blows out a sigh and then asks, "What are we doing?"

Just as he did when she broke the silence earlier, he doesn't respond with his words. He lifts his hand away from her back, traces his fingertips along her hairline, and tucks a few silky strands behind her ear. His touch is tender. So tender, it makes her want to cry.

"I'm a mess," she whimpers. "And—you and me—I…"

"No more secrets," says Khalohn, holding the back of her head in his palm. "No more lies. No more *deal*." He locks his gaze with hers, staring unwaveringly as he goes on to say, "You and me."

"But we don't even—"

"There are no promises here, Jessica. Not from me. Not from you," he interrupts, certain her rebuttal holds no merit. Especially not after what they shared in the very bed they still lay in, both of them still naked. "You want to walk away, you say the word. You want to stay—you want to see where this goes? I'm right here. I'm not going anywhere."

When she extracts her fingers from his hair in order to grab hold of his wrist, Khalohn's fingers twitch around the back of her head as he touches his forehead to hers. She nods, as much as his hold will allow, and then she reaches for a kiss.

The conversation that follows starts at a whisper.

A while later, it ends with a gasp and a groan.

JESSICA WAKES UP in bed alone Wednesday morning. She lays on her side, staring at the spot where Khalohn laid, thinking about what it means that she knows he's likely up for a swim. It's such a small part of who he is—his morning routine—but it's something he's given her. Something she holds onto, just as she intends to hold onto him.

There are no promises here, Jessica.

You want to stay…I'm right here. I'm not going anywhere.

She rolls onto her back, sucking in a deep breath, remembering how they spent all of the previous evening. The sex had been an escape. It injected a spark of life into her body, reminding her of her need to *move*. The cuddles afterward were a comfort. Being in Khalohn's arms was good for her soul.

Now, a new day dawning, she thinks of all the unknown that lays ahead of her. Jessica's life must go on. Empty as her loss makes her feel, she acknowledges she can't hide in Khalohn's penthouse forever. It's not who she is. But that truth only seems to beg a series of questions…

Who am I without her? Am I the same? Is it even right to try to be?

The realization that these are questions she can't ignore is daunting, but she's been avoiding them for days. Staring up at the ceiling, Jessica makes up her mind. With this new day, she'll at least try to ponder what the answers might be. Beth has been laid to rest, which means all Jessica can do now is search for peace.

She closes her eyes, and her memory of Khalohn's gym fills her mind. After he brought her to his place, it took her a couple days to wander around. It was on Sunday, when she couldn't find Khalohn, that she ventured to the third level of the penthouse. Along with his indoor pool, he's got a fully outfitted gym, all of which is bordered by a terrace with the perfect view. However, as she remembers the space—it's not the view, the pool, or the gym equipment that calls to her. It's the vacant floor space at the center of his gym. Floor space where she can *move*.

Jessica's heart aches at the thought of dancing. She's confident it'll bring her just as much joy as it will sorrow; it'll wring out emotions she's been harboring for days. It'll hurt—but it'll also give her clarity. It always has.

I'm a dancer. With or without mom—because of mom—I'll always be a dancer.

Certain as she is, procrastination feels easier. When her stomach growls, she clings to the excuse to hold off from heading upstairs. Her appetite has been almost nonexistent for more than a week. Hunger feels like healing, and she's content to indulge the feeling.

Climbing out of bed, she walks naked toward the bathroom, making a pit-stop in Khalohn's extravagant dressing room. The bag Stefano brought was unpacked by the woman who cleans Khalohn's home once a week. She plucks a pair of panties out of one of the dresser drawers in the middle of the room and steps into them. Then, rather than hunt for something clean to wear, she finds the NYU hoodie she's been wearing, pulls it over her head, and continues her journey to the bathroom. She's just finishing up rinsing her face when Khalohn appears.

His dark hair is slicked back. Wet as it is, the deep brown mane looks almost black in the morning light pouring into the bathroom. Water is still dripping down his chest and back, falling around every hard ridge and crevice of his defined muscles. He's got a towel wrapped low around his waist, cluing her into the fact that he's naked underneath, and Jessica's nipples tighten as she drinks him in.

"Morning," he mumbles, coming straight to her.

He presses a kiss to her temple as she manages a feeble, "Hi."

"Got a meeting I need to dial into in an hour. Went out and got you breakfast earlier. It's in the kitchen, if you're hungry. I've got to shower. You need anything?"

Jessica frowns a little, shaking her head as she looks up at him and inquires, "You got me breakfast? And you went for a swim? Already?"

"Had a call at six with a partner company in Italy. Been up for a while, precious."

It's all he says before he steps around her, drops his towel, and starts his shower. She stares at him, that warm ache he causes in her chest igniting. It amazes her how anyone could think he's not enough. He's hardly left her side in a week. When he does, it's so he can get work done or see to her needs. She still doesn't fully understand how much he's sacrificing for her; but as she watches him duck underneath the showerhead, she's sure he's more than enough for her.

I owe it to mom to pick myself up and start living again. I owe it to myself. But after all he's done—pretty sure I owe it to him, too.

Forcing herself to look away from him, she picks up her brush, runs it through her hair a few times, and then leaves to go see about breakfast.

As soon as she reaches the kitchen, she sees the bakery bag on the counter. She assumes there are bagels inside; but when she approaches the bag and looks inside, she gasps at the sight of two boxes of apple pie. When a giggle bubbles out of her mouth, it surprises her—but she doesn't run from it. She allows herself to feel it, and then she goes about serving herself a piece of pie for breakfast.

Jessica is sitting on a high stool at the island in Khalohn's sleek kitchen, savoring her last bite of pie and contemplating another slice, when she hears his landline ring. It's a sound she's only heard once before, when Stefano came by to drop off her things. The sound of the phone echoes from where it sits—on the hallway table of Khalohn's foyer, right across from the private elevator. Aside from the phone in his office, it's the only one she's seen. Frowning in its direction, she wonders if Khalohn is expecting anyone. Glancing over her shoulder and up the stairs, she wonders if Khalohn is finished with his shower.

The phone stops ringing for all of about two seconds. When it starts up again, Jessica pulls her lower lip between her teeth, shifts her attention back in the direction of the foyer, and then decides maybe she should answer it. She's halfway across the room when she hears the elevator chime between rings. At the sound of the man's voice, she stops dead in her tracks.

"Khalohn, boss man, what the fuck?" he calls, the sound of his shoes against the hard floors signaling his approach. "Been trying to reach you. Stopped by your office. Maribelle says you're working from *home* all week? Since when do you—"

An attractive man with long hair, tied back at his nape, and dressed in a navy-blue suit, tailored to perfection, comes to a halt in the middle of the hallway at the sight of Jessica. Her eyes grow wide as she watches him do a full body scan. Her cheeks burn with a blush when she remembers what she's wearing. Or, more accurately, what she's *not* wearing.

His dark eyes are practically molten when they return to hers. A disarmingly smug smirk tugs at the corner of his mouth as he mutters,

"Well, hello, gorgeous. You explain a lot and yet pose a plethora of questions I can't begin to conjure at the moment."

Uselessly, Jessica tugs at the hem of Khalohn's sweatshirt and stammers, "Uh, who—who are you?"

"I'm the guy who knows the code to the elevator, which means I've been around a lot longer than you. I think the better question is: who are *you?*"

After he explains how he got up to the fifteenth floor, Jessica realizes the phone in the foyer has long since stopped ringing. Before she can decide what to say next, his familiar voice fills the hallway.

"My name's on the deed. Perhaps the questions should be left to me."

Relief washes over Jessica for about two seconds. Then she turns to see Khalohn. One look at him, and her heart seizes, sputters, and then races at the same time her stomach drops, tingles, and twists. She forgets to breathe, all of her attention captivated by the most gorgeously handsome face she's ever seen.

Jessica barely notices as he closes the distance between them, too captivated by the perfect, high cheekbones she couldn't see before. She's mesmerized by the way his eyebrows seem thicker and darker somehow, making his blue eyes more striking and beautiful.

"Breathe, Jessica," Khalohn insists, sliding a hand around the side of her neck.

She sucks in a deep breath, her lungs rejoice, and then Khalohn's lips twitch in amusement. The muscle movement is so minute, she would have missed it before. Absentmindedly, she reaches up to graze her fingers down his freshly shaven cheek, wondering how many expressions she's missed, each one hidden beneath his beard.

"You—you shaved," she whispers breathlessly.

Khalohn's eyes drink in the awe lighting up her face as she reaches up with both of her hands to cup his bare cheeks.

Fuck, he thinks, his grip tightening around her neck. *If I'd known she'd respond like this, would have gotten rid of the beard weeks ago.*

Completely forgetting their audience of one, he lifts his free hand, gently clasping his fingers around one of her wrists as he admits, "You wanted to know who I was beneath the beard. Thought I'd show you."

"You're beautiful," she says on a sigh.

A small smile pulls at his mouth, and her gaze drops down to watch instantly. He's about to kiss her when they're interrupted.

"Hate to break up this—whatever it is," Porter begins to say. "But seeing as how that beard has been around almost as long as I've been slummin' it with you, I think I'm entitled to know who this gorgeous creature is who inspired your baby face."

At the sound of his voice, Jessica sucks in a sharp breath, pulling her hands away from Khalohn's face as she looks over at Porter. Khalohn does the same. Rather than letting Jessica go, he moves his hand from her neck and wraps his arm around her shoulders, tucking her into his side.

Ignoring Porter's comment, Khalohn simply inquires, "What are you doing here?"

"There are so many more pertinent questions than that right now," scoffs Porter.

The two men stare at one another for a long moment, and then Khalohn heaves a sigh. He knows Porter won't relent. It's not in his character. With this in mind, he gives Jessica a squeeze, beckoning her attention. Once he has it, he regretfully suggests, "Maybe you should put some clothes on."

She nods and then slips out of his hold, hurrying toward the bedroom. He watches her until she's out of sight, then he shifts his attention back to his uninvited guest, who's grinning like a fool.

"You've been holding out on me," he teases. "She's a stunner. Where'd you find her?"

Khalohn ignores his questions, again, and turns to head into the kitchen. As he suspected he would, Porter follows close behind.

"Come on. Give me something. There's a story here. I mean, what, you took her to bed, decided you didn't want to see the light of day until you'd had your fill, so you quit the office for the week?"

"Don't be an asshole," demands Khalohn as he goes about making a batch of French press coffee.

"Answer my questions, and maybe—"

"Her mother passed," he interrupts, looking his friend straight in the eye. "She's going through a tough time."

"Shit," mumbles Porter, instantly somber.

The truth earns Khalohn a moment of silence before his broker pipes in again.

"Honestly, though—what's the deal with you two? You dropped everything, so I'm guessing it's serious."

"I haven't *dropped* everything. And what it is, is none of your business."

"Five years I've known you. Not once have I found a woman in this place. Not once."

"Read into it what you will," Khalohn begins to say. At the sound of her light footsteps, he glances toward the stairs and sees Jessica making her way down. He takes her in from top to toe, her toned legs now adorned in a pair of pale pink leggings, the side of her white sports bra visible in the loose fitting, dove gray tank top that drapes from her shoulders. Without taking his eyes away from her, he informs his friend, "You likely won't be too far from the truth."

As soon as Jessica reaches the bottom of the stairs, she doesn't stop until she's tucked under Khalohn's arm. After she got dressed, she had half a mind to stay out of sight. Curiosity getting the better of her, she couldn't help herself. So much of her relationship with Khalohn has been restricted to the bedroom. While the last week has brought about quite a bit of change, she's not met anyone in his life, aside from Atzel. Wanting to know everything there is to know about the man at her side, she decides to stay close.

"I'm sorry to hear about your mother," says the stranger, catching Jessica off guard.

She flinches in Khalohn's hold. He feels it and tightens his arm around her as she replies, "Thank you."

"Jessica, this is my broker—Porter Hunt. Porter, Jessica."

His smug smile returns as he replies, "Broker and only friend. He likes to leave that part out."

"I'm still trying to figure out why you're *here*."

"You canceled our standing lunch last Friday, you've been ducking my calls since—there's a gala Friday night you agreed to attend, and I'm just wondering if you'll be there or not. You're an idiot if you don't show. Everyone with any power in this city will be there, along with those stupid enough to think they've got power, but rich enough to get through the door."

Khalohn inhales deeply and Jessica looks up at him as her arms move with the puff of his chest. The muscles in his cheek jump as he clenches his jaw closed tight, and she's fascinated by the sight. So much so, she almost misses his reply.

"I don't know. Maybe."

Suddenly aware of why he might back out of a party he's already agreed to attend, Jessica inserts herself into the conversation. "If you're thinking of not going because of me, you should go."

Dropping his gaze to find hers, he mutters, "I'm thinking of not going because I find these events insufferable."

"The price you pay for being among the upper echelon of Wall Street's businessmen," says Porter. "Look, you deal with a handful of these dinners a year. It's good for your reputation."

"Good business is good for my reputation, and I've got that in spades."

Shaking his head in both amusement and annoyance, Porter counters, "You know what I mean. Good business breeds a good reputation; but attending parties with the powerful stimulates *good business*. This is why you keep me around, boss man—because I know what I'm talking about. Because I drag you to these things. Hell, *I'm* good for business."

Khalohn frees a sigh, triggering Porter to switch tactics.

His eyes drift over Jessica and a mischievous smile plays across his lips. "You know what else would be good for business? If you showed up with a stunner on that arm of yours. Bring your girl," he says, jerking his chin in her direction. "Bet you'll find the gala more bearable with the right company. Besides—nothing cheers a woman up like a new gown and a night to show off, am I right?"

Khalohn's body grows stiff at the suggestion. Jessica feels it, but she's not sure what to react to—Porter thinking a fancy party will cheer her up, or Khalohn bristling at the idea of taking her to a party.

"Careful," Khalohn grumbles.

Porter is not deterred. "*The* Khalohn Morgan with a gorgeous brunette on his arm? You'll make *Page Six* headlines."

Jessica's eyes close in a slow blink. Their conversation is information overload. She wonders if he's serious. Just the thought that she could end up in a tabloid is absolutely outrageous to her.

"Hey," murmurs the man in her arms. Jessica forces her head up before Khalohn continues, "I would never ask that of you."

"You'd never ask me to a party?"

His arm glides from her shoulders down to her waist, his grip tightening as he replies, "As my date? Yes. As my arm candy? No."

Jessica considers this. Peeking over at Porter, she recognizes *this* is what Khalohn is sacrificing for her. Not merely a night out with the man who claims to be his only friend—but a networking opportunity that's important to men like him.

"If it's important, you should go," she tells Khalohn. Drawing in a breath, she steels herself to add, "And if you want me, I'll be your date."

"Jessica—"

"See? It's settled," Porter exclaims with an obnoxious clap.

Khalohn glares at the man before informing Jessica, "We'll discuss it later." He doesn't give her a chance to respond as he pulls away from her, looks back at his broker and states, "If that's all you came for, I've got a meeting. I'll see you out."

A crooked smile lights up his eyes, and he signals his acquiescence with a nod. As he and Khalohn make their way toward the elevator, he calls out, "I'll see you Friday, gorgeous."

Jessica is still trying to sort through the finer details of all that just happened when Khalohn returns to the kitchen. He goes straight to his French press, pushing down on the knob to separate what is now the coffee from the grounds.

"Would you like some?" he asks, turning to grab a mug.

"Please." She watches him pour them each a serving and then tells him, "I meant what I said about the gala. I know you're a busy man. I know this week you've been *less* busy because of me. I won't pretend I can give back what you've given me, but I owe you."

"You don't owe me anything."

"Actually..."

She pauses, an acidic feeling swelling in her belly as *reality* settles there. Among the things she's been avoiding are her financial responsibilities. Nothing has been easy as she's waded into life as an orphan; but shoving aside what she's certain will be her money problems has definitely been easier than addressing them.

"We should probably talk about that. I mean, what I owe you. I know you paid for mom's funeral. She had life insurance at her old job, but when they let her go—"

"Jessica, look at me," he demands.

He says the words, and she realizes how intently she's staring down into the black liquid of her mug. When she forces her gaze up to find his, the hard expression in his eyes causes the burn in her stomach to intensify.

"You do not owe me for your mother's funeral. And since we're on the topic, the hospital debt she incurred over the course of her three-week stay, that's been settled, too."

Shock hits her like a jolt, and she rocks back a step as she gasps, "What?"

"I took care of it."

"I—no, I—I can't let you do that. You shouldn't have done that."

"It's done."

"Look," she starts and then she stops. Letting go of her coffee, she takes hold of her side with one hand, using her other to rake her fingers through her hair, pulling it away from her face. She keeps a tight hold of the strands, as if doing so will help her hang on to her emotions, keeping her from falling into hysteria. "I get it. I get that you've got lots of money and you're trying to be nice—but you didn't even know her. You never met her. And if you did—I told you. I told you about her, so you know I mean it when I say—she wouldn't want your handouts. She wouldn't, and I can't—Khal, just tell me how much I owe you."

"No," he replies flatly.

"No?"

"It's done. I took care of it. You don't owe me anything."

The sick feeling in her belly wanes as the burning rises to her chest. The ache is undeniable, as is the sting of tears that prickles the back of her eyes.

"I don't want to argue about this. Please. Tell me how much I owe you."

He takes a step toward her, all but eliminating the space between them. When he reaches up and buries his fingers in the back of her hair, holding her still as he stares unrelentingly into her eyes, her arms drop to her sides helplessly.

"We're not going to argue because there's nothing to argue about. I wanted to pay for your mother's funeral, and so I did. I wanted to pay for her hospital stay, and so I did. I remember the way you kissed me when you got the news that sent you running to her bedside; and for the last week, I've watched you crawl through the mire of your pain.

"In case I didn't make it perfectly clear how I feel last night, you're mine. I laid it out, you made your choice, and so you're mine. When a woman is mine, I see to it that she's taken care of. This is not about money. Do you hear me? This is about you, spending the last few years of your life doing everything within your power to help support the woman who raised you. This is about you, being so fucking loyal you offered me your body to make ends meet.

"The way I see it, you've got an apartment in Brooklyn you need to deal with, you've got no job—which, technically, is my doing—and the last thing you need is to carry the financial burden of the woman you lost while you're trying to see your way through your grief.

"This is not a handout. This is me, offering my loyalty to you the only way I know how. So, for the last time, you don't owe me anything. And I told you last night—there are no promises here. I'm not playing games with you, either. You can take it or leave it—but when I tell you I'm here and I'm not going anywhere, it means I see you. I see the kind of woman you are, I'm giving in, and I'm holding on. *This is not about money.*"

When Khalohn is finished, he lets her go, grabs his coffee, and starts for his office without a backwards glance. Jessica blinks, hardly aware of the tears racing toward her chin as she stares into the empty space he occupied. She's so overwhelmed by all he said, she feels numb. Then, slowly, her fingers and toes start to tingle. With each breath she sucks in, she feels more alive, until her chest is burning.

Sealing her eyes closed tight, she blindly reaches out in search of every emotion coursing through her veins. Grief. Regret. Loss. Fear. And love. Above all the rest, *love.* Homing in on it causes it to spread, until the amount of love she feels is so much it hurts.

In that moment, she knows there's only one way to get through the pain.

There's only one way to process all Khalohn said and the depths to which she feels his declarations. Gone is her desire to take the easy way out. To procrastinate. To avoid.

It's time to face the music.

Jessica turns on her heel, leaves her coffee behind, and heads to the gym—to dance.

Chapter Thirty-Three

JESSICA DANCES UNTIL HER body begins to protest, then she drags herself to the shower. She cries the entire time she bathes. When she's finished, still wrapped in only a towel, she wanders back into the bedroom in search of her phone. She pulls up their thread of messages, props herself against the side of the unmade bed, and types out what feels like a desperate plea.

Our place? 2:00?

She doesn't have to wait long before Stefano's reply arrives.

I'll be there. You okay?

Jessica doesn't answer right away. Her phone still gripped in her hands, her legs carrying her slowly back to the bathroom, she takes stock of her emotions. She's halfway through the day, but she feels like it's been days since she woke up, the events leading up until now yanking her all about mentally.

Just need to see you.

It's the best answer she can give, so she leaves it at that. It's nearly an hour later when she makes her way to Khalohn's office. Upon reaching the door, she hovers timidly, peeking in on him where he sits behind his desk. Just the sight of his clean-shaven face is enough to make her heart skip a beat. When he lifts his gaze, giving her his perfectly blue eyes, her feet move of their own accord.

Khalohn smells her perfume before he looks up and sees her standing at the threshold of his office. He takes her in, assessing her. It's been a couple hours since their confrontation in the kitchen. As unsure as he's been about whether or not he was too harsh with her, given her fragile state, he doesn't regret a word he said. Studying her at her approach, his doubts evaporate.

She's dressed in a pair of jeans, cut low around her hips. A sliver of bare skin is on display in the gap between her jeans and her cropped, loose fitting, ACDC t-shirt. Her long, thick hair is loose—full and slightly wavy as it falls down her chest and back. Her face bears a hint more color than he's seen recently; and while her makeup is barely noticeable, her natural beauty taking center stage, he still notices a touch of it is there.

"Do you have a minute?" she inquires, halfway to his desk.

"Yes," he returns, shifting his chair in subtle invitation.

Jessica comes to stand beside him, propping her backside against the front of his desk. She looks down at her feet, tucking a bit of hair behind her ear as she informs him, "I'm going to go out for a little bit. Stefano and I—we have this place…" Her voice trails off, she shakes her head and then sighs, "I just need to see him."

"Do you need a ride? I can arrange for Atzel—"

"No, please," she insists, lifting her head and giving him her brown eyes. "Thank you. I, um, I'll find my way. I—I don't know. It might sound stupid but—I kind of want to get lost in the city. The feel of it. I miss it."

Khalohn stares at her silently before replying with slight dip of his chin.

"I was planning on coming back here after, if that's okay."

A slight scowl causes a crease between his eyebrows as he lifts a hand from his lap and takes hold of her waist. Squeezing her gently, he mutters, "Why wouldn't that be okay?"

She hesitates to respond. When she does, it's not in the way Khalohn expects. The instant her lips press against his, the scowl tugging at his brow lifts, as does his unoccupied hand, which finds its way into her hair. He follows her lead, allowing her to express what she must. At the first tease of her tongue, he takes over. Her faint whimper is all the assurance he needs that she doesn't object. It's not long before she's in his lap, her arms locked around the back of his neck, her tongue tangled with his.

When she pulls away, she does so abruptly before pressing her soft cheek to his smooth one. He can feel her rapid breaths at his ear as she blindly lifts a hand to hold the opposite side of his face. Half distracted by the erection, not the least bit concealed with her pressed against it, he almost misses the significance of her touch. Then her thumb grazes back and forth across his cheek as she presses her own closer.

"I see you, too," she whispers, a slight tremble in her voice. "I'm giving in. I'm holding on. I'm yours, Khalohn. I think I always have been."

He doesn't get a chance to respond. She brushes a feather soft kiss against his jaw, and then she's gone.

An hour later, as Jessica emerges from the 36th Street Station, she does so mindlessly. Just as she told Khalohn she would, as she traveled from one borough to another, she let herself get lost along the way. The numbing sensation that accompanies her escape is welcome, and she clings to it until she's on the sidewalk just outside the diner. Her feet slow to a halt when she looks through the window and spots Stefano sitting alone in a booth for two. The sight of him is like a shot of reality injected directly to the vein.

He looks different in the light of day, but those are just details. His long, dark locks are pulled back into a careful twist at the nape of his neck, allowing her an unobstructed view of his elegant profile. He's dressed down in a pair of black, holey, skinny jeans, a t-shirt, and a distressed jean jacket she's sure is designer. It fits his lean frame perfectly. He takes a sip of his coffee, and then—as if he can feel her—he turns and spots her standing. Staring. His hazel eyes lock with hers, and she's taken back to that night.

The night it all began.

The beginning of the end.

She hardly notices when he jumps up to come outside. Her vision grows blurry as the whirlwind of the last several weeks flashes before her eyes. When Stefano folds her in his arms, she sucks in a strangled breath, breathing in the familiarity of Bleu de Chanel wafting from his skin. A sob clogs her throat as she grips hold of the sides of his jacket. She holds on tight as she accepts the truth; as she accepts the point at which she finds herself. She's come full circle. She's hit the bottom. Now her only option is to climb her way out. To fight. To survive. To solider on—like she always has.

Sucking in a breath through her nose, she shoves Stefano away from her, lifting her gaze to stare into his eyes.

"Dove," he murmurs, resting his hands on her shoulders.

She jerks her head in a sharp shake. "Coffee," she manages.

A ghost of a smile softens the worry in his eyes as he cups her face and wipes away her tears. Without a word, he carefully detaches one of her hands from his jacket, wraps his fingers around hers, and leads her inside. After they fill the booth, he waits until she's got coffee in front of her before he speaks.

"Talk to me, Jess."

Jessica takes a slow sip of her hot beverage. Staring into it, she blurts out the first thing that comes to mind.

"He paid mom's hospital bill."

"*What?*"

Peeking up at Stefano through her lashes, she replies, "Yeah. And he won't hear of me paying him back for that or the funeral."

His face scrunched in a frown, he scoffs, "I don't—I don't know what to say."

"I know you don't trust him." Jessica watches as Stefano's spine straightens. He opens his mouth to speak, but she beats him to it. "You don't have to say the words, Huey. You're my best friend. I know. I also know—I know you've known him longer than me, in a very different capacity. To you, he's a man with money who sleeps around."

"A lot," he interjects. "With a fee."

"Yeah," she whispers with a nod. "But then he met me."

"Jess—"

"I get it, why you think it's not real. I do. And I don't blame you. But you don't know him like I do."

"Fuck," he breaths. His brow dips as concern weighs down his eyes. Stefano leans across the table, resting his hands over hers as he says, "Dove, I don't mean to be a dick, but you're in a really vulnerable spot right now. He swoops in, throws his money, and—"

"Huey, it's not like that."

"Jessica, I can't. I can't see you get hurt because of him. It was me who put you in his path, and—if he hurts you? With everything you're going through? I just can't let that happen."

Adjusting her hands so her fingers are laced between his, she holds onto him and promises, "He won't. He won't hurt me. Not on purpose, anyway."

The doubt she sees in his eyes begs her to admit the truth. She doesn't know how badly she needs to say the words until she does.

"I'm falling in love with him."

A moment of silence settles between them. As they stare at one another, the tension that eases in her chest—a tension she tried her damnedest to dance away—finally releases.

"Jess…"

"Maybe it sounds ridiculous or reckless or just flat out stupid. I mean, he's only known my real name for a week, and my mom just died, and I'm…a mess." Stefano grows blurry as her eyes fill with tears. She blinks, needing to see him clearly as she tells him, "But this thing we have—it's real. I know it is. You're just going to have to trust me, okay?"

"And if you're wrong?"

Forcing a smile that doesn't reach her eyes, she shrugs and says, "It's like I said. You're my best friend. If it all falls apart, I know you'll come hold my hand and help me pick up the pieces."

"Yeah," he agrees resolutely.

With a sniffle, Jessica untangles their fingers so she can dry her cheeks. She then takes another slow sip of her coffee and prepares herself for what she intends to tell him next.

"So—I've got a lot of things to figure out. I barely know where to begin. And I know what I'm about to ask might sound crazy, but you can't say no."

Stefano smooths his hands over his hair, leaning back against the booth as if the last ten minutes alone have already exhausted him. "Say no to what?"

"I need to go shopping for a dress. Not just any dress—but the kind of dress the likes of which could hang with the Gucci in Stefano Neal's closet."

Quirking an eyebrow, he mutters, "Excuse me?"

"You can't say no…"

Unable to curb his inner smartass, he inquires, "Was there a question I missed?"

"Will you go shopping with me? Please?"

"Now you're just playing me," he says, folding his arms across his chest. "You know I like to shop."

This time, when a smile pulls at each side of Jessica's mouth, the expression reaches all the way up to her eyes.

Chapter Thirty-Four

KHALOHN STRAIGHTENS HIS black bow tie, then reaches for his black, Christian Dior tuxedo jacket. He slips it on, adjusting his shirt cuffs as he tries to make sense of what he's doing. Somehow, Jessica has convinced him to attend the gala.

Maybe it was the Ralph Lauren gown she brought home the day before yesterday, he thinks to himself as he prepares to make his way to his dressing room.

Given tuxedos aren't his first choice of attire—as a tuxedo usually means he's on his way to an event meant only to remind the public of his success—he doesn't keep them hanging with any of his other suits. This, along with the fact that Jessica's gown *is* in the dressing room, was all the excuse he needed to finish getting ready in his second closet. With their departure time imminent, he assumes Jessica must be about ready. However, when he darkens the door of his dressing room, he stops short at the sight of her.

He's seen the dress. After she brought it home and convinced him she wanted to accompany him to the gala, she'd hung it, leaving the garment bag zipped closed. The next morning, while she was still sleeping, he snuck a peek. He knew what the Audrey cape gown looked like. What he didn't know was his woman *in* the dress would steal his ability to conjure words, restrict the flow of oxygen to his lungs, and send a rush of blood to his groin so fast, he would question if he was thirty-five or fifteen years old all over again.

Sensing him in the doorway, Jessica turns to face him directly, smoothing her hands down the front of her gown. It's sleeveless, her shoulders completely bare, while the top of the dress clings to her chest, around her upper arms and back. The front is simple, hugging her curves until the fabric drops from her hips down to the floor. It's the cape which defines the dress. It starts at her arms and extends around her back, the excess material draping to the floor and extending behind her in a short train.

She's curled her hair in big waves, all of which she's styled over one shoulder. Her makeup is dramatic, but not overly so. It's fitting for the occasion, and he thinks she looks absolutely beautiful—even as she fidgets nervously.

"I was actually looking for a black dress. I thought it might be more appropriate. But then Stefano insisted I try this one on and…"

"Red suits you," says Khalohn, finally finding his words. "You look gorgeous."

"Thank you." Turning slightly, she looks over her shoulder and asks, "Will you zip me up all the way?"

"Of course."

Khalohn can't remember the last time he helped a woman *into* her clothes, but he doesn't want to remember. Right here, right now, he only wants to remember her. After he's pulled the zipper to the top, he slides his hands over her shoulders, holding her gently as he leans down and presses a kiss against her exposed neck.

"I have something for you," he admits, his lips still grazing her skin.

"You do?"

"Yes. Wait here."

He doesn't go far, the small parcels he hid after his errand the previous afternoon tucked into a drawer of his dresser. When he holds out the first Harry Winston box, Jessica doesn't move to open it, but looks between it and him repeatedly.

"Khalohn…"

"If you insist I must go, and if you do me the honor of being my date, then it is my duty to ensure that when you walk into the room, you won't be the only one not dripping in diamonds."

Her gaze now zeroed in on the still closed box, she whispers, "*Diamonds.*"

"That is what Harry Winston is known for."

"I—this—tonight is supposed to be me saying thank you. Me making sure you don't sacrifice anything else for me. Me making sure you don't miss something important. I—diamonds?"

A hint of a smile curls the corner of his mouth and he tucks the box he extended beneath his arm before opening the second. He doesn't miss the soft gasp she sucks in at the sight of the tennis bracelet, matching the long linear drop earrings he purchased after he snuck a peek at her gown. Extracting the piece from the box, he sets the container aside and reaches for her right wrist before clasping on the bracelet.

"This gala is a parade, precious. You'll see." He pauses, this time opening the earring box on her behalf as he continues, "Your gratitude is noted, but that doesn't make these diamonds any less yours. And if you feel obligated to express more gratitude than the humble manner in which you're receiving these gifts now, it won't be in a room full of people at a party. My preference would entail you and I alone—naked. Now…" Khalohn dips his chin down at the box and insists, "Put them on. Atzel will be waiting by now."

"Right. Okay," she breathes, reaching for the earrings with shaking hands.

It takes her a minute to screw on the backs once they are in her ears, but the effort is well worth it. When they're both ready, he takes her hand in his, draws her close and murmurs, "Priceless. Positively priceless."

As they walk into the ballroom, Jessica's unoccupied hand tucked into the crook of Khalohn's elbow, her belly twists with her rising anxiety. Since Porter mentioned the gala—where *everyone with any power in this city will be*, along with *those stupid enough to think they've got power, but rich enough to get through the door*—she thought she could scrounge up the courage to stand by Khalohn's side for the night. After all, she's getting used to what it feels like to be around power. Her first night with Khalohn until now, he's not lost a bit of that confidence which seems to leak from his pores, making him even more sexy than his entire body broadcasts all on its own.

However, it doesn't take long to *feel* the power and money in the room. It's hard for her to suck down a full breath, the atmosphere so thick it's overwhelming. Looking around, she feels like a total fraud. Her heartbeat picks up speed, her grip around Khalohn's arm tightening as she tries not to panic.

Someone's going to notice.

I'm just a girl from Bay Ridge.

I'm no one special. No one noteworthy.

These diamonds are real, I'm wearing Ralph Lauren, but I do not belong here.

"Hey." Khalohn's voice breaks through her thoughts as he covers her hand with his own. He doesn't speak another word until her eyes find his. He then lifts his eyebrows, signaling what he's about to say is serious. "When you're ready to go, you say the word and we're gone."

"We just got here," she whispers, trying to hide her nerves.

"Precious—you say the word and we're gone."

She stares at him for a long moment. Part of her wants to tuck tail and run. Then she remembers all he's done for her over the last week. Not just the bills he paid, but how attentive and gentle he's been. Certain she needs to see this through, she admits, "I think we should stay. I'm just nervous."

"You've no reason to be nervous. You look stunning. Stay close, and we'll both make it through the night."

A small smile helps her relax a little as she promises, "I'm not letting you go."

"Good," he replies with a wink.

Khalohn escorts her further into the elegantly decorated room, successfully resisting the pull into any of the ongoing conversations while doling out polite nods hello. Jessica notices the soft music which fills her ears is being played by a small live band, and there are servers mingling amongst the crowd with trays of champagne. She's never really had a taste for champagne, but she can't deny a little liquid courage might go a long way—especially with the amount of over-the-shoulder glances being casted in her direction.

"Khal?" she whispers.

"Jess?"

When she called his name, her focus was still bouncing around the room. At his use of her nickname, her head jerks to look up at him, her small grin unavoidable. It's the first time he's ever said it, and she hopes it's not the last.

God, I love my name on his lips.

Shaking off her reaction, she leans close and asks, "People are staring. I'm not imagining that, am I?"

"No. But don't let it bother you. Half the people in here who know me probably don't recognize me."

"Oh," she sighs, feeling relieved. "No beard."

"Precisely."

As if to prove his point, their attention is drawn a few feet away from them when a woman calls, "Khalohn? Is that you?"

Jessica's feet stop moving and it takes every brain cell she's got to keep her jaw from falling open as Naomi Gray makes her way toward them. Until this very moment, she's only ever seen the Grammy award winning artist on television or on the internet. The fact that Naomi and Khalohn are apparently on a first-name basis makes her feel more out of place than she already did.

"Naomi, back in the city already?"

She coughs out a laugh, her big, beautiful smile lighting up her round eyes. "I get it. Me, home, in the city—hasn't happened a lot in the last year. But *you*—Khalohn Morgan sans beard? Is this what you've been hiding?" she asks, gesturing toward his face. "You look—dashing."

Khalohn merely shakes his head, as if he finds her amusing.

"Then again," she continues, folding her arms across the front of her gorgeous, gold gown, "Maybe it's the woman on your arm who makes you look so good."

Reflexively, Jessica's hand tightens and then loosens in Khalohn's bent elbow.

"Naomi, Jessica," he introduces without further prompting. "Jessica—"

"Naomi Gray. Yeah. Anyone who doesn't know who you are is seriously disconnected," Jessica blurts.

Naomi stares at Jessica openly, taking her in from head to toe before she shifts her gaze back to Khalohn. "I've got to admit—she came in on your arm, and for that alone I didn't like her. Upon closer inspection, I've changed my mind," she teases before holding out her hand. "It's so nice to meet you, Jessica. Honestly, I've never seen this man with anyone. You being here says more about you than you know."

"Thanks," breathes Jessica, letting go of Khalohn long enough to return Naomi's gesture. "It's nice to meet you, too."

"Are you here with Porter? I haven't seen him, yet," asks Khalohn, mercifully changing the subject.

"Oh, he's around here somewhere; working the crowd, as usual. But to answer your question, no. I'm not here because of him. I'll actually be performing after dinner."

"Looking forward to it."

Someone calls Naomi's name, she glances over her shoulder and then excuses herself, promising to catch up with them again before the end of the night. Jessica is still a little star-struck when someone beckons Khalohn's attention. Following his lead, she turns to face a small group of people coming to speak to him. It's the man who seems to be acquainted with Khalohn. He introduces the woman on his arm as his wife, Scarlett, and the second woman as his sister, Christina. At first glance, Jessica thinks Christina looks vaguely familiar. It's not long before she decides—in a crowd like this—there's no way she knows her.

"I would say it's nice to meet you, but I'm afraid that wouldn't be true," says Christina.

"Chris," chastises her brother.

Even though she addresses her sibling, it's Khalohn she stares at as she replies, "Charlie, you're selling our legacy to this man and his company. Pier House Resorts will lose everything that makes it unique once it bears the name Khalohn Morgan. You know it, I know it—and if you weren't such a coward, maybe we wouldn't be losing the business that's been in our family since we were children."

"Christina, we agreed," interjects Scarlett.

"Right. A peaceful evening." She finally pulls her fixed stare away from Khalohn only to pin it on Jessica. After giving her a very deliberate once over, she shakes her head and mutters, "If you'll excuse me."

"I apologize," says Charles. He casts a small smile at Jessica and adds, "I didn't mean to put a damper on your evening. Just wanted to be polite."

"Don't worry about it," Khalohn assures him. He offers Charles and Scarlett a nod, then begins to walk around them as he says, "I hope you enjoy the rest of the gala."

"What was that about?" asks Jessica when they're out of earshot.

"Just business. At least, it's just business for me. For them, it's a little more complicated—but *that* is not my business."

"Oh," mutters Jessica distractedly. She can't help but look in the direction Christina went. Whatever *business* he's referring to is obviously complicated. The way she was staring him down made Jessica feel uncomfortable. She hopes that was the first and last time they will cross paths.

When everyone is called to their seats for the dinner hour to begin, Jessica is relieved to have a reason to sit. She and Khalohn are seated at a table with Porter and a handful of other businessmen and businesswomen along with their spouses. She's, quite obviously, the youngest at the table, but she tries not to dwell on it. It's during the first course when someone asks Jessica what she does for a living. Not at all prepared for the question, she hesitates just long enough for Khalohn to inform the table she's been spending all her time caring for her ailing mother. She's relieved only until a follow-up question leads her to confess, she buried Beth a few days ago. For what it's worth, this stops any and all questions from being tossed in her direction for the duration of the meal.

Dancing commences shortly after dessert is served. Jessica watches as the guests couple up and sway to the sound of music and the hum of chatter. She tunes out the conversation at their table and allows her thoughts to wander. Unintentionally, memories of Beth crowd her mind. She wonders what her mother would think if she saw her now—all dressed up in a room full of the wealthy and powerful. It's a completely different world than the one in which she was raised.

"I feel compelled to rescue you from whatever it is that's on your mind," says Porter, appearing at her side. Jessica looks up as he extends a hand and asks, "Shall we dance?"

She hesitates, glancing at his outstretched hand before looking at Khalohn. It's his eyes she's staring into when Porter says, "He snoozes, he loses. I asked first."

Khalohn tilts his head to one side, as if to say, *he's got me there.* Taking this to mean he doesn't mind, and appreciative of the distraction, Jessica decides a dance might be nice. It feels strange being in another man's arms, with Khalohn across the room watching, but she tries to relax and let her body feel the music.

"Are you having a good time?"

"I guess," she replies with a slight shrug. "I don't exactly fit in here."

Porter chuckles, the sound emanating from deep within his chest, causing a vibration between them. His dark eyes smiling down at her, he says, "Haven't you figured it out yet? Nobody fits in here. We just like to pretend." Pulling her a little closer, he leans down until his lips are grazing her ear. "As the most beautiful woman in this room, you were never going to fit in."

Warmth spreads across Jessica's cheeks, and she pulls in a deep breath as he straightens to full height. Not entirely certain how to feel about his compliment, she instinctively looks back toward their table. When she doesn't spot Khalohn, her nerves start to get the better of her again. That is, until she feels a second warm hand graze the small of her back.

"I think I'll cut in now," says Khalohn, stealing her right out of Porter's hold.

He lifts his hands in surrender, winking at Jessica before he goes in search of another partner.

"He's harmless, but he's still a shameless flirt."

Resting both hands against Khalohn's chest, Jessica melts against him and confesses, "I'd rather dance with you anyway."

He tightens his hold, and she turns to rest her cheek between her hands. As she does so, she inadvertently finds her gaze aimed at Christina. A chill races down her spine at the sight of her pale green eyes staring right at them. Fortunately, Khalohn's steps guide them in a different direction, putting his back to the woman. Before they come full circle, the current song comes to an end. A round of applause erupts a second later as Naomi makes her way out on stage. For the next fifteen minutes, no one dances, too transfixed by the hypnotizing sound of her uniquely amazing voice. Jessica loves every minute of the performance. Partly because it's Naomi Gray; partly because she's listening to Naomi Gray while tucked into Khalohn's side.

It's then that it hits her...

This is some first date.

After Naomi finishes her short performance, Jessica excuses herself to the ladies' room. She's not surprised by the elegant design of the bathroom, but she is taken aback when she finds the pristine space all but empty upon her entrance. While she's closed in a stall, someone finishes up and takes her leave while someone else occupies the stall next to hers. It's after she handles her business and is at the sink, washing her hands, that the second woman appears. Jessica doesn't notice who it is until she picks up a paper towel to dry her hands. When she sees Christina's reflection cast in the mirror, she jumps a little in surprise. This only causes a snide smirk to cross the woman's lips before she reaches up to swipe at her nose.

"You don't remember me," she says, speaking to Jessica's reflection.

Jessica doesn't move, staring in an attempt to place her face in a memory.

Christina sniffs, tilts her chin up, then looks down her nose as she says, "He pretends like he doesn't remember me, but that's part of the deal. Clandestine's is like *Fight Club*. Then again, I was one of many—and I only had him twice. Maybe I'd need to be naked for him to remember me."

Jessica's fingers clench the paper towel in her hands tightly, but she tries not to give away any signs of a reaction. She doesn't want Christina to know her heart is racing, her lungs are shrinking, and all she wants to do is run away. She's about to open her mouth to speak when the reflection of the blonde turns into a memory. Then she remembers.

She's seen those pale green eyes looking down that nose before, her first night at Clandestine's.

He must not have liked you.

Jessica didn't understand it then—how or why this woman knew she'd been with Khalohn and for how long. As the faded memory becomes clearer, she sees the way Christina looked her up and down that night, not altogether different than the way she eyed her a couple hours ago.

Thinking back on the way Christina had been staring at her and Khalohn on the dance floor, she says, "He's hard to forget—even if you've only had him twice. I can understand your jealousy. But if you think you're going to screw with my head about him, you picked the wrong girl. Needless to say, he's never pretended to forget me."

"Yeah, well—I'm going to see to it that he remembers me."

Turning to face her directly, Jessica boldly asks, "What is that supposed to mean?"

"It means fuck boy should have stayed out of my business. Fortunately for me, I don't have to sully my name to get what I want. Guess that's what he gets for taking home the *trash*."

Jessica's head snaps back at the thinly veiled threat. Admittedly, she can't fully comprehend what the woman is saying, but it doesn't take a genius to surmise *Jessica* is the trash to which she's referring. As much as she wishes she could come up with a dig just as biting as hers, she can't. She's had enough, and the last thing she wants is to get into a verbal sparring match with someone whose beauty and privilege has made her ugly and desperate.

Without saying another word, Jessica snatches up her clutch, tosses her used paper towels, and hurries out of the restroom. She spots Khalohn almost as soon as she returns to the party, and she hurries to close the distance between them. He's in the middle of a conversation at their table, but she doesn't care. Whatever Christina is planning, she doesn't want to be anywhere near her.

Leaning over his shoulder, she whispers, "Can we go?"

Khalohn doesn't even look at her as he apologizes to the couple he was speaking to and stands to his feet. He bids them goodnight as he clasps his tuxedo jacket closed. Finally looking at Jessica, he reaches for her hand, and then they're heading for the door.

A couple minutes later, in the back of the Maybach, Atzel merging into traffic, she asks, "Christina, the woman who was rude to you earlier?"

"What about her?"

"Did you recognize her?"

Khalohn frowns, shakes his head, and mutters, "Should I?"

Staring down in her lap, Jessica fidgets with her fingers as she asks,

"Are you playing dumb because you don't want to upset me? Or do you really not remember you had sex with her?"

As soon as the question is out of her mouth, she closes her eyes, as if bracing herself. Before Khalohn speaks, she feels his fingers wrapped around her chin, turning her face in his direction.

"Look at me," he demands softly. She complies, certain she can't ask for the truth and hide from it at the same time. "My sexual past cannot come as a surprise to you."

"That's not what I asked," she whispers.

"Meeting her tonight, it was in a completely different context. No, I didn't recognize her. Maybe that makes me an asshole—but I never made it my business to remember them. That wasn't the point."

Jessica nods as much as his grip will allow. She's not sure what to say, and she expresses as much as she casts her gaze down her cheeks.

"Does that change *this*?" he asks, releasing her chin.

Rather than spout the answer she *wants* to be true, she pauses and honestly considers his question. The fact that he even asked is simply confirmation he's not playing games with her. He's being honest.

Isn't he always?

He's right. He's never hidden himself from her. Given how they met, she'd be a fool to want to know how many women he's slept with. Nonetheless, she can't judge him for his past any more than he can judge her for hers.

A frown knitting her eyebrows together, she peers through the darkness into his eyes and replies, "Maybe it makes me a slut—but no. It doesn't change this."

"Precious, you are so far from a slut. I never want to hear you say that again," he insists, grazing the back of his knuckles down her cheek. "Christina should never have approached you."

"Yeah, well—she did more than that. She threatened me. Or *you*. Or maybe both of us? I don't know."

"What'd she say?"

Jessica frees a sigh and then relays the entire bathroom exchange with him. When she's finished, he sits silently for a moment, staring out the window.

"If she says anything to anyone, it'll be a breach of contract. The consequences aren't cheap. Beatrice saw to that."

"I remember."

Wrapping his fingers around hers, Khalohn brings her hand into his lap and instructs, "I don't want you to worry about it, okay? I'll handle it."

Something about the way he says it puts her at ease. She's sure when he says he'll handle it, he will. Then she recalls she's holding hands with the man who didn't know her name but tracked her down and made her his anyway. Scooting closer to him, she rests her head against his shoulder and semi-repeats to herself:

No. Nothing could change this.

I'm giving in.

I'm holding on.

And I'm not letting go.

Chapter Thirty-Five

A T SEVEN-THIRTY ON MONDAY morning, Maribelle knocks on Khalohn's office door before granting herself entrance, in order to deliver his breakfast. As she sets the tray on the far side of his desk, she greets, "Good morning, dear. It's nice to have you back."

He calls to mind the early hours of the morning—his usual routine executed with one welcome addition. For the first time in more than a week, he felt confident leaving Jessica behind. The kiss he plays back in his head reawakens a longing he'd spent the drive in tamping down. She was fully naked and half sleep. He could think of no better way to leave her than tangled in the sheets of his bed.

"It's good to be back," he replies, offering her a small smile.

She lingers for a minute, her hands clasped together in front of her, and Khalohn surmises her mind must be buzzing with questions. He's certain she won't ask. In all the time they've been acquainted, she's never inquired about his love life. She teases him about the company he keeps, she offers unsolicited but thoughtful advice about his workload, and she inquires about his sleep—but she's always respected his privacy. It's one of the many reasons he respects and trusts her as much as he does.

As if she only needs a minute to quell her curiosity, she returns his smile, takes a deep breath and then says, "Your morning is light until nine, upon which time you've got a meeting with your lawyers. Shall I give you a ring five minutes prior?"

"Please. Thank you, Maribelle."

"Of course." She nods and then leaves him to his breakfast. Before the door closes behind her, she calls out, "It's nice to see your face, Morgan."

Smiling, he returns to his emails as he eats, reading and responding as necessary. He's opening a report from the previous week when his phone rings. Recognizing the page from his secretary, he knits his eyebrows together. There's no way he lost an hour of time. He checks the clock, sees it's barely past eight, and looks at the device before answering.

"Yes?"

"It's Lorelai. She says it's urgent. May I send her in?"

"Yes."

No sooner is the word out of his mouth than the sound of Lorelai's heels, approaching in haste, meets his ears. She comes to an abrupt halt in front of his desk, and he hears her small gasp as her eyes widen at the sight of him. If he wasn't so focused on why she was barging into his office first thing in the morning, he might be amused. She recovers quickly then throws something in front of him before planting her hands on her hips. Taken aback by the irritated expression which sweeps away her response to his clean-shaven state, he doesn't look down, but continues to stare at her as he waits for her to speak.

"Sir, I mean no disrespect when I say—what the fuck?"

"I'm going to need more than that," he replies, still not breaking his stare.

"That was just delivered to me by courier," she says, pointing at what she threw on his desk. He still doesn't look as she goes on to explain, "The Pier House deal is almost locked in—but we're still redlining, and now

Christina Winslow is trying to fuck with us. I'm sorry, Morgan—I know this deal is mine, but I don't know what to do."

Khalohn's blood runs cold at the mention of *Christina Winslow*. Finally, he looks down at what Lorelai dropped in front of him. His jaw locks as his own irritation washes over him.

He hasn't forgotten what Jessica told him Friday night. Saturday morning, he spent a little time doing some light digging into what he could find on the woman. From the beginning, Pier House Resorts has been a project he gave to Lorelai. He's trusted her, and she hasn't let him down—which means he knows what he needs to know about the business, its major players, and the details of the acquisition. Now he knows a little more.

After studying the picture of Christina he'd found on the internet, it didn't take him long to remember the last time he saw her. What he told Jessica still holds true. He doesn't remember the two nights they spent together. He remembers the *third* night she *tried* to get from him. It was only a couple months ago—shortly before he met Jessica.

He didn't need to, but he went over the NDA Beatrice had him sign years ago, reviewing the terms so they were fresh in his mind. What he found was enough to assure himself one meeting with their lawyers, and he could have the woman muzzled. Yet, considering how long he'd managed to go without anyone other than his accountant knowing about his investment in Clandestine's, he decided to wait to call his lawyer until he felt he had no choice.

Staring angrily at the paper in front of him, it isn't his lawyer he's thinking about.

Involving my lawyer would be too cordial.

The paper in front of him is a copy of *Page Six* from Saturday's edition of *The New York Post*. Khalohn curses under his breath as he recalls Porter's flippant joke about he and Jessica appearing in print. Turns out, he wasn't wrong. They aren't the main story—but in a short article in the bottom left corner, there's a photograph of Khalohn and Jessica arriving at the gala. In it, her hand is tucked into his elbow, and she's looking up at him. The seemingly insignificant headline reads: *Is Wall Street's Most Eligible Bachelor Off the Market?*

He doesn't bother reading what the journalist wrote. He doesn't care. Instead, he reads the handwritten script on the Post-It note just above the article.

I know who she is, and I'll talk. Cut ties with Pier House Resorts, and your secret will be safe with me. You've got 48 hours.
   – Christina Winslow

To Khalohn, it's bad enough Christina cornered Jessica in the bathroom Friday night. She'd made it personal. Delivering her threat to his office is like declaring war.

"I'm on it," he says, reaching for his cell phone.

"Sir?"

He pauses, glances up at her and repeats, "I'm on it. See what you can do to hurry the redlining process along. I want this done, and in my name, as soon as possible."

"You got it."

Before she reaches the door, Khalohn's already found the contact he's after. He initiates the call, bringing the phone to his ear as he waits impatiently for the man to answer.

"Adams," he greets on the fourth ring.

"How's your plate? I need you to look into someone, and I need all you can get me in twenty-four hours."

Brett Adams chuckles softly before replying, "Sounds like a dare. Who am I after?"

JESSICA TAKES A deep breath as she steps foot into her apartment. Standing just beyond the door, she looks around, waiting for the tears to come. When they don't, she nods to herself and makes her way into the middle of the living room. She stares at the couch but doesn't sit on it. It feels like a lifetime ago when she regularly folded up the bed each morning, in a feeble attempt to create more space in the room. She can't even clearly remember the last time she slept on the pull-out. Between the hospital, the loft, and the penthouse, it's been a long time since her life has felt *normal*.

Until she came home, she wasn't sure what she intended to do with the place. Now there's no doubt in her mind. She doesn't want the apartment or most of the things in it. Looking around, she's sure there's nothing that won't fit in a suitcase that she will miss. Clothes, Beth's books, a few photos—those are the only things that hold any value to her. She decides to donate the rest.

If anyone will take it, she thinks, staring at the couch once more.

Without thinking twice about it, she goes rummaging for Beth's big, old suitcase and starts to fill it. The rent is paid for the next three months; but after she leaves, she doesn't have any intention of coming back, if she can help it. Where she'll go, she's not entirely sure—but this isn't home anymore.

The penthouse?

It's a possibility she considers only as long as it takes her to think of it. She discards it immediately. Generous as Khalohn has been, she has no intention of moving in with him. They're in a good place, in spite of everything, and the last thing she wants is to mess it up by taking their relationship one step too far too soon. She's been in his bed for more than a week, but she's not naïve. She needs her own place just like she needs to figure out what she intends to do about a job. Mooching off her man isn't something she intends to do.

An hour after she's arrived, she's filled the old suitcase with Beth's belongings, and she's stuffed a trash bag full of her clothes. When she looks around at what she's accomplished, she feels the absence of Beth so profoundly, her chest hurts. She needs to get out of there. She wrestles with her load until she's out on the street. Channeling her pain into her frustration, she stubbornly shoulders her burdens until she can flag down a cab. It's when she slides into the backseat that she knows where she's going.

Another hour later, she sits on the floor in the middle of unit 601 and lets her tears fall. They don't last long, as if her body knows crying won't offer her the solace she's after. When she's calmed down, she thinks twice about where she is—just a block away from Miah's. Almost as soon as the realization settles, she's grabbing her purse and heading for the door. Jessica doesn't know what time it is, but it's not a scheduled class she's craving when she walks the short distance to the studio. More than anything, she just wants the space to *move*.

Pulling open the front door to Miah Michael's Dance Studio, she's relieved when she spots the owner bent over the shoulder of the person sitting at the computer behind the front desk. They both look up at her entrance, but Jessica only has eyes for Miah. She straightens, and the way her eyes soften at the sight of Jessica, she guesses Kierra shared the news about Beth.

"Hi, honey," she says, making her way out from behind the front desk.

"Miah, if you hug me, I'll just start crying again—and I didn't come here to cry."

Miah's step doesn't even falter. "If you think you can come in here, for the first time after your loss, and I'm *not* going to hug you, you've got another thing coming."

She wraps her arms around Jessica, and she surrenders, bending a little to rest her chin against the woman's shoulder. The tears come, but as Jessica embraces Miah, she closes her eyes tight in an effort to keep them from falling.

"Tell me what I can do, Jess."

"Got an empty room I can borrow for a couple hours?"

She pulls away, moving her hands so they grip Jessica's arms as she nods. "It's a smaller space, and it's booked up all afternoon, but it's yours until then."

"Perfect."

"Come with me."

Miah escorts her up the stairs to the studio at the end of the long stretch of the narrow hallway. Music from the other occupied spaces wafts through the crevices around the doors they pass. That feeling of *home* tickles the back of her neck, sending a tremble down her spine.

"Dance it out, girl," says Miah before leaving Jessica alone.

She drops her purse on the floor and stands staring at her reflection in the wall of mirrors before her. She hadn't planned on finding herself in the dance studio when she got dressed that morning—but she's dressed for it anyway, in a pair of cropped leggings, a sports bra, and a t-shirt of Beth's she'd swapped with her own while she was packing. It's too big, the material hanging loose around her body, but the worn, soft garment smells like her mother. She breathes in the scent and then reaches up to tighten her ponytail. Staring into her eyes, she sees the root of her pain looking back at her. The longer she stares, the greater the ache in her chest.

Dance it out, girl.

Jessica reaches for her phone and opens her music app. Without even thinking about it, she chooses the song she'd been dancing to in Khalohn's gym a few days ago. As "Waves" by Dean Lewis starts to play, she turns up the volume as high as it'll go. Closing her eyes, she listens to the entire song once, every muscle in her body relaxing as her mind takes her through the steps she started to piece together. When the song starts over again, she tosses her phone on the floor and backs into the middle of the room.

He sings the first word of the first verse, and her body starts to move. It's not long before she's completely lost in the music. An hour passes, and then another—the song playing over and over again as she channels every emotion bottled up inside of her, granting each one its own movement until she's choreographed the extent of her pain.

The song starts again, and her back is to the door. Jessica is breathing so heavily she doesn't hear it when it opens. As she begins to work her way through the dance, she can't stop—even when she sees her audience. When she's done, it's not just Miah filling the doorway, but a small crowd of four other dancers she's never met, all of whom take her by surprise when they break out in applause.

Jessica scrambles across the room, stopping the song from playing again before she sweeps a loose tendril of hair away from her sweaty face. She's still breathing hard, at a loss for words as she meets Miah's unwavering stare.

"Are you teaching that?" asks one of the female dancers as she casually enters the room. "I love that song."

"Um, I'm—I'm still working on it," Jessica manages to say. Her gaze flicks to the group now preparing for their session and then quickly returns to Miah.

She's still staring at Jessica as she says, "I want you back here tomorrow. I want to see that again."

"You do?"

"Hell yes, I do. Tomorrow. Eleven. Can you be here?"

"Yeah. Sure," she agrees, still taken aback.

"All right. See you then."

Jessica nods and grabs her purse as she slips her feet back into her shoes. She's not conscious of how sweaty she is until she steps outside, and the warm afternoon breeze hits her skin. Uncertain as she may be about what just happened or what to expect the next morning, she's without a doubt she needs a shower. Feeling lighter than she's felt all day, she heads for the loft to do just that.

It's nearly eight when Atzel pulls up to the curb outside the loft. Khalohn grabs the take-out order he picked up moments before and steps out of the Maybach, bidding his driver goodnight as he walks inside. He takes the elevator to the sixth floor alone, the smell of dinner making his stomach groan in hunger. When he lets himself into 601, he locks the door behind him, discards his keys on the hall table, and heads straight for the kitchen.

Setting the food on the island, he looks for Jessica and finds her curled up in one of the leather armchairs. She's sleeping, her arms clutched around a paperback book with tattered edges. Khalohn shrugs his way out of his suit jacket as he begins to close the distance between them, draping the garment over one of the dining room chairs along the way. Memories of the last time he was in the apartment filter through his mind, and he glances toward the closet. He knows the mess he made has long since been managed, but he stops short when he notices the closet isn't merely straightened—it's *full*.

From where he stands, he pauses long enough to take a closer look at his surroundings. Aside from the closet full of Jessica's clothes, he notices a couple picture frames on the nightstand, and a couple more on the coffee table. Against the far wall, behind where Jessica is sleeping, there are two small stacks of books on the floor, as if waiting for the installation of a bookshelf. His eyes settle on his woman, piecing together clues as to how she must have spent part of her day.

Having been without her company for as long as he can stand it, he continues to cross the room until he's kneeling beside her. "Hey," he calls tenderly, tucking a bit of hair behind her ear. "Precious…"

Jessica comes out of sleep slowly, blinking her eyes open lazily before her focus settles on him. "Hi," she whispers.

"You hungry?"

He watches as she considers his question and then offers him a sleepy nod. A crooked smile curls his lips, and he carefully extracts the book from her grasp, setting it on the coffee table behind him before he stands to full height. He holds out his hand, and she accepts the gesture, using him to help her to her feet. As soon as she's standing, Khalohn tilts his head and leans in for a kiss. He's not disappointed when she responds in kind.

"Missed you," she confesses as he pulls away.

He can tell by the dreamy look in her eyes her words slipped out, unfiltered. He likes this and expresses as much as he buries his fingers in the back of her hair, holding her head still as he presses his lips to her forehead.

"Let's eat, beautiful."

Khalohn doesn't know if Jessica likes salmon. When she takes a small helping of everything he ordered from the Greek restaurant a few blocks away, he's confident he ordered well. She then settles herself at the dining room table, and he follows her lead, taking the seat next to her at the head of the table with enough chairs for eight.

"How was your day?" she inquires, breaking the silence between them.

Christina's threat is the first thing to pop into his head. Suddenly, the weight of the phone in his pocket is hard to ignore. It's been hardly more than twelve hours since he put Adams on her trail. The soonest he'll hear from his PI is the next morning, but that doesn't make him any more patient.

"The woman from the gala?" He avoids using her name on purpose. "The threat she threw at you Friday was meant for me. She followed through this morning."

"What?" Jessica gasps, sitting up straighter in her chair.

"I'm not telling you so you'll worry, Jess. I'm handling it, as I said I would."

"Okay."

She watches him closely as he takes another bite of his dinner, and he recognizes it's time to change the subject.

"You moved in," he states matter-of-factly.

"Oh," she breathes, setting down her fork. "Actually—I didn't mean to. I mean, I was going to talk to you about it." She turns in her chair, facing him more directly as she anxiously gathers all her hair to one shoulder. "I went back to my apartment. I don't want to keep it. I took what I wanted, and I brought it here, not sure where else to go. Then I left for a couple hours, and when I got back, the cleaner had been by. She unpacked my things."

"You've always been welcome to live here; you know that."

"That was before, Khalohn," she responds, her voice hardly above a whisper.

"I'm happy to keep the apartment. It's a solid piece of real estate. As long as you want to, it's yours to call home. Not to mention, I already have a key."

She licks her lips before tugging the bottom one between her teeth. He thinks he sees a hint of a smile at his comment before she says, "I don't want to stay here for nothing."

"Jess, I'm not—"

"I'm not a freeloader. You know that. And this place? If I move in here and don't pay rent, it won't feel any different than it did before—but things *are* different."

"I know they are."

"So you know there's no *deal* here. It's just us. And you've claimed yourself a woman who wants to stand on her own two feet. You *have* to let me stand on my own two feet."

Khalohn is speechless for a second, too distracted by the raw desire which fills his chest. It presses against his ribs, as if it's uncontainable, and he wonders how it's possible he found someone so genuine and integrous—a woman so beautiful, both inside and out, that her value is immeasurable.

When he was younger and nothing but a student, he stood on his potential. That was the promise he made to Hollie; if she was to rely on anything, he had his love and his work ethic to offer. When that ended, when he was no longer enough, he kept his head down and his sights focused. For years now, when women look at him—it's not his potential they see. It's the cut of his suit. The designer of his watch. The make and model of his vehicle. It's why he was so drawn to Clandestine's. Underground, none of that mattered. His desirability was built on a reputation of a different sort.

Then he met Jessica. When he looks at her, he sees a woman who looks at him and sees a man. It's that simple. It's that pure. It's an unmatchable quality he wouldn't trade for anything.

He drops his fork and reaches for the bottom of her chair. She lets out a started cry as he yanks her toward him, putting her in kissing distance. Her lips still parted in surprise, he doesn't hesitate to slip the tip of his tongue into her mouth for a taste.

He lingers only a short while before he pulls away slightly and catches her eyes with his own. "The apartment is yours, free of charge, until you've got a job that enables you to stand on you own. When you do, we'll renegotiate. Agreed?"

This time, it's Jessica who stares at Khalohn before she reaches up to hold the side of his face and leans in to steal a kiss. Only, she *does* linger— to which he has no objections.

Chapter Thirty-Six

"Got a minute?" Adams asks when Khalohn picks up his call. It's five minutes before ten, nearly twenty-six hours since he last heard from his PI. Khalohn's on his way into a conference room for a meeting, but he stops shy of the doorway and turns his back to the glass wall.

"Yes."

"As soon as I end this call, everything I've got will hit your inbox. And what I've got is a loaded gun."

"Well?" mutters Khalohn impatiently.

"Blow."

His brow dipping in a deep scowl, Khalohn hisses, "Excuse me?"

"Yeah. I'd say I'm good, but I think luck was on my side this time. She's adept at hiding her extracurricular activities. Just so happens I caught her with her dealer late last night. Took me a bit to piece it all together, and there may still be a few holes in my theory, but it's the best I can do in twenty-four."

Adams frees a sigh and then explains, "Her trust is just about gone.

Looked back at her family tree, and I don't have to know how much she had access to when she was granted control at twenty-one to know it should have been enough funds to last a lot longer than seven years.

"She's been living off the shares she's got in Pier House Resorts along with some miscellaneous income I can't trace. Between maintaining the reputation of her last name and her constant flow of snow, she's doling out a lot of dough. More than she's got coming in with no real job. Add to that the outrageous amount she seems to be feeding her lawyers recently, and she's just about dry."

Khalohn reaches up and grabs hold of the back of his neck, staring down at his shoes as he surmises, "What you're saying is, the minute Khalohn Morgan acquires Pier House Resorts, the equity she has now—which is currently shit, given the state of the business—will be cashed out, effectively putting an end to her only traceable income."

"That about sums it up."

That's why she's fighting so hard. Without the family business, she's out of money—and with no money, she's nothing more than a hooker with a drug problem.

"You'll send this over?" Khalohn asks, returning to his office.

"On its way."

"Include your invoice," he instructs before he disconnects. As soon as he's in earshot of Maribelle, he says, "I need lunch reservations for three. I also need you to get in contact with Charles Winslow. Tell him to meet me. Inform him it's an urgent matter and he should come with his lawyer."

"Anything else?" she asks, making quick note of his request.

"Yes. As soon as I step into my next meeting, I'm going to forward you an email. It should have an invoice from Brett Adams; see to it he gets paid. As for the rest, print it—two copies. One for me, one for Lorelai."

"Instructions for Lorelai?"

"I'll deliver those myself." Dipping his chin in a nod of thanks, Khalohn turns on his heel, making his way to the bullpen. It's rare that he's seen maneuvering his way through the associates' desks, but it's not difficult for him to find his intended target.

"Mr. Morgan," says Lorelai upon his approach. She's quick to stand to her feet, and she smooths her hands down the front of her skirt as she looks at him in question.

"I'm late for a meeting, but this can't wait."

"Okay," she replies with rapt attention.

"Within the next hour, Maribelle will have a file on your desk. It's what we need to call off Christina Winslow. You are to have it delivered—be it by courier or personally, it's up to you. However, the timing is crucial. Do you have lunch plans?"

Speaking through a half smile, she replies, "I think you're about to make them for me."

"I'll be meeting Charles to hand off the same documents at lunch. Check with Maribelle for what time. I don't intend to dine, just deliver a warning: get her to back off, or I tank the deal. By that I mean, as soon as the company is mine, I'll dismantle Pier House without thinking twice about it."

"Wow." Lorelai lifts her eyebrows in surprise, folding her arms across her chest. "She struck a nerve, didn't she?"

"She made it personal."

"You mean—because of the woman in the photo?"

Khalohn stares at his associate, saying all he needs to in the silence. When he's certain his point has been made, he continues with his plan.

"I don't want her to know before he does."

"Right. Well, I think I can lure myself a lunch date," says Lorelai mischievously.

"I trust you will."

Having said all he needs to say, he turns without another word and heads to his meeting. It lasts just shy of an hour. As the room clears, he checks his phone, glancing at his calendar. He doesn't have time to stop at his office before his next appointment, but he sees Maribelle came through—as she always does. He's got a lunch reservation at twelve-thirty, and he intends to be the first in his party of three to arrive.

Before his next meeting begins, he makes it known he's on a tight schedule. He expects everyone to stick to the outlined agenda. As usual, what the boss wants is what the boss gets, and he's heading to Maribelle's desk at noon on the dot.

"Everything you asked for," she says, holding out the printed file before he comes to a full stop. "Mr. Zúñiga has been notified and should be waiting for you now."

With a sharp jerk of his chin, he takes hold of his ammunition and starts for the elevator. It's been a long time since he's gone to war for a deal. Negotiations are one thing, and the best business transactions are won in battle; but pulling out the big guns is a tactic he only uses as a last-ditch effort. This time, just as Lorelai surmised, a line was crossed. Thinking back to Friday night, to the ride home after the gala, he remembers what Jessica said.

Maybe it makes me a slut—but no. It doesn't change this.

To Khalohn, it doesn't matter where they met or how their relationship began, his woman is not a slut. For Christina to threaten him, not simply by exposing his connection to Clandestine's, but exposing *Jessica's* arrangement as well—it's foolhardy, at best. His business reputation is too powerful to take a major hit from rumors in regard to his personal life. But Jessica cannot say the same, and he won't see her name dragged through the tabloids out of spite.

However many steps ahead Christina thinks she is, she's wrong. She saw Jessica on his arm, and she's stupid enough to think she has leverage. It's almost laughable how she believes he would ever cower to her. She tried to bend him to her will once before, and she failed. Khalohn isn't a vindictive man, but she needs to be checked.

Atzel is waiting with the door open as he approaches the Maybach. Picking up on Khalohn's sense of urgency, they're on their way in no time. It takes fifteen minutes for them to reach their destination, and Khalohn doesn't wait for his driver to open his door before he climbs out and steps onto the sidewalk in front of the restaurant.

He's seated five minutes before twelve-thirty, and he takes advantage of his moment alone. A waiter comes by and offers him a water, which he accepts. It's the only thing he intends to ingest before he returns to the office. When he looks to the front entrance and see's Winslow and Shephard being escorted his way, Khalohn draws in a breath and looks to the file atop the table in front of him. He doesn't stand to shake hands upon their arrival but offers them each a curt nod in greeting.

"Your secretary informed us this was urgent," says Barry, unbuttoning his jacket as he takes his seat. "I was just on the phone with Lorelai this morning. Shouldn't be long now, and all the paperwork should be complete."

"I'm here to make it clear, if you don't get Christina to back down, Pier House Resorts will be dismantled, piece by piece, before you can spend a dime that comes from me."

"Christina?" mutters Charles. He leans forward, a worried frown tugging at his brow. "We've handled her. Even if she wanted to take over—"

"She came after you, and you settled for tying her up in red tape." Khalohn picks up the folder and stands, both men gaping up at him. He takes a step toward Charles and does him the curtesy of holding the file in offering. "I'm not a small business looking to bail you out and *partner* with you; I'm an enterprise, and I don't need red tape. She backs off, or it won't be me the papers are interested in. People will be too busy gossiping about the Winslow scandal—until your name and your father's legacy are meaningless."

Charles is quick to open the file, his eyes moving frantically over Adams' findings. Khalohn, confident he's made himself clear, doesn't stick around for further discussion.

He closes his jacket, smoothing his hand down his tie as he says, "Afternoon, gentleman."

AFTER AN HOUR in the studio, Jessica walks out the front doors, every cell in her body zinging through her blood stream. She's more excited than she feels she has a right to be, but it can't be helped. Wanting to share the news, she digs her phone out of her purse and finds Stefano's contact information, initiating a call as she starts for the loft. When it rings through to his voicemail, she's disappointed—but she barely feels the sting, her buzz still in full force.

"Huey, call me when you get this. I want to see you. I have something to tell you. Something good." Her voice drops to a whisper as she gushes, "Something really, really good. Love you."

She clutches her phone to her chest, crossing the street in a hurry. When she reaches the other side, she glances down at her phone as she thinks about calling Khalohn. It only takes a few steps for her to decide she doesn't want to tell him on the phone. A pang of longing zips right through her, thinking back to the previous week, when he was only just down the hall.

He had time for me then, who's to say he won't have time for me now?

Too excited to be intimidated at the thought of stepping foot into his Wall Street office, she hurries up to 601 to get a quick shower. When she's finished and wrapped in a towel, she uses dry shampoo on her hair before she styles her dance-wrecked waves into big, loose curls. By the time she's finished, she's too impatient to commit to a face full of makeup. She settles for some mascara, grabs a tube of lip gloss, and makes her way to her closet.

Biting her bottom lip, she hesitates for a minute. She doesn't know what a woman is supposed to wear to her man's office. Her eyes flick over the empty garment bag, which housed the suit he put on that morning. She then considers her collection of dresses. Given she's never worked in an office, most of what she's got is more appropriate for outings after dark. The most modest dress she's got is the one she wore to her mother's funeral. Thinking about putting that thing on again puts a damper on her mood. Then she remembers it's hanging in a closet on the Upper East Side, and she shakes off her negative thoughts.

Her impatience to share her news reignites her buzz, and she decides to just be herself. Ten minutes later, she's dressed in a pair of white skinny jeans, a plain, gray, cotton tank top, that hugs her breasts but drapes comfortably around her hips, and a cropped denim jacket, the sleeves rolled up her forearms. She tucks her feet into a pair of pale-gray, suede, heeled booties, snatches up her purse, and takes her leave. After she locks up, her phone sounds with an alert. On her way to the elevator, she pulls it from her purse to find a message from Stefano.

Meet at my place in an hour?

She smiles to herself, quickly typing out her reply. Hoping Khalohn will be able to spare her a few minutes, she guesses she'll have just enough time to see him before heading to Brooklyn. On her way through her building's lobby, she looks up the exact address of his office. Five minutes later, she's rattling off her destination to the taxi driver. Ten minutes after that, the buzz of excitement which fueled her adrenaline wanes as her belly twists nervously.

You've come this far, she tells herself, craning her neck back to take in the length of the skyscraper.

Jessica closes her eyes, remembering the hour she spent with Miah, and that's all it takes. Her heels clip loudly against the hard floor of the cool, sleek lobby. Ignoring the anxious feeling in her belly, she walks with confidence to the elevator bay and waits for the lift car that'll take her to the fifty-second floor. When she arrives, she steps out slowly, her eyes looking everywhere, curiosity begging her to take in every detail.

Walking through the front entrance, she sees a woman in a fancy, fitted blouse and tons of blonde hair look up from where she sits behind the reception desk. Jessica doesn't blame the green-eyed stranger for looking at her strangely. She guesses it's not everyday someone walks in wearing *jeans*.

"Hi. Can I help you?"

Jessica reaches up to hold the strap of her purse over her shoulder and forces her feet to carry her across the distance between them. "I'm here to see Khalohn Morgan."

The receptionist's expression changes in an instant. She quirks an eyebrow, her eyes suddenly more judgmental than a second ago.

"Do you have an appointment?"

"No. I'm just stopping by." A little annoyed by the way the woman is looking at her, she insists, "Could you maybe just call him? Tell him—tell him Jessica Chapman is here to see him."

The blonde coughs out a laugh under her breath but reaches for her phone anyway. Jessica's grip around her purse tightens, but she stands tall, refusing to cower.

"Hi, Maribelle? Is Mr. Morgan available?" Her green eyes glance at Jessica and then back at the phone as she says, "There's someone here to see him. A Jessica Chapman?" She pauses, then the expression on her face falls before she nods and hangs up. A disingenuous smile spreads across her lips before she instructs, "His office is that way, at the end of the corridor."

The victorious grin pulling at Jessica's mouth feels too good to resist, so she doesn't. Finally relaxing, she thanks the blonde and turns in the direction the woman pointed. As she goes, Jessica absorbs as much as she can of the space. It's beautiful and sophisticated; modern and unique. Remembering it's all Khalohn's calls to mind the confidence and power he exudes—it's not for nothing.

"Miss Chapman?"

Jessica's pace slows to a stop as an older woman comes out from behind her desk. She's a little shorter than Jessica, even in her heels, but her presence is impossible to ignore. Standing as tall as her body allows, she's dressed in an awesome skirt and blouse, her makeup flawless, her red lipstick on point, and her dark hair streaked with gray. Jessica almost forgets to speak.

"Y-yes."

"I'm Maribelle, Khalohn's secretary," she says, extending a hand.

Jessica returns the gesture, deciding then and there she really likes this woman. Even more, she loves that Khalohn's secretary is a beautiful woman likely twice her age—and not blonde.

"Hi," she murmurs through a smile.

Maribelle studies her openly, but the gentle expression on her face while she does it encourages Jessica to endure it. "It is lovely to meet you, dear. But I'm sorry to say, Khalohn had a lunch engagement this afternoon. He's not—"

"I'm right here."

At the sound of his voice, Jessica's belly tingles. She twists her neck in time to see him approach. When she finds his blue eyes locked in on her, she forgets to breathe for a second.

When he's within reaching distance, he places a hand on the small of her back, encouraging her forward. Without breaking his stride, he tells Maribelle, "Hold my calls. Ten minutes."

After crossing the threshold into Khalohn's private office, he shuts them inside. She barely gets a chance to look around before he's standing in front of her, one of his hands buried in her hair at her nape, his eyes dancing around her face.

"What are you doing here? You okay?"

Tentatively resting her hands against his abdomen, she asks, "Is it okay that I'm here? I really wanted to see you. Just for a minute."

His grip in her hair tightens as his free hand takes hold of her waist, pulling her closer. "Are you okay?" he repeats.

It doesn't go unnoticed how his question isn't exactly confirmation her presence is welcome, but she decides to focus on the feel of his hands on her instead. "I have news."

"What news?"

Pressing into him further, she balls her hands into fists and tells him, "I went to the dance studio this morning to meet with Miah, to show her a piece I've been working on. She really loved it. I taught it to her, and she helped me make it better."

As she speaks, she watches as Khalohn's gaze softens, growing warmer, causing a familiar ache in her chest—an ache she clings to as she presses on.

"She offered me a part-time job. She wants to take me on as one of her choreographers. The pay is hardly anything, but she says when I'm ready— she'll take me on full-time." Saying the words out loud for the first time is overwhelming. When her eyes fill with tears, it's without warning; and as a knot forms in her throat, she has to swallow hard before she continues. "Khalohn, all I've ever really wanted to do is dance. This is like—the beginning of a dream come true. A dream I'd all but given up on. And it sucks so bad that my mom's not here for this, but I'm so excited. I'm so excited, and I had to tell someone. I had to tell you."

An almost imperceptible smile curls up the edges of Khalohn's mouth, and Jessica stares, thankful there's no beard under which he can hide the small movement of muscle. He stares, too, not saying anything at first. Silently, he extracts his hand from her hair and tenderly wipes away her tears. Molding his hand warmly against her cheek, he leans down and presses a soft kiss to her lips.

"You amaze me," he mutters as he pulls away slightly.

Jessica doesn't know what to say, so she simply moves her arms until they're wrapped around his middle.

"Sounds like we should celebrate."

"Really?" she breathes.

"If you're up for it," he says with a nod.

She considers his proposal. It seems odd to think of celebrating anything just a week after laying her mother to rest. But Jessica can't deny she's having a *great* day. In her heart, she knows Beth would be happy for her. Even more, she'd be proud. If that's not something to celebrate, she's not sure what is.

"Yeah. Yeah, I'm up for it."

"Good. I'll make reservations for eight."

"'Kay," she whispers. Tightening her grip around him, she presses up on her tiptoes and murmurs, "Looks like we'll be renegotiating my lease agreement sooner than we thought."

He chuckles, the sound deep and delicious, the smile that lights up his eyes mesmerizing. She stares at it, knowing *this* is what she came for.

"Khal?"

"Hmm?" he hums, his fingers finding their way back into her hair.

"Thanks for giving me a minute."

He tilts his head, lining up their lips as he mutters, "By my count, we've got five more." His mouth grazes hers teasingly and then he promises, "I never want to be too busy for you, precious. Never."

Jessica smiles until the tip of Khalohn's tongue goes in search of hers. It's not long before her arms are around his neck, her body flush with his—one of his hands in her hair, the other molded around her backside. As she gets lost in his kiss, she realizes she's got her answer.

Yeah. It's okay that I'm here.

Ten minutes later, as she heads to the elevator—Jessica makes no attempt to hide her swollen, pink lips. Feeling wildly confident, she even tosses a wink to the front desk receptionist on her way out.

Epilogue
One Year Later

KHALOHN SITS WITH HIS BACK propped against the pillows, his legs folded beneath him, and his hard length buried inside of his woman. Jessica's thighs hug his hips, her bare breasts are pressed against his chest, and her hands frame his face as she stares deep into his eyes. She grinds her hips down, whimpering softly—desperately. She feels perfect. Hot and wet. Tight and soft. He glides his hands down her smooth back, grazing her ass, then her hips, tracing his fingers along her thighs before starting all over again. All the while, she moves slowly. It's the most beautiful form of torture.

"*Khalohn*," she breathes, grinding against him again. She drags one of her hands from his cheek, until her fingers are pressed to his lips. He opens up and licks her fingertips. She moans and then dips her middle and ring finger into his mouth. He sucks them deep, watching as her eyes grow wide before her brown irises seem to catch fire. Her gaze drops and she frees another moan as she grinds her hips down harder. When she throws her head back and bucks against him with a new intensity, he wonders if it's because of her fingers in his mouth—or the sight of the diamond he slid on her hand just a couple hours ago.

"I'm—I'm close," she pants. "I didn't—*baby*—I didn't think I could come like this."

Khalohn takes hold of her wrist, pulling her hand away from his mouth before he demands, "Eyes on me, precious."

She obeys immediately, wrapping both arms around his neck as she continues to roll her hips. He can feel her desperation growing, like she can't get close enough.

"I love you," she declares as her body begins to tremble. "Oh, god— *Khalohn.*"

Wanting to see her topple over the edge, he slides a hand between them, pressing his thumb against her slick, swollen clit. The instant he makes contact, he loses her eyes as she surrenders to her pleasure. Khalohn frees his own groan, the feel of her sex constricting around his too good for words.

When she comes down from her orgasm, he takes hold of her hips and pulls her from over his stiff penis. He settles her on her back with ease, finding his way between her legs before he submerges himself fully into her core. She gasps, arching her spine, her nails digging into the small of his back as she holds on tight.

Fuck, I adore her.

Having had enough of their slow pace, he thrusts in and out of her hard and fast, his eyes locked on hers the whole time. Every moan and whimper that passes from her lips sends a rush of desire down his spine. He's so aroused, his shaft so hard, there's only one way this will end.

He can feel himself losing control as his own growing sense of desperation takes over. He loses his rhythm, slamming into her as deep as he can manage. Then her strangled sob hits his ears a second before she comes again, and he can't hold back a moment more. The groan which claws its way out of him originates so far down inside his chest, he barely recognizes the sound. His orgasm hits so fiercely, he can't see straight; and he comes so hard and long, his whole body trembles from the exertion.

Khalohn collapses on top of her, burying his face in her neck as he tries to catch his breath. They stay like this until he finds the strength to shove an arm beneath her, taking her with him as he rolls onto his back. Jessica lets out a deep exhale as she rests her head against his shoulder, and Khalohn turns until his lips are touching her forehead.

He closes his eyes, his memory taking him back a year. He remembers telling her—*There are no promises here.* Now, that couldn't be further from the truth.

He wholeheartedly believes he doesn't deserve her. She's so genuine, the light inside of her so precious, it still amazes him how they found each other. A year ago, when he finally met *Jessica*—when the lie of Bryn van Doren was shattered—he knew then how loyal she could be. But the loyalty she exposed him to, the faithfulness others had earned from her— it's nothing compared to the experience of being on the receiving end of her devotion to him. Her loyalty runs so deep, it's impossible not to return.

It took him a while to catch on to the fact that his devotion to her is the root of his love. Khalohn told her there were no promises between them because he didn't know if he could fall in love again. Now he knows he wasn't wrong to doubt what's possible. The truth is, he doesn't love her like he loved Hollie. His desire to marry her doesn't feel comparable to what he felt the first time around—not simply because they're different women, but because the love he has for her only exists because she's *his Jess.* She's the only woman who could convince him, without asking, bargaining or negotiating, that she's worth promising the world.

In his arms is the most incredible woman he's ever loved, and he's never letting go.

"Never going to let you go," he murmurs, his lips grazing her warm skin.

Lifting her head, she waits for him to find her eyes before she whispers, "Promise?"

"I promise."

She responds with a kiss and then rests her head back on his shoulder, freeing a contented sigh. Silence settles around them until she asks, "I guess it's time to give this place up, huh?"

Reaching up to run his fingers through her hair, he stares at the ceiling above them, picturing all the ways in which she's made the loft her home. Since the night she moved in, they've spent most nights together. More times than not, they find themselves on the Upper East Side during the week and in Tribeca over the weekend. When he's traveling for work, he knows she's at the loft, even though she has full access to the penthouse. She prefers what she considers *their* space over his—but there are amenities the loft lacks that he's decided he doesn't want to live without.

"Precious, you want to settle in Lower Manhattan, we will. We both work on this end, and I can sell the penthouse."

He feels it when her body goes stiff on top of his. "Really?"

"If it's what you want."

This time, she props herself up against him—folding her arms across his chest as she stares down at his face. His hand falls away from her hair, but he merely circles his arms around her instead.

"Are you saying—are you saying you'll give up the penthouse for the loft?"

"No, Jess. I'm saying, if you don't want to move into the penthouse on the Upper East Side, we'll find one we like down here."

Her eyes light up as she fights a smile, and it makes him want to kiss her. Before he gets a chance, she guesses, "A penthouse…with a pool?"

"You know there are few things in life I'd rather not give up."

"A private pool and me," she says, speaking through a grin.

"Not in that order."

Jessica touches her lips to his. "Can we start looking this weekend?"

"Yes."

"You know I love you, right?"

She doesn't give him a chance to respond before dipping her tongue into his mouth for a taste. His arms around her tighten, and his penis starts to harden as she moves her legs to straddle his waist.

"I love you more," he manages to sneak in between kisses.

She hums, taking hold of either side of his face as she breathes, "I love you *most*."

He doesn't argue. He doesn't need to. She's right. No one's ever loved him more.

"Be right back," says Jessica, leaning across the short distance between them for a kiss.

"Take your time. We're not in a hurry."

Her heart swells at his response, and she doesn't deny herself another kiss before she steps out of the backseat of the Maybach. She offers Atzel a smile in thanks, then makes her way through the cemetery with a fresh bunch of flowers. It's only been a couple days since her last visit, the first anniversary of Beth's death having just passed. Still, she never comes without flowers—and she couldn't wait. Not for this.

When she reaches the familiar headstone, she kneels down and arranges the new flowers among the existing blossoms in the cemetery vase. It's late enough in the day that the dew from morning has evaporated, so Jessica doesn't hesitate to sit for the conversation she's been waiting for all morning.

"Hey, mom," she murmurs.

Jessica never feels silly talking to her mother's headstone. Beth is gone, but she chooses to believe her spirit lives on. That's all the hope she needs, and her visits comfort her.

"The love of my life asked me to marry him last night." She pauses to look down at the huge rock he slid on her finger at the restaurant after dinner. Speaking through a smile, she confesses, "I said yes, of course. I mean—there was no other answer, you know? I'm his. I always have been, and I always will be.

"I wish you knew him. I'm sorry I kept him from you. He's…he's become my whole heart. He sees me, mom. He sees me like no one else does. And he believes in me. He supports me. No way I'd be choreographing for Miah's dance studio if it wasn't for him. When I was still part-time? Making less than I did when I was tending bar at Moby's Dive—god, remember that hell hole? Anyway, without him, I would have been working at least two other jobs to make ends meet; and if I was working all the time, I couldn't have focused solely on dance, and I wouldn't have made it.

"I don't know. I guess what I'm trying to say is, he's special. Man like him? Smart and driven and successful—a businessman who can command a room because he's *that* good at what he does? Not to mention, mom— he's *hot*. It's unique for a man of his caliber to look at me and believe in my talent. And I don't mean that, like, I don't have any pride in who I am and where I come from. But I'd be naïve not to admit, I don't come from much. I've had to work really hard to get where I am; and it took the pain of losing you for me to really break out of my shell. He knows that. He understands it. He tells me all the time that I amaze him. And the way he watches me when I dance—I think you'd love him just for that. I do. For that and so many other reasons."

She pauses, glancing over her shoulder in the direction of the car. After they leave the cemetery, she and Khalohn are planning on meeting a few friends for cocktails at a rooftop bar in Midtown. Porter will be there—*he always is when Khal invites him out*—and he says he's bringing Naomi, since she's in town. This, Jessica is convinced, will make Stefano's *year*. Kierra will be there, too, with the guy she's been seeing the last several months.

Returning her gaze to the headstone, Jessica admits, "I'm happy, mom. I miss you like crazy, but life is good. It's full. And in a few weeks, I'll be a *Mrs.* Khal and I agreed on a short engagement. I don't want a big wedding. Not without you. Besides, if we go big, we might end up in the society pages or something. I kind of hate it when that happens. Khalohn does, too. To the outside world looking in, I'm just his arm candy. They have no idea what we have. How real it is. How beautiful…

"Anyway, we're going to go to City Hall. I'm going to ask Stefano to be my best man. But you knew that. I'll invite Jackie, too. I promise. And I'll be back—on whatever day our wedding falls, I'll come see you. I know, if you had any other choice, you wouldn't miss it for the world."

Jessica stands, wiping at the back of her sundress before she frees a sigh. She then presses her fingertips to her lips, kissing them before using the same hand to touch the top of Beth's headstone.

"Bye, mom. Love you."

Thank you so much for reading! I hope you enjoyed

The Lies of Bryn van Doren. If you did, I would love to hear your thoughts. Please consider leaving a review.

Oh—and one more thing! I may have written a bonus chapter for Khalohn and Jessica. You know, just a little peek into their future. If you want more of these two, subscribe to my newsletter and I'll send you what I've got!

https://mailchi.mp/rcmartinbooks/bryn-bonus

Also by R.C. Martin

Heartless
The Bridgewater Case
Stealing Home

Foolish at Heart Series
Fool for Him
Fool for Her
Fools in Love

Savior Series Duet
Guarded
Tethered

Vollucci Security Series
Severed
Wired

Tennessee Grace Series
Background Noise
Backwoods Belle
Rock-N-Roll Christmas

Mountains & Men Series
Encore Worthy
Worthy of the Harmony

Worthy of the Dissonance
Worthy of the Melody

Made for Love Series
The Promises We Keep
Reckless Surrender
The O'Conners
So Much More
Chasing After Me